A BIG SKY CHRISTMAS

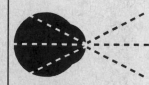

This Large Print Book carries the
Seal of Approval of N.A.V.H.

A BIG SKY CHRISTMAS

WILLIAM W. JOHNSTONE
WITH J. A. JOHNSTONE

THORNDIKE PRESS
A part of Gale, Cengage Learning

GALE
CENGAGE Learning·

Detroit • New York • San Francisco • New Haven, Conn • Waterville, Maine • London

GALE
CENGAGE Learning®

Thorndike Press® Large Print Western.
The text of this Large Print edition is unabridged.
Other aspects of the book may vary from the original edition.
Set in 16 pt. Plantin.

LIBRARY OF CONGRESS CATALOGING-IN-PUBLICATION DATA

Johnstone, William W.
  A Big Sky Christmas / By William W. Johnstone with J.A. Johnstone. — Large Print edition.
      pages cm. — (Thorndike Press Large Print Western)
    ISBN-13: 978-1-4104-6481-1 (hardcover)
    ISBN-10: 1-4104-6481-4 (hardcover)
    1. Montana—Fiction. 2. Christmas stories. I. Johnstone, J. A. II. Title.
PS3560.O415B54 2013
813'.54—dc23   2013037091

Published in 2013 by arrangement with Pinnacle Books, an imprint of Kensington Publishing Corp.

Printed in the United States of America
1 2 3 4 5 6 7 17 16 15 14 13

A Big Sky Christmas

PROLOGUE

Montana, 1947

The roar of gunshots seemed to hammer against the old man's ears. Alexander Cantrell couldn't hear well anymore. Time had taken its toll on him, as it does on everyone. But he could plainly hear — or at least thought he could — the dull boom of pistols going off and the ear-splitting crack of rifle fire. The smell of burned powder was strong in his nose.

Likewise his vision wasn't what it once had been, but that didn't stop his bleary eyes from making out the sight of dozens of Indians charging toward him, their faces painted for war and contorted with hate as they attacked, yelling and whooping at the top of their lungs. Some people might say he was imagining them, but at this moment, they were as real to him as they had ever been.

Behind them leaped giant flames, as if the

old man were looking straight into the mouth of Hell itself. . . .

"Blast it," the old woman standing beside him said. "Have you gone to sleep on your feet again?"

"What? No. No, I'm not asleep." The old man shook his head and smiled at his sister Abigail. They were twins, and even at their advanced age, the resemblance between them was obvious. "Just remembering how things used to be."

"Good memories, I hope."

Alexander thought about the violence that had wracked this land and the blood that had been spilled. "Well, I don't know."

But in a way she was right, he mused. There were plenty of good memories to go along with the bad. In the end, the good outweighed the bad. The violence was the price that had to be paid for the long, happy life that followed.

Brought back to the present by the exchange with Abigail, he looked around. They stood side by side at the top of a slight rise. The grassy slope in front of them led gently down into a broad, lush valley bordered by wooded hills on the far side. A crooked line of trees in the middle of the valley marked the meandering course of the stream that watered the range and made it such fine grazing land. There was no more beautiful place in all the world, the old man thought, than this vast ranch where he and his sister had spent much of their childhood.

About fifty yards down the slope was a level stretch of ground surrounded by a wrought iron fence. Inside the enclosed area, the grass was cut short and carefully tended. Here and there were bright spots of color where wildflowers had grown up and been left to bloom. The place had a serene beauty about it, surrounded as it was by rangeland and roofed by the huge, arching vault of the blue Montana sky.

Big sky country, they called it, and there was no truer description than that. The Montana sky was the biggest and bluest to be found anywhere, and the rich cobalt shade was made even more striking by the white clouds that sailed in it like ships. As a young man he had lain on grassy hills like this one and looked at the clouds and actually seen ships in them, and every other shape under the sun as well.

"There you go drifting off again," Abigail said. "If you're not careful the young folks will start thinking you're a senile old man who ought to be stuck in a home somewhere."

Alexander snorted. "I'd like to see 'em try."

He was tall and spare, with crisp white hair under his Stetson and a white mustache that stood out in sharp contrast against his lean face that the elements had tanned permanently to the color of old saddle leather. He wore a Western-cut suit and boots and looked like he could still leap onto a horse and gallop across the rolling landscape.

He was just as glad he didn't have to, though. He knew it would hurt like blazes if he did.

The small, birdlike old woman beside him had white hair, too. When it was loose it hung down her back to her waist, but she wore it in long braids that were wound around her head. A stylish hat perched on those braids. She wore a wool dress and jacket that helped keep her warm, even though the day wasn't really cold. Old blood didn't flow as well as young.

Alexander glanced over his shoulder at the group of men, women, and children who were waiting a respectful distance away beside the dirt road that led to the ranch and the two big Packards that had brought all of them, his children and grandchildren in one vehicle and Abigail's in the other. He linked arms with his sister and said gruffly, "Come on, we might as well get this done."

"You don't have to make it sound so much like a chore. I enjoy coming here to see Ma and Pa."

"I do, too," the old man admitted in a quiet voice. Soon enough, he would be coming and staying, like the others laid under the good Montana soil, their final resting places marked by weathered stone monuments.

Stiff-kneed, they started down the slope to the small private cemetery. The afternoon was achingly quiet, so quiet he could hear the faint rumble of trucks on the highway more than a mile in the distance. Overhead an airplane cut a trail through the sky.

The world had changed so much in the time that he'd been alive, the old man thought. Now you could hop in a car and drive clear across the country, and if you wanted to get where you were going even faster, you could get on an airplane and be at your destination in a matter of hours.

People didn't appreciate how lucky they were. It hadn't been like that when he was young, that was for sure. In those days, if you wanted to move across the country, you loaded your belongings in a covered wagon, hitched up a team of horses or mules or

11

oxen, and set off on a journey that would take months. Months of hardship and danger . . .

Those journeys had been filled with courage and honor and love. Heroes strode through those days like warrior gods of ancient mythology, towering men who protected the weak and innocent, who stood up for what was right, who brought justice and peace to a lawless land with hard fists and fast guns.

CHAPTER ONE

Kansas City, Missouri, 1873

People stood aside from Jamie Ian MacCallister. His sheer size alone would have prompted most folks to get out of his way. He was a head taller than most men and had shoulders as wide as an ax handle was long. Despite the fact that he was getting on in years, the comfortable old buckskins he wore bulged with muscles. Strength and power radiated from him.

Anybody who wasn't intimidated by how big he was might take a look at the weapons he carried and conclude that he was a man to step lightly around. Holstered on his hips were a pair of Colt .44 Army revolvers, the Model 60 conversion. Tucked under his left arm was a Winchester "Yellow Boy" rifle, also in .44 caliber. A hunting knife with a long, heavy blade rode in a fringed sheath behind the right-hand gun. Jamie was, in the parlance of the time, armed for bear, and those weapons would kill a man even quicker and easier than they would a big old silvertip grizzly.

But size and weaponry aside, the real reason most folks naturally left Jamie alone was the intensity of the gaze that came from his deep-set, eagle-like eyes. Those piercing orbs peered out from under shaggy brows and dominated his craggy, unhandsome, but powerful face. They had seen everything, the eyes seemed to say. Seen the elephant and then some. When angered, they could turn dark and threatening as a thunderstorm rolling across the prairie.

The thing of it was, when folks got to know him, Jamie's eyes could twinkle with humor or shine with compassion. He was every bit as big and rugged and dangerous as he looked, but his greatest strength was the magnificent frontiersman's heart that beat in his massive chest.

At the moment, he was striding down one of the streets in Kansas City, taking a look around on a beautiful, crisp autumn afternoon. He had visited the town before, but it had been awhile. The place had grown quite a bit from the rude frontier settlement that had started life as a fur trading post known as Chouteau's Landing. It was an honest-to-God city and even had a railroad bridge that had opened a few years earlier spanning the Missouri River.

Civilization, Jamie thought. He didn't mind it as much as some of the old-time mountain men did, but despite its advantages it would never be able to hold a candle to the prairies, the mountains, and the deserts of the West where he had grown up and lived his life.

He had left his rangy, sand-colored stallion Sundown and his pack horse tied in front of a general store to take his *pasear* along the street. He passed a big open area where dozens of covered wagons were parked. The teams were gathered in a large corral nearby.

Men worked on the vehicles, making repairs on things that had broken during the first part of their journey. Women stirred cook pots simmering on campfires. Soon it would be time for supper. Kids ran here and there, playing and enjoying not having to be in school like their peers who were tied down to one place.

A lot of immigrants traveled by train these days, since the completion of the transcontinental railroad a few years earlier, but there was still plenty of country where the trains didn't go. If somebody wanted to settle in one of those places, they had to travel by wagon, the same way other pioneers had done for decades.

Jamie supposed these pilgrims were on their way somewhere, although he hoped for their sake that their destination wasn't too far off. It was awfully late in the year to be starting a long trek anywhere. Travelers shouldn't cross the plains after winter settled in.

A group of riders jogged past him in the street. He glanced over at them, the long-standing habit making him take note of everything that happened around him. A man who had made as many enemies as he had over the years needed to keep a close eye out for trouble. That was one reason he'd stayed alive as long as he had.

The riders looked like they might be trouble for somebody, all right. There were about twenty of them, all roughly dressed and well armed. Even though Jamie had never seen any of them before, he recognized the sort of hard-planed, beard-stubbled faces they bore. Drifters, hardcases, maybe out-and-out owlhoots.

He felt an instinctive dislike for the men, fueled by the damage similar hombres had done to his family, but as long as they steered clear of him, he wouldn't bother them.

One of the men said, "My mouth's so dry I'm spittin' cotton, Eldon. How many saloons are we gonna ride past before we get to one that suits your fancy?"

The man riding slightly in the lead of the group turned in the saddle to frown at the one who had spoken. He was a tall, raw-boned man with a lantern-jawed face and tufts of straw-colored hair sticking out from under a black, flat-crowned hat with a concho-studded band.

"Just keep your shirt on, Jake," he snapped. "We'll stop when I'm good and ready, and if that don't suit *your* fancy, you know what you can do about it."

The man called Jake grinned and held up a hand, palm out. "Whoa. Didn't mean any offense. You know I'm fine with you callin' the shots."

"You better be. It's worked out pretty good so far."

"That it has," Jake agreed, but Eldon had already turned back around and was ignoring him.

The group rode on down the street.

Jamie continued on his way, too, forgetting about the hardcases. In the next block, he paused to tip his head back and study the big fancy sign that stretched along the front of the building where he had paused.

In gilt letters, it read CHANNING'S VARIETY THEATER. The building was fancy, too, with two stories and a lot of elaborate scrollwork and trim on its front. It had double doors with a lot of glass in them and a window where people could buy tickets to go inside.

Posters had been tacked up next to the ticket window announcing that a troupe of actors and entertainers headed by that noted thespian Cyrus O'Hanlon would be performing at the theater. Troubadours and terpsichoreans would put on a show, according to the poster, and after a moment Jamie figured out that was a highfalutin' way of saying singers and dancers. The troupe would also perform excerpts from famous plays through the ages, ranging from Sophocles and Aristophanes to the immortal bard of Avon, William Shakespeare himself.

There were pictures of the various players, including several women. Jamie knew that most people considered actresses to be little better than whores, an attitude that had always irritated him because one of his daughters was an actress and she was as fine a young woman as anybody would ever want to meet.

He might take in the show while he was in Kansas City, he told himself. If he stayed around long enough. Never could tell when he might take the notion to just up and go.

That was what he'd been doing for a while.

Drifting.

Ever since he had finished the grim chore of avenging his wife Kate's murder.

Over the course of several years he had tracked down and killed forty-four members of the gang of outlaws responsible for Kate's death. It had been a long, hard, bloody road he had followed, and the taking of it had drained something from him.

When his quest had come to an end, he could have returned to MacCallister's Valley in Colorado and settled down to live out his life on the ranch there, surrounded by his and Kate's children, grandchildren, and great-grandchildren. It would have been a quiet, comfortable life.

But that wasn't Jamie Ian MacCallister's way.

He had stayed home for a while, long enough to visit with all the young ones, then he'd slapped a saddle on Sundown, the horse he'd gotten from his son Falcon. Some folks considered Sundown a killer horse, but he and Jamie had come to an understanding and the stallion had served the big man well.

From Colorado, he had set out on a journey of memory, determined to revisit many of the places where he had been in his long life, places that were important to him. He'd started out by riding all the way down into East Texas, to the place where he and Kate had been married, where their first child, a daughter named Karen who hadn't survived infancy, was buried. Knowing that he might never get back there, he had found the grave site, carved a new marker for it, and said his final farewell to his little girl.

Then he'd turned Sundown's nose west, an appropriate direction considering the horse's name.

On across the Southwest he'd gone, adventuring a mite along the way. Then a great loop to the north and back down the Great Plains. Jamie had considered going all the way to St. Louis, then decided that Kansas City was far enough east for him. He could resupply there and he and Sundown could rest for a few days, then they would head back to Colorado.

Assuming something more interesting didn't come along first.

CHAPTER TWO

Dusk was settling down over Kansas City and lights were being lit in most of the buildings. None were brighter than those in the Bella Royale Saloon. The place was so big it took up an entire block, with its entrance situated on one of the corners. Gaily colored lamps hung along the board-walks on both streets that flanked the double doors.

As Jamie paused to watch, a fellow in a swamper's apron went along lighting those lamps with a long match. Even though the doors were closed, Jamie could hear music and laughter coming from inside the place. Obviously, folks had a good time in the Bella Royale.

He had planned to return to the store where he had left his horses, put in an order with the proprietor for a load of supplies, and then ask the man for recommendations of good places to eat and sleep, as well as a livery stable where his animals would be cared for properly.

As he looked at the gaudy saloon, though, he realized that he had a thirst. It wouldn't hurt anything to wash some of the trail dust out of his throat before he got around to those other things, he decided.

Once Jamie had made up his mind, he didn't wait around. He strode across the street, opened one of the doors, and stepped into the Bella Royale.

Noise and smoke filled the air, along with the odors of beer, whiskey, bay rum, unwashed flesh, and human waste. The sawdust sprinkled liberally on the floor couldn't soak up all of that typical saloon smell.

Jamie's nose wrinkled slightly. Anybody who had ever taken a deep breath of early morning, high country air like he had thousands of times in his life could never be satisfied with this . . . stench. But he could put up with it long enough to down a mug of beer. Then he'd go on about his business.

He had seen a lot of horses tied up at the hitch rails outside the saloon, so he wasn't surprised that the place was doing a brisk business. He recognized some of the men lined up along the bar as the ones who had ridden past him in the street a few minutes earlier.

The one called Eldon, who seemed to be their leader, stood with his back to the bar, his elbows resting on it as his eyes scanned the room. His gaze lighted on Jamie, but stayed there for only a second. Evidently he didn't consider the big man in buckskins all that interesting.

That was fine with Jamie. He walked to the bar, found an empty spot where he could belly up to the hardwood, and nodded to the apron-wearing bartender who came along to take his order. The man had a pleasant, round face that seemed even rounder because he parted his thinning brown hair in the middle and slicked it down.

"What can I do for you, mister?" the bartender asked as Jamie laid the Winchester on the bar. The man looked at the rifle, but didn't say anything about it.

"If your beer's cold I'll take a mug of it."

"Coldest in Kansas City," the bartender replied with a grin. "At least that's what they tell me. I can't say as I've sampled all of it to know for sure. That'd make a good hobby for a man, wouldn't it?"

"If he didn't have anything better to do," Jamie said with a grunt. He had always been

23

plainspoken and didn't plan to change his ways.

The bartender raised his eyebrows and then shrugged. "Whatever you say, my friend." He filled a mug with beer from a tap and slid it in front of Jamie. "That'll be six bits."

"Think mighty highly of the stuff, don't you?"

"I don't set the prices," the bartender said as he spread his hands and shrugged. "I just work here."

Jamie took a couple coins from the buckskin poke he carried and dropped them on the bar. Then he picked up the mug and took a long swallow of the beer. It *was* cold and had a good flavor to it, to boot. Maybe it was worth six bits, after all.

"Are you callin' me a liar?" The loud, angry voice came from one of the tables where men were sitting and drinking, as opposed to the gambling layouts in the rear half of the big room.

Jamie barely glanced over his shoulder at the disturbance. Men got their dander up in saloons all the time. It went hand in hand with guzzling down cheap liquor. As long as the ruckus didn't have anything to do with him, he made it a habit to mind his own business.

Another man at the table said, "I didn't call you a liar, Ralston. I just said you'd have a hard time gettin' those wagons to Montana before winter sets in."

The man called Ralston smacked a big fist down on the table so hard it made the glasses on it jump. "And I'm sayin' I'll do it!" he insisted. "I'll have those pilgrims in their new homes by Christmas, by Godfrey! An' if you say I can't do it, then you're callin' me a liar!"

Judging by the loud, slurred quality of Ralston's voice, he was drunk. Jamie watched in the bar mirror as Ralston leaned over the table and made his point by jabbing a blunt finger against his fellow drinker's chest. That man swatted Ralston's hand away impatiently, and Ralston seized that as an excuse to start the trouble he obviously wanted to. He lunged out of his chair, fist cocked to throw a punch.

Jamie sighed, set his half-finished beer on the bar, and turned around. "Hold it!" he snapped.

Ralston stopped with his fist poised. He was a thick-bodied man with a round-crowned, broad-brimmed hat tilted back on a thatch of sandy hair. A soup-strainer mustache of the same shade drooped over his mouth. His face was red, the nose swol-

25

len from habitual drunken binges. "Who in tarnation are you?" he demanded as he glared at Jamie.

Good intentions to avoid trouble notwithstanding, Jamie didn't like the conversation he had just overheard. He stepped toward the table.

Sensing a possible ruckus in the offing, a lot of the saloon's patrons had quieted down to see what was going to happen. The girls who worked there, dressed in short, spangled dresses, moved well clear of the table where Ralston stood glowering at the big stranger.

Jamie didn't answer Ralston's question about who he was. Instead, he asked one of his own. "Did I hear you say that you're taking that wagon train to Montana?"

"That's right. What business is it of yours?"

"You're the wagon master?" Jamie's tone of voice clearly registered his disbelief and disapproval.

"Damn right I am! Jeb Ralston, finest wagon master on the frontier!"

Jamie's skeptical grunt made it plain how he felt about that claim.

From the corner of his eye, he saw one of the saloon's front doors swing open. A slender man stepped inside quickly and closed it behind him. He wore a black suit and hat and a collarless white shirt, and a pair of spectacles perched on his nose. He looked utterly harmless, and Jamie barely took note of him since nearly all of his attention was focused on Jeb Ralston.

"Look, I'm not trying to pick a fight," Jamie told Ralston. "But it's too late in the year to be starting out to Montana from here. You won't make it before winter, and you don't want to be up there on those plains when the northers start sweeping down from Canada."

Ralston sneered at him. "How do you know so much about it?"

"Because I've been there myself," Jamie said harshly. "I nearly died in a few of those blizzards."

"This doesn't concern you, old man. You'd better shut up and go back to your beer."

Jamie wasn't in the habit of backing down when he knew he was right. "If you start to Montana now, you'll be risking the lives of every one of those pilgrims."

"They paid me to do the job, and by Godfrey, I'm gonna do it!"

"Then they made a bad mistake by hiring a drunken fool like you."

He knew Ralston wouldn't stand for that

27

insult. He didn't care. It was true, and Jamie Ian MacCallister was a man who spoke the truth.

Ralston's face flushed darker. His eyes widened with outrage. He drew in a deep breath, bellowed in anger, and charged Jamie like a maddened bull.

CHAPTER THREE

Jamie expected the attack. Ralston was big
— although not as big as Jamie — and probably plenty strong. More than likely he had
plenty of experience brawling in saloons.

But Jamie had fought for his life in desperate battles hundreds of times. He stepped
aside, grabbed Ralston, and used the man's
own momentum to heave him up and over
the bar.

Ralston let out a startled yell as he sailed
through the air. The crash as he landed
against the back bar cut off that yell and
replaced it with the sound of bottles shat-
tering. Ralston bounced off and landed in
the floor behind the bar.

The slick-haired bartender stood a few
feet away, his eyes bugging out as he stared
at Jamie. The man babbled, "You . . . you
just picked him up . . . and threw him!"

"Yeah," Jamie said. "Sorry about all the
damage. I'll pay for it."

He could well afford to. During his wanderings over the past five decades, he had cached small fortunes in gold and silver in numerous places across the West. In addition, he had an entire cave full of Spanish treasure that had been hidden there a couple of centuries earlier. All of that didn't include the money he had made from his ranch and the other successful businesses in which he had invested, many of them operated by family members. The MacCallisters were a dynasty, and a mighty wealthy one, at that.

Jamie was aware that the room was completely silent as he took out his poke and counted five double eagles onto the bar. That was more than enough to cover the cost of the spilled liquor. He glanced at his still half-full mug of beer and decided he was in no mood to finish it.

"When that fella wakes up" — he nodded toward the area behind the bar where Ralston had fallen — "somebody ought to try to talk some sense into him about starting for Montana this late in the year. If he won't listen to reason, somebody needs to warn those pilgrims he plans to lead them right into trouble."

"Nobody talks sense to Jeb Ralston, mister," the bartender said. "He has his own ideas, and he's not shy about using his fists to defend them."

"Well, it backfired on him this time, didn't it?" Jamie turned away from the bar to leave the saloon.

He had taken only a couple of steps when somebody yelled, "Look out!"

Jamie whirled around, and saw that Ralston had regained his senses and climbed to the top of the bar. He leaped from it in a diving tackle aimed at Jamie.

Unable to get out of the way in time, Ralston's weight slammed into Jamie's left shoulder, the collision's impact making Jamie stagger. He stayed on his feet, though, planted his left hand in the middle of Ralston's chest, and shoved him back a step. With enough room, Jamie swung a right-hand punch that landed on Ralston's jaw like a pile driver.

The blow jerked Ralston's head to the side but didn't put him down. Drunk he might be, but it surely wasn't the first fight he'd had when he was full of booze. He hooked a right fist of his own into Jamie's mid-section. The punch landed with considerable power. Ralston could hit.

Jamie sent a short, sharp left into the wagon master's face. Ralston came back with a left of his own that tagged Jamie on

31

the chin. For several long moments as the saloon filled with cheers and shouts of encouragement on both sides, the two men stood toe to toe and slugged it out.

They were pretty evenly matched, but Jamie was a little taller and heavier and had a slightly longer reach. Those things gave him an advantage.

The wagon master fought with the intensity of a crazed animal, though, and for one of the few times in his life, Jamie found himself being forced to give ground a little.

His back came up against the bar. Bracing himself against it, he hunched his shoulders to protect his head and snapped two quick lefts into Ralston's face. Ralston's nose was redder and more swollen, but it was from being hit, not drinking. Jamie whipped a right into Ralston's solar plexus.

The wagon master leaned forward, his face going gray from the shock of the blow. He lowered his head and plowed forward. The top of his head rammed Jamie's chin, forcing his head back.

Jamie grabbed hold of Ralston and pulled him in closer, grappling with him. He got his arms around Ralston's waist and swung him into the air again. The muscles of Jamie's arms, back, and shoulders swelled so much from the effort it looked almost like they were about to burst through the buckskin shirt he wore.

Once Ralston was off his feet, he couldn't get his balance to fight anymore. Jamie turned him upside-down and then lifted the wagon master into the air above his head. It was an amazing feat of strength, the stuff of which legends were made. As he supported that massive burden, Jamie took a couple of stiff-legged steps and then smashed Ralston down onto one of the empty tables. Wood splintered and cracked as the table collapsed under the impact.

Ralston lay there senseless among the wreckage of the table.

He wouldn't be getting up any time soon, Jamie thought.

A frown creased his forehead as he saw just how true that was. Ralston's right leg was twisted at an odd, unnatural angle. Something white stuck out through a bloody rip in his trousers.

Jamie drew in a deep breath as he realized it was the jagged end of a bone. He had broken the wagon master's leg.

He wasn't the only one to notice that. A man in the crowd yelled, "Holy cow! Look at Ralston's leg!"

"Somebody better fetch a doctor!" another man added excitedly.

Jamie scowled. He had set plenty of broken bones in his time and had no doubt that he could do a passable job on Ralston's leg, but he reminded himself that he was in the middle of a good-sized city where there were probably a number of doctors practicing medicine. It would be better to leave the job to one of them.

He noticed the fellow who had come into the Bella Royale just as the fight was starting. The man edged forward to stare at Ralston's unconscious form. His eyes were big with horror behind the spectacles he wore.

One of the saloon's patrons nudged the man with an elbow and asked, "What's the matter, mister? Ain't you never seen somebody with a busted leg before?"

"Yes, but . . . but . . ." the man stammered. "That . . . that's a piece of *bone* sticking out!"

He suddenly clamped a hand over his mouth, whirled around, and sprinted for the door as several of the customers guffawed at him.

The door was still open from the man's hasty departure when another man stepped in, this one a burly, middle-aged individual with a badge pinned to his coat lapel. He had a revolver on his hip and a shotgun tucked under his arm. He strode toward the bar and said in a loud voice, "All right, all right, everybody just settle down. What happened here?" He stopped and frowned at Ralston. "Good Lord, that man's leg is broken!"

One thing you could say about folks in Kansas City, Jamie thought. They seemed to have a firm grasp of the obvious.

The constable or deputy or whatever he was glared around the room and demanded, "Somebody tell me what happened here. Who busted this man's leg?"

Jamie saved everybody the trouble of pointing him out by saying, "That was me."

The lawman looked him up and down, still frowning darkly. "And who might you be?"

"Name's Jamie Ian MacCallister."

Despite the lawman having told them to be quiet, that announcement brought a stir from the crowd. Probably not everyone in the Bella Royale recognized the name, but a lot of them did. Jamie was one of the most famous men on the frontier, and his recent campaign of vengeance against the Miles Nelson gang had added to his already staggering reputation.

"MacCallister, eh?" the lawman said after a moment. "What did Ralston do, look crossways at you?"

The bartender spoke up. "That's not fair, Deputy. Ralston started the fight. He was drunk and obnoxious, as usual, and he attacked Mr. MacCallister. Mr. MacCallister was just defending himself."

"I suppose Ralston should be glad you didn't defend yourself with those Colts," the deputy muttered. "How many men is it you've killed now?"

"I don't keep count," Jamie replied curtly. "But I never killed a single one that didn't need killing."

The deputy looked like he wanted to say something in response to that, but he didn't. He looked around at the crowd. "Has anybody gone for a doctor?"

The saloon's customers looked back at him mutely.

"Well, what in blazes is wrong with you?" the deputy roared. "Somebody go and do that!"

Several men hurried out of the saloon.

The lawman went on. "Anybody here want to argue with the claim that MacCallister acted in self-defense? No?" He blew out an exasperated breath and turned back to Jamie. "I reckon there's no point in arresting you. Under the circumstances, a judge would just dismiss any charges against you."

"And justifiably so," the bartender put in. "Nobody's gonna shed any tears over what happened to Ralston. This wasn't the first fight he's caused in here over the past few years, since he showed up and started guiding those wagon trains west. He just picked the wrong fella to try to buffalo this time."

The lawman looked at Jamie through narrowed eyes. "Just try to stay out of trouble the rest of the time you're in town, MacCallister. I know your reputation. Anywhere you go, all hell seems to break loose."

"That's hell's choice, not mine," Jamie said.

The deputy stomped out.

As the customers returned to their drinking and gambling and flirting with the saloon girls, the bartender said, "Let me set you up with a real drink, Mr. MacCallister. On the house, of course."

"I'm obliged, but what I'd really like is a good meal. Where's the best place to eat in this town?"

"Herbert's Steak House, three blocks up and one to the right, is mighty good," the bartender said. "Tell 'em Clancy sent you. That's me."

"I'll do that," Jamie promised. He took one more look at Ralston, who was still sprawled on the floor, shook his head, picked up his rifle, and walked out.

The room buzzed behind him as people talked about having seen the famous Jamie Ian MacCallister in action.

He had never thought of himself as being any sort of famous personage, even though he was. He just went about his business and did what had to be done.

As he stepped out onto the boardwalk in front of the saloon, movement to his left caught his attention. He stopped and turned that way, his right hand going to the Colt on his hip. His fingers closed around the gun's grips, but he didn't draw it.

The bespectacled man who had run out of the saloon a few minutes earlier stood there. His face was pale and drawn, and he looked scared. He took an involuntary step back and held out his hands, palms toward Jamie. "Please, Mr. MacCallister! Don't shoot me!"

CHAPTER FOUR

Jamie frowned at the stranger for a second, then took his hand away from his gun and said sharply, "Take it easy, mister. I'm not in the habit of going around shooting people unless they shoot at me first."

"That . . . that's good to know. I mean you no harm, Mr. MacCallister."

Jamie grunted. The fellow was about half his size and didn't look like any sort of gunslinger or knife artist. The chances of him being able to do any harm were about zero.

Jamie wasn't rude enough to point that out, however. "How do you know my name? You ran out of there before I said what it was."

"The deputy left the door open some when he went in. I listened to what was going on inside after I . . ." He looked toward the alley. "Well, after my . . . my digestion settled down. From the way people in there

39

were acting, they seemed to recognize your name."

"You don't?"

"No. I'm sorry, I'm afraid I don't."

A grin split Jamie's rugged face. "Nothing to be sorry about. I don't know your name, either."

"Oh. That's right. It's Moses. Moses Danzig."

Jamie extended his right hand. "Pleasure to meet you, Mr. Danzig." His big paw pretty much swallowed up the other man's hand.

Moses Danzig looked nervous, like he was afraid that Jamie would crush his fingers, but Jamie took it easy on him.

After they'd shook, Moses said, "Obviously, you're some sort of frontiersman."

"Some sort, yeah," Jamie agreed.

"Would you happen to be looking for work?"

Jamie rubbed his chin. "Not really. But what did you have in mind?"

Moses took a deep breath and went on. "I'm traveling with the wagon train that's supposed to pull out tomorrow. We're going to have to find a new wagon master and guide." He paused, then added dryly, "Somebody broke the leg of the one we had."

Jamie looked at the smaller man for a moment, then burst out laughing. Moses Danzig might not be very big and his stomach might be a little delicate at the sight of blood, but he had some sand in his craw, that was for sure.

"Well, Mr. Danzig, that is a problem, but I can't help you. In fact, I was thinking as I left the saloon just now that it was a good thing Ralston jumped me the way he did. I didn't want trouble with him, but at least with him laid up, that wagon train will be stuck here until spring."

"But we can't wait until spring," Moses insisted. "We have to get started to Montana now."

Jamie shook his head. "It's too late in the year. You can't get there before winter sets in. Ralston ought to have known that. It's too dangerous."

"Mr. Ralston promised he could get us to our destination by Christmas."

Jamie snorted and shook his head. "Even if he managed to do that, it's still five or six weeks too late. You *might* be able to travel up until the end of November, but even that's mighty chancy."

"He said winter was going to be late this year. He'd studied the almanac and all the signs and that if we made it by Christmas we would be all right."

"And you'd trust your life to some drunk saying that?" Jamie asked. "Because that's what you'd be doing."

"It doesn't matter," Moses said, his voice growing hollow with despair. "We can't stay here, you see. There's no money. Everyone with the wagon train . . . spent everything they had to get this far and buy supplies for the rest of the trip."

"You've got those supplies," Jamie pointed out. "Live on them until spring."

Moses shook his head. "They won't last that long, and even if they did, we couldn't afford to buy more for the rest of the journey."

"Sure you could. Some of the folks could get jobs and work over the winter."

"Most of the families saved for *years* to afford to come out here, Mr. MacCallister. They couldn't make enough in a few months. No, they have to reach those homesteads waiting for them in Montana or give up their dreams."

"Then maybe that's just what they should do," Jamie said bluntly.

"Would you?" Moses asked. "I don't know you, Mr. MacCallister, but you don't strike me as the sort of man who would give up on much of anything you wanted."

That was true enough, Jamie thought. When the Good Lord made him, He'd put in a few extra pinches of stubbornness. Sheer muleheadedness, Kate would have called it. And she had, on more than one occasion.

"What is it you want me to do?"

"You're a frontiersman," Moses said. "Evidently quite an accomplished one, from the way the people in the saloon were acting when they found out who you are. It seems to me that the answer is simple."

"I'm listening," Jamie said.

"You can take us to Montana."

CHAPTER FIVE

Jamie didn't know whether to laugh or let out a disgusted snort, but he did neither. "I told you, Moses, I'm not looking for work."

"I'll wager that you've guided wagon trains before, though, haven't you?"

Jamie's broad shoulders rose and fell in a shrug. As a matter of fact, he *had* guided several wagon trains to where they were going, but that didn't mean he wanted to do it again, especially under these circumstances.

"And you know the country," Moses went on. "You told Mr. Ralston you'd been up there."

"I've been to Montana Territory," Jamie admitted. "Where are the homesteads you people are claiming?"

"They're in a place called Eagle Valley. Do you know it?"

Jamie frowned slightly. "I know it, all right. It's a beautiful little valley with plenty of decent land for farms and ranches. The last time I was there, though, it was covered with buffalo. The Sioux and the Blackfeet considered it part of their hunting grounds and fought over it now and then."

"Mr. Hendricks was assured that the Indians in the area had been pacified."

Jamie snorted disgustedly. "Who's this fella Hendricks?"

"The captain of the wagon train. His name is Lamar Hendricks."

Jamie knew that wagon train captain was an elected position, making Hendricks the leader of the immigrants, but it was a title without much real power. The wagon master was really the one in charge.

And this bunch didn't have one, since, as Moses had correctly pointed out, Jamie had broken the son of a gun's leg.

"Who told Hendricks the Indians weren't a threat?"

"Someone with the government. The Bureau of Indian Affairs, I believe. I don't really know the details."

That answer didn't surprise Jamie. There must be something in the water in Washington, D.C., that made all those bureaucrats think they knew better about everything than everybody else. Darned fools was what they really were.

"I wouldn't go so far as to say that the

Indians are pacified. From what I hear, there hasn't been much trouble up there lately, but that's because the big buffalo herds have moved north into Canada and most of the bands have followed them. They could come back any time, and then it's liable to start all over again."

"Captain Hendricks and his people just want to live peacefully. I'm sure they'll make every effort to get along with the Indians."

Jamie didn't say anything in response to that. All across the frontier, settlers had risked their lives moving into areas where the Indians didn't want them. Running such risks was just part of being a pioneer. The choice was up to them.

He was curious about something else, though. "You mentioned Hendricks and his people. Aren't you one of 'em?"

Moses smiled and pushed his spectacles up on his nose. "Not really. I'm just traveling with their wagon train, and they agreed to let me stay with them in Eagle Valley until the spring. But when winter's done I'll be moving on to Oregon. I'm supposed to take over a synagogue in Portland."

"That's like a Hebrew church, isn't it?"

"That's right. I'm a rabbi."

Jamie grunted. "First one I've ever met, I reckon. I figured you were a farmer like most homesteaders are."

"I am. It's just the crop I help to cultivate consists of people's souls. It's a calling that I've followed all the way from my home in Poland."

"From Poland all the way to the American frontier. That's quite a journey."

"And it's not finished yet," Moses said quietly. "But I need your help to get where I'm going, Mr. MacCallister. All of us with the wagon train do."

"Eagle Valley, eh?" Jamie mused.

"Yes. If you could find it in your heart to at least talk to Mr. Hendricks and meet the others . . ."

"Well, I suppose that wouldn't hurt anything." Even as he said it, Jamie wondered if he was making a big mistake. He wasn't the sort of man to brood over such things, though, so he put that uncertainty out of his mind. All he'd agreed to do was talk to Lamar Hendricks. He could try to convince Hendricks that it would be best to lay over in Kansas City until the spring. By then, they ought to be able to find another wagon master.

Shoot, if it came right down to it, he could help those pilgrims out with enough money to tide them over. He'd never miss it. As long as he had enough for food and ammunition and a few other supplies, that was all he needed while he was on the drift.

Moses had a big grin on his face. "That's wonderful, Mr. MacCallister. Come with me and I'll introduce you. You'll stay for supper and get to know everyone. You'll see what a fine group it is."

"I need to fetch my horses first and find a livery stable for them."

"Bring them with you," Moses suggested. "You can put them in with our livestock. I'm sure you'd all be welcome to spend the night."

"You're bound and determined to rope me into this, aren't you?"

"It just seems like such a fitting solution. I mean, since you're the one responsible for Mr. Ralston's injury —"

"He brought that on himself," Jamie said.

"I know, I know. I'm just saying that everything works out for a reason. Like tonight, when Captain Hendricks asked me to look for Mr. Ralston and I had a feeling I'd find him in that saloon —"

"I was wondering what you were doing there."

"I was looking for the man who's going to lead us to the promised land." Moses chuckled. "And I think I found him, just not the one I intended."

As they started walking along the street, Jamie scowled. "If I remember right from reading the Good Book, it was an hombre named Moses who led the Israelites to the promised land. Maybe your name is the Lord's way of saying that *you* should have the job."

"Me?" Moses said with a squeak in his voice. "The biblical Moses took the Israelites to Canaan, all right, but he never set foot in it himself. All he could do was look across the River Jordan at it and see that it was good." A worried note came into his voice. "Do you think that's a bad omen for me, Mr. MacCallister? That I'll make it to Montana but never set foot in Eagle Valley?"

Jamie didn't know how to answer that. His ideas of faith and spirituality came more from the Indians than from any of the so-called organized religions.

He slapped a big hand against Moses's back hard enough to make the smaller man stumble a little. "Don't worry about that. For now, let's try to figure out the best way to get there."

"Does that mean —"

Jamie shrugged. "It means I'll talk to those folks and think about it."

CHAPTER SIX

Inside the Bella Royale Saloon, people were still talking about the brutal fight between Jeb Ralston and Jamie Ian MacCallister. It wasn't every day folks got to see a brawl involving a legendary frontiersman like MacCallister who was known from one end of the West to the other. It was something many of them would tell their grandchildren about.

Eldon Swint didn't seem too impressed. He sat at one of the tables with several of his men, a bottle and glass in front of him. He filled his glass again, then leaned back in a chair and stretched out his long legs. "People talk about that fella MacCallister like he was Davy Crockett and Jim Bowie and Kit Carson all rolled into one. He didn't look so dang special to me. Just another old man who ain't had the sense to die yet." Swint downed the drink and licked his lips.

"You must be joshin', boss," Three-Finger Jake Lucas said. He was a handsome young man with a quick, cocky grin and a full head of brown hair under his tipped back hat. The last two fingers of his left hand were gone, pinched off cleanly when he got them trapped between his rope and saddle horn as he took a dally to stop a runaway steer during a drive up the trail from Texas. It was a mistake many cowboys had made, which was why many of them were missing a finger or two.

Jake had taken the accident hard. It had embittered him, and when the herd he was with reached Abilene and the Texas crew started home, Jake hadn't gone with them. He had stayed in Abilene, spent all his wages on a monumental drunk, and vowed never to return home in his mutilated state.

In the four years since then, he had fallen in with bad company, as they say. His best friend Bodie Cantrell knew that . . . because he was a member of that so-called bad company himself.

Bodie was sitting at the table with Swint, Jake, and three other men, all of them drinking heavily. Bodie had a pretty fuzzy glow going from the liquor. He didn't like to get drunk as much as some of his companions did, but from time to time he gave in to the

51

urge, anyway. The whiskey usually helped him forget what had happened in Kansas a couple weeks earlier.

It wasn't helping so much that night.

"It's just a little flag stop out in the middle of nowhere," Eldon Swint said. "There's only one man on duty at night. He's the telegrapher, ticket agent, and baggage clerk, all in one. When we throw down on him, he'll put that flag up, you can bet a hat on that."

"Yeah, but will the train stop?" one of the men asked.

"It's not an express. It'll stop," Swint said confidently. "That's what it's supposed to do."

"Why would they ship all that money from the mint on a train that's not an express?" Bodie asked. "That doesn't make sense to me."

"Because they're tryin' to be tricky. They don't think anybody'll suspect the shipment's on a local like that. They got a whole series of 'em set up to get the money from Denver to St. Louis."

The outlaws sat their horses on a slight rise looking north toward a small settlement on the rolling Kansas plains. The railroad tracks ran straight as a string east and west, disappearing in the distance in both directions.

A small depot sat next to the tracks on the north side, and behind it was the settlement's short, single street with half a dozen businesses on each side. At the far end of the street stood a whitewashed church that doubled as a schoolhouse during the week. Maybe two dozen residences were scattered around haphazardly.

Bodie didn't know the name of the place. It was so small it didn't really deserve one, although he was sure it had some sort of official designation on railroad maps since there was a station there.

One of the men said to Swint, "You're sure you can trust the fella who told you about all this, boss?"

"I'm sure," Swint said with an ugly grin. "He thought he was sellin' out the government for a share of the loot, so he didn't have any reason to lie. He sure was surprised when he found out that his share was a bullet!"

Swint's *haw-haw* of laughter made Bodie's guts clench. He was well aware that he wasn't riding with a bunch of choir boys, but Eldon Swint making a joke out of cold-blooded murder rubbed him the wrong way.

Bodie had done plenty of things he wasn't proud of in his life. He had been on his own since he was nine years old, when both his parents had died of a fever while the family was on its way west. The only way he had survived the fifteen years since was by doing whatever it took, even if that meant breaking a few laws. He had stolen money and food plenty of times, and after he got older he had stuck a gun in men's faces and made them hand over their valuables.

But he had never killed anybody while committing his crimes, or any other time, either. Maybe he'd just been lucky that things had worked out that way, but he liked to think it was more than that. He hoped he still had a shred of decency left in him.

Nobody would ever say that about Eldon Swint. The man had a reputation for being cunning and ruthless, and it was well deserved. The gang he led had been growing for several years, its latest recruits being Bodie Cantrell and Jake Lucas.

The two young men had quickly become good friends. Jake had opened up a little to him during long nights standing guard while the gang was on the run from the law. It was how Bodie knew about the bitterness hidden behind Jake's easygoing grin.

They were on the verge of pulling their biggest job yet. According to the information Swint had gotten, almost $80,000 in new gold coins would be on the train coming through Kansas tonight, on their way to several banks in St. Louis. Even divided among the almost two dozen men in the gang, that was more than three grand apiece. Bodie could hardly conceive of having that much money.

Once he had his share of the loot, he could quit the gang, head farther west, maybe even start a little spread somewhere. After a decade and a half of drifting around, struggling to survive, getting in and out of trouble, the idea of settling down and trying to forge a real life for himself held a powerful appeal.

"The east bound's due to come through a little after eight o'clock tonight," Swint went on. "If we all ride in there before that, it's bound to raise some suspicions. So here's what we'll do. Four of us will ride in. Me, of course" — he looked around the gang — "and Charley."

Charley Green was one of Swint's top lieutenants. He had been in the gang for a couple years.

Swint pointed to another man. "You, too, Hinkley, and . . . Cantrell. You'll be the fourth man."

Bodie nodded. He wasn't sure what Swint had in mind for the four of them to do, and he would have just as soon not been picked by the boss outlaw, but he would go along with whatever he needed to do. He wanted that stake.

"We'll ride in as soon as it gets dark," Swint continued. "Maybe have a drink in the saloon

55

and size the place up. Then we'll drift over to the depot one by one and get the drop on the fella working there. Once he's raised the flag to get the eastbound to stop, we'll signal the rest of you. You'll be waitin' up here. As soon as the train pulls in, all of you charge down to the station and make sure nobody interferes with us while we're gettin' that loot out of the express car."

Bodie had to admit, the plan sounded like it would work. If everything broke their way, they would ride off into the night $80,000 richer, without a shot being fired.

It would be a good way to end his career as a desperado, he thought.

CHAPTER SEVEN

Later that afternoon, while they were waiting in a small grove of cottonwoods for night to fall, Jake came over to Bodie. "I wish the boss had picked me as one of the four to go into town tonight."

"It doesn't really matter," Bodie said. "You'll get your share either way."

"Yeah, I know, but you boys get to have a drink first, maybe even pat some calico cat on the rump while you're waitin'. I get to hang around out here with a bunch of stinkin', whiskery ol' owlhoots."

"I'll be sure to drink a shot of whiskey and flirt with a soiled dove for you," Bodie said with a grin.

"Yeah, you do that." Jake grew more serious. "Just keep your eyes open, Bodie. Could be you'll have a chance to slip a few of those double eagles in your pocket without Eldon noticin'. I'll expect you to share your good fortune if you do."

Bodie frowned. "I'm not sure I'd risk that, even if I did have a chance. Eldon would put a bullet through a man's head, sure as sin, if he tried to help himself to more than his fair share."

"Maybe," Jake said with a shrug. "And maybe it'd be worth the risk."

Bodie didn't say anything else about that, and neither did Jake. Bodie worried, though, that sooner or later his friend would give in to temptation and try to double-cross Swint. That could lead to bad trouble.

Bodie felt himself getting tense as night approached. The time seemed to go by fast.

Too soon, Swint was calling out, "All right, boys, mount up. Time for us to go."

The three men he had picked to accompany him swung into their saddles. They circled west of the settlement, crossed the railroad tracks, and came in from that direction.

The saloon didn't have a sign on it, just the word *SALOON* painted in big letters on the upper part of the false front. Swint, Bodie, Hinkley, and Green tied their horses at the hitch rail in front of it and went inside.

The place wasn't very busy. Four men were playing poker at a table; three more stood at the bar drinking while a single bartender lazily polished glasses with a grimy rag. Bodie didn't see a woman in the place, so if he told Jake any stories about flirting with one, he'd have to lie.

The bartender wasn't talkative like a lot of drink jugglers were. He brought their beers and left them alone, which was fine with Bodie. He'd hoped the beer would calm his nerves a little, but that didn't seem to be the case.

He would be glad when the robbery was over and done with. Despite all the things he had done, maybe he wasn't cut out to be an outlaw.

When it was good and dark, Swint downed what was left of the beer he'd been nursing and wiped the back of his hand across his mouth. "See you later, boys."

The other three knew what that meant. Swint was on his way to the depot. The rest of them would follow at short intervals. Green would go first, then Hinkley, and finally Bodie.

Soon he was the last of the quartet in the saloon, and it occurred to him that he could go outside, get on his horse, and ride away. The other three were all waiting down at the train station. They wouldn't be able to stop him. He didn't have to go through with it. He could put this life of banditry behind him right here and now.

But where would he go and what would he do? Not nearly as far or as much as he could with $3,000, he told himself.

No, he would do what he'd said he would do, he decided. He wasn't going to run out on his partners.

He left the saloon and strolled toward the station in apparent innocence. As he neared it, a hiss came from the thick shadows beside the building. Bodie darted into the gloom and found the other three men waiting there for him.

"All right," Swint whispered. "Cantrell, you go in and ask the fella if the train's on time. That'll distract him while we come in the platform door."

Bodie nodded, realized that Swint couldn't see him in the darkness, and said, "I understand."

He left them there and stepped back into the dim glow of the lantern that hung over the depot's entrance. Trying not to look as nervous as he felt, he went inside and found himself in a small, dusty waiting room with a ticket window to the left and a storage room to the right. A door on the other side of the waiting room led out onto the platform. The night was warm, and the platform door was open to allow some cross-ventilation.

If the agent was behind the ticket window, Bodie would have to lure him into the waiting room some way. Luck was with him, though, and the man emerged from the storeroom, dusting his hands off from moving something around in there. He was a middle-aged, balding man wearing a green eyeshade. With a friendly smile, he asked Bodie, "Something I can do for you, young fella?"

"Is the eastbound train on time?"

The agent scratched at his jaw. "Yeah, I reckon. Haven't heard anything saying otherwise. You need to buy a ticket? I can flag it down for you if you do. Ought to be here in another fifteen, twenty minutes."

While the man was talking, Swint and the other two catfooted into the depot from the platform behind him. Bodie had to use all his willpower not to look directly at them and give the game away.

Of course, it wouldn't really matter if he did. They outnumbered the agent four to one, and he didn't even appear to be armed.

Swint put the barrel of his revolver against the back of the man's neck and eared back the hammer. The metallic ratcheting echoed sinisterly in the small room. "Oh, you'll flag down the train, all right, friend. Now don't you move."

The agent stiffened and his eyes widened in fear.

Bodie felt sorry for the man. He drew his gun and told him, "You just do what we tell you and you'll be all right."

The agent's mouth opened and closed, but he didn't say anything.

Swint prodded him with the gun again. "You understand, friend?"

"S-Sure," the agent stammered. "Just don't kill me."

"I won't shoot you," Swint promised. "Not as long as you cooperate."

"What is it you fellas want? That train's not carrying anything except freight and a few passengers. There's nothing special in the express car."

Swint laughed. "That shows how much you know, amigo. The railroad don't tell you little fellas about the deals it makes with the government. They probably figure it's safer that way, keepin' you in the dark. Might have been, too, if somebody hadn't sold 'em out."

"Mister, I don't have the slightest idea what you're talkin' about."

"That don't matter. Just come with me and raise that flag so the engineer'll know to stop. You be sure to give him the right signal, too. No mistakes or you'll be mighty sorry." As Swint started to take the agent out onto the platform, he glanced back at Bodie and added, "Go get the horses."

Bodie nodded, pouched his iron, and hurried out of the depot.

He was back in less than five minutes, leading all four horses. He tied them outside the station and went back in. Hinkley and Green were standing watch just inside the door, in case any of the townspeople should show up, but Bodie saw right away that wasn't the case. The depot was just as empty as he'd left it.

Swint waited on the far side of the waiting room by the platform door. Bodie frowned as he realized he didn't see the agent. Then he glanced toward the storeroom door, which was still partially open, and stiffened as he saw a pair of legs on the floor.

"What in blazes?" Bodie muttered. He pushed the door open farther and drew in a startled breath as light from the waiting room spilled over the man's motionless body. A dark pool of blood was spreading slowly around his head. Bodie could see the gaping wound where the man's throat had been cut.

He turned his shocked gaze toward Swint. "You told him you weren't going to kill him."

"I said I wouldn't shoot him," Swint replied with a leering grin. "I didn't. That trusty knife of mine did the trick and made sure he wouldn't try to warn anybody."

A ball of sickness rolled around Bodie's guts. He had seen violent death before, more times than he liked to think about, but this was cold-blooded murder and he didn't like it. "They

63

hang men for things like this."

"Only when they catch 'em," Swint said. "And nobody's gonna catch us, Bodie."

In the distance, a train whistle sounded, a long, wailing cry that seemed to Bodie like the howl of a lost soul. . . .

The noise faded from his memory and blended in with the racket from a piano in a corner of the Bella Royale that a sleeve-gartered entertainer had started pounding. Bodie was back in Kansas City again, sitting at the table with Swint, Jake Lucas, and several other members of the gang.

The rest of the robbery had gone off without a hitch, a couple weeks earlier. The train had rolled in and stopped just like it was supposed to, and the rest of the gang had swarmed over it, taking control of the engineer and the fireman in the locomotive cab, the conductor in the caboose, and the travelers in the two passenger cars.

Swint, Bodie, Green, and Hinkley got the drop on the messenger in the express car. The man had thought about putting up a fight, but with four guns staring him in the face, he had thought better of it.

And so they had ridden away just as Bodie had hoped, without firing a shot.

Even so, they had left a dead man behind

them, a dead man whose face still haunted Bodie's dreams from time to time.

What made it even worse was that he hadn't been able to leave the gang like he'd planned. Swint was dragging his feet on divvying up the loot. He had said they would do it once they got to Kansas City.

Bodie hoped that was true. He wanted to get away from these men. He hoped he could persuade Jake to take his share and come with him. If they partnered up, they could start a fine ranch somewhere with the money they'd have.

"I sure wouldn't want to tangle with MacCallister," Jake was saying. "No telling how many badmen he's sent over the divide in his time."

"Stories like that always get blown up bigger than they really are," Swint insisted. "I ain't afraid of that old man, or anybody else for that matter. He'll get his comeuppance one o' these days, and if he ever crosses me, I'll give it to him myself. I'll blow his lights out, I will."

Part of Bodie would have liked to witness such an encounter. He thought Swint was completely wrong about Jamie Ian MacCallister, and it might be satisfying to watch the results.

Swint changed the subject. "Did you boys

notice that theater when we were comin' into town? Posters out front said there was gonna be a show. I hope we haven't missed it."

CHAPTER EIGHT

"Hark! What light through yonder window — Dadblast it! Who put that board there? I almost tripped and broke my bloody neck! We open tomorrow night, my friends. We can't have things like this happening!"

Savannah McCoy put a hand over her mouth to stifle the laughter she felt trying to bubble up her throat. The sight of Cyrus O'Hanlon's portly figure in tights and doublet was pretty ridiculous to start with, and the way he had stumbled as he crossed the stage and nearly fallen on his face made him seem even more like a comedian. He would have made a good one, Savannah thought, if he hadn't considered himself the greatest dramatic actor of his generation.

Of course, great dramatic actors didn't head up troupes that played in second-rate variety theaters and opera houses across the Midwest, occasionally venturing as far out on the frontier as Kansas City, which seemed like the Wild West of penny dreadful fame to Savannah.

She pushed back the rich brown ringlets of hair that kept trying to fall in front of her face when she leaned through Juliet's "window," which was part of the set the troupe had erected on the stage of Mr. Channing's theater. She pulled up the neckline of her dress. Cyrus had designed the costumes, of course. He had a hand in everything the troupe did. He'd had the neckline cut low enough to display what Savannah considered a scandalous amount of cleavage, especially when she leaned forward to say her lines.

"Give the rubes in the front row what they want to see," he always said.

Savannah didn't like it. Most people already considered actresses to be little better than harlots. They didn't see that it was a true calling, like any other artistic endeavor. She didn't think it was a good idea to reinforce their prejudice by dressing like a saloon girl.

So she pulled the dress up as much as she could, but in the end, Cyrus was the boss. That was why, at the age of fifty-five, he was playing the stripling youth, Romeo. Savannah, though six or seven years older than Juliet was supposed to be in the play, was at least a lot closer to the right age.

Cyrus took off the hat with a tired-looking feather plume that he wore, ran his fingers through his mostly gray hair as he recovered his composure, and pulled the hat back on. "We'll begin again," he said in a loud, ringing voice. He was so accustomed to projecting to the back of the house that he talked that way all the time.

He launched once again into Romeo's balcony speech, and Savannah tried to concentrate on what he was saying so that she couldn't miss her cues. It was difficult to keep her mind from wandering. She had been doing this scene for months, ever since the platform behind the "window" had collapsed during a performance in Chicago, dumping Cyrus's wife Dollie, the previous Juliet, on her amply padded rear end.

Even though she hadn't been injured in the fall, following that accident Dollie had declared that she was too old to be clambering around on scenery and told Cyrus to find himself a new Juliet. The role had fallen to Savannah, who had been with the troupe for about a year.

After Cyrus had made that announcement, Dollie had taken Savannah aside and told her, "Cyrus sometimes gets carried away and thinks his love scenes with his leading ladies ought to continue offstage. In fact, that's how the two of us wound up married."

"Oh, I'm sure that won't ever happen," Savannah had said. "Mr. O'Hanlon is much too professional."

"It had better not," Dollie had warned her. "If it does, you're liable to find yourself stranded in some backwater with more livestock than people. Don't think your acting talents would help you then."

Since that day, Savannah had learned that there was some truth to what Dollie had told her. Cyrus had made some advances — subtle ones, to be sure — but unmistakable in their intention. Savannah had gotten quite skilled in fending them off without seeming to do so.

She realized that Cyrus had paused and knew it was her line. For a split second, she couldn't think of where they were in the scene, but then it came back to her. Her acting instincts were good and hardly ever let her down. She leaned out the window and delivered her line, and below her on the stage Cyrus started emoting once more.

Savannah's mind strayed again, back to the stately white mansion in the Georgia city that had given her name to her. At least, the name she was currently using . . .

■ ■ ■ ■

"No daughter of mine is going to be an actress!" William Thorpe thundered as he stalked back and forth in his study.

Her father was good at thundering, Gillian Thorpe thought as she steeled herself against his rage. He preferred to shout rather than discuss anything in a calm, rational manner. He seemed to think that whoever was the loudest in any argument was going to prevail. And to be fair, that was usually what happened when William Thorpe was involved. Goodness knew his wife Helen, Gillian's mother, had long since given up ever trying to convince her husband of anything. He would just shout her down.

Arguing with a man who was always right, at least in his own head, was just a waste of time and energy.

"Of course, Father," Gillian said. "I understand."

He stopped short and frowned at her in surprise. "You understand? Does that mean you're going to give up this mad idea of parading yourself on a stage like a painted woman in a house of ill repute?"

For a second Gillian wanted to ask her father how he knew so much about painted women and what went on in houses of ill repute, but she decided not to, probably wisely.

"No, Father, I understand why you feel the way you do, but I haven't changed my mind. I still believe that it's my destiny to become an actress."

"Destiny!" he snorted. "Romantic claptrap! I realize you're just a female, Gillian, and as such it's your nature to bury yourself in folderol and foolishness, but good Lord, girl, I thought better of you than this! I thought I'd raised you better!"

Again Gillian had to restrain an impulse, the urge to pick up one of the paperweights on his desk and throw it at him. *Just a female,* indeed!

"You're not the only one who raised me, Father," she pointed out.

"I know," he said with a scathing sneer. "And I'm not really surprised that your mother filled your head with so many foolish notions."

"She taught me to do what I believe to be right."

"You have no business believing anything except what I tell you to believe."

That summed it up, all right, Gillian thought. She had a brain in her head, a good brain, but her father didn't want her to use it. As long as she lived under his roof, he wouldn't allow her to use it. So the solution was simple.

Terence had been right. If she wanted to do anything worthwhile with her life, she had to get out of there. She had to run away.

With him.

Terence Flanagan was an actor, a breathtakingly handsome man. Gillian had met him backstage after a performance of a play she and her mother had attended. She had been impressed with him right away and very pleased that he took an interest in her. From that moment on, a friendship had developed between them . . . a friendship that Gillian sensed Terence wanted to turn into something more. She hadn't yet made up her mind about that, but the two of them had gotten close enough that she had confided her ambitions to him.

He had been receptive to the idea right away. "There's a spot for you in the company to which I belong, Gillian dear. All you have to do is say the word and I'll speak to the director. We'll soon be leaving on an extended tour, and I'm sure he'd be willing to take you along."

"I don't know, Terence. Leaving home seems like such an extreme step. . . ."

They were sitting on a bench in one of Savannah's lovely, gracious parks. The city hadn't suffered as much damage in the Late Unpleasantness as Atlanta and Richmond, for

73

example, and these days it looked much the way it had before the war.

With so many people around on the bright, beautiful day, Terence had to be discreet, but he reached over and rested his hand on Gillian's. "I want you to have a chance to fulfill your dreams, my dear. How about this? Perhaps a small role in one of our productions while we're performing here in Savannah? That would allow you to see what the theater is really like, firsthand."

The idea held great appeal for Gillian. And the thrill that went through her when Terence's hand pressed warmly against hers made her long for the opportunity to get to know him better.

All she had to do was convince her father. . . .

Bringing up the idea led to a war on a much smaller scale, but no less passionate. The two of them had gone around and around about it for more than a week, and finally it was too late. The troupe had left the day before, continuing on to the next stop on their tour — Nashville.

But Gillian had a plan, and the final confrontation with her father convinced her that she had no choice but to go through with it. She wished that she could tell her mother she was leaving, but she knew if she did, the older woman would just try to talk her out of it.

Gillian couldn't blame her for that. She wouldn't have wanted to be left alone with William Thorpe, either.

Her father always retired early. He had very lucrative interests in a shipping concern, a bank, and a number of warehouses, and he liked to be at his office before anyone else in the morning. That way he could see when all the employees arrived . . . and the ones who made a habit of being later than William Thorpe thought appropriate would pay for their tardiness.

Gillian knew that if she waited until her father was asleep, he wouldn't be aware of what was going on until it was too late to stop her. She had already checked the railroad schedule and knew there was a train for Nashville leaving at ten o'clock.

She packed a bag, taking as little as she thought she could get by with, then slipped stealthily down the rear stairs and out of the house.

Chapter Nine

It was frightening to walk to the train station in the darkness. Her heart was in her throat the whole way. But people who never took risks never accomplished anything worthwhile in life, she told herself, and she clung to that thought for strength as she made her way to the depot.

Once she was there, she ran into an unexpected obstacle. She had plenty of money, but there were no compartments available on the train. She had to purchase a ticket that allowed her to sit up in one of the regular passenger cars.

It was a frightening ordeal, and it lasted a lot longer than the walk to the station had. Several of the male passengers leered at her as she made her way to her seat, and she knew what they were thinking. An attractive young woman, traveling alone . . . well, there was only one sort of woman she could be, as far as they were concerned. She sat stiffly and avoided their eyes, hoping that her chilly demeanor would be enough to keep any of them from approaching her.

Atlanta, Chattanooga, the whole trip was just a blur to her. She didn't dare let herself go to sleep so she was utterly exhausted by the time the train pulled into Nashville in the middle of the next day. But she had made it, and all she had to do was find the hotel where she knew the acting troupe was staying.

Hansom cabs were lined up outside the station, and she had brought enough money with her to afford one. The driver knew the hotel, and when they got there Gillian was surprised to see that it was rather rundown. She would have thought the troupe would stay somewhere better.

She went inside and inquired at the desk for the number of Mr. Flanagan's room. The clerk gave her a smug, knowing smile that irritated her, but he told her the number. Gillian climbed to the third floor and knocked on the door.

At first she thought Terence must be out, perhaps at the theater, because no one answered. But then a thick voice said, "Whass . . . who . . . hold on."

That was Terence, or at least she thought it was. She heard him muttering curses under his breath as he approached the door.

Then abruptly he jerked it open and stood

there wearing only the bottom half of a pair of long underwear. His hair was in disarray, his face was puffy and flushed, and his eyes were bleary. Obviously, he had been sleeping, and before that he'd been drinking . . . a lot.

But he recognized her and exclaimed, "Gillian! My God. I'd given up on you. Finally worked up the gumption to run away from the old goat, eh?"

Before Gillian could answer, a woman's voice said, "Terence? Who is it?"

He half turned, so Gillian could see past him into the hotel room. A woman with tousled blond hair was sitting up in the bed, holding the sheet around what was apparently her nude body.

"Look who's here, darling," Terence said to her. "That young ingénue I was telling you about. Come on in, Gillian, and I'll introduce you to our leading lady. I'm sure the two of you will enjoy getting to know each other."

Gillian was too shocked and stunned to move. It was like her feet were nailed to the floor. What had happened to Terence? All his charm and sophistication had disappeared, leaving only crudeness behind. She couldn't believe she had left her home and come all this way, only to find that he . . . he . . .

"Come on, Gillian," Terence said, sounding a little impatient. "It'll be all right. We'll take good care of you."

Gillian turned and ran down the dingy hotel corridor, her bag bumping against her leg. Terence stepped into the hall and called out behind her, but she ignored him. The blond woman said something else, and he went back into the room and closed the door.

If the trip from Savannah had been a blur, the next few minutes were even worse. Gillian wasn't sure how she made it back downstairs and out of the hotel. She had no idea what she was going to do. She could go home, of course, but if she did she would have to listen to her father browbeat her about her foolishness for the rest of his life. She knew he would never let her forget it.

But what else could she do? She was hundreds of miles from home, in a city where she didn't know anyone, and she was scared and desperate. . . .

She didn't see the well-dressed older man until she bumped right into him on the sidewalk outside the hotel. She might have fallen if he hadn't reached out and caught hold of her arm to steady her.

The elegant-looking woman with the man said worriedly, "Are you all right, dearie? You look like you've had quite a fright."

"No, I just . . . I was going to join an acting troupe . . ."

The man wrinkled his nose. "Not Flanagan's Players, I hope. They're a sorry lot, if I do say so myself. Den of iniquity and all that. Not the least bit professional, like O'Hanlon's Traveling Company."

Gillian shook her head. "I . . . I'm afraid I'm not familiar with them."

"Are you an actress?"

"Well . . . I want to be."

The man was wearing a top hat, which he swept off and held in front of him as he performed a half-bow. "Cyrus O'Hanlon, at your service, miss."

The woman with him laughed.

"This is my wife, Dollie. If you'd care to discuss joining our troupe, we'd be glad to talk to you. We can always use another player. If you're truly devoted to your craft, that is."

"I hope I would be. I think it would be wonderful to be an actress."

"Well, you've got a lot to learn," Dollie O'Hanlon said. "But if you throw in with us, at least you'd be learning around decent folks. Not like that lecher Flanagan."

Gillian swallowed hard. Her father was right about one thing. She really did believe in destiny and other romantic notions like that. "I think I might like that."

"What's your name, dear?"

Gillian had thought about that. When her

father found out that she was gone, he might hire detectives to look for her. She didn't want to be found, didn't want to return home until it was on her own terms. She had decided that she ought to use a different name to make it harder to find her. But she hadn't settled on a name.

She had no time to ponder the question further. She glanced across the street at McCoy's Hardware Store, thought about her hometown, and put a smile on her face as she told the O'Hanlons, "Savannah McCoy. My name is Savannah McCoy."

And so it had been ever since, until even she thought of herself by that name, through performances in countless towns and in Kansas City as the troupe ran through its dress rehearsal before the opening performance, which was the next night.

She had been lucky. That hotel in Nashville had catered to the theatrical trade, and the O'Hanlon Traveling Company was staying there, too. Cyrus and Dollie had gone out to eat and had been returning to the hotel when she literally ran into them.

She'd gone with them to the troupe's performance that night and been welcomed by all the members of the company. Cyrus liked to say that they were like a family and

81

he was the paterfamilias, and it was true. Romantic notion or not, Savannah felt like she had found a home with them.

She couldn't imagine anything changing that, at least not any time soon.

It would take a new twist of fate, a new rendezvous with destiny, to do that.

She figured she was through with such things.

CHAPTER TEN

Jamie went back to the hardware store where he had left Sundown and the pack horse tied to the hitch rack. Nobody had bothered the animals, which came as no surprise to him. When anybody but Jamie approached the big sand-colored stallion, Sundown got proddy. Any time he bared his teeth and started moving around skittishly, folks tended to make a wide circle around him.

"That's an impressive-looking horse," Moses Danzig said as he looked at Sundown with admiration.

"He's mean as all get out," Jamie said bluntly. "But he'll run all day if he has to. Run until his heart busts if that's what it takes. He's got as much grit as any horse I've ever seen." He handed the pack horse's reins to Moses. "Here, you can lead this one. He won't give you any trouble."

They headed for the open area where the

immigrants were camped. As they approached, Jamie heard loud, boisterous music. It sounded like several fiddlers were scraping their bows across the strings of their instruments with great enthusiasm, if not a great deal of talent, and the lively tune made Jamie's blood perk up. He had always enjoyed dancing, although he hadn't done any in quite some time.

Not since before Kate died, actually.

He put that thought out of his mind and watched the couples spinning and whirling around near the big campfire in the center of the area between the circled wagons. People who weren't dancing had gathered around to watch, too. They clapped in time to the music and called out encouragement to the dancers.

Not everybody seemed to be enjoying themselves, though. Jamie noticed one man standing off to the side with a glare of disapproval on his stern face. He was tall and heavily built, with a barrel chest and prematurely white hair that grew in a tangle on his head. He wore a sober black suit, and his big hands rested on the shoulders of two children who stood with him — a boy and a girl about ten years old. Jamie looked closer at the resemblance between the youngsters and realized they were twins.

Jamie turned to Moses and nodded toward the glowering man. "Who's that? Not your wagon captain, I hope."

"No, certainly not. That's Reverend Bradford. He's on his way to Montana, too, with his children. I'm afraid he doesn't approve of the dancing and has made that clear to Captain Hendricks. He says it's sinful for men and women to cavort around together like heathens. But the captain thinks it's good for the group's spirits to have these little celebrations of life from time to time."

"Is that what they're celebrating? Just life in general, nothing in particular?"

"Well, in this case," Moses explained, "there's another reason. There was a wedding earlier today. R.G. Hamilton married Alice Dennison. R.G. is one of the single men traveling west — or at least he was — and Alice is the daughter of one of the immigrant families. They're a fine couple and an excellent match, and everyone is happy about it."

"Except that fella Bradford," Jamie said with another nod toward the preacher.

"Oh, he doesn't mind the marriage. Actually, he performed the wedding ceremony. He just doesn't like dancing . . . among other things."

From the sound of that comment, Jamie

thought that Moses didn't get along very well with Reverend Bradford. He didn't pursue that question, however, since it was none of his business.

As the three fiddlers — two whiskery old-timers and a skinny, gangling man who was much younger — came to the end of the merry tune they had been playing, people laughed and applauded. One couple seemed to be at the center of the dancers, and Jamie ventured a guess that they were the ones who'd gotten hitched earlier.

Moses confirmed it, then pointed out the wagon train captain. "There's Captain Hendricks." As the musicians took a break and the immigrants began to mill around and talk he nodded in Hendricks's direction. "Come on, I'll introduce you."

Lamar Hendricks was a tall, fair-haired man with a rawboned, middle-aged face under a broad-brimmed brown hat. He wore a brown leather vest over a homespun shirt. As the two men approached him, he said, "There you are, Moses. I was starting to wonder what had happened to you. Where's Mr. Ralston?"

"That's an, um, interesting story, Captain," Moses replied. "By the way, this is Jamie Ian MacCallister. He's quite a famous frontiersman."

Hendricks grunted. "Is that so?" Obviously, he hadn't heard of Jamie. He held out a hand. "Pleased to make your acquaintance, Mr. MacCallister."

"You, too, Captain," Jamie replied with a nod as they shook hands.

Hendricks turned back to Moses. "Were you not able to find Mr. Ralston?"

"Oh, I found him, all right. But there's been . . . an accident. Mr. Ralston is injured."

A look of alarm instantly appeared on Hendricks's face. "An accident? What sort of accident?"

Moses looked pretty uncomfortable at the prospect of answering that question, so Jamie saved him the trouble. "I broke the varmint's leg."

Hendricks's eyes widened in surprise. "Why in the world would you do something like that?"

"Because he was trying to do the same or worse to me."

Moses said, "Mr. Ralston attacked Mr. MacCallister, Captain. I found him in that saloon he frequented, just as I feared I might. He had been drinking heavily. When Mr. MacCallister disagreed with him about something, Mr. Ralston started a fight. I saw the whole thing. Mr. MacCallister was

87

only defending himself. He didn't do anything wrong."

"Well, maybe not," Hendricks said with a frown, "but don't expect me to be happy about what you did, MacCallister. We were counting on Jeb Ralston to get us to our new homes in Montana."

"Then you were counting on a drunken bully," Jamie said, not mincing words.

Hendricks controlled his anger with a visible effort. "You'll have to excuse me. I need to start figuring out what we're going to do now. We have to find another wagon master as quickly as possible."

"You see, that's just it, Captain," Moses told him. "I've asked Mr. MacCallister if he would consider guiding us to Montana Territory."

Hendricks looked surprised again, and still angry. "You had no right to do that, Moses. I'm the captain of this wagon train. We need an experienced guide —"

"Ask around town," Moses suggested. "Mr. MacCallister is a famous frontiersman, much more well known and respected than Mr. Ralston. And probably much more capable of leading the wagon train to Montana, I suspect."

"No offense, MacCallister," Hendricks said grudgingly. "I'm not aware of your reputation."

"I never asked for a reputation," Jamie said. "Just to be left alone to live my life. But I don't control what folks say about me. I can tell you one thing — setting out for Montana this late in the year is a mighty foolish thing to do, and I'd bet this old hat of mine on that."

"We have no choice." Hendricks's voice was as stiff as his back seemed to be. "We can't afford to wait for spring. Besides . . . I promised everyone that we'd be in our new homes in Eagle Valley by Christmas."

"Maybe you shouldn't make promises you can't deliver."

The air of tension between the two men was thick. Moses stepped in. "In your opinion, Mr. MacCallister, what would it take for us to reach our destination in time?"

"Well, you'd have to leave pretty quick," Jamie said. "First thing tomorrow morning, if you can."

Hendricks shook his head. "That's impossible. It'll take at least another day to finish making repairs on our wagons."

"Day after tomorrow, then," Jamie said. "And you may wish later on you had that extra day back."

"What else?" Moses asked.

Jamie's eyes narrowed in thought. "You'd

have to push hard, and I'm talking about livestock and human folks as well. The days on the trail would be mighty long ones, from as soon as it's light enough to see in the morning until it's too dark to go on. Under normal circumstances, you could afford to stop and lay over for a few days every now and then, mainly to give the stock some time to rest. If you leave now, you can't risk doing that. You'll have to push on every day without any breaks. By the time you get there, your teams will be worn down to a nub . . . and so will most of your people."

"But we could do all that if we have to," Moses insisted. "Couldn't we, Captain Hendricks?"

"We'll do whatever's necessary," Hendricks said with a curt nod. "We all knew when we started out that there would be hardships along the way."

Jamie said, "You'd need plenty of luck, too. Luck that you don't run into any Indian trouble, and that the weather cooperates. That last is the main thing. Winter would have to hold off, at least the worst of it. Where you're going, nothing will kill you quicker than a Great Plains blizzard."

"We have faith," Hendricks said. "The Good Lord watches over us."

"He'd have to, for you to have a chance of getting there."

Moses turned to Jamie. "But you could do it," he insisted. "With God's help, of course. You could make all those things happen and lead us to Montana."

"I can't do anything about the weather," Jamie said.

"But if it did get bad, you could tell us what we need to do to survive. And then when conditions improved, we could move on again."

"It would depend on how bad things got" — Jamie's brawny shoulders rose and fell — "but yeah, maybe. If anybody could get you through, I reckon I can."

"Then it's settled, right?" Moses said eagerly. "Mr. MacCallister has the job, Captain?"

Hendricks peered at Jamie. "Do you *want* the job, MacCallister?"

"Not particularly," Jamie replied, being honest as always. "But this young fella tells me that you'll be setting out for Montana Territory anyway, whether I go with you or not."

"That's true. We don't have any choice."

"And I can't stand by and wind up with the lives of . . . how many in your bunch?"

"Two hundred and seventeen souls, Mr.

91

MacCallister. Men, women, and children."

"I won't have the lives of that many people thrown away if there's anything I can do about it. I'll take you to Montana."

There. It was done. His earlier idea of paying for them to stay in Kansas City until spring and then set out on their journey was forgotten, and he had a pretty good idea why he had discarded it. Jamie Ian MacCallister wasn't a vain man, but he was a proud one, and Moses had played on his pride in a shrewd manner. That one was plenty smart.

"It's settled, then," Moses said again. "You can put your horses with our stock, since you're one of us now. Isn't that right, Captain?"

"Yeah, I reckon," Hendricks said, still not completely convinced it was a good idea. Apparently he was going to make the best of it, though. "Then I'll introduce you around. People will need to know what's happened."

After taking that short break, the musicians were starting up again. The strains of their new tune filled the night air. Jamie felt one of his booted toes begin to tap slightly in time to the music. It would be a long, hard trail to Montana, he thought, and these pilgrims had no real idea of what they were facing.

Let them enjoy what time they had left, before they set out on what might be a trail to disaster.

CHAPTER ELEVEN

Moses Danzig invited Jamie to share his wagon, but Jamie told the young rabbi that he would just spread his bedroll underneath the vehicle. "I'm pretty sure it's not going to rain, and I've spent many a night sleeping on the ground. Maybe that's not as comfortable for these old bones as it once was, but it doesn't bother me all that much."

"Suit yourself, Mr. MacCallister," Moses said.

"Call me Jamie."

"All right, Jamie. Since we didn't get around to meeting everybody, I'll introduce you to the rest of the group in the morning."

"You're acquainted with everybody in the wagon train, are you?" Jamie asked.

"Well, most of them, anyway. Once you get to know me, you'll see that I'm the gregarious sort."

"Does that mean friendly and talkative?"

Jamie asked, even though he knew that was exactly what the word meant.

"Yes, it does."

"Reckon I'd sort of figured that out already," Jamie said dryly.

He had put his horses in the corral after unsaddling Sundown and moving his supplies from the pack horse to the back of Moses's wagon. He would use the pack animal as an extra saddle mount if he needed one and eventually press it into service again as a beast of burden once he parted ways with the immigrants after they reached Montana Territory . . . although he might not be leaving Eagle Valley right away, he realized. That would depend on the weather. If snowstorms closed the passes, it was possible he might have to remain with the pilgrims until spring, unable to reach his home in Colorado until winter was over.

He spent the night under the wagon, and as he had predicted, he slept just fine. His muscles creaked a little and his joints popped when he crawled out of his bedroll the next morning, but there was nothing uncommon about that.

As usual, he was up well before dawn, had a fire going and his coffeepot boiling by the time Moses crawled out of the wagon with his hair rumpled and a sleepy expression on his face.

"What time is it?" Moses asked.

"Time for folks to be up and stirring around," Jamie told him. "Most of them already are."

It was true. The women had cook fires blazing, and the men were tending to the animals. Jamie had already checked on his horses and knew they were all right.

Moses dropped from the tailgate to the ground and ran his fingers through his tangled hair. He put his hat on and hunkered next to the fire. The days were still pleasant some of the time but the nights were almost always cold. His breath fogged a little in front of his face as he held his hands out toward the fire's heat.

Jamie handed him a tin cup of Arbuckle's. "That'll warm you up."

Moses sipped the strong black brew gratefully.

"Once we're on the trail, we'll be moving by this time of the morning every day." Jamie waved a big hand toward the arching gray vault of the eastern sky. "There's enough light for the men handling the teams to see where they're going. That's all we really need."

"You weren't joking when you said that the days would be long ones, were you?"

"Not one blasted bit. What do you usually do for meals?"

"I, uh, prevail upon the generosity of some of my fellow pilgrims, and in return I provide them with some supplies. I'm afraid that I'm not much of a cook myself."

"Well, no need for you to do that anymore. I'll fix us some flapjacks and fry up a mess of bacon."

"Uh, Jamie . . . I don't exactly eat bacon . . . You know, because of my religion . . ."

Jamie vaguely recalled hearing something like that about the Hebrew religion. He wasn't sure how anybody could live without eating bacon or salt jowl, but he supposed that was Moses's business, not his. "We'll just stick with the flapjacks, then, if they're all right for you to eat."

"Sure," Moses said with a smile. "Actually, that sounds really good."

After they had finished breakfast, Moses offered to clean up.

Jamie thanked him. "While you're doing that I'll go talk to Cap'n Hendricks. Point me to his wagon."

"Of course." Moses told him how to find the captain's wagon, and he began to walk around the big circle that formed the camp.

He had passed about a dozen of the

covered vehicles when a figure stepped out from behind one of them and confronted him. Jamie recognized the man Moses had identified as Reverend Bradford. He and the two children with him had disappeared by the time Moses had started introducing Jamie to the rest of the group the previous night.

It appeared that Bradford was intent on meeting him. He planted his feet and stood with a stern expression on his face.

Jamie could have moved him out of the way if necessary, but it would have taken a little work.

"You're MacCallister," the big man said bluntly. "The new wagon master and guide."

"That's right." Jamie didn't feel any instinctive liking for the reverend, but he was willing to wait and see what the man had to say, so long as Bradford didn't waste too much of his time. He held out his hand to see if Bradford would shake.

"You've befriended the Israelite," Bradford went on, ignoring Jamie's hand and making the words sound like an accusation of some sort.

"If you're talking about Moses, I believe he's from Poland," Jamie said as he lowered his hand. His eyes narrowed. It seemed that his initial dislike of Bradford had been right on the money.

"I don't care where he's from, he's a Hebrew, and someone like that has no place among decent, God-fearing folks like the ones with this wagon train."

"Now hold on a minute," Jamie snapped. "He's got a right to be here, same as anybody else —"

Before Jamie could go on, rapid footsteps sounded behind him. He whirled around, instinct making his hand flash to the butts of the .44s holstered at his hips.

CHAPTER TWELVE

He stopped before he made the draw, as two youngsters skidded to a halt in front of him. Their eyes widened at the sight of the big frontiersman looming over them in a slight crouch, clearly ready to jerk his Colts from leather and set those deadly smoke-poles to work.

"Good Lord!" Bradford exclaimed. "Mac-Callister, no! Those are my children."

Jamie straightened, took his hands away from his revolvers, and willed the snarl off his face. He drew in a deep breath and smiled as he nodded to the children. "Sorry, younkers. I didn't mean to spook you. It's not a good idea to come running up behind an old-timer like me, though. We spook easy."

The boy swallowed. "That's all right, mister. We didn't mean to scare you."

That brought a genuine chuckle from Jamie. "That's all right. Just don't do it again."

"This is a perfect example of why we don't need some gunman accompanying this wagon train," Bradford said from behind him. "Guns never bring anything but trouble."

Jamie glanced over his shoulder at the reverend. "If you ever get set upon by Indians or road agents, you'll be mighty happy to have somebody around who knows how to handle a shooting iron. Now, why don't you introduce me to these young'uns of yours?"

Grudgingly, Bradford performed the introductions. "This is my son Alexander and my daughter Abigail."

"We're twins," Alexander told Jamie.

Jamie nodded. "I can see that. How old are you?"

"We're ten," Alexander replied.

"And our mama's dead," Abigail added.

Jamie looked at Bradford again. "I'm sorry to hear that."

"It's true that I'm a widower," the preacher said. "My dear wife, rest her soul, went to be with our Lord more than a year ago."

"So you've been raising these little ones by yourself since then?"

"That's right," Bradford said. "Bringing

them up in the way they should be raised."

Alexander said, "We're not so little."

"That's right," Abigail said. "We're just the right size for our age."

Jamie grinned down at her. "I reckon that's true, missy. I didn't mean any offense."

"That's all right," Abigail said graciously. "You're pretty big for *your* age, aren't you?"

"I reckon you could say that."

Bradford asked, "What do you children want? I thought you were going to play with the Harper youngsters today."

"We were," Alexander said, "but we saw you talking to Mr. MacCallister. Billy Harper says that he's a famous gunman and Indian fighter. We wanted to get a look at him close up."

"Do you think the Indians will scalp us, Mr. MacCallister?" Abigail asked.

"Don't you worry about that," Jamie told her. "It's my job to see to it that nobody hurts you, Indians or anybody else."

"You'll take care of us, then?"

"Well . . . that's really your pa's job. But I'll help him any way I can."

"All right," Alexander said, evidently satisfied by Jamie's answer. "Let's go, Abby. Billy said he knew where there was a dead frog we can look at."

The two children turned and ran off. Jamie watched them go, then looked at Bradford. "That's a couple of fine youngsters you got there. I've got quite a few children myself, and a passel of grandchildren and great-grandchildren."

"You and your wife must be proud of them," Bradford said stiffly.

"My wife's dead, too," Jamie said, his voice hard and flat. "So I reckon we got that in common, Reverend. Because of that I won't take any offense about what you had to say about my friend Moses . . . this time."

Bradford glared, but he didn't say anything else. He just turned and stalked off.

Jamie shook his head as he watched Bradford walk away. He hadn't known many Jewish fellas in his life, but Moses Danzig seemed like a decent hombre and Jamie was willing to give any man the benefit of the doubt.

Bradford, on the other hand, rubbed him the wrong way. Jamie would try to keep things civil between them because he liked the man's kids. Bradford must not be all bad, he told himself, if he'd had a hand in raising Alexander and Abigail.

Jamie started toward Lamar Hendricks's wagon again, but he hadn't gone very far before he was intercepted again. Three men stepped up and barred his path. They wore belligerent expressions and planted their feet as if they didn't intend to move until they'd had their say, whatever that was.

Jamie stopped and studied them. The one on his left was tall and lean, but the ropy muscles of his arms and shoulders testified to his strength. His hands were clenched into knobby-knuckled fists. The one on the right was tall, but broad-shouldered and powerful-looking. He sported a bristly black beard, while the other two were clean shaven.

The man in the middle probably looked shorter than he really was, since he was standing between the two tall men. He seemed almost as broad as he was tall, and small, piggy eyes were buried in deep pits of gristle above a prominent nose in his round, sunburned face.

He was the one who spoke. "You're Mac-Callister."

"That's right."

"The man who attacked Jeb Ralston for no good reason and broke his leg."

"Well, you've got that half right," Jamie drawled. "Ralston started the fight. As for breaking his leg, that wasn't my intention. It just sort of happened in the heat of battle." Jamie's voice hardened. "But I didn't lose any sleep over it last night."

"Jeb is a good man and a top-notch wagon master. He deserves better."

"I don't plan on wasting my time arguing with you," Jamie said. "Step aside."

"No, sir," the piggish man snapped. "We hired on with Jeb as scouts. We've worked with him before. Now we hear you figure on waltzin' in here and takin' over."

"Agreeing to take this train to Montana wasn't exactly my idea. But I've said that I'll do it, and that's what I plan to do, with you men or without you. It makes no never mind to me. We'll get there either way."

"One of us should've got that job, blast it! It's not right that you cripple Jeb and then take his job!"

"You've seen Ralston?" Jamie was mildly curious about the man's condition. "How's he doing?"

"The sawbones says it'll be months before he can walk normal again, if he ever does. He may not ever get over what you done to him."

Jamie shrugged. "He should've let it go after I threw him over that bar, instead of coming after me again." In a voice like flint, he added, "He's lucky I didn't kill him."

"Mister . . . by the time we get through with you, you're gonna wish it was the other

105

way around!"

All three men attacked at the same time, charging at Jamie with fists swinging.

CHAPTER THIRTEEN

That didn't surprise Jamie. He'd been able to tell as soon as the men got in his way that they were on the prod. They'd just taken a few minutes to talk themselves up into doing something about it.

At least they hadn't come after him with guns or knives. Maybe he wouldn't have to kill the stupid varmints.

That thought flashed through his brain as he planted his feet and hit the short man first, since he was the closest of the three hombres. Jamie's fist crashed into that prominent nose and flattened it. Blood spurted hotly across his knuckles. The blow rocked the man's head back and stopped him as abruptly as if he'd run into a stone wall.

The lanky man with the malletlike fists darted in quickly. Jamie didn't have time to block the punch he threw. All he could do was lean his head to the side and let the man's bony fist scrape along the side of his head. That hurt his ear a little but didn't do any real damage.

Jamie hooked a hard left high into the man's midsection, just under the heart. The man hunched over and his face turned a sick shade of gray. He tried to throw another punch, but it was wide and flailing.

After dealing with the first two, Jamie couldn't hope to avoid taking a punch from the third man. His fist landed solidly against Jamie's jaw, sending him staggering to the side as his hat flew off his head. The bearded man was the biggest of the three, and he hit hard.

Still on his feet, Jamie's head and eyesight were clear. He grinned at his opponent. "That the best you got, son? Can't even put an old, old man like me on the ground?"

That gibe had the desired result. The man roared angrily and charged. Jamie twisted out of the way, grabbed the man's shoulder, and slung him up against the nearest wagon. The man crashed headfirst into the heavy side boards and bounced off. He fell on the ground and rolled over, stunned.

"Look out, Mr. MacCallister!" a little girl's voice cried.

Jamie wheeled around in time to meet another charge from the short, broad man who had recovered his wits after the painful blow that had broken his nose. Blood streamed from his nostrils, smearing the bottom half of his face and giving him a fearsome look. He threw punch after punch as he bored in at Jamie, landing some of them.

The big frontiersman shrugged off the blows, and threw a couple of his own, a left-right combination that landed on the attacker's gut and chin. Jamie would have hit him again, but a couple arms like thick cables wrapped around him from behind, pinning his arms to his sides.

"I got him, Keeler!" a harsh voice yelled in Jamie's ear. It belonged to the tall, lanky man recovered from Jamie's initial blow. "Teach the old codger a lesson!"

A vicious grin split the bloody face of the short, piggish Keeler. He laughed, clenched his fists, and rushed at Jamie, obviously intent on dealing out a lot of damage.

Jamie let him get fairly close, then lifted his right leg and planted his boot heel in Keeler's belly. The collision made Jamie's leg bend, but his muscles caught the weight and straightened his leg.

That sent Keeler flying away from him, and drove him and his lanky captor backward. The man tripped and lost his balance.

When he fell, Jamie's massive form came crashing down on top of him.

Jamie rolled away, came up on hands and knees, and surged to his feet. All three of his opponents were still on the ground, stunned. A lot of the immigrants had gathered around to watch the battle, although he hadn't been aware of that while he was fighting. All his attention had been focused on his opponents.

Some of the people looked excited, as if the brawl were a welcome break from the monotony of their journey. Others appeared to be shocked and upset by the violence.

Reverend Bradford stood to one side, the usual frown of disapproval on his face. Jamie picked up his hat and slapped it against his leg to get some of the dust off of it. "What's the matter, Reverend? Fighting bother you just as much as dancing does?"

Bradford snorted. "To tell the truth, Mr. MacCallister, I didn't really expect any better of you."

Before Jamie could respond to that, Lamar Hendricks hurried up and demanded, "What's going on here? Someone told me there was a fight."

"If you can call it that, Captain," one of the immigrants said. He waved a hand at the men on the ground. "Mr. MacCallister just whipped all three of these fellows!"

"Is that right?" Hendricks asked Jamie.

"Seems they hold a grudge against me because of what happened to Ralston. They ran their mouths some, then jumped me." Jamie shrugged and nodded toward Keeler. "Well, that fella there is really the one who did all the talking."

"Keeler," Hendricks said, making a little face as if the name tasted bad in his mouth. "I'm not surprised. He's a hothead and too fond of drink, just like Ralston. It's no wonder they're friends. But Ralston swore these men were good scouts."

"Maybe they are. You can be good at your job and still be a polecat."

Hendricks frowned. "Do you want me to discharge them? I'd assumed they would work for you the same way they were going to work for Ralston, but if there's going to be trouble between you all the way . . ."

"That's up to them," Jamie said. "I don't hold a grudge against any man over a little ruckus like this."

He didn't say it, but he reserved his grudges — and his vengeance — for animals like the outlaws who had murdered his wife.

The three men were groaning and moving around on the ground. Hendricks strode over to them and said sharply, "Keeler! Holcomb! Gilworth! Get up."

The three men gradually climbed to their feet and shook their heads as they tried to get their wits back about them. Keeler and Holcomb, the tall, lanky one, glared murderously at Jamie, but big, bearded Gilworth looked sort of confused as he stood there shaking his head slowly.

"What's the meaning of this?" Hendricks snapped at them. "You had no call to attack Mr. MacCallister."

"Ain't you even gonna listen to our side of the story, Cap'n?" Keeler asked in a whining tone.

"That's what I'm doing. Why did you attack our wagon master?"

"Because he hadn't ought to be the wagon master!" Holcomb said. "Jeb's the rightful wagon master, and we're his scouts."

"Not anymore. Mr. MacCallister has the job now, and you'll work for him and take his orders."

"Damned if I will!" Holcomb said.

"The same goes for me," Keeler rumbled in his gravelly voice.

"Then you can gather your gear and get out of here," Hendricks said with a curt nod. "And since we haven't left Kansas City yet, you won't have any wages coming to you."

"That ain't right," Keeler insisted. "It's been four days since Jeb hired us. That's four days we could've been workin' at some other job."

"No, it's more likely four more days you would have spent lying around whatever saloon or house of ill repute Ralston found you in. Get out of this camp or I'll summon the authorities."

With surly, hate-filled glares, Keeler and Holcomb stumbled off. The crowd parted to let them through. Several of the women looked repulsed by the two men.

Hendricks looked at the third man. "Well, how about you, Gilworth? Do you have anything to say for yourself?"

"Yeah, I do."

Gilworth took a step toward Jamie.

The crowd drew back a little, and a mutter of anticipation went through the group of immigrants. They expected to see more fighting.

Gilworth stuck out his big paw of a hand. "Sorry, Mr. MacCallister. I went along with the others 'cause they got so worked up about what happened to Ralston, but to tell you the truth I was never that fond of the fella myself." He grinned sheepishly. "I reckon I like a good fight, too. From what I'd heard of you, I figured we'd get one."

113

He grunted. "Never figured you'd whip all of us, though. I mean, one —"

"One old man?" Jamie finished for him when Gilworth stopped short in his sentence.

"Well, yeah. No offense, but you ain't no spring chicken, that's for sure."

Jamie snorted. "I'm not ready to be put out to pasture yet, either." Gilworth's hand was still out, so he gripped it. "Jamie Ian MacCallister."

"Hector Gilworth. I've heard a heap about you, Mr. MacCallister, and I'm mighty pleased to make your acquaintance."

"You want to scout for this wagon train and work with me, Hector?"

"Yes, sir. I'd plumb admire to," Hector said with a decisive nod. "That is, if you'll have me."

"You don't make a habit of getting liquored up, do you?"

"Not when there's a job to do. Don't get me wrong, Mr. MacCallister. I like to blow off steam just as much as the next man, but I reckon there's a time and place for it."

Jamie clapped a hand on Hector's shoulder. "You'll do — at least until you give me reason to think otherwise. And you can call me Jamie."

"That'd be an honor. I've heard a whole

heap about you, Mister — I mean, Jamie. I won't let you down."

Jamie looked over at Hendricks. "There's still a problem. We'll need a couple more scouts, since those two quit."

"If you know anyone . . ." the captain began.

"That's just it, I don't," Jamie said. "I didn't know a soul in Kansas City until yesterday, and I've been a mite too busy to make any acquaintances except here among your bunch."

Hector said, "I might know somebody."

"Friend of yours?"

"My cousin. Name of Jess Neville. I don't think he ever worked as a wagon train scout before, but he's been a fur trapper and a prospector and a bullwhacker and done plenty of wanderin' around. Reckon he probably knows the ground between here and Montana about as well as anybody else would."

"He's here in Kansas City?"

"Yes, sir, and he's at loose ends. He just quit workin' for a freight outfit not long ago."

Hendricks said, "He wasn't fired for drinking or causing trouble, was he?"

"No, Jess is the one who up and quit. He never did like stayin' in the same job for too

115

long. When we were growin' up, folks said he was shiftless, but I think it's more like he gets tired of doin' the same thing."

Jamie said, "If you can hunt him up, I'll talk to him. If I like the look of him, we'll give him a job, but he'll have to stay with it until the wagons get where they're going. He can't just go wandering off if he feels like it."

"Yes, sir. I'll make sure he understands that."

"Even if you hire this fellow Neville, you'll still need at least one more scout, won't you?" Hendricks asked.

"That's right," Jamie said with a nod. "Hector, let's go see that cousin of yours, and while we're at it we'll see if we can't come up with somebody else."

"I really appreciate you puttin' so much faith in me, Jamie."

Jamie grinned. "I like to think I can size up a fella's character pretty good, especially after I've swapped punches with him. You'll do. At least, like I said, until you prove different."

"You don't have to worry about that," Hector said fervently. "If you want to go hunt up Jess right now, I know where he's been stayin'."

As the two big men, one young and one

old, were leaving the wagon camp, they passed a group of children who stopped playing to gaze up at them in awe-struck admiration. Jamie spotted the Bradford twins among them and paused to say, "Abigail, that was you who called out that warning to me a little while ago, wasn't it?"

The little girl looked embarrassed and didn't say anything, but Alexander replied, "It sure was, Mr. MacCallister. She just beat me to it, though. I was about to yell for you to look out when Abby did it."

"I appreciate the two of you looking out for me," Jamie told them. "How about we make the two of you honorary wagon train scouts?"

Their faces lit up with grins. Abigail said, "You mean it, Mr. MacCallister?"

"I'm not in the habit of saying things I don't mean," Jamie said. "But that's a serious job I'm giving you. You've got to keep your eyes open for trouble, and if you see anything that doesn't look right, you come find me or Mr. Gilworth or Captain Hendricks and tell us about it, all right?"

They nodded solemnly in unison, and Alexander promised, "We sure will."

Jamie lifted a hand in farewell, and he and Hector walked on.

Hector said, "Those are cute kids. The

preacher's young'uns, ain't they?"

"That's right."

Hector made a face. "I probably shouldn't say it, but I'm not all that fond of their pa."

"Can't argue with you there," Jamie said. "Come on, let's find your cousin."

Chapter Fourteen

Hector Gilworth led Jamie to a rundown hotel on one of the side streets. "I know the place has seen better days, but I reckon it's all Jess can afford right now."

"There's no shame in a man being poor," Jamie said. "There's been plenty of times in my life when I didn't have two pennies to rub together." He didn't mention that these days he had more than two pennies to his name . . . a lot more. This was one of many situations in which he'd found himself where how rich he was didn't matter one blasted bit.

They went up stairs that sagged a little under their weight and down a dusty hallway to the door of Jess Neville's room. Hector banged a fist against the panel and called, "Jess? You awake in there? It's me, Hector."

Jamie heard shuffling footsteps on the other side of the door. It swung open, and a man slightly below medium height peered out at them with bleary, confused eyes. He had thinning brown hair, a couple day's worth of beard stubble, and looked thoroughly unimpressive.

Jamie didn't smell liquor, though, so he was willing to give the man the benefit of the doubt and figure that his bleary eyes came from being sleepy, not hungover.

"What time is it, Hector?" the man asked as he dragged fingers through his hair.

"Sun's been up a couple hours," Hector replied.

"Well, the sun may have been up, but I ain't." The man frowned at Jamie. "Who's this big old galoot?"

"Jamie Ian MacCallister," Jamie introduced himself.

Vague recognition stirred in Jess Neville's eyes. "I think I heard of you, mister. Can't rightly recollect what it was that I heard, though."

"He's the new wagon master for that bunch of immigrants I signed on with," Hector explained.

"What happened to that fella Ralston?" Neville asked.

Hector pointed at Jamie with a thumb and grinned. "Mr. MacCallister — I mean, Jamie — happened to him. Ralston started a ruckus with him in the Bella Royale, and he wound up with a broken leg."

"Ralston did?"

"Yep. You don't see Mr. MacCallister hobblin' around with a broken leg, do you?"

Neville shook his head. "This early in the mornin', I don't trust my eyes not to be playin' tricks on me, so it don't matter what I see. What is it you want?"

"The other two fellas who were supposed to be scouts up and quit because of what happened to Ralston. I thought maybe you'd be interested in one of the jobs."

Neville hadn't invited them into the room, but that was all right with Jamie. He could look past the man's shoulder and see that the room was sparsely furnished with a chair, a rickety table, and a bed with grimy sheets that were so tangled they resembled a rat's nest.

Neville put a hand on the door like he was about to shut it and said, "Dadgum it, Hector. You know I just quit that bullwhackin' job a few days ago. I ain't ready to go back to work yet."

"You mean you ain't completely out of money yet."

"Same thing, ain't it?" Neville tried to swing the door closed.

Hector wedged a big, booted foot between the door and the jamb. "Here's the thing,

121

Jess. We're in sort of a bind. We need a couple scouts, and like I told Jamie, you know the country."

Neville frowned. "Where is it those pilgrims are goin' again?"

"Montana Territory. A place called Eagle Valley."

Neville scratched at his patchy beard as his forehead furrowed in thought. "I think I've heard of it. Wouldn't rightly know how to find it, though."

"Cap'n Hendricks has a map. He's the fella the rest of the immigrants elected to be in charge."

"I know where it is," Jamie said. "I can get the wagons there. It'd be a lot easier with some good help to scout out the trail, though."

"Well, you could get an argument about whether or not I fall into that category, mister." Neville squinted up at him. "Did this big ol' grizzly of a Gilworth tell you that I'm just about the laziest human bein' on the face of the earth."

Jamie glanced at Hector and said dryly, "No, I don't reckon he mentioned that."

"Well, he should have. It ain't that I don't do my work. I do, and you can ask anybody I ever drew wages from about that. But when I ain't workin', I'm not of a mind to do much of anything except take it easy. That seems to rub most people the wrong way."

"You do your job and I don't care how much you sleep," Jamie declared. "That's not any of my business."

"Now, see, that's a reasonable attitude. Most folks I work for, they just ain't reasonable."

"I'm not most folks," Jamie said flatly.

Neville glanced up and down Jamie's tall, rugged frame. "Yeah, I can see that."

"You want the job or not?" Hector asked.

"Now, don't rush me, don't rush me. That's another problem folks have these days. They're in too much of an all-fired hurry all the time. It don't hurt to just slow down and ponder things for a while 'fore you make up your mind."

"The wagon train's leaving at first light tomorrow," Jamie said. "We don't have any time to waste. If you're not coming with us, Neville, we'll need to find somebody else."

"Well, if you're gonna put it that way . . . I promised my aunt Sadie, his mama — Neville nodded at his cousin — that I'd look after ol' Hector here. He's big as an ox, but he ain't much more'n a babe in the woods, you know what I mean?"

"Blast it," Hector said. "I been around.

You make it sound like I'm some sort of tenderfoot, Jess."

Neville ignored that outburst and went on. "I reckon I can come along. Can't stay here in Kansas City, that's for sure. If I did, I might have to take a job clerkin' in a store or something else that's inside. I can't hardly abide havin' walls and a roof around me all the time."

"You won't find many walls and roofs on the prairie between here and Montana Territory," Jamie said.

Neville grinned. "No, that's sure enough true." He put out his hand. "Count me in, I reckon, Mr. MacCallister."

"Call me Jamie." As they shook hands, Jamie went on. "I don't suppose you know somebody else we can hire as a scout."

"I surely don't. Sorry."

Hector said, "Get your possibles together and come on over to the wagon camp today. You can stay there tonight. Might as well save the cost of this hotel room, and that way there's no chance you'll sleep too late."

"Leavin' at first light, you said?" Neville winced a little. "I sure do hate to hear that, but I'll be there. And my word is good."

As they were headed back downstairs, Jamie asked Hector, "Is he telling the truth about his word being good?"

124

"Yeah. Jess has got his faults, no doubt about that, but he's honest as the day is long. If he tells you he'll do something, you can count on it." With a note of worry in his voice, Hector asked, "What are we gonna do about findin' another scout?"

"We'll just have to look around, maybe check in some of the saloons and hash houses. If we don't find anybody" — Jamie's brawny shoulders rose and fell — "I reckon we'll start out with three scouts, counting me, instead of four. Maybe somebody who's already part of the wagon train would take the job. Some youngster, eighteen or so, who's traveling with his folks."

"Scoutin' on the plains is pretty dangerous for somebody who's inexperienced."

"Setting out for Montana at this time of year is pretty dangerous for everybody involved," Jamie pointed out. "They all seem bound and determined to do it, though."

They left the hotel and turned back toward the main business district. Jamie figured they would have a look in the Bella Royale first. It was early in the day, but there might be somebody already in there who'd be interested in a scouting job.

As they passed the variety theater, he glanced at two young men who were looking at the posters for the show that was starting that night. They were dressed like cowboys, which meant they probably had experience with long days in the saddle, and he thought about asking them if they'd like to sign on with the wagon train.

They turned away before he could say anything, though, and he didn't go after them. There was bound to be somebody else in Kansas City who wanted to go to Montana.

CHAPTER FIFTEEN

Now that the gang was in Kansas City, Bodie thought Edwin Swint would go ahead and divide up the loot from the train robbery, as he had said he would. But Swint seemed to be in no hurry to do so.

The money, in the form of twenty dollar gold pieces, had been packed in a chest in the express car. He had split the loot between five sets of saddlebags so it could be carried away. All those saddlebags were safely cached in Swint's hotel room, and a couple men guarded them around the clock, everybody in the gang taking a turn at that duty.

The night before, Swint had kicked the guards out of the room when he came back to the hotel from the Bella Royale with one of the soiled doves who worked there. He'd told the guards to stay right outside in the hall, just to make sure nobody bothered him and his lady friend . . . and the money.

Bodie heard about that from his friend Three-Finger Jake Lucas, who'd heard the story from one of the guards Swint had booted out of the room. The two young men were sitting at a table in a nearby café over a late breakfast.

Jake sipped his coffee. "I'm startin' to wonder if the boss plans to double-cross us and just keep all that loot for himself. Otherwise why don't he go ahead and divvy it up like he promised he would?"

"I guess he's got his reasons," Bodie said.

Jake grunted skeptically. "Yeah, like bein' a dang crook. Think about who you're talkin' about, Bodie. A man like Eldon Swint can't be trusted." Jake's eyes narrowed in thought. "If a man was smart, he might try to get his hands on those double eagles himself and not wait for somebody to just hand him his share."

Bodie frowned and put down his coffee cup. "You'd better not be thinking what it sounds like, Jake. Swint would kill anybody who tried that. We've talked about things like this before."

"Yeah, and I haven't changed my way of thinkin' about it, either." An easy grin flashed across Jake's face. "But shoot, don't worry about it. I'm just talkin', is all. I'd never go against a pard." He paused. "The thing of it is, Eldon ain't really a pard. He's the boss."

Bodie changed the subject. "Are you going to that show tonight?"

"To see some singin' and dancin' girls? You bet I am! We've been out on the trail long enough I'm ready for some entertainment."

They had stopped by the theater on their way to the café. The place was closed, but Bodie and Jake had stood on the boardwalk in front of the building, looking at the posters tacked up next to the ticket window. The posters had drawings of the members of the troupe on them, and Bodie had been particularly intrigued by one of them, a young woman with a mass of dark, curly hair.

Miss Savannah McCoy, her name was, according to the poster.

He didn't know which parts she played in the show, but he was looking forward to finding out. Thinking about her and the performance they were going to watch that night made him forget all about the fortune in double eagles for the time being.

Even though she had been a member of the troupe for more than a year, Savannah still got nervous before each performance. The butterflies, as Cyrus called them, weren't as bad as they had been starting out, but they were still potent enough to force her to stand backstage with one hand pressed to her stomach while she made herself take deep breaths. She closed her eyes and imagined how the night's performance would go, letting it all play out inside her head.

Perfectly, of course.

After a while, the routine began to calm her. She was ready.

When Dollie bustled past and smiled at her, Savannah was able to return that smile and mean it.

"I just snuck a glance at the crowd," Dollie said. "Looks like we're going to have a full house."

"That's good," Savannah said.

"You bet it is. We need to do well here."

Savannah thought she heard a trace of worry in the older woman's voice. The troupe hadn't been doing as well financially in recent months. Quite a few of the performances in various cities hadn't sold out, and it seemed like the expenses of traveling and staying on the road just kept going up. She didn't think the troupe was in any real danger of folding, but that unwelcome possibility lurked in the back of her head, anyway. If that ever happened, she didn't know what she would do.

She had a little money saved up; she could always return to her home in Georgia. But if she did that, it would mean admitting defeat. Worse, there was the chance that her father wouldn't *allow* her to come home. For all she knew, William Thorpe might have disowned her. She hadn't had any contact with him in more than a year.

With a little shake of her head, Savannah put all that out of her thoughts. Concentrate on the thing that was at hand, she told herself, and that was tonight's show. That was the only thing she could do anything about at the moment.

A minute later, Cyrus parted the curtain and walked out on stage to loud applause, dressed in his Shakespearean costume. He swept his plumed hat off his head and gave the audience his usual welcoming spiel, then launched into Hamlet's famous "To be or not to be" speech.

The crowd listened politely, but as she waited behind the curtain Savannah could hear them growing slightly restless toward the end. She knew that some of the men in the audience had come mostly for the singing and dancing, and to look at her and the other female members of the troupe.

Cyrus concluded the famous passage and

said, "Now, ladies and gentlemen, a beautiful rendition of one of your favorite melodies by our lovely songbird of the South, Miss Savannah McCoy!"

Savannah stepped through the curtains and out onto the stage. She smiled as she walked forward, letting her eyes sweep over the audience. As she began to sing Stephen Foster's "Jeanie with the Light Brown Hair," her gaze settled on a man about four rows back, in the middle of the theater.

She had learned that her performances were always better when she pretended to be singing directly *to* a member of the audience. It was largely a matter of luck who that person happened to be. As long as they were in a good place, that was all Savannah cared about.

The person on the receiving end of her song happened to be a young man who looked a few years older than her, with dark hair and a hard-planed face. He was dressed like a cowboy, as was the young man who sat beside him. The other man was more handsome, but there was something compelling about the man Savannah had selected.

Singing to him was no trouble at all.

CHAPTER SIXTEEN

"I swear, she's lookin' right at you." Three-Finger Jake dug an enthusiastic elbow into Bodie's ribs. "She must be sweet on you!"

"I don't even know the girl," Bodie protested. "I mean, I know she's Miss Savannah McCoy, but that's all."

"That's what the fella said when he introduced her."

"I would have known it anyway. I would have recognized her from her picture on the poster."

It was true. The artist had done a good job of capturing Savannah McCoy's likeness. If anything, she was even prettier in person than she was on the poster, although before he saw her Bodie wouldn't have thought that was possible.

She sang beautifully, too. Cyrus O'Hanlon had been right to describe her as a songbird. Savannah was lovely and talented, and if Bodie hadn't known better, he might have said that he was smitten with her.

But that was loco, of course. He could tell just by looking at her that she was a real lady, despite the immoral reputation that actresses and entertainers sometimes had. She wouldn't ever have anything to do with a lawless ruffian like him. For all he knew, she might already be married to one of the other members of the troupe.

Just sit back and enjoy the show, he told himself, and stop thinking about things that could never be.

The show was certainly enjoyable. After Savannah's song, a couple jugglers came out and entertained the crowd for several minutes while the curtains were closed behind them. Bodie heard people moving around back there and figured they were getting ready for something else.

He was right. When the jugglers finished and the curtains were pulled back, several fellows with what looked like bed sheets wrapped around them were standing on steps with white-painted columns at the top. One of them stood a little apart from the others and started talking, but as he did so, several of his companions took out knives and began to sneak up behind him with evil expressions on their faces.

"What the Sam Hill!" Jake exclaimed.

"They're gonna stab that hombre like they was red Injuns!" He reached for the gun on his hip. "I'll stop 'em!"

Bodie's hand shot out and closed around Jake's wrist before Jake could draw the revolver. "Hold on!" Bodie whispered. "I think it's all part of the show."

Not everybody in the audience figured that out as quickly as he did. Several men shouted warnings, which the sheet-wrapped figures on stage ignored. A nervous tingle ran through Bodie's brain. What if he was wrong? What if they were about to commit cold-blooded murder right there on the stage?

That was loco, of course, and a moment later he saw proof of that as the men with knives pretended to stab the fellow who was spouting words. They didn't even do a very good job of pretending, but it was enough to make the audience hoot and holler in enthusiasm. The supposed victim of the assault staggered around and made a real production of dying.

Once he had slumped onto the steps and wasn't moving anymore — except for a twitch every now and then that Bodie could see — Cyrus O'Hanlon came out again, dressed in a sheet like the others, and started making another long speech about burying Caesar. Bodie couldn't follow all of what O'Hanlon said, but the whole thing was stirring, no doubt about that.

O'Hanlon finally shut up and the curtains closed again. An older but still attractive woman came out and sang a song. She was good, Bodie thought, but not as good as Savannah. Then she danced with a young man while another man with a walrus mustache played a piano at the edge of the stage. She was pretty light on her feet, despite her hefty build.

After that, everything started to run together a little for Bodie. There were more dramatic scenes, more singing, more dancing, even some acrobats, one of whom was a gal in a scandalously scanty costume that exposed her knees. But he was waiting to see Savannah McCoy again, and when she didn't appear he began to get a little impatient.

Cyrus O'Hanlon came out in that silly hat with the feather on it again. "Finally, ladies and gentlemen, to conclude our performance tonight we are proud to present one of the most famous scenes in the illustrious history of the theater . . . the balcony scene from the great tragedy *Romeo and Juliet,* as written by Mr. William Shakespeare. It will be performed by yours truly and Miss

136

Savannah McCoy."

Bodie sat up straighter in his seat and thought that it was about time.

Jake elbowed him again. "She's the only one you like, ain't she?"

"Shhh," Bodie said. "They're about to start."

The curtains parted and went back. Some fake bushes had been placed around the stage to represent a garden of sorts, and to one side rose a wall with a window in it. Bodie edged forward in his seat as Savannah appeared in that window and leaned through it so the audience could get a good look at her.

She was worth looking at, wearing a thin gown that was cut almost sinfully low in front. Bodie felt vaguely embarrassed for her having to wear such a getup, but at the same time he couldn't take his eyes off her. She was so attractive that just looking at her felt almost like a punch in the gut to him.

Cyrus O'Hanlon strode onto the stage, wandered through the fake bushes toward the wall, and stopped to throw out an arm and bellow, "Hark! What light through yonder window breaks? 'Tis the east, and Juliet is the sun!"

Savannah was as bright and pretty as the sun, that was for sure, Bodie thought. He could have sat there and watched her all night, but the scene was over all too quickly as far as he was concerned. The curtains swept across the stage again. Bodie sighed. He didn't want the performance to be finished, but there was nothing he could do about it.

The whole troupe came out for a curtain call as the audience cheered, whistled, and applauded, so he got to see Savannah again, if only for a moment.

Finally, the audience began to file out of the theater.

As they left, Jake said, "Now, ain't you glad we came to Kansas City? If we hadn't, you never would've seen that brown-haired gal. You were practically droolin' over her all night like a dog with a big ol' soup bone."

"No, I wasn't," Bodie said. "I think she's pretty, but —"

Jake's snort interrupted him. "I reckon you'd marry her if you got the chance — which is a durned fool way to feel, if you ask me. You know what actresses are like. You might as well marry a —"

Jake stopped short as Bodie stiffened. He had seen enough gunfights to recognize Bodie's stance as that of a man who was ready to hook and draw.

"Sorry," Jake muttered quickly. "I reckon

I was all wrong about Miss McCoy."

"I reckon you were," Bodie snapped. He forced himself to relax. Jake Lucas was his only real friend in the gang, and he didn't want to lose that friendship. He put a smile on his face, even though he was still a little irritated.

As they reached the sidewalk in front of the theater, a very well-dressed man with dark blond hair under his black hat and a neatly trimmed mustache of the same shade bumped hard into Bodie's shoulder. "Watch where you're going, cowboy," the man snapped as he brushed past.

"Hey," Jake said angrily. "You're the one who ran into my pard, mister."

A couple of larger men in cheap suits were trailing the well-dressed gent. Bodie noticed them and realized they were probably bodyguards. Bulges under their coats told him they were carrying guns.

The blond dandy glared at Jake and demanded, "What did you say, Tex?"

"I'm not from Texas," Jake shot back as he squared himself up for trouble.

Bodie put a hand on his friend's arm. "Let it go, Jake."

"But this galoot ran into you and then acted like it was your fault," Jake protested.

"It's not worth causing a ruckus over."

Bodie steered Jake away from the dandy.

The man gave them a sneering smile as they turned to leave. "That's right. I'm an important man in this city. Trifle with me and you'll regret it."

Jake looked back over his shoulder and said hotly, "Oh, yeah? Well, you'll regret —"

"Come *on*." Bodie lowered his voice and added, "We don't want the law talking to us, now do we?"

"Oh," Jake said in sudden understanding. "No, I reckon we don't."

Bodie glanced back at the dandy. The man's arrogant attitude rubbed him the wrong way. If it came down to a fight, Bodie figured he and Jake could have held their own against the bodyguards, whether with fists or guns.

But that would have almost certainly landed them in trouble with the law, and they sure didn't need that. If they were arrested, somebody might figure out they were part of the gang that had held up the train in Kansas. At the very least, Eldon Swint might take it as an excuse to split their shares among the rest of the outlaws . . . or just keep that money for himself.

Bodie wouldn't forget the blond man's face, though. Maybe one of these days their trails would cross again under different circumstances. If that ever happened, Bodie figured he would give Mr. High-and-Mighty a little lesson in manners. If that meant gunplay, then so be it.

In the meantime, he told himself to forget about that hombre and think about Savannah. He just wished there was some way he could let her know how much he had enjoyed her performance.

CHAPTER SEVENTEEN

Since there were only a few female members of the troupe, they used the same dressing room, with the exception of Dollie who shared a dressing room with Cyrus. Savannah was sitting at one of the tables in front of a mirror, removing the makeup she had worn as Juliet, when Cyrus knocked on the door and poked his head into the room.

"Ah, ladies, you're all decently attired," he said.

As usual, Savannah couldn't tell if he was relieved or faintly disappointed by that.

"Savannah, a word with you, my dear?"

"Of course. Was there something wrong with my performance tonight?"

Cyrus shook his head. "Not at all, not at all. Quite the contrary, in fact. There's a gentleman out here who was in the audience. He wishes to convey his compliments to you in person."

Savannah frowned slightly. That was

unusual but not unheard of. Sometimes members of the audience — usually middle-aged or even older men — came backstage and tried to approach the women in the troupe, probably because of the reputation that stubbornly clung to actresses.

Cyrus fended them off most of the time, but now and then — when he judged that the would-be suitor had plenty of money and might be persuaded to make a donation to the troupe — he allowed them to talk to the women.

That bothered Savannah, but she recognized it as a part of her job. She had to be nice to the people who bought tickets. That didn't mean she had to go beyond politeness and surface friendliness, and she never did. "Would you like for me to talk to this man, Cyrus?"

"I think it would be a good thing if you did. It shouldn't be too terrible an ordeal. He's rather attractive, you know, and much younger than some of your, ah, admirers."

She supposed it wouldn't hurt anything. She nodded. "All right."

"The rest of you ladies, let's give Savannah some privacy, shall we?" Cyrus ushered the other female performers out of the dressing room, leaving Savannah alone.

She picked up a dressing gown and

shrugged into it. She was still wearing the costume she wore as Juliet, which was daring enough onstage. In close quarters, it definitely would be immodest.

A moment later a man appeared in the open doorway, holding his hat in one hand. Savannah could tell that the suit he wore was very expensive. He had the unmistakable look of wealth about him, from his carefully barbered dark blond hair to the soft hands to the shoes on his feet that probably cost as much as Cyrus paid her in a year.

"Miss McCoy," he said, his lips smiling under the neatly trimmed mustache, "I can't begin to tell you how much I enjoyed your performance tonight."

She returned the smile. "I believe you just did, Mister . . . ?"

"Kane. Gideon Kane."

He moved closer to her and put out his hand, and without thinking she reached to take it. Instead of shaking hands with her, he turned her hand, held it, lifted it, and pressed his lips to the back of it.

She had played scenes where a man kissed the back of a woman's hand, but she had never seen it happen in real life, only on the stage of a theater. Certainly she had never had it happen to her. She wasn't sure

144

whether to laugh or be touched by the melodramatic gesture.

She settled for saying, "I'm Savannah Mc-Coy."

"I know. Just as I knew when I saw your picture on that poster outside the theater that I had to attend tonight's performance. Kansas City is a rather squalid place, Miss McCoy. I'm not sure a sight as lovely as you has ever been seen here before."

Savannah forced a laugh. "You're flattering me, Mr. Kane —"

"Call me Gideon," he suggested. "It's not flattery when it's true."

She tried to change the subject. "You're in business here?"

His smile twisted a little. "My family is. We own stockyards and slaughterhouses and have interests in the railroad as well as other enterprises. All quite successful, of course. None of it particularly interests me, though. I'm more fond of the arts, such as the theater."

"It's my calling," Savannah said.

"Anyone can tell that by watching you perform. You bring such life and passion to your roles, and you sing wonderfully. I plan to be in the audience every night while your troupe is in Kansas City."

"Oh, you wouldn't want to do that. The

show doesn't really change. Of course, there are minor differences in every performance, but really, if you've seen one of them —"

"Seeing you once is not nearly enough," he broke in. "I don't care about the rest of the performance. I want to see you. Every night."

She was starting to get uncomfortable. She had been looked at by men often enough to recognize lust when she saw it. In Gideon Kane's eyes it bordered on obsession. It was time to ease him out of the dressing room. . . .

Using the heel of one of those expensive shoes, he closed the door behind him.

CHAPTER EIGHTEEN

Savannah felt a tingle of alarm as the latch clicked shut. "Please, Mr. Kane —"

"Gideon."

"Please, Mr. Kane," she repeated, "it's inappropriate enough for the two of us to be alone in here. To have the door closed is simply unacceptable."

"Not to me. However, I don't want to make you uncomfortable. I'll step out into the hall if you'll agree to have a late supper with me."

"I didn't know any restaurants were still open."

Kane shook his head. "I'm not talking about going to a restaurant. My carriage is right outside the theater. We'll go to my house. I've already sent one of my men with word for my cook to prepare a meal —"

Savannah was shaking her head. "No, I simply couldn't do that. It wouldn't be proper. We just met tonight."

She saw the fingers of his hand holding the hat tighten a little on the expensive material.

"When I see something I want, it doesn't take me long to make up my mind to have it. Besides, I'm willing to purchase a large block of tickets for every performance, and from the way O'Hanlon talked when I asked him about you, the troupe can use the money. You won't have to do anything . . . unpleasant . . . to insure those sales, Miss McCoy, I can promise you that. Actually, I think you'd thoroughly enjoy spending time with me."

He stepped closer to her, and if his blatant lechery hadn't been enough to start her heart pounding with anger and fear already, that would have done it.

Once again the wild thought that this was like something out of a melodrama crossed her mind as she said coldly, "I think you've mistaken the sort of woman I am, Mr. Kane."

He smiled. "I doubt it. What can I do to get you to call me Gideon?"

"Nothing. The only thing I want you to do for me is to leave this dressing room."

"Not until I get what I came here for. At least part of it, anyway." He tossed the hat onto the dressing table and reached for her.

"A kiss, at the very least —"

Savannah had dealt with persistent, unwanted suitors before. She supposed every woman in the theater had at one time or another. Somehow, though, she sensed that Gideon Kane was more dangerous than most.

She didn't hesitate. She still wore Juliet's slippers, but that didn't stop her from kicking him in the groin.

The blow seemed to take him completely by surprise. As her heel sunk into his flesh, he grunted in pain and bent forward. His hand shot out, grabbed the dressing gown, and ripped it open. Some of the costume came with it, exposing even more of Savannah's skin. She jerked back and pulled free from him, and while he was off-balance she gave him a hard shove that sent him falling back toward the door. He landed against it with a heavy thud.

Close by in the backstage corridor, Cyrus called worriedly, "Savannah, are you all right?"

Kane held one hand to his painful nether region while the other pressed against the wall to hold himself up. He glared at her and grated, "You little bi. . . ."

"Cyrus!" Savannah called.

He flung the door open and stood in the

doorway with several members of the troupe crowding up behind him, including a couple burly stagehands. "Are you all right, lass?" Still wearing Romeo's costume, he put his hand on the hilt of the prop sword that hung sheathed at his waist.

"I'm fine," Savannah said as she pulled her garments closed again, calling on her skills as an actress to sound a lot more calm than she really felt. "Mr. Kane was just leaving."

Kane said, "You'll —"

"Regret this?" Savannah interrupted him. She shook her head. "I don't think so."

"Good night, Mr. Kane," Cyrus said. "The time for backstage visits is over."

Kane glared murderously at both of them, then straightened with a visible effort and stepped unsteadily toward the door. Cyrus moved aside to let him out.

"Oh, wait!" Savannah picked up Kane's hat from the dressing table, and when he turned back toward her, she tossed it to him. "You wouldn't want to forget your hat."

He caught it awkwardly, and his glare grew even darker. He put the hat on and moved slowly past the members of the troupe in the hallway, all of whom frowned menacingly at him.

Dollie looked like she would have cheerfully taken a knife to him and carved him up like a turkey.

When Kane was gone, Savannah said, "I'm sorry about the tickets he promised to buy, Cyrus. I know the troupe could use the money."

Before Cyrus could reply, Dollie said briskly, "Nonsense. We don't need the money of scoundrels like that. Did he hurt you, dear?"

"He never laid a finger on me," Savannah replied honestly. "Well, except when he kissed the back of my hand."

"He what?" Cyrus exclaimed. "What does he think this is, some French farce?"

"Never mind about that." Dollie took her husband's arm. "Come on, everyone. Let's let Savannah get dressed. We'll see you back at the hotel, dear."

"Of course," Savannah said with a nod.

The others left, and she closed the door and quickly got dressed in her regular clothes. As she did, she worried about what Gideon Kane might do. He hadn't struck her as the sort of man to just forget about what had happened tonight.

Even though she had no proof that he was as rich and powerful as he'd said, she didn't doubt it for a second. It took real wealth for

151

a man to display the sort of cruel, careless arrogance that he had. As usual, when the will of someone like that was thwarted, he had started to bluster and threaten.

It was possible that Kane might go to the owner of the theater and pressure the man to cancel the rest of the troupe's engagement and refuse to pay them. She had seen men employ tactics like that before when they held a grudge.

Actually, it was the sort of thing her father might have done if someone angered him, although William Thorpe would never make improper advances toward a young woman.

Savannah stepped out of the dressing room and looked for the others. She didn't see anyone backstage, so she supposed they were waiting for her out front.

But Dollie had said they would see her back at the hotel, Savannah recalled. They could have gone on, figuring that she would catch up with them. The hotel was less than two blocks away, after all.

Even so, she felt nervous as she walked through the darkened theater. Her footsteps echoed from the cavernous ceiling. Lamps still burned here and there, casting enough light for her to see her way without any trouble.

An old man was sweeping up. He nodded

to her as she passed. "Good night, miss."

"Good night," Savannah told him. For a second she thought about asking him if he would walk her back to the hotel, but then she discarded that idea. That wasn't his job, and she didn't want to inconvenience him.

She went out through the theater lobby, past the box office, and stepped onto the sidewalk. The street was fairly dark, but again, she could see well enough to get where she was going. From where she stood, the hotel was even visible a short distance up the street, a warm yellow glow coming from its lobby windows.

There was also enough light for her to see the carriage that suddenly pulled up beside her and stopped on the cobblestone street. Two men, large and threatening in the gloom, stepped out of it, and one of them rumbled, "You're comin' with us, Miss McCoy."

CHAPTER NINETEEN

Bodie couldn't get Savannah McCoy out of his mind. From the theater he and Jake had gone to the Bella Royale for a drink and to see if any of the other boys were there. The saloon had become the gang's unofficial headquarters while they were in Kansas City waiting for Eldon Swint to divide the loot.

Bodie nursed a beer at a table with Jake and a couple other outlaws, Clete Mahaffey and Dave Pearsoll. They were playing a desultory game of poker, but Bodie couldn't concentrate on his cards. His thoughts kept straying to Savannah.

Jake grinned as he raked in another pot after winning a hand from Bodie. "You know why our pard here keeps losin', boys?" Without waiting for an answer he went on. "It's because he's distracted. He's too busy moonin' over a gal to think about playin' poker."

"What gal's that?" Mahaffey asked. "That redheaded soiled dove called Dora who works here, maybe? She knows some tricks that'd sure keep a man's mind occupied . . . among other things." He guffawed with laughter.

Pearsoll joined in, and Bodie wished Jake would just shut up about the subject.

But Jake wasn't going to do that. "Naw, it's an actress we saw at the theater tonight. We took in the show, and it was a good one. But Bodie here didn't have eyes for nobody but this brown-haired Southern belle named Savannah."

The other two men hooted even more.

Glaring across the table at his friend, Bodie scraped his chair back. "I don't reckon I feel like playing anymore. Deal me out."

"You're gonna quit just because I was hoo-rawin' you a little?" Jake asked. "That ain't like you, Bodie."

"I'm just tired, that's all," Bodie said with a shake of his head. "Think I'll head for the hotel and turn in."

Jake shrugged. "Suit yourself." He seemed a little insulted.

But Bodie didn't really care. He didn't appreciate being made sport of. As he turned to walk away from the table, he heard Jake say to Mahaffey and Pearsoll,

"There's somethin' I've been wantin' to talk to you boys about."

Bodie didn't hear any more. The hubbub in the saloon swallowed up the rest of Jake's words. Whatever the conversation was, Bodie didn't know or care anything about it.

He drew in a deep breath of night air as he stepped out of the saloon. Kansas City wasn't the most fragrant place in the world; the vast stockyards on the edge of town took care of that. The pungent smells that came from there drifted over the whole town.

But even so, the air outside seemed cleaner to Bodie than that inside the Bella Royale. After pausing on the sidewalk for a moment, he turned toward the hotel.

When he reached the next corner, his steps carried him in a different direction. He realized he was heading toward Channing's Variety Theater.

No point in going there, he told himself. The show had been over for a while. All the performers, including Savannah, would have left already and gone back to wherever they were staying or to get something to eat. All he could do was stand in front of the darkened theater and gaze at it, remembering what he had seen inside earlier.

It would have to be enough, he decided, and walked a little faster. It wasn't far to the theater.

As he approached, he saw the carriage that had pulled up in front of it. Several shadowy forms were moving around on the sidewalk between the street and the theater. Something about the situation made the hackles rise on the back of Bodie's neck.

A second later, a woman's voice rang out clearly. "Gideon Kane sent you, didn't he?"

"Never you mind about who sent us, gal," a rough male voice answered. "You just come on with us, and there won't have to be no trouble."

"Get away from me. I'll scream!"

"Look out. She's gonna run! Grab her!"

Bodie was already moving. He'd recognized Savannah's voice when the woman first spoke.

She lunged away from the two men, but they were too fast for her and had her hemmed in against the building.

Bodie left his feet in a diving tackle. His shoulder rammed into the back of the nearest man. The impact drove the man toward his companion. They crashed together, and their feet got tangled up. All three men fell to the sidewalk.

Bodie scrambled to his feet first. Savannah stood a few feet away, gaping at him in surprise. His hat had come off when he tackled the first man, so he snatched it off the sidewalk and grabbed Savannah's arm with his other hand. "Come on, Miss McCoy! I'll get you out of here!"

He didn't know who the two bruisers were, except that Savannah thought they worked for Gideon Kane, whoever that was. It didn't matter. They had threatened her, and he had to get her away from them.

But as they turned to run, one of the men regained his feet and shot out a hand to snag Bodie's shirt collar. Bodie felt himself being jerked backward, away from Savannah. He was whirled around, and a punch exploded against his jaw, knocking him back against the carriage.

The big man bored in, obviously intent on keeping Bodie pinned against the carriage with his bulk while he hammered the young outlaw with his fists. Bodie sensed as much as he saw another powerful blow rocketing at his face and dropped desperately out of its path.

The punch went over his head and smashed into the side of the carriage. The man howled in pain and danced back, shaking his injured hand.

Bodie looked around for Savannah but couldn't locate her. The second man blocked his view, looming up to throw a roundhouse punch that would take Bodie's head off if it landed.

Once again, Bodie avoided the blow at the last second, weaving aside so that the man's fist barely scraped the side of his head. He buried the toe of his boot in the man's belly, doubling him over. Moving fast, he clapped his hat back on his head, clubbed his fists together, and brought them down on the back of the man's neck, driving him to the ground.

Bodie took a step away from the carriage but didn't even have time to think about finding Savannah and hustling her to safety. Something crashed down on his back from above, knocking him off his feet.

The small part of his brain that was still working realized the carriage must have a driver, and that man had leaped from the high seat onto him. The next instant, the man's weight came down hard enough on Bodie to force all the air from his lungs. The world spun crazily and the night turned red in front of his eyes for a second, and he knew he was close to passing out.

If he lost consciousness, the three men might stomp him to death. Even worse, they might succeed in kidnapping Savannah.

With that thought fueling his efforts, he forced himself to ram an elbow up and back, into the midsection of the man who had tackled him. At the same time, he heaved up with his other arm and his legs.

Bodie wasn't big, but he had the lean, muscular build of a panther and had spent years taking care of himself and learning how to survive. He was stronger than he looked, and he was able to throw his opponent off to the side.

He surged to his feet, but the other two men had recovered enough to attack him again. He was trapped between them as their fists crashed into him. He couldn't block all the blows, couldn't get set to throw some punches of his own.

One man screamed suddenly and reeled backward, pawing frantically at the side of his neck, startling his companion enough to give Bodie an opening. He jabbed a stinging left into the man's face and followed it with a right cross that landed solidly on the hombre's jaw, sending him spinning to the sidewalk.

The one who had started yelling staggered into a slanting ray of light coming from a window in a nearby building, and for the first time, Bodie got a good look at his face. A second later, he realized where he had seen the man before.

Earlier, the big bruiser had been with the

rich, blond gent who had bumped into Bodie outside the theater. That meant the second man was probably the other bodyguard.

Based on what Savannah had said, the rich, arrogant son of a gun would be Gideon Kane, Bodie supposed. Not that it mattered. Anybody who wanted to hurt Savannah McCoy, for whatever reason, was his enemy.

The yelling man finally plucked whatever was bothering him from his neck and shouted, "Shoot him! Shoot that cowboy!"

CHAPTER TWENTY

For a second, Bodie didn't know who the man was talking to, then from the corner of his eye he caught a glimpse of the driver fumbling under his coat, trying to pull a gun.

Nobody would ever mistake Bodie Cantrell for a real gunfighter like Wild Bill Hickok, but he could get his Colt out of its holster fairly fast, and he usually hit what he aimed at. He drew the revolver and smoothly eared back the hammer as the barrel came up. He had beaten the carriage driver cleanly to the draw, so he expected the man to give up.

But the driver fumbled out a pistol and thrust it toward Bodie.

That took the decision out of Bodie's hands. He squeezed off a shot before the man could pull the trigger. The Colt roared and bucked against his palm.

The bullet smashed into the man's shoulder and slewed him around. He yelled as the pistol flew from his fingers.

Savannah grabbed Bodie's arm and tugged on it. "Come on!" she urged. "Maybe they won't chase us as long as you've got that gun!"

Bodie didn't figure they could count on that. He fired again, aiming low so that the bullet hit the sidewalk near the two men who were still on their feet. The one going after the driver's pistol forgot about it for the moment as they both leaped for cover.

Bodie wheeled around and started to run. He took Savannah's arm and pulled her along, making sure he didn't outdistance her with his long-legged strides.

He was a little surprised she was still there. He had hoped she would take off running as soon as she got the chance. But she had waited for him and they needed to put as much distance as they could between themselves and the three men.

Bodie didn't know where he was going. He wasn't familiar with any of Kansas City except the area around the hotel, the Bella Royale Saloon, and the theater. But as an open stretch of ground loomed up to his right, he saw the wagons parked there and steered Savannah in that direction.

"We'll hide among those wagons," he told

her in a whisper. "They won't be able to find us."

She didn't say anything, but she went with him willingly. Even though he knew perfectly well who she was, she wouldn't have any idea as to his identity. All she knew was that he was trying to help her, and he supposed that was enough for the time being.

They ducked around the closest of the big, canvas-covered vehicles. The wagons were arranged in a rough circle, the same formation the immigrants would use when they were traveling out on the prairie. The difference was that away from town, the livestock would be kept inside the circled wagons, not in a corral adjacent to the lot where the wagons were parked.

The big campfire in the center of the circle had burned down to mostly embers and a few faintly flickering flames that didn't cast much light. The wagons were dark and quiet. Everybody in the camp seemed to be asleep.

Bodie led Savannah farther away from the street. When he thought they were deep enough in the camp, he dropped to a knee beside one of the big wheels and urged Savannah to kneel beside him. He didn't like the idea of her getting her dress dirty, but they needed to hide in the shadows in case the three men came looking for them.

He leaned closer to her, and suddenly felt a little lightheaded from the fight or from the clean, tantalizing scent of her thick brown hair. He didn't know which.

"Are you all right?" he asked in a whisper. "Did those varmints hurt you?"

"No, I'm fine," she replied, keeping her voice as quiet as his. "Just scared."

"You don't have to be scared, Miss McCoy. I won't let them get you."

"You know who I am?" She sounded a little surprised.

"Why, sure I do. I was in the audience at the theater tonight. Right in the center on the fourth row."

Their shoulders were touching as they knelt beside the wagon. He felt her tiny start of surprise and wondered what it was about.

She whispered, "I saw you while I was singing my first number."

"It was a mighty pretty song. My name's Bodie, by the way. Bodie Cantrell."

"I'm pleased to meet you, Mr. Cantrell. Under the circumstances, very pleased indeed."

They crouched there for a moment in silence, catching their breath. Then Bodie asked, "Why were those fellas trying to grab you?"

"To take me back to their employer's mansion, I expect. They work for a man named Gideon Kane."

"Fancy dressed fella with blond hair and a mustache?" Once again he felt Savannah react slightly.

With a note of worry in her voice, she said, "That's him, all right. He's not a friend of yours, is he?"

"Not hardly. Me and a pard of mine had a run-in with him earlier this evening. I didn't like him then, and now that I know he likes to have girls kidnapped, I don't cotton to him that much more."

"I think he's probably a bad man to have for an enemy."

"I've heard it said you can judge a man by his enemies. In this fella's case, I reckon it says some pretty good things about us."

She was quiet for a second, then she laughed softly. Bodie had seldom heard a nicer sound.

"I think you're right about that, Mr. Cantrell."

They were quiet again, and Bodie listened intently, searching the night for any indication that Kane's men were coming after them. When he didn't hear anything that seemed unusual, he asked, "Do you know how come that fella started screaming and grabbing at his neck?"

"I certainly do. I stuck a hat pin in the side of his neck as hard as I could."

It was all Bodie could do not to burst out laughing. He held it in check and chuckled softly. "I didn't notice you wearing a hat."

"I wasn't. But I always carry a hatpin in my bag, anyway, just in case. Tonight it came in handy."

"It sure did," Bodie agreed. "That was pretty brave of you, jumping in like that. They had me in a pretty bad spot. I might not have been able to get away from them if you hadn't given me a hand."

"You were risking your life to help me. It was the least I could do."

Bodie was about to tell her that he would have given his life to save her, but he didn't get a chance to say anything else. At that moment, an arm looped around his neck from behind, closed on his throat like an iron bar, and jerked him to his feet. He felt the cold, hard ring of a gun muzzle pressed to the side of his head.

CHAPTER TWENTY-ONE

One thing about growing older, Jamie had discovered, was that he didn't seem to need as much sleep as he once had. He found himself awake at night fairly often, and he wasn't the sort to just lie there in his bunk or bedroll and stare at the darkness. He felt better getting up and moving around. He liked to stay busy, always had.

Besides, even though the wagon train was camped in a city and surrounded by civilization, it didn't mean there were no dangers lurking in the darkness. In some ways, the situation was more precarious than if the immigrants had been out on the prairie. The threats were just different, that's all.

For those reasons, Jamie was up and taking a pasear around the camp when he spotted a couple figures skulking beside one of the wagons.

They might be two of the immigrants, he told himself. Maybe a boy and a girl who weren't supposed to be courting had slipped out of their families' wagons for a midnight rendezvous. In that case, it wouldn't be any of his business. Young love could run its course — or not — without any meddling from him.

However, in one way of looking at it, anything that happened involving the wagon train was the wagon master's business, he thought. Anyway, something about those two struck Jamie as suspicious, and he had long since learned to trust what his gut was telling him.

With the same stealth that had allowed him to sneak up unnoticed on countless enemies over the past five decades, he approached the two shadowy forms. One of his Colts came smoothly out of its holster with only the faintest brushing of steel against leather.

The two people were whispering to each other and seemed to have no idea he was right behind them. Jamie's eyes, still keen despite his years, made out the fact that one of the figures was male and the other female, but they didn't sound like a couple of love struck kids.

Actually, they were talking like they were in some sort of trouble, maybe with the law. Regardless, they were strangers and didn't belong there. Since Jamie had taken the job of getting the pilgrims safely to Montana Territory, his first responsibility was to protect the wagon train.

Because the man was armed, Jamie decided the best thing to do was make sure he couldn't yank that gun out and start blazing away. With so many folks around, flying lead could tear through the canvas covers on the wagons and would be a real danger.

When Jamie made his move, it was swift and sure, grabbing the man from behind, hauling him to his feet, and pressing the Colt to his head. "Take it easy, mister," he rasped into the man's ear. "It wouldn't take much to make this gun go off and splatter your brains all over that canvas."

The woman sprang to her feet, and for a second Jamie thought she was going to bolt.

But she didn't. She said urgently, "Please don't kill him! He doesn't really have anything to do with this. Just let him go and . . . and I'll go with you to Mr. Kane's house."

The fella Jamie had hold of made a squawking sound, like he was trying to object to what the woman had just said, but he couldn't get any words past Jamie's iron grip on his throat.

"Miss, I don't have any idea what you're

talking about," Jamie told her. "I don't know anybody named Kane. I just want to know why you're sneaking around these wagons. You plan on robbing some of them?"

"No!" the woman exclaimed. "We're not thieves, I swear. We're just trying to hide from some men who . . . who wanted to kidnap me."

The story came pouring out of her in disjointed fashion, some wild yarn about her being an actress and a rich fellow who had taken a fancy to her and was used to getting what he wanted, even if that meant taking it by force.

Jamie could believe the part about the woman being an actress, because the story she told sounded like something out of a play penned by some crazy scribbler. When the flow of words from her finally ran down, he asked, "So who's this hombre I've got hold of?"

"His name is Bodie Cantrell. He risked his life to help me get away from those terrible men. That's all I really know about him."

Despite being a little lurid, the woman's story had the ring of truth about it. Jamie had a hunch she wasn't lying to him, and since he was in the habit of following his hunches, he let go of Bodie.

171

There was nothing wrong with being careful. Now that he had a hand free, Jamie reached down and plucked the man's revolver from its holster before Bodie had a chance to stop him. The man was too busy at the moment dragging air back into his lungs after being choked for a couple minutes.

Jamie had been careful not to squeeze hard enough to kill him or even make him pass out, so he recovered quickly. Still a little breathless, he asked, "Who . . . who are you?"

"Jamie Ian MacCallister. Wagon master for this bunch that's headed to Montana."

"You didn't have to try to kill me," Bodie complained.

Jamie chuckled coldly. "Mister, if I wanted you dead, you wouldn't be standing there right now. You'd already be shaking hands with St. Peter."

He was about to say something else when one of the numerous dogs that belonged with the wagon train started to bark. None of the curs had raised a ruckus when Cantrell and the woman, whatever her name was, had sneaked into the camp a few minutes earlier, but several of them began to carry on.

A shaft of light played around the camp

172

from the direction of the street. Somebody had a bull's-eye lantern, Jamie realized. The light darted toward them like a searching finger in the night.

CHAPTER TWENTY-TWO

"Get under the wagon," Jamie told the two strangers in a low, urgent voice.

"What?" Bodie said.

"Under the wagon," Jamie repeated. "That's probably the varmints who were after the gal."

They didn't need any more urging. Bodie took hold of Savannah's arm and helped her crawl underneath the wagon. Jamie moved so that his buckskin-clad legs would help shield them and planted his feet solidly on the ground as several men approached. One of them carried the lantern.

The Colt .44 was still in Jamie's hand. He raised the weapon, pointed it at the intruders, and called softly, "Lower that light, by God, or I'll shoot it out!"

The light played over him, but only for a second before it dipped toward the ground. It was long enough for the men to have seen that he had the drop on them.

174

"Take it easy, mister," one of them said. "We're not lookin' for any trouble."

"You may have found it anyway," Jamie snapped. "I'm the boss of this wagon camp. Who are you, and what are you doing here?"

"We're looking for a woman," another man said. "She's a thief. She stole something from our boss, and we're just tryin' to get it back."

"That's right," the first man added. "She's got this cowboy with her. I think he's an outlaw. He must be in on it with her."

Once again Jamie's instincts passed judgment on what he was hearing . . . and he didn't like it. These men were lying — which meant Cantrell and the woman were probably telling the truth.

"Well, there's nobody like that around here," Jamie told the three men. "I've been standing guard all night, and I'd know."

The man with the lantern came closer, but he kept the light pointed toward the ground.

"No offense, old-timer, but we're not going to just take your word for it. We'll have a look around —"

"I don't think so." Jamie's voice was hard, flat, and dangerous as he interrupted.

"Look, you may have a gun, but there are three of us —"

"Which means I'll have two bullets left over in this old Colt of mine when I get through with you, since I carry the hammer on an empty chamber." There was no mistaking the threat in Jamie's voice. He wasn't bluffing. The men were strangers, and they had bullied their way into the wagon camp uninvited. As far as he was concerned, he would be well within his rights to ventilate all three of them.

The moment stretched out tensely until one of the men muttered, "That old coot sounds crazy enough to do it. I've already been shot at once tonight, and I ain't in the mood to have it happen again."

The man with the lantern argued. "The boss won't like it if we come back without—"

"He's smart. He can figure out what to do about it. Come on," interrupted the other man who had spoken.

Two men started backing away, and the one with the lantern wasn't going to stay there and take on Jamie by himself. He blustered, "You don't know how much trouble you're getting yourself into, mister," then turned and followed his companions out of the camp.

After a few moments, Jamie said quietly to the couple under the wagon, "You two stay right where you are until I get back."

He walked to the edge of the camp where he could look along the street and make sure the three intruders were gone. He saw them walking quickly away from the camp, already more than a block away. He supposed they were on their way to report to the man who had ordered them to kidnap the young woman. If she had told him her name, he had missed it.

He pouched the iron and turned back to the wagon where he had left her and her rescuer. He knew it was possible they might have crawled out and lit a shuck without waiting for him, as he had told them to do. However, when he reached the right wagon and said, "Come on out of there," they emerged from under the vehicle.

Bodie stood up first, then helped the woman to her feet. "Are they gone?"

"Yeah. I made sure of that. Of course, they might circle back and try to slip into the camp again, so why don't the two of you come with me?"

"Where are you taking us?" the woman asked nervously. If what she had told him earlier was true, Jamie didn't blame her for not being very trusting.

"I want to get the two of you out of sight while we hash this out. We'll go to my friend

Moses's wagon. He won't mind us disturbing him. He's a preacher, sort of, so he ought to be used to folks waking him up and needing his help in the middle of the night." Jamie led them across the camp and stopped beside one of the wagons. It was a little hard to tell them apart in the dark, so he hoped he had the right one as he hissed Moses's name through the opening above the tailgate.

A moment later, he heard a sleepy mutter from inside the wagon, then Moses stuck his head through the opening. "Jamie? What's going on? It's awfully late."

"Yeah, I know. I've got a couple people here who need a place to get out of sight for a little while. Reckon you can let them stay here?"

"Well . . . sure, I guess so. Climb on in, folks. These are hardly luxury accommodations, though."

"We don't care about that," Bodie said.

Jamie lowered the tailgate, and Bodie helped the woman climb into the wagon. Moses gave her a hand, too.

When the younger people were inside, Jamie perched a hip on the tailgate. "All right, Cantrell, introduce the lady to Moses and me."

"We really just met tonight, too, Mr. Mac-

Callister, but this is Miss Savannah McCoy. She's part of the troupe of entertainers that's performing at Channing's Variety Theater, down the street."

"I remember seeing the place," Jamie said with a nod. "It's a pleasure to meet you, Miss McCoy."

"Indeed it is," Moses added. "May I offer you something to drink?"

"No, but thank you," Savannah said. "I just want to get back to the hotel where my friends are staying."

"We'll see that you get there safely," Jamie promised. "First, though, I want to hear more about those three hombres who were after you."

"I'm afraid it's very simple. Their employer, like too many other people, believes that actresses are the same as prostitutes."

"My daughter's an actress," Jamie said curtly. "I don't cotton to people who think like that."

Bodie shook his head. "Neither do I. Once you're safe, Miss McCoy, I think I might have to look up this Gideon Kane and teach him a lesson."

"Oh, no," Savannah said quickly. "You've already done enough for me tonight, Mr. Cantrell. More than enough. You risked your life by fighting those men. And you saved me from being dragged off by them and turned over to that . . . that . . ."

"No-good polecat will do," Jamie finished for her. "I reckon I can say that even though I never met Gideon Kane."

"You got that right, Mr. MacCallister," Bodie said. "If anything, you're not being fair to the polecats of the world."

Jamie laughed. He felt an instinctive liking for this young man. If he had seen the same thing going on, a young woman being threatened, he would have jumped right into the middle of the fracas just like Cantrell had. "What are you doing here in Kansas City? You wouldn't happen to be looking for a job, would you?"

Jamie and Hector Gilworth had spent all day trying to find someone else who was willing to sign on with the wagon train as a scout, but they hadn't had any luck. Jamie was prepared to set out with just him, Hector, and Jess Neville to handle the scouting chores, but it would be better if they had at least one more good man.

Cantrell hesitated, then said in reply to Jamie's question, "No, I reckon not. I'm not working at anything right now, but I've got some possibilities coming up soon."

"Well, if you change your mind between now and first light, let me know," Jamie told him. "I'm looking for another scout to help me get these wagons to Montana."

Brodie let out a low whistle of surprise. "Montana's a long way off. You're setting out this late in the year?"

"It's their idea," Jamie said. "I've warned 'em about it. Seems like we're going, though, one way or the other."

"There's really no choice," Moses put in.

Jamie let that pass. There was at least a chance they would make it, and if anybody could get those immigrants where they were going, he knew it was him. That wasn't boastful on his part, just a realistic acknowledgment of his abilities.

Savannah said, "I hate to inconvenience you even more, Mr. Cantrell, but do you think you could accompany me back to my hotel?"

"Sure," Bodie answered without hesitation. "I planned to all along."

"And I'm coming, too," Jamie said. "With both of us along, I don't reckon anybody's liable to bother you. How about you, Moses?"

"Well, I wouldn't be any good in a fight, but I'll come along," the young rabbi said. "Strength in numbers, eh?" He fingered the nightshirt he was wearing. "Just let me put some pants on."

Bodie and Savannah climbed out of the wagon. Moses joined them a couple minutes later. Together, the four of them left the wagon camp and walked toward the hotel where the O'Hanlon troupe was staying.

Jamie kept his right hand on the butt of the Colt on that side, but he didn't need the gun. No one bothered them. When they reached the hotel, he was about to turn back when Savannah said, "If you could just come into the lobby with me. Those men might be waiting."

That was true, Jamie thought. It would be a shame to get Savannah this close to safety and then have Gideon Kane's men grab her after all.

The lamps in the lobby were turned low, and no clerk was on duty at the desk. It was bright enough in the room for Jamie to get his first good look at Bodie and Savannah. The young woman was a beauty, all right, even with her dress disheveled and dirty from crawling around under a covered wagon. Bodie Cantrell was a medium-sized young man in range clothes, with black hair under his tipped-back hat.

The four of them had just entered the lobby when a man stood up from a chair next to a potted plant where he'd obviously been waiting. He started toward them, but clearly he was no threat. Middle-aged and portly, he sported a black eye, and there was dried blood around his mouth. "Savannah!" he exclaimed. "Thank God! We didn't know what had happened to you or if you were all right."

Savannah caught hold of his extended hands and gaped at him in surprise. "Cyrus, what happened to you? You look like you've been in a fight!"

"I have," Cyrus O'Hanlon said grimly. "Gideon Kane and his men have been here, Savannah . . . and they were looking for you."

CHAPTER TWENTY-THREE

The news hit Savannah hard. She gasped as if she'd been punched in the stomach. Beside her, Bodie put a hand on her arm to steady her.

"Oh, Cyrus, I'm so sorry," she was able to say after a moment. "Are you hurt badly? Was anyone else hurt?"

Cyrus waved a hand. "Don't worry about me, child. This isn't the first time I've been roughed up. I'll be fine. Harry Sennett has a broken arm, but no one else suffered anything except bumps and bruises."

Bodie asked, "Why would they do something like that?"

"Because they were looking for me," Savannah answered before Cyrus could say anything. "Isn't that right?"

"Aye," Cyrus answered with a shrug. The gesture made him wince. "Kane demanded to know if you were here, and when I told him you weren't, he said that I was lying.

One of his men hit me, and Harry jumped into the fight. He wasn't any match for them, though. The commotion drew the rest of the troupe. We tried to give a good account of ourselves, but" — he shrugged again — "we're performers, not brawlers."

"Wish I'd been here to lend you a hand," Jamie MacCallister growled.

Cyrus looked him up and down. "My, you're big as a mountain, aren't you, friend? I wish you'd been here, too. Who's this, Savannah?"

"This is Mr. MacCallister. He's the wagon master for that wagon train camped down the street. He helped us after Mr. Cantrell got me away from Kane's men to start with."

"I'm afraid I'm not acquainted with young Mr. Cantrell, either . . . although you do look a bit familiar, sir."

"I was in the audience at the show tonight."

"Ah! That explains it." Cyrus still looked puzzled, though. "You're a friend of Savannah's?"

"He is now," she said. "He risked his life fighting Kane's men when they tried to kidnap me. We got away and hid among Mr. MacCallister's wagons."

"I'm starting to get the players straight,"

Cyrus said with a nod. He turned to Moses Danzig. "And you are . . . ?"

Moses introduced himself, then added, "I'm going to Montana Territory with Jamie and the rest of the wagon train."

Jamie asked, "Did anybody send for the law while that ruckus with Kane's men was going on?"

Cyrus nodded. "One of our people did. But that just made things worse. When the police came in —" He had to stop and draw a deep breath. "When the police came in, Kane and his men claimed that *we* had attacked *them.* He accused us of being criminals. He said we had pickpockets working the crowd and that we were no better than gypsies."

"Let me guess," Jamie said with a frown. "The law believed them."

Cyrus spread his hands helplessly. "Kane and his family are rich. Of course the authorities believed him. The officers threatened to run us out of town . . . but Kane said he didn't want to cause trouble for us and told them he didn't want to press charges. After the police left, though, he said he would see to it that we were all thrown in jail unless we turned Savannah over to him. Then he told us we had until morning to find her and take her to his house."

Savannah felt sick and light-headed. If not for Bodie's hand on her arm, she might have collapsed. How could things have taken such a bad turn, so quickly? She hadn't done anything to cause it. She'd just been going about her job, following her calling, practicing her art. Then suddenly, without any warning, Gideon Kane had walked into her dressing room, and with him had come pure evil.

That was just the way things were in life, she told herself. Bad things happened for no apparent reason.

But understanding that and being able to accept it were two different things. It wasn't fair for Cyrus and the other members of the troupe to suffer just because Gideon Kane had decided he had to have her.

"Listen," she said, speaking quickly so she wouldn't back out on going through with the idea that had just occurred to her. "I have to leave the troupe."

"What?" Cyrus said with a confused frown. "No! You don't need to do that. We'll figure some way out of this —"

"There isn't any other way out of it," she told him. "Kane will use the law against you, and you know he'll get away with it, too. At the very least, he'll have you run out of town. At worst, you'll all be locked up. I can't stand to have that on my conscience, Cyrus. I just can't."

"We'll fight him," Cyrus insisted. "I'll hire a lawyer and fight him in court."

Savannah shook her head. "No lawyer worth anything will want to go up against the Kane family. There's just no other answer, Cyrus, and you know it."

He looked miserable as he tried to come up with something else to say and couldn't. Finally he managed to ask, "But where will you go?"

Savannah turned to look at Jamie Mac-Callister. "To Montana Territory. You can find a place for me in your wagon train, can't you, Mr. MacCallister?"

"It's not really my wagon train," Jamie replied. "I don't have any say over who stays and who goes, as long as they follow my orders once we're on the trail."

"I can follow orders. I'm good at taking direction, aren't I, Cyrus?"

"You're a quick study," Cyrus admitted. "You won't be playing a part, though, Savannah. You'd really be an immigrant."

With a faint smile, she said, "Isn't all life just playing a part, at least to a certain extent? We know what we're supposed to do because we've read it in books and seen it onstage. And then as we live it, it becomes real."

"I suppose you could look at it like that," Cyrus said grudgingly. "But I don't want to lose you. Neither will the others."

"It's for their own good. The troupe has to come first." Still smiling, she added, "The show must go on."

Cyrus winced again. "To have such a hoary old chestnut used against me." He sighed. "Very well. You'll probably be safer with a behemoth such as Mr. MacCallister rather than with a bunch of actors. No offense intended by that behemoth comment, sir."

"None taken," Jamie said with a grin. "I know I'm a big galoot." He grew more serious. "I'm not sure about you being any safer, though, Miss McCoy. We're talking about going all the way to Montana, not on some picnic lunch. Hundreds of miles of riding in a wagon that's not very comfortable, miserable weather, maybe hostile Indians and outlaws. Lots of bad things can happen."

"Something bad *will* happen if I stay here," Savannah pointed out. "Gideon Kane has seen to that. Besides, maybe I wouldn't have to go all the way to Montana. The troupe's next stop is Des Moines, isn't that right, Cyrus?"

"Yes, we'll be there in a couple weeks."

"I could travel with the wagon train for a week or so, long enough for Kane to give up on finding me, then leave and join the troupe again in Des Moines."

"You can't go gallivanting across the prairie by yourself." Bodie looked at Jamie. "You still interested in hiring another scout, Mr. MacCallister?"

Jamie regarded him with narrowed eyes. "A temporary scout? Just for a week? I don't know about that. But I don't reckon I can stop you from coming along, if that's what you want. You'll have to talk to Captain Hendricks about it, though. He's in charge of the bunch."

Savannah frowned. "Mr. Cantrell, I can't ask you to —"

"You're not asking me to do anything," Bodie interrupted. "I'm volunteering." He paused. "I'll have to talk to some friends of mine, though, and let them know that I'm leaving."

"It's very thoughtful of you to want to help me. I really appreciate it."

"Hey, I don't like that fella Kane, either," Bodie said. "Anything I can do to put a burr under his saddle, I'm all for it."

Moses spoke up. "I don't want to throw

cold water on these plans, but how are you going to convince Kane that you're gone, Miss McCoy? He's liable to think that the troupe is just hiding you."

Savannah frowned again. "I hadn't thought about that. I know. I'll write him a letter telling him that I'm leaving Kansas City and leaving the troupe. You can give it to him, Cyrus."

"Even if you do that, there's no guarantee that he'll believe it."

"He can search the hotel and the theater. He can come to all the performances. I really will be gone, so when he can't find me he'll have no choice but to believe it."

Cyrus rubbed his chin and frowned in thought. After a moment he said, "Hmm. It *might* work. . . ."

"It's the only chance we have to keep him from causing more trouble for the troupe."

"You won't tell him where you're going, just that you're leaving town?"

Savannah glanced at Jamie and Bodie. "That's right. I don't want to cause trouble for those immigrants, either."

"I'm not worried too much about some rich young wastrel like that, miss," Jamie told her. "I reckon I've dealt with a lot worse in my time."

"All right, it's settled then. I'm starting to

191

Montana with the wagon train. That is, if I can find someone to let me travel with them . . ."

Moses said, "That shouldn't be a problem. There are plenty of families who ought to be willing to make room for you. These are good people, Miss McCoy."

"I'm sure they are." She put a hand on Cyrus's arm. "And if I don't show up in Des Moines, you'll know not to wait for me. Just go on with the tour."

"What are you talking about?" he asked. "Why wouldn't you join us?"

"Well, something might happen. As Mr. MacCallister pointed out, a trip like this could be dangerous." Savannah smiled. "Or you never know . . . once I'm on the way, I might decide that I want to be a pioneer woman!"

CHAPTER TWENTY-FOUR

"We'd better go out the back way," Bodie suggested before they left the hotel. Savannah had gone upstairs and quickly packed her carpetbag. Luckily, the troupe's nomadic existence had taught her the art of traveling light. "Kane could've posted somebody outside to keep an eye on the place."

Jamie said, "I thought of the same thing. That's why I had a good look around when we came up. I didn't see anybody skulking around, but it's possible I missed something. We'll go out the back just to be sure."

Bodie had a hunch it would be hard to out-think Jamie MacCallister, and it was mighty unlikely that he would miss anything, too. He had heard of the big frontiersman. Anybody who had been around as long as Jamie had, leading that sort of adventurous life, was bound to be pretty cunning, not to mention experienced in all kinds of trouble.

Savannah had found pen and ink and paper behind the registration desk and quickly written a note for Gideon Kane, telling him that she was quitting the troupe and leaving Kansas City, to boot. She didn't tell him where she was going, but she warned him not to try to find her. She read the message out loud to the others, then sealed it and gave it to Cyrus O'Hanlon to have it delivered to Kane.

Cyrus insisted on calling the rest of the troupe down to the lobby so they could say good-bye to Savannah. It was an emotional farewell, full of hugs and tears, and it bothered Bodie that she had to abandon the life she enjoyed just because of some worthless skunk like Gideon Kane.

Finally Savannah was able to tear herself away from her friends and colleagues. She and Bodie, along with Jamie and Moses, went to the hotel's back door.

Jamie said, "Better let me go out first and have a look around, just to make sure Kane's men haven't set up an ambush for us."

"I'll come with you," Bodie said.

"No, you stay here. In case anything happens to me, you'll have to look out for Miss McCoy."

194

"What about me?" Moses asked.

"Have you got a gun?"

"Well . . . no."

"Ever fired a gun?"

"Actually, I haven't."

"Then you'd best stay here with Cantrell and Miss McCoy," Jamie said. "Stick to doing whatever it is rabbis do and let me burn any powder that needs burning."

"When you put it like that, I see your point," Moses said.

Jamie slipped out the door, moving with unusual grace for such a big man, and returned after a few tense minutes to report that the coast seemed to be clear. "Kane's probably convinced that he spooked your friends so bad they won't have any choice but to turn you over to him, Miss McCoy."

"Since we're all going to be traveling together, why don't you call me Savannah?" she suggested. "And the three of you will be Bodie and Moses and . . . Mr. MacCallister."

That brought a chuckle from Jamie.

Savannah smiled. "It's just that you're old enough to be my, well, my father."

"I'm older than that, girl," Jamie said. "I could be your grandpa. But I've never cared much what folks call me, as long as they don't call me late for supper."

Bodie grinned. "I figured you were going to say that."

Savannah changed the subject. "Kane is underestimating just how tough Cyrus and the others are. They'd never help him."

"They wouldn't as long as he didn't box 'em in where they didn't have any choice. Maybe that letter of yours will keep that from happening."

They went into the alley behind the hotel. It was pitch black, but Jamie led them through it as if it were bright as day. A short time later, they were back at the wagon train camp, which was still dark and peaceful.

Jamie went to one of the wagons, knocked softly on the tailgate, and called, "Cap'n Hendricks."

A man with tousled hair stuck his head out of the wagon. "Who's there?" He thrust the twin barrels of a shotgun over the tailgate.

Jamie grasped the barrels and shoved them skyward. "Take it easy with that greener," he snapped. "It's MacCallister and Moses Danzig. We've got a couple more pilgrims for your expedition, and one of 'em's going to be my third scout, at least for the time being."

Wearing a long nightshirt much like the one Moses had been sporting earlier, Captain Hendricks climbed out of his wagon and listened as Jamie introduced Bodie and Savannah and explained the situation.

When Jamie was finished with the story, Hendricks said, "Normally when a person joins a wagon train, they have to contribute something —"

"I can pay," Savannah broke in. "I have a little money saved up."

Hendricks smiled and shook his head. "I was about to say that under the circumstances, I think we can forget about that, at least for now. Since it's possible you may not be with us for long, there's even less reason to worry about it." The wagon train captain scratched his angular jaw. "Now, there's the matter of finding you a place. . . ."

"What about with the Binghams?" Moses suggested. "There's just the two of them, so they'd probably have room in their wagon."

"Yes, that might work." Hendricks turned to Savannah. "They're a couple getting on in age, really probably too old to have pulled up stakes and started west like they did, but their children are all grown and Edward Bingham wanted to see some new country. Can't say as I blame him. I feel sort of the same way myself."

"Once a man's feet get restless, there's

not much he can do about it except move on," Jamie said. "I know that feeling mighty well."

So did Bodie. He had been pretty fiddle-footed himself since his parents' deaths had left him alone, but it was from necessity, not choice. As filled with trouble as his life had been, he'd had to stay on the move.

That thought reminded him that he still had something to do before morning, something pretty important. He had to see about getting his share of the train robbery loot from Eldon Swint.

Now that they had obtained Captain Hendricks's approval for joining the wagon train, Moses took Savannah to the wagon belonging to the elderly couple. Before they left, Bodie said to her, "I'll see you later."

"I really hate to disrupt whatever plans you had," she said.

"Trust me, I didn't have any real plans, and you're not disrupting a thing."

That was true. For her sake, he hated what Savannah was having to go through, but it was a good excuse to leave the gang. He had never been that comfortable riding with Swint and the others, and after the cold-blooded murder of that station agent, Bodie wanted more than ever to get away from them.

As Savannah and Moses walked off, Bodie hung back with Jamie. "There's something I have to do before I can leave in the morning."

"Yeah, you said something about that before. You need a hand with whatever it is?"

That was just the sort of man Jamie MacCallister was, thought Bodie. Jamie had to at least suspect that Bodie's business might involve some degree of danger, but he'd volunteered to come along anyway, without the slightest hesitation. By that, Bodie could tell that Jamie already considered him a friend, and it was a good feeling.

He shook his head. "No, I can handle it. But I'm obliged to you for the offer."

"We're pulling out at first light. You'll need to be back here by then."

"I will be," Bodie promised.

CHAPTER TWENTY-FIVE

He left the wagon camp and headed back to the hotel where the gang was staying, which was seedier than the one being used by the troupe of performers. Swint might be there, or he might be at the Bella Royale. Bodie thought the odds were good that he would find the gang leader at one place or the other.

On the second floor of the hotel, he found Clete Mahaffey and Dave Pearsoll sitting on ladderback chairs in the hallway outside Swint's room. "I didn't know you fellas had first shift on guard duty tonight."

"Yeah, that's us — just sittin' here while the rest of the boys are out havin' fun," Mahaffey groused.

"You need something, Cantrell?" Pearsoll asked.

Bodie nodded. "I'm looking for the boss. Is he in his room?"

"Nah, we haven't seen Swint for a couple

hours. Check the saloon."

"That was going to be my next stop. Much obliged."

"Wait a minute," Mahaffey said. "Is something wrong, Cantrell?"

"No, not at all," Bodie lied. "I just need to talk to him for a few minutes."

Clearly, both men were curious what was going on, but they weren't going to poke their noses in another man's business. They just grunted as Bodie lifted a hand in farewell and headed back downstairs.

He should have asked them where Jake was, he thought as he left the hotel. Jake was the only member of the gang he considered a friend — one that he wanted to say good-bye to before pulling out with the wagon train.

He could find Jake later, he decided. It was more important to settle things with Swint.

The hour was getting really late, but the Bella Royale was still busy. Bodie entered the saloon but didn't see Swint anywhere, so he went to the bar and asked the bartender if he'd seen the boss outlaw.

The apron nodded toward a closed door. "There's a poker game going on in that private room back there. Swint and some of his boys are sitting in on it. Say, aren't you one of his bunch?"

"I was," Bodie said. All that had changed tonight.

He hadn't known it at the time, but it had changed the moment he first laid eyes on Savannah McCoy.

With that thought in mind, Bodie went to the door and knocked on it. A voice he didn't recognize told him to come in.

When he stepped into the room he saw that it was windowless and dark except for a lamp that cast a cone of light over a round table topped with green baize, the cards and money scattered on it, and to a lesser extent, the men who sat around it. Swint sat on the far side of the table, facing the door.

That came as no surprise to Bodie; Swint wouldn't want anybody coming in behind him where he couldn't see them. That was just common sense for someone with a lot of enemies and a price on his head.

To Swint's right was a frock-coated man Bodie didn't know, probably a professional gambler. To the gambler's right was another man Bodie didn't know who had the well-fed look of a successful businessman. The other three men at the table were members of the gang: Charley Green, who was usually Swint's second in command when the gang pulled a job, a gunman from Arizona named Jack Perkins, and Joe Guerra, a 'breed from the border country down in Texas.

It appeared that a hand had just concluded and the frock-coated gambler had won. He finished pulling in the pot, then glanced up at Bodie. "We don't have a chair open right now, but you're welcome to stay and watch in case one of these gents drops out."

"I'm not goin' anywhere," Swint said irritably. "Not until I've had a chance to win back that money I lost."

The gambler took a slender black cigarillo from his vest pocket, put it between his lips, left it unlit, and rolled it from one side of his mouth to the other. "That's the sort of talk I like to hear. It shows you're passionate about the game, my friend . . . and it tells me I'm going to have a chance to take even more of your money."

Swint scowled, and Bodie thought that the gambler didn't really know what sort of loco hombre he was dealing with. Swint was quick to take offense, quick to reach for the gun on his hip.

The boss outlaw's reaction lasted only for a second before he controlled it and forced a grin. "You just go ahead and think that way, amigo. We'll see who's rakin' in the pot next time." He glanced up at Bodie. "Did you want somethin', Cantrell, or do you plan to just stand there?"

"I need to talk to you for a minute," Bodie said. "In private."

Swint's scowl came back. "You got somethin' you can't say in front of these fellas? I'm not sure I like the sound of that."

"It's just business, that's all."

Swint drummed the fingers of his left hand on the table. "My luck's due to change. I can feel it in my bones. If I sit out this next hand, that luck's liable to pass right over me."

"Why don't we take a short break?" the gambler suggested. "That way you can talk to your friend, I'll go get another bottle from Horace, and we can all stretch our legs."

"All right," Swint said as he scraped back his chair. "But don't start again without me, you hear? Cantrell, this isn't gonna take very long, is it?"

"It shouldn't," Bodie said. Just long enough for you to go upstairs, get the money that you owe me, and hand it over, he thought.

Swint stood up. "Come on. We'll step out into the alley."

They left the private room and went out through a side door into the narrow passage between the Bella Royale and the building next to it. Swint left the door open so that a rectangle of light slanted through it and the glow lit up most of the alley.

"All right," Swint said. "What is it you want?"

"My share of the money," Bodie replied bluntly.

Swint's scowl got even more fierce. "You know we'll divvy up that loot when the time is right. And I'm the one who decides when that is, Cantrell, not you."

"I'm not saying you have to divvy up with everybody."

"That wouldn't be fair to the others. What makes you so dang special, anyway?"

"I'm leaving the gang," Bodie said.

Swint stared at him for a second as if he couldn't comprehend what Bodie had just said. Finally he repeated, "Leaving the gang?"

"That's right."

Swint's eyes narrowed, and his face began to flush with anger. "What's the matter, we ain't good enough for you anymore? You gonna go out and start your own gang, show ol' Eldon what it's like to be a famous owl-hoot?"

"It's not like that." It wasn't going as smoothly as Bodie had hoped, but to tell the truth he hadn't really expected Swint to take the news very well. "In fact, I plan to give up being an outlaw altogether."

"So you really do think you're too good for the likes of us. But when it comes to the money the rest of us took off that train, you ain't so high and mighty that you'll turn your back on it, are you? You're just as greedy as the rest of us where that loot's concerned."

Bodie felt a flash of anger of his own. "Listen here, I did everything you told me to do during that holdup. If there had been trouble, my neck would have been on the line just like yours. So I think I've got a right to my share."

Swint hooked his thumbs in his gun belt and sneered. "Only members of the gang get shares. You walk away now and you won't have a damn dime comin' to you."

"Now hold on! You never said anything about that before."

"Never figured I'd have to explain it. It's just common sense."

Actually, it was a chance for Swint to get his hands on an extra share, Bodie realized . . . assuming that the leader of the gang didn't mean to hang on to *all* the loot. Chances were, Swint didn't really care whether Bodie stayed or went. He had never been any great shakes as an outlaw. Swint could replace him with any of a hundred drifting hardcases.

Swint had his pride, though, and he felt insulted. For that reason alone, he was willing to make it an issue.

Both men stood tensely in the mixture of dim light and shadows in the alley. It was bright enough for Bodie to see the anticipation of violence in Swint's stance. He knew that if he made even the slightest move toward his gun, Swint would slap leather, too. The killing lust burned in the man's eyes.

Suddenly, Bodie felt sick. His guts clenched. But it wasn't from fear. He and Swint were pretty evenly matched when it came to gun speed, he thought.

What gripped him was revulsion. He was ready to kill or be killed over money stained with the blood of that murdered station agent. The whole thing was loco.

Besides, Savannah McCoy needed his help to stay safe. Sure, if he got himself killed over a pile of ill-gotten loot, Jamie MacCallister, Captain Hendricks, and Moses Danzig would still do their best to look after her. Bodie had a feeling that Jamie would be more than a match for any threat the wagon train might run up against.

But even so, there might come a time when he was all that stood between Savannah and disaster, like when Kane's men had tried to grab her earlier. He couldn't afford to run the risk of not being there.

He drew in a deep breath. "You know what, Eldon? Keep my share. I don't care."

Swint's eyes narrowed with suspicion. Obviously he couldn't comprehend such a decision. "Is this some sort of trick?"

Bodie shook his head. "No trick. There are other things I need to do, and they're more important than any stack of gold eagles. You keep my share and divide it up among the other men. Or just keep it for yourself. It doesn't matter to me either way, as long as you're all right with letting me walk away from the gang."

"I don't give a damn whether you're in the gang or not," Swint snapped, confirming what Bodie had thought a few moments earlier. "I still think you're tryin' to put somethin' over on me, though."

"I'm not. I give you my word." Bodie stuck out his hand. "I'll even shake on it."

Swint hesitated, but finally he clasped Bodie's hand. "What is it you've got to do?"

Bodie opened his mouth to explain about Savannah, Gideon Kane, and the wagon train, then thought better of it. Swint didn't have any reason to know about any of that. "Just some personal business to take care of."

"Fine. It ain't like I care. You remember one thing, though, Cantrell. You walk away from me, and we're done. We ain't partners no more, and if you ever cross me in the future, I'll kill you just as quick as I would a total stranger."

Bodie wouldn't have expected anything less from the man. He didn't see any reason his trail ought to cross that of Eldon Swint any time in the future, though. It would be perfectly fine with him if he never saw the lantern-jawed outlaw again. "I understand. You won't have any trouble from me, Eldon."

Swint snorted contemptuously. "I'd better not, or you'll wind up filled full of lead, you got that?"

Bodie thought back and realized that he had never seen Swint engage in an actual gunfight. The outlaw had killed several men, but always from ambush or when he already had the drop on them. Maybe Swint wasn't quite the deadly pistoleer he always bragged about being.

None of that mattered, Bodie told himself. He was going with Savannah, and he would never see Swint again.

"You know where Three-Finger Jake is?" he murmured. He still hadn't given up on the idea of saying good-bye to his friend.

"I ain't got the slightest idea. It's not my job to keep up with the whereabouts of a bunch of no-account road agents when they're not pullin' a job for me."

"All right. If you see him —" Bodie stopped and shook his head. He didn't want to tell Swint that he was going to be traveling with the wagon train. Even though it was unlikely, that might somehow put Kane on Savannah's trail. Bodie wasn't going to take the chance.

"So long, Eldon. That's all."

"You're loco, you know that?" Swint growled as Bodie turned away. "Givin' up that loot just don't make sense."

"It does if maybe you've found something more valuable," Bodie said, thinking about Savannah McCoy.

CHAPTER TWENTY-SIX

Jamie was up long before dawn the next morning, making sure people were awake and getting ready to depart from Kansas City. He had said that he meant for the wagons to roll at first light, and he meant it. As far as he was concerned, the eastern sky barely had to turn gray for it to count as first light.

As he was making the rounds of the camp, he came up to one of the cook fires and found Moses Danzig and Bodie Cantrell hunkered beside the flames, sipping coffee from tin cups. The pot was sitting at the edge of the fire, keeping warm.

"Some coffee, Mr. MacCallister?" Moses asked.

"Don't mind if I do," Jamie said. He'd already had a cup with Captain Hendricks, but a man couldn't have too much coffee when he planned to spend a long, long day in the saddle.

Moses went to his nearby wagon and brought another cup, filled it from the pot, and handed it to Jamie.

He sipped gratefully at the strong black brew. "Did you get your business taken care of last night, Cantrell?"

"Yes, sir, I did," the young man replied.

Jamie nodded. "Glad to hear it." He didn't press for any more information. He felt an instinctive liking for Bodie Cantrell, but the young man's affairs were his own and Jamie didn't intend to interfere in them. "Seen Miss McCoy this morning?"

Bodie shook his head. "No, but I'm sure she's fine with the Binghams. I wouldn't want to intrude on her."

"Moses, you mind going and checking on her? I want to make sure she didn't change her mind about going with us."

"Sure," Moses said with a shrug. He ambled off toward the Bingham wagon.

Bodie said, "I don't think Miss Savannah would just up and run off."

"She was pretty scared last night," Jamie pointed out. "It's hard to tell what somebody will do if they get spooked bad enough. I've seen animals bolt right into danger instead of away from it, all because they were too scared to think straight."

Bodie looked worried. He drained the last

of his coffee from the cup and rose from his position beside the fire. "Reckon I'll go make sure, too —"

"I told Moses to do that," Jamie cut in. "What you need to do is make sure your horse is ready to ride. We've got to get moving soon, or the day's going to be half gone."

Bodie squinted and frowned at the eastern sky, which was still almost pitch black with plenty of stars showing. He figured Jamie was a little loco, and a bit of a slave driver, to boot.

But like the others in the group, he didn't fully grasp what a difficult undertaking it would be to get the wagons to Eagle Valley in Montana Territory before winter closed in around them and stranded them. Jamie would have to use every available minute of every day to accomplish that goal, and it was going to be hard on everybody, human and livestock alike. They might as well get used to that, right from the start.

Bodie went to see to his horse, as Jamie had suggested, and the big frontiersman continued making sure that everything was ready for the journey. Any time he found immigrants who weren't preparing fast enough, he prodded them into hurrying without being overly harsh about it. He was prepared to lay down the law to them if he had to, the law of the trail according to Jamie Ian MacCallister, but they seemed a fairly well disciplined bunch, so he didn't want to do that . . . yet.

Once they got started to Montana it might be a different story.

Not everyone was completely cooperative. When he got to the Bradford wagon, he found the twins, Alexander and Abigail, struggling to get the team of oxen hitched to the vehicle. The huge, stolid beasts dwarfed the children and paid little attention to their efforts to get them into the traces.

"Where's your pa?" Jamie asked the youngsters. "He should be doing this."

"He's in the wagon reading the Bible," Alexander said.

"Pa always reads some in the Good Book every morning and every night," Abigail added.

Jamie scowled. Being spiritual was all well and good, but there was a time for that and a time to get earthly work done, he thought. After all, the book said that the Lord helped those who helped themselves.

He stepped to the back of the wagon and saw that a candle was burning inside. "Reverend Bradford?"

"What is it?" Bradford answered without

lifting the canvas flap over the opening at the rear of the wagon. He sounded clearly annoyed.

"We'll be rolling soon. You need to get your team hitched up. Those kids can't do it by themselves." And even if they could, they shouldn't have to, Jamie thought.

Bradford pushed the canvas aside and glared out, looking as irritated as he'd sounded. "The needs of a man's immortal soul won't wait, Mr. MacCallister. These wagons will."

"That's where you're wrong," Jamie said, making his voice as hard as flint. "If you're not ready to go when the rest of us are, we'll leave you here. Whether or not you catch up is up to you."

"You'd abandon us here?" Bradford demanded in obvious outrage. "I won't hear of it. I paid my fee to join this wagon train, just like everyone else. I'll speak to Captain Hendricks about this high-handed behavior."

"Go right ahead," Jamie told him. "It won't change anything. I'm wagon master now, and we leave when I say we leave. It's your responsibility to be ready." He didn't like speaking to Bradford this way in front of the man's children, but facts were facts and they needed to get on the trail.

"Very well," Bradford said disgustedly. He set aside his big, leather-bound Bible, pushed the canvas flap back farther, and clambered out of the wagon. "But I still plan to speak to Captain Hendricks."

"Go right ahead," Jamie invited. It wouldn't make any difference, and he knew it.

He waited a moment to make sure Bradford was going to help the two youngsters hitch up the team. When he was satisfied about that, he moved on to the area where the saddle horses were picketed.

Bodie was there, tightening the cinches on his saddle. So were Hector Gilworth and his cousin Jess Neville, who were also getting their horses ready to ride.

"Did you fellas introduce yourselves to each other?" Jamie asked the scouts.

"Sure did," Hector replied. "I'm glad you found somebody to help us with the scoutin', Jamie."

"I'll try to live up to the responsibility," Bodie said.

"Keep your eyes open and don't do anything foolish, and you'll be fine," Jamie told him.

"Are you takin' the point today?" Hector asked.

Jamie nodded. "That's right. Bodie, you'll

be with me. Hector and Jess, you fellas take the flanks."

"Nobody bringing up the rear?" Bodie asked.

"Not today. Once we've gotten farther from town, one of us will drop back from time to time to check our back trail. I don't really expect much trouble from behind, though. It's what'll be in front of us that we'll have to worry about."

"Meanin' Injuns?" Neville said.

"And outlaws and bad weather and flooded streams and buffalo stampedes and just about anything else you can think of," Jamie said with a grin. "This isn't going to be an easy trip. If all four of us make it to Montana Territory alive, we'll be doing pretty good." Of course, Bodie might not be going that far, he reminded himself.

That all depended on Savannah McCoy.

CHAPTER TWENTY-SEVEN

Edward Bingham was a tall man who had once been handsome. With his gray hair and close-cropped, grizzled beard, now he was distinguished, Savannah thought. His tiny, birdlike wife Leticia had long gray hair twisted into braids and wound around her head. The two of them were a good couple. They suited each other, in Savannah's opinion.

They were happy to make room for her things in their wagon and give her a place to sleep, as Moses had suggested they would. They had sold most of their goods before they left their long-time home in Reading, Pennsylvania, bringing with them only what they needed for the journey and to set up basic housekeeping in Montana, avoiding the trap of trying to take everything that some immigrants fell into.

As Mrs. Bingham prepared breakfast, Savannah offered to help, even though her cooking skills had never been anything to boast about. Living on the road with the troupe as she had, there hadn't been many opportunities to better them.

"There'll be plenty of chances for you to pitch in once we're on the trail, dear," the older woman said. "This is your first morning with the wagon train, so I'll take care of this."

Savannah suspected that Mrs. Bingham had her own way of doing things and didn't want anybody interfering with that routine. She could go along with that for now, but she was determined to carry her weight during the trip, for as long as she was with the wagon train.

She'd expected to see Bodie Cantrell again this morning, she thought as she sipped coffee and ate the hotcakes and bacon Mrs. Bingham had cooked. So far, though, she hadn't seen the young man. She supposed he was busy with whatever duties he had as one of the party's scouts.

The most important thing, she told herself, was that she hadn't seen Gideon Kane or any of his men. She would have liked to think that he had already given up searching for her, but she couldn't bring herself to believe that. She had seen a look of pure obsession in Kane's eyes. The look of mad-ness, almost.

"Mrs. Bingham, do you happen to have a sun bonnet I can borrow?" Savannah asked when they had finished breakfast.

"Of course. You don't need it now, what with the sun not being up yet, but you will before the day's over, I'm thinking."

That was true, but the main reason Savannah wanted the bonnet was so that it would obscure her face if any of Kane's men came by the wagon camp looking for her. She had put on her oldest, drabbest dress, and if she wore the bonnet and kept her face turned away from the street as much as possible, she thought there was a good chance she could go unnoticed. "I just want to get used to wearing one."

"All right. I'll fetch one of my extras," Mrs. Bingham said.

When Mr. Bingham went to hitch up the oxen, Savannah offered to help with that, too. He gave her a dubious frown. "No offense, Miss McCoy, but you don't strike me as a farm girl. Have you ever handled oxen before?"

"No, sir, but I'm a quick —" She started to say she was a quick study, then switched from that theatrical term. For the time being, she wasn't an actress.

She was a fugitive.

"I learn quickly," she said. "And I'm not afraid of hard work, even though I have to admit I'm not exactly accustomed to it."

He thought about her offer for a moment, then nodded. "All right. I can always use a helping hand. Just be careful. Those great brutes are peaceful and slow-moving most of the time, but they can be surly beasts now and then." He smiled. "Sort of like people."

Jamie MacCallister stopped by the wagon when they were almost ready to go. "Everything quiet the rest of the night?"

"Quiet as can be, thanks to you and Mr. Cantrell," Savannah said. "Speaking of Mr. Cantrell, I haven't seen him yet this morning. . . ."

"He's around," Jamie said vaguely. "You'll be seeing plenty of him during the trip." He smiled. "I like that bonnet. You look like a real pioneer woman."

Savannah smiled. "I suppose for now, that's exactly what I am."

A short time later, the wagons began pulling out of their places in the circle and lining up. As captain, Lamar Hendricks had the first spot in line. The others pulled in behind him as they were ready. The Bingham wagon was about halfway along the column by the time the train had finished forming up.

Savannah was sitting on the lowered tailgate as Jamie and Bodie rode past. She lifted a hand and waved at them. Jamie nodded and touched a finger to the wide brim of his hat. Bodie followed suit. He didn't smile; his face was serious in the gray light of approaching dawn.

That was all right, Savannah told herself. He was handsome in his rugged way, even when he didn't smile. She was looking forward to the chance to talk with him again.

But that wouldn't come for a while. Jamie and Bodie rode to the front of the train, where the big frontiersman paused and lifted his right arm above his head. His powerful voice carried along the length of the train as he bellowed, "Wagons . . . *hooooo*!"

With a shuffling of hooves, a creaking of leather, and a rasp of wheels turning, the wagons lurched forward into motion.

They were off to Montana.

CHAPTER TWENTY-EIGHT

Jamie could tell that the big sand-colored stallion Sundown was glad to get out on the trail and stretch his legs again. To tell the truth, so was he. He was even happier to have a destination and a goal again. The drifting he had done since the end of his vengeance quest had felt right at the time, but after a lifetime of getting things done, he was ready to accomplish something again.

If he got the pilgrims safely to where they were going, that would be an accomplishment, all right. A mighty big accomplishment.

The wagons followed a well-defined trail along the Kansas River westward, keeping the stream to the left. Jamie and Bodie rode about a hundred yards in front of the lead wagon.

It wasn't really necessary to do any scouting yet. Their route was easy to follow, and as the sun rose behind them, its golden light washed over the plains and revealed the way before them. Once the wagons were out of town, the trail would lead through farming country for the next few days, so there weren't any significant dangers to watch out for.

That would change once they swung to the northwest. The country would become more sparsely settled, and they would be traveling through regions where it was still possible to run into roving bands of Pawnee and Cheyenne that might prove hostile.

As they rode, Bodie said, "I'd sure like to hear about some of your adventures, Mr. MacCallister, if you don't mind talking about them."

"Make it Jamie. And who said I'd had adventures?"

Bodie frowned. "Well . . . just about everybody who's ever heard of you, I reckon."

Jamie chuckled. "I'm just joshing you, son. I guess I've run into my fair share of trouble. Ever hear of a place called the Alamo?"

"Well, sure."

"I was there for a spell, before it fell to the Mexicans, of course. A long, long time ago."

Jamie reminisced about that and some of his other exploits as he was growing up a child of a wild, young country. It was a sign that a man was growing old when his own kids didn't want to listen to his stories anymore, but Bodie was an eager audience, paying rapt attention to the yarns Jamie spun. There had been a time when his boy Falcon had been like that, before he had grown up and become one of the most dangerous gunfighters west of the Mississippi.

Jamie hipped around in the saddle and peered along the line of wagons from time to time, checking their back trail.

Bodie followed that example. "You're making sure Kane isn't following us, right?"

"Would you put it past him, if he thought there was a chance Miss McCoy had joined the wagon train?"

"Not for a minute. From what I saw of the man, he's loco . . . and poison mean."

Jamie nodded. "I haven't met him, but I've got a hunch you're right."

The wagons rolled along steadily for several hours before Jamie called a halt to let the livestock rest for a short time. He and Bodie went to Captain Hendricks's wagon, where Jamie asked the man, "Have you got a map of the route you were supposed to follow? I know where Montana is, right enough, but if you were supposed to go a certain way we'll try to stick to it . . . as long as I don't know a better trail."

"Actually, yes, I have a map that Mr. Ralston prepared," Hendricks replied. "I'll get it."

While they were waiting for him to do that, Jamie glanced eastward behind the wagon train again, just out of habit, and stiffened in the saddle as he spotted several riders following the trail along the river and coming toward them. He caught Bodie's attention, lifted a hand, and pointed.

A worried frown appeared on Bodie's face as he looked at the riders. "Kane's men?"

"Could be. Let's go find out."

Hendricks had climbed over the seat into the wagon to look for the map. As Jamie and Bodie turned their horses toward the rear of the train, he stuck his head back out. "Where are you going?"

"Just to check something out," Jamie said. "We'll have a look at that map later."

He heeled Sundown into a lope. Bodie rode alongside him. Some of the immigrants waved and called greetings to them as they went past the wagons.

Hector Gilworth and Jess Neville had come in from the flanks when the train stopped. They saw Jamie and Bodie approaching, and Hector asked, "Something wrong, Mr. MacCallister?"

"Probably not, but come along with us anyway."

The four of them reached the end of the wagon train when the newcomers were still about a quarter mile away. Jamie's keen eyes didn't recognize any of them as men he had seen the night before, but that didn't have to mean anything. Gideon Kane was wealthy enough to hire any number of men to do his bidding.

Bodie suddenly let out a startled exclamation. "I know those fellas."

"Friends of yours?" Jamie asked.

"Well, one of them is, anyway. And the others are all right, I think."

The four wagon train men reined in and waited for the riders to come to them. As the men approached, Bodie moved his horse out in front of his companions and called, "Jake! What in the world are you doing here?"

The riders came up and halted. The one in the lead grinned and said to Bodie, "I'll bet you didn't expect to see me again so soon, did you, pard?"

"That's right. I didn't." Bodie glanced around at Jamie. "Mr. MacCallister, this is my friend Jake Lucas."

"Three-Finger Jake, they call me, and you

227

can see why." He held up his left hand with its missing digits. "I blame an old brindle steer and my own dumb luck for that. Call it a souvenir of my cowboyin' days."

Bodie introduced the other two men. "These hombres are Clete Mahaffey and Dave Pearsoll. Boys, this is Jamie Ian MacCallister, Hector Gilworth, and Jess Neville."

The men exchanged nods. Jamie studied the newcomers, sizing them up. Jake Lucas seemed to be a brash, cocky young cowboy, while Mahaffey and Pearsoll were older, more hard-edged.

"I thought you were staying back in Kansas City," Bodie said to them. "You know, until that other business got cleared up."

Jake shook his head. "There's nothin' I hate worse than sittin' around, Bodie, you know that. When I heard that you'd left town, I reckon it put ideas in my head. We got everything squared away and decided to come after you."

A frown creased Bodie's forehead. "I didn't tell anybody I was leaving with this wagon train."

"Well, where else would you have gone?" Jake asked with a laugh. "That sounded like something you'd do, takin' off with a bunch of pilgrims bound for Montana. There's a lot of talk about it back in town. In fact, we were thinkin' we might just throw in with you."

Jamie watched Bodie's face, but the young man seemed to be keeping his features carefully impassive. Even as insightful as he was, Jamie couldn't tell how Bodie felt about the idea Jake Lucas had just come out with.

Bodie shrugged. "That's not up to me. Mr. MacCallister is the wagon master, and the immigrants have a captain they've elected. They'd be the ones to decide who comes along and who doesn't."

Something nagged at Jamie, just a vague feeling that maybe not everything was as it appeared to be on the surface. But having three more experienced men along on the journey might not be a bad idea. The wagons were bound to run into trouble somewhere along the way, the sort of trouble that meant gunplay. Even though Mahaffey and Pearsoll had a rough, hard-bitten look about them, they might make good allies. "If it's all right with Captain Hendricks, it's all right with me. That is, if you vouch for these fellas, Bodie."

"Sure," Bodie said. "Why wouldn't I?"

That was something Jamie wondered about, and he resolved to ask Bodie about it later, in private.

"One thing," Jamie went on. "You boys will have to earn your keep if you travel with this train. Bodie's signed on as a scout, and I could use some more pairs of eyes and ears, if you're interested."

"Why, that sounds like a bang-up idea, Mr. MacCallister," Jake said. "We'd be glad to work as scouts, wouldn't we, boys?"

"Sure," Mahaffey said, and Pearsoll just shrugged and grunted his assent.

Jamie turned Sundown toward the front of the train again. "Come on," he told the newcomers. "We'll go see Captain Hendricks and make sure it's all right with him. I expect it will be, though."

In a matter of moments, he had gone from having barely enough scouts to maybe having too many, Jamie thought as he rode toward the front of the train. But considering the wild country they would be traversing before they reached their destination, maybe it wasn't possible to have too many scouts.

Or too many men who were good with a gun.

CHAPTER TWENTY-NINE

Bodie's head was spinning. Of all the people he might have run into on the way to Montana, Jake Lucas, Clete Mahaffey, and Dave Pearsoll were just about the last ones he would have expected. He had a bunch of questions for them, starting with their reasons for leaving the gang . . . and whether or not they had managed to get their share of the loot from Eldon Swint.

That had to wait until later, though. He couldn't say anything about it while Jamie or the other scouts were around. He didn't want to reveal his outlaw past to them. The wagon train was his chance to start over. Maybe his last chance.

When he dared to let himself think about it, he thought that Savannah might be a chance to start over, too. She needed one, and so did he.

Why not together?

Bodie put that thought out of his head for

the time being. When they talked to Captain Hendricks, he acknowledged that he and Jake and the other two men had been acquainted for a while and that he trusted them.

"That's good enough for me, I suppose," Hendricks said. "I realize I've known you only a very short time, Mr. Cantrell, but Mr. MacCallister seems to trust you. That carries a great deal of weight with me."

"Thank you, sir," Bodie said. "I'll try to live up to his trust, and yours as well."

He didn't get a chance to talk to Jake privately until the wagons had stopped for the midday meal and to let the teams rest again. Jake was standing on the riverbank, watering his horse, when Bodie walked over to join him.

"I don't reckon I've ever been as surprised in my life as I was when I saw you," Bodie said quietly.

"Why?" Jake asked. "You didn't think I was gonna stay with that lobo wolf Swint forever, did you?"

"You never said anything about leaving."

"Maybe that's because you never put the idea in my head until now," Jake said with a shrug. "When Swint told me you were gone, I asked myself why not? It was as good a time as any to make a break. I'll be honest with you, Bodie. Sooner or later, Eldon was gonna land us smack-dab in some trouble that we couldn't shoot our way out of. I don't want to wind up dancin' at the end of a rope, thrown in a cheap pine box, and stuck in some potter's field. That's what was gonna happen if we kept ridin' the owl-hoot."

"Where we're going, wolves may wind up scattering your bones."

"That's a chance I'll take. When I said I was leavin', Clete and Dave wanted to come with me. They're as tired of Swint's bull as I was."

Bodie lowered his voice to a whisper. "What about the money? Did you get him to give you your share?"

"We did better than that," Jake said with his quick grin. "We talked him into givin' us your share, too, so we could deliver it to you when we caught up. He tried to pull that ol' business about how if somebody left the gang, they didn't get what was comin' to 'em. That didn't fly, and we told him so. He backed down."

Until his own confrontation with Eldon Swint, Bodie might not have believed that was possible. He had seen for himself, though, that Swint might be more bluster than real threat, especially when the odds weren't overwhelmingly on his side. He could believe that Swint hadn't wanted to stand up to Jake, Mahaffey, and Pearsoll.

"You must have been mighty sure I was with the wagon train, if you figured on bringing my share of the loot with you."

Jake chuckled. "Well, if we guessed wrong and hadn't found you, I reckon we would've just had to keep that money ourselves. It would have been a shame, but we could've brung ourselves to do it."

Bodie let out a wry laugh and shook his head. "Well, you're here now, and that's all that matters, I reckon. You plan to stay with the wagon train all the way to Montana?"

"We'll have to wait and see about that. Right now all that matters is that we're on the move again, and it feels mighty good. I was already tired of that town. Too many people crowdin' around all the time. I'm a Texas boy. Used to wide open spaces all around me, you know."

Bodie nodded. "From what I've heard, there'll be plenty of those where we're going."

CHAPTER THIRTY

Back in Kansas City, Eldon Swint stirred in the grimy sheets of his hotel room bed. Somebody muttered and moaned beside him. Unable to recall which of the soiled doves he had brought from the Bella Royale the night before, he raised himself on an elbow so he could look over at his companion.

The tangled mass of hennaed hair on the other pillow looked vaguely familiar. Harriet? Hermione? Helen, that was it, he told himself . . . not that it really mattered to him what the dove's name was.

He reached over and smacked a beefy hip under the sheet.

Helen groaned again, rolled over, and opened her eyes to slits, wincing at the morning light coming in through the gap between the threadbare curtains over the room's lone window. "What time is it?" she muttered.

"Time for you to get up and haul yourself out of here," Swint told her.

She didn't seem to have heard his answer. "You can't expect to go again this mornin'. You didn't pay me that much, honey."

"I didn't say I wanted to go again. I said you need to get out."

To emphasize his point, Swint planted a bare foot against her rump and shoved. Helen let out a yelp of dismay as she slid out of the bed. The thud as she hit the floor cut off her cry.

She came up angry, exclaiming, "You son of a —"

Swint had already swung his legs out of bed and stood up. Standing on the far side of the bed, his bony frame clad only in the bottom half of a pair of long underwear, he turned his head to look at her. The ice-cold menace in his slate-gray eyes made her shut up in a hurry.

"You don't have to treat me so mean." Helen pouted as she started looking around for her dress. She still wore stockings rolled just above her knees, and those stockings, her slippers, and the dress were the only things she had been wearing when Swint brought her to the hotel the previous night.

The bare wood floor was cold against the soles of Swint's feet as he went over to a small table where some of his gear was piled. He pawed through it until he found one of the thin black cheroots he favored and a match. He snapped the lucifer to life with his thumbnail and set fire to the gasper. He didn't have any interest in watching the soiled dove get dressed. The night before, he had thought she was beautiful, but a bottle of rotgut whiskey improved any woman's looks immeasurably.

"Are you coming to the Bella Royale tonight, honey?" Helen asked behind him.

"More than likely," Swint replied without looking around. He stared out the window instead.

"Well, I'll be there. You'll look for me, won't you, honey?"

"We'll see," Swint said dully.

His mouth tasted like something had crawled into it and died. His head was throbbing a little from all the who-hit-John he'd guzzled down the night before. His guts roiled unpleasantly. He had hoped the cheroot would help with those problems, but it wasn't doing a blasted bit of good.

Helen tried again. "I had a mighty fine time with you last night."

"Forget it," Swint snapped. "Just get out."

She sniffed angrily, and a moment later the door slammed behind her on her way out of the room. Swint grimaced as the noise made his head throb harder. It felt like imps straight from Hades were capering around inside his skull, banging on it with ball-peen hammers.

Another memory stole back into his thoughts. Bodie Cantrell had quit the gang last night, he recalled with a scowl. That infuriated him. After all he'd done for Cantrell, only to be treated like that!

At least Cantrell hadn't insisted on getting his share of the loot. Swint would let the rest of the gang think that he had. That way Swint could pocket it for himself.

Thinking about the money made him turn away from the window. When he'd brought Helen back to the hotel, he had hefted the saddlebags before they got down to business. No matter how drunk he was, he always checked on the loot.

As the cheroot dangled from his lips, he had the urge to let some of those double eagles trickle through his fingers. That always made him feel better. He went to the wardrobe where he'd stashed the saddlebags, reached inside, and picked up one of them. The weight was comforting, and so was the clink of coins as he set the bags on the table. He unfastened one of the pouches and thrust his hand inside.

He knew instantly that something was wrong. His fingers touched coins, all right, but they weren't the right size to be double eagles. And there was something else in the pouch . . .

Rocks.

Swint's teeth clamped down on the cheroot so hard that he bit off the end and the thin black twisted cylinder fell onto the table next to the saddlebags. Swint ignored it and spat out the piece left in his mouth. He upended the pouch and stared in shock and disbelief at the rocks that fell out onto the table, along with a handful of pennies.

After a moment, he ripped the other pouch open and dumped its contents as well. More rocks and pennies spilled out. Bellowing a curse, Swint lunged for the wardrobe to get the other saddlebags.

A minute later, he had confirmed the awful truth.

Somebody had stolen all the loot.

Choking with fury, Swint yanked his revolver from the holster attached to the coiled shell belt lying on the table. He threw the door open and ran out into the hall, still wearing just the long underwear.

Two doors down the corridor, Swint hammered on the panel of Charley Green's room and yelled, "Charley! Damn it, Charley, get out here!"

When Green opened the door wearing a pair of baggy long-handles, he looked just as bleary-eyed as Swint had been upon first awakening. He coughed and cleared his throat. "Eldon, what's wrong?"

Swint started to blurt out that the loot was gone, but then he stopped himself. It might not be smart to let the others know what had happened until he figured it out himself. He grated, "Who was standin' guard here last night?"

Green raked his fingers through his tangled hair and frowned. "I dunno," he said after a second. "You must've seen 'em when you came in."

"Yeah, but I can't remember —" Swint stopped short as a couple faces locked into place in his mind. "Wait a minute. Mahaffey and Pearsoll. They were the ones."

"Well, there you go, then," Green said as he started to turn away and close the door. Clearly, he didn't grasp the depth of the problem.

Swint slapped his free hand against the door. "Where are they?" he demanded.

"What? Who?" Green gave his head a violent shake as if he were trying to clear the cobwebs from his brain. "Oh, you mean Mahaffey and Pearsoll. Shoot, I don't know.

240

I don't keep track of where everybody is."

"We've got to find them," Swint said. "Get dressed. Now!"

He stomped back to his room and started pulling on his clothes. Once he was dressed and had his gun belt strapped around his hips, he rousted out the other members of the gang. Green, still confused, helped him.

Within ten minutes, everybody was gathered in Swint's room, with three notable exceptions: Clete Mahaffey and Dave Pearsoll, who had been guarding the loot the night before . . . and Three-Finger Jake Lucas.

Swint questioned his men, his angry voice lashing them like a whip. Nobody admitted to having seen Mahaffey, Pearsoll, or Lucas since the previous night. Swint ordered them to spread out through the area and conduct a search. There were plenty of saloons, brothels, dance halls, and gambling dens where the three men might be.

He had an unhappy feeling that they wouldn't be found in any of those places.

By mid-morning the conclusion was inescapable. Lucas and the other two were gone. Only one reason for their disappearance made sense. They had stolen the loot from the train robbery and lit a shuck out of Kansas City.

241

Swint had no choice but to break the news to his men. They took it with startled curses, followed by bitter anger.

"What are we gonna do, Eldon?" Charley Green asked when the hubbub in Swint's room subsided.

"I'll tell you what we're gonna do. We're gonna find those damned double-crossers and get our money back! And when we do . . . those three are going to wish they'd never been born."

CHAPTER THIRTY-ONE

Gideon Kane was in the habit of rising late. There was no reason for him not to, since he had never done an actual day's work in his life. Things like that were for lesser men.

In the mansion on the outskirts of Kansas City, breakfast and coffee were waiting for him on a table covered with a fine linen cloth in the sitting room next to his bedroom, even though it was late enough that most people were starting to think about their midday meal. He belted a silk dressing gown around his waist and sat down to eat.

A bell pull hung within reach. Kane tugged on the cord, and a moment later his butler, Jenkins, appeared in the doorway. "Yes, sir?"

Kane sipped from the fine bone china cup and then asked, "Is Harrison here?"

"Yes, sir, he's in your study. He arrived a short time ago and said that he had a report for you when you woke up. I assumed that's where you would want to receive it after you'd eaten."

"Normally, yes. I'm feeling rather impatient this morning, however. Send him up here."

Jenkins inclined his head forward. "Yes, sir. Right away."

Kane went back to his breakfast.

A few minutes later a knock sounded on the partially open sitting room door. Kane called, "Come in."

Eli Harrison stepped into the room. He was a tall, heavy-shouldered man with massive fists and a face like a slab of raw meat. He had worked for the Kane family in a number of capacities over the years, starting out as a stableman.

Now he worked exclusively for Gideon Kane as a troubleshooter of sorts. Whenever Kane had a problem, no matter what it was, Harrison found a way to take care of it. He was brutal when he had to be and utterly ruthless.

Without looking up, Kane said, "I hope you're here to tell me that you've located that girl and brought her here."

"I wish I could, Mr. Kane," Harrison said bluntly, "but my men haven't turned up any sign of her yet."

"You kept watch on the hotel where that

troupe of entertainers is staying?"

"I sent a couple men to do that." Harrison didn't sound happy about what he had to say next. "They got sidetracked. One of 'em felt like he had to stop and pay off a gambling debt. They wound up, ah, gettin' mixed up in a game for a while."

Kane frowned as he laid aside the spoon he had been using. "So the hotel went unguarded?"

"Not for long. Only about an hour."

Kane felt his face warming with anger. Harrison knew as well as he did that a lot of things could happen in an hour.

"I want those two fools fired," Kane snapped.

"Already done it, sir." Harrison lifted one of his huge fists. The knuckles were skinned and raw. "Had a talk with 'em about falling down on the job, too."

"You have men watching the hotel now?"

"Yes, sir. If she's still there, we'll pick her up whenever she goes out."

Jenkins stepped into the doorway behind Harrison. He cleared his throat. "A note was delivered for you earlier this morning, sir."

"Who's it from?"

"I don't know." Jenkins lifted a piece of paper that was folded and sealed with wax.

"I have it here."

Kane pushed his empty plate aside and made a curt gesture toward the table. Jenkins crossed the room and placed the note on the linen. Kane picked it up and ripped the seal open.

His eyes scanned the words written in a feminine hand on the paper. More anger welled up inside him. He started to crumple the note, then stopped, set it down again, smoothed the creases from it. "Bring me O'Hanlon," he said softly.

"Sir?" Jenkins murmured.

"I'm talking to Eli." Kane stared coldly at Harrison. "O'Hanlon, the head of that acting troupe. Bring him here. Now."

Harrison nodded and left the room.

By the time Harrison returned to the mansion, Kane was dressed and waiting downstairs in his study. He had been pacing back and forth angrily, but he forced himself to regain his composure when Jenkins announced that Harrison was there and had brought Cyrus O'Hanlon with him as ordered. Kane gave the butler a curt nod to indicate that he was ready for them.

Harrison gave O'Hanlon a little shove as they came into the study, making the actor stumble. O'Hanlon caught himself before he fell. Drawing himself up straighter, he glared at Kane. "The authorities will hear about you having me kidnapped like this, Mr. Kane."

"Kidnapped?" Kane repeated. He smiled coolly. "I don't know what you're talking about. I asked Mr. Harrison to request that you honor me by visiting my home, and that's all that happened, Mr. O'Hanlon."

"You know good and well that's not true," O'Hanlon blustered. "This bruiser of yours practically dragged me bodily out of the hotel. My wife witnessed the incident, and so did other members of my troupe."

"We've had this discussion before," Kane chided. "As far as the law is concerned, my version of events is what actually happened, not the fantasies of some wild-eyed actor. Now . . ." His voice hardened. "Where is Miss McCoy?"

"I have no idea."

Kane leaned over and picked up the note from Savannah that he had brought down with him from the sitting room. "You arranged for her note to be delivered to me."

"I don't know what you're talking about."

"Please. You look after her. You must know where she's hiding." Kane tossed the paper back onto the desk. "I don't believe for one second that she's left town. You've just got her stashed away somewhere, that's all."

Stubbornly, O'Hanlon shook his head. "She left the troupe," he insisted. "I hated to see her go, but you made it impossible for her to do anything else, you . . . you . . ."

Harrison's big hand came down heavily on O'Hanlon's shoulder as the actor sputtered, searching for a suitable epithet.

"I'll find her," Kane said confidently. "I'll involve the law if I have to. The police can scour the entire city for her. Or you can save us all a great deal of trouble by telling me where she is."

"I can't tell you because I don't know. And if I did know, I wouldn't tell you!"

Kane looked at him for a second, then sighed and nodded to Eli Harrison.

The big man kicked O'Hanlon in the back of the right knee. O'Hanlon cried out in pain and toppled to the side as his right leg collapsed under him. Harrison kicked him again as he fell, digging the toe of his boot into O'Hanlon's shoulder blade. O'Hanlon lay on the floor, writhing and making little noises as he tried to keep from crying.

"I'll ask you again," Kane said. "Where is Miss McCoy?"

"G-go to hell!" O'Hanlon spat out between clenched teeth.

"You'll regret that you didn't cooperate

with me, O'Hanlon," Kane warned.

"I already regret that I ever saw your damned face!"

Kane nodded to Harrison again.

By the time the big man finished, O'Hanlon had passed out. There wasn't a mark on his face to indicate that he'd been beaten, but Kane wouldn't have worried if there had been. No one was going to believe the actor's story.

Harrison stood over the unconscious O'Hanlon and frowned. In his rumbling voice, he said, "I'm startin' to think that he's tellin' the truth, boss. If he knew where the girl was, he'd have spilled it by now."

"I believe you may be right." Kane picked up the note again. "But if she's abandoned the troupe and left Kansas City, where could she have gone?"

Jenkins cleared his throat again. The butler had been standing to one side during the brutal beating, his unlined face as imperturbable as ever. "I beg your pardon, sir, but I have a thought."

Kane turned to face him. "You're a smart man, Jenkins. What is it?"

"Miss McCoy has been traveling with this troupe of actors and entertainers, which means she's accustomed to having a group of people around her. I have my doubts that she would set out all alone from a strange place. Didn't your men report that they pursued Miss McCoy and that unknown cowboy to a place where a wagon train was camped? A wagon train that, I believe, departed from Kansas City this morning?"

"That's right." Kane closed his eyes for a second and made a face. "Of course! She went with the wagon train!"

"That would be my guess, sir."

Kane flipped a hand at O'Hanlon and told Harrison, "Take him out and dump him somewhere. If anyone ever asks, he was fine when he left here after our visit. Thieves must have attacked him on his way back to the hotel."

"It'll look more realistic if he doesn't have any money left on him," Harrison pointed out.

"Fine, fine, I don't care about that. Just put together a group of men and get after that wagon train. Stop it and search it." A thought occurred to Kane and put a smile on his face. "Not right away, though. Let it get several days away from here." He laughed. "That way Miss McCoy will believe that she's gotten away from me. How delicious it will be when she's dragged back here."

Harrison nodded slowly. "There's just one

problem we might have with that, boss."

"I pay you very well to take care of problems," Kane snapped. "What are you talking about?"

"From what I've heard, a fella named MacCallister took over as wagon master for that bunch of pilgrims. He's supposed to be a pretty tough gent. A real ring-tailed roarer."

"Mr. Harrison . . . did you ever see a man who was tougher than a bullet from a gun?"

"Well, no, sir, I haven't."

"There's your answer, then," Kane said. "No problem at all. If this fellow MacCallister or anybody else gets in your way, just kill him."

CHAPTER THIRTY-TWO

As Jamie expected that it would, life on the trail soon settled into a routine. He had the immigrants up early every morning, and they broke camp and the wagons rolled when the sky was still gray. Other than short breaks to rest the teams, he kept them moving all day.

Unfortunately, the sun slipped below the horizon a little earlier each day, cutting down the time that they could travel.

Late every afternoon, the wagons pulled off the trail and formed a big circle next to the river. He and some of the scouts stood guard while the livestock was watered and then driven into the circle.

The train had come far enough from Kansas City that the land was sparsely settled with a few isolated ranches in the area. Jamie didn't think there was any real danger from Indians yet, but it never hurt to be careful.

And outlaws, of course, could strike anywhere.

Once everyone had eaten supper, they turned in for the night, tired from the long day on the trail. There was no big center campfire where the immigrants gathered to play music, sing, and dance the way they had done back in Kansas City. They didn't have the energy for diversions like that anymore. The hard pace that Jamie established saw to that.

He set up guard shifts at night, drawing on volunteers from the wagon train along with his scouts. Moses Danzig was always willing to pitch in and do whatever was needed. He wouldn't be much good in a fight, Jamie knew, but he could stay alert and give the alarm in case of trouble as well as anybody else.

So far Lucas, Mahaffey, and Pearsoll had worked out fairly well. Mahaffey and Pearsoll weren't very friendly with the immigrants and the other scouts and kept to themselves most of the time. But they didn't cause any trouble and they did what Jamie told them without any arguments.

Jake Lucas, on the other hand, seldom stopped talking and always had a friendly word for everybody. He flirted with all the teenage girls whose families were part of

253

the group and even with some of the married women, which Jamie thought might lead to problems sooner or later. He asked Bodie to have a word with his friend about it.

Bodie agreed to do so, but he added, "Jake doesn't mean anything by the way he acts. That's just how he is. He's friendly with everybody."

"Get too friendly with a married woman and punches can get thrown," Jamie cautioned. "That's if you're lucky. If you're not, guns go off."

"I'll talk to him," Bodie promised.

Lamar Hendricks and Jamie had gotten together and studied the map that Jeb Ralston had drawn before they left. The route Ralston had laid out turned northwest away from the Kansas River, followed the Oregon Trail for a good long ways, then cut almost due north, crossing the Platte and continuing to skirt the Rocky Mountains to the east as they headed for Montana.

Once they were there the wagons would turn west again, travel through the foothills and on into Eagle Valley. It was a route without any extremely rugged terrain to cross, just plains and rolling hills, which meant the wagons could move fairly fast over it.

Jamie planned to follow that route. Ralston might have been a braggart and a bully, and reckless to boot, but he had sketched out a decent trail for the immigrants he was supposed to lead.

Several days out of Kansas City, they camped where the Blue River flowed into the Kansas from the northwest. It was where the Oregon Trail turned away from the larger stream.

That evening Jamie called his scouts together. "We haven't had much to worry about so far, but from here to the Platte we'll have to be a mite more watchful for trouble. Wagon trains have been taking this trail for a long time, so the Indians are used to seeing them, but you never know when some band will take it into their heads to get proddy." He paused to emphasize the next point. "The important thing is that if we do run into any Cheyenne, Arapaho, or Pawnee, everybody needs to stay calm until we see what they've got in mind. That goes for us as well as the pilgrims. No shooting unless I say so. More blood's been spilled because of itchy trigger fingers than any other reason."

The men nodded their agreement, even the normally taciturn Mahaffey and Pearsoll.

"Get a good night's sleep," Jamie added. "We'll all be in the saddle early tomorrow."

CHAPTER THIRTY-THREE

"And where are you off to, my friend?" Moses asked as Bodie stood up from their supper fire after they finished eating. "As if I didn't know."

"I've hardly gotten a glimpse of Savannah — I mean, Miss McCoy — since we left Kansas City. And I sure haven't gotten a chance to talk to her. I want to see how she's doing."

"Do I need to come with you to serve as a chaperone?" Moses asked with a grin.

"I just want to talk to her," Bodie said, slightly irritated. "I don't plan to do any sparking with her, or anything else that'd need a chaperone." He paused. "Besides, I reckon Mr. and Mrs. Bingham will be right there."

"I don't know, maybe you could convince her to go for a walk with you around the camp. I'm just saying . . ."

Bodie waved a hand at his friend, clapped

his hat on his head, and went to look for the Bingham wagon. He wasn't exactly sure where in the big circle it was parked.

He was walking past the area where the saddle mounts were picketed when he heard a murmur of voices. Something about the sound struck him as secretive, so he circled around the horses to see what was going on.

Several figures stood in the deep shadows next to a wagon. They seemed familiar to Bodie, and as he came closer he recognized Jake Lucas, Clete Mahaffey, and Dave Pearsoll. They were having an animated discussion, but Pearsoll noticed Bodie coming and said something curt to the others, who immediately fell silent.

Jake turned to greet Bodie. "What's up? Is MacCallister lookin' for us?"

"No, not as far as I know," Bodie replied. "What are you fellas doing?"

"Oh, nothin' that amounts to anything," Jake said with a laugh. "This 'tarnal idjit here" — he jerked a thumb at Mahaffey — "is tryin' to claim that he saw a panther today while he was scoutin'. I told him we're a heck of a long way from anywhere that a panther would be. Likely you just saw a coyote, Clete."

"Or a prairie dog," Pearsoll added in an

uncharacteristic display of dry humor.

"You lunkheads are both wrong," Mahaffey snapped. "I know what I saw."

"Where are you headed, Bodie?" Jake asked.

"I, uh, thought I'd go see how Miss McCoy is doing," Bodie admitted.

Jake grinned. "At least we know now why you left the gang back yonder in Kansas City."

"I don't want to talk about that," Bodie said as he quickly glanced around to see if anyone was within earshot. "That part of my life is over."

"Don't worry. It's the same way with all of us, pard. Although I wonder sometimes if you can ever leave behind who you really are."

"Sure you can," Bodie said. He hoped that was true, anyway.

He said so long to the three men and moved on toward the Bingham wagon. As he did, he wondered about the conversation they had been having. Even though he hadn't been able to make out any of the words, it had sounded to him as if they were arguing.

But somehow he wasn't convinced that they had been arguing about panthers.

Thoughts of Savannah crowded back into

his mind and made him forget about the encounter with Jake and the other two former outlaws. When he reached the Bingham wagon, Savannah and Mrs. Bingham were cleaning up after supper. The cooking fire had burned down to a small blaze, but it gave off enough light for Bodie to see how pretty Savannah was, even with her face flushed slightly from washing dishes in an iron pot of hot water.

"Hello, Bodie," she said brightly. "How are you?"

"Fine. How about you?"

"Oh . . . all right, I suppose."

He realized how stilted and uncomfortable this exchange was, but he couldn't seem to bring himself to relax around her. "I haven't had much of a chance to talk to you since we left Kansas City."

"I know. Mr. MacCallister must keep you really busy with your scouting duties."

"He does. He's not overbearing about it, though. He just wants to keep the wagon train safe."

Leticia Bingham came up beside Savannah. "Goodness, you two need to start talking to each other like actual human beings. Savannah, let me finish up here. You go visit with Mr. Cantrell."

"Are you sure?" Savannah asked. "Because

I really don't mind —"

"Go," Mrs. Bingham said again. "Sit on the wagon tongue. It's a nice night, just a little chilly. If you sit close, you won't be too cold."

The thought of sitting close to Savannah made Bodie's pulse race a little faster. He was grateful to Mrs. Bingham for suggesting it.

"All right." Savannah dried her hands on the apron she wore, then walked with Bodie to the front of the wagon. They sat down.

"I've been keeping an eye on our back trail," Bodie said. "You know, just in case Kane sends anybody after us."

"After me, you mean. He probably doesn't have any idea who you are. You haven't seen anyone following the wagon train, have you?"

"Not so far. And it's been several days. I think if they were back there, they would have caught up by now."

"I hope that means my note worked and that Kane has given up on finding me," Savannah said. "But I don't want to talk about him anymore, Bodie."

"I don't blame you. I don't want to talk about the no-good scoundrel, either." He grinned. "How do you like traveling with the wagon train?"

She smiled back at him. "Well, it's not like I never traveled by wagon before. The troupe travels from city to city in wagons, so I'm used to riding in one. Although Mr. MacCallister certainly has us covering more ground quicker than Cyrus ever did."

Bodie chuckled. "Jamie MacCallister isn't one to let grass grow under his feet, that's for sure."

"You sound like you admire him."

"I've never met anybody else quite like him. The places he's been, the things he's seen and done . . . I could listen to him talk about them all day. I find myself thinking . . . a fella could do a lot worse for himself than trying to be like Jamie Ian MacCallister."

Savannah's voice was quiet as she said, "I think you're doing fine just being Bodie Cantrell."

"It's nice of you to say so, but —"

She silenced him by leaning closer to him and kissing him.

That took him by surprise. He wouldn't have thought she would be so daring with the Binghams only a few yards away. But he certainly didn't pull back from her, instead lifting a hand to rest it lightly on her shoulder as he enjoyed the sweet warmth of her lips on his.

"I told Moses we wouldn't need a chaperone," he whispered when she finally broke the kiss after a long, delicious moment.

"We don't." Savannah stood up. "I'll be turning in now, Mr. Cantrell. I'll say good night."

"Good night to you, too, Miss McCoy," he replied, his voice thick in his throat.

He stood there while she went to the rear of the wagon and climbed in. If he was going to tell the truth, he had been thinking about Savannah and wishing he could kiss her ever since they'd left Kansas City. Now that he had . . .

Now that he had, he realized as a grin broke across his face, he was ready to do it again.

CHAPTER THIRTY-FOUR

"Forget about sharin' the loot with Cantrell," Clete Mahaffey said as the three former outlaws resumed their conversation once Bodie had walked off toward the Binghams' wagon. "That fool doesn't care about money, anyway. The only thing he can think about now is the girl."

"She's worth thinkin' about," Jake said. "She's a mighty pretty gal."

Dave Pearsoll grunted and declared, "A big pile of double eagles is prettier. That's what we've got, and I agree with Clete. I ain't inclined to share 'em with Cantrell. He didn't do anything to earn a share."

"He was with us when we took them off that train," Jake pointed out. "Shoot, he helped Eldon and the others take over the depot and make sure the train stopped. We wouldn't have that pile of double eagles if they hadn't done that."

"But he wasn't there when we risked our

necks to steal them from Swint," Mahaffey said. "Anyway, he quit the gang back there in Kansas City. That was his own decision."

"So did we," Jake reminded him. "But I'm not gonna argue about it with you boys. Bodie don't know we've got the loot, and as long as he don't know he can't say that we're cheatin' him out of anything. So I'll go along with whatever you say. When the time comes to leave the wagon train, we'll go our own way and leave Bodie behind."

"Yeah, well, when's that gonna be?" Pearsoll asked.

That was the question they had been wrangling about when Bodie came up to them a short time earlier and caused Jake to come up with that story about the panther. Mahaffey and Pearsoll thought it was already time to leave the wagons behind and disappear in the middle of the night with the loot they had liberated from Eldon Swint, but Jake wanted to wait and stay with the train a while longer.

"We'll reach the Platte River in a few weeks," Jake said. "By then, we'll know for sure whether or not Eldon's gonna come after us. If we haven't seen hide nor hair of him, we can figure he doesn't know where we are and go wherever we want from there.

San Francisco, Mexico, wherever suits our fancy."

Despite the fact that he was younger and less experienced than the other two outlaws, he was in charge and he didn't want them to forget it, so his voice hardened slightly. "Until then, we'll stay with the wagons. If Swint and the rest of the gang show up lookin' for us with guns in their hands and blood in their eyes, we'll need all the help we can get fightin' 'em off. Bodie and his new friends will pitch in on our side, I'm sure of that. Those pilgrims will think they're under attack by owlhoots, and that'll be the truth. They just won't know the reason why."

"All right, all right," Mahaffey muttered. "I reckon what you say makes sense, Jake. That big varmint MacCallister worries me, though."

"Me, too," Pearsoll agreed. "Sometimes when he looks at me, it feels like he can see right through me, Jake. Like he knows everythin' I'm thinkin' or feelin'. Man's got eyes like a hawk . . . or an eagle."

"Don't worry about Jamie MacCallister," Jake said. "He's just like Bodie." He grinned. "He don't suspect a thing."

CHAPTER THIRTY-FIVE

Moses was checking the hubs on his wagon wheels to see if they needed to be greased again when he heard rapid footsteps coming up behind him.

He straightened and turned quickly, not really expecting trouble right in camp but knowing that it was best to be careful. He relaxed when he saw the two children who had just run up to his wagon.

"Hello, Mr. Danzig," Alexander Bradford said.

"Hello," his sister Abigail added.

"Good evening to you, children," Moses told the youngsters with a solemn nod. "What brings you to see me? Shouldn't you be back at your father's wagon, getting ready to go to sleep? You know how Mr. MacCallister likes to make an early start in the morning!"

"We were hopin' you could show us that toy again," Alexander said.

"You know, the spinning one," Abigail said.

Moses grinned. "Ah, you mean the dreidel. Let me get it."

They had seen him idly spinning the dreidel one day back in Kansas City. It helped him to think, and he had explained a little about it to them during that conversation.

He climbed into the wagon over the lowered tailgate and emerged a moment later to hop back down to the ground. Motioning for Alexander and Abigail to come closer, he poised the four-sided top on the tailgate. "Here we go."

Grasping the little shaft that stuck up from the dreidel, he flicked it between his thumb and index finger and gave it a spin. The top whirled so fast that the four Hebrew letters painted on it, one on each side, blurred and became unreadable.

Not that the children could have read them anyway, Moses thought. He was quite probably the only member of the wagon train who could.

But they enjoyed watching the top spin. Abigail clapped her hands together and giggled. Alexander grinned and fidgeted, shuffling his feet back and forth. Moses knew the boy was anxious to try spinning the top himself.

"We use the dreidel to play a game during one of my people's holidays," Moses told them.

"Like Christmas?" Abigail asked.

"Well, not exactly. Our holiday is called Hanukkah, which means the Feast of Lights, and even though it comes at about the same time of year as Christmas, it's different —"

"Alexander! Abigail!" The angry bellow came from Reverend Bradford, who stalked toward Moses's wagon with his hands clenched into knobby-knuckled fists.

The children scurried away from the tailgate, obviously not wanting to incur any more of their father's wrath than they already had by being there. Moses frowned. He didn't like to see children acting so frightened. He worried that they had good reason to be scared.

The dreidel had stopped spinning and fallen over onto its side. Moses picked it up and held it in his hands where Bradford could see it and hopefully realize that he had just been entertaining the youngsters with a harmless toy. "Good evening, Reverend."

Bradford came to a stop and glared at him. "What are you doing with my children?"

"I was just showing them the dreidel," Moses explained. "I was going to let them play with it."

"You were preaching your heathen religion to them!"

Moses shook his head. "Not at all. I wouldn't do that. They're just children."

"I heard you telling them about your Hebrew holiday, the one you celebrate instead of Christmas." Bradford stabbed a blunt finger toward the dreidel. "Look at it! It's got religious symbols painted on it!"

"They're just Hebrew letters —" Moses stopped and drew a deep breath. It was true that the markings on the dreidel had some significance in his faith, and as a rabbi he could have explained all that to Bradford in a calm, rational manner, but he knew the man didn't want to hear it.

Instead he said simply, "I'm sorry. If you'd rather the children not play with it, I'll honor your wishes, of course."

"I'd rather that they not have anything to do with the likes of you," Bradford snapped. "If they come around here again, you send them packing, you hear?"

Moses made an effort to hang on to his temper. "All right. They're your children."

"And don't you forget it."

Bradford turned and stalked off across the

camp. Alexander and Abigail had already disappeared, no doubt scurrying back to their wagon.

Moses watched the man go and shook his head. It was a shame that Bradford had to be so hostile, but with some people, once they made their minds up there was no changing them.

"The reverend's lucky you didn't take a swing at him."

The quiet voice made Moses jerk his head around. The huge shape that loomed up in the firelight was instantly recognizable as that of Jamie Ian MacCallister.

"Mr. MacCallister," Moses said. "I didn't hear you." He had wondered before how a man as large as Jamie could move so silently. The big frontiersman was as stealthy as Moses supposed an Indian to be.

"I was keeping an eye on things. If Bradford had jumped you, I would have stepped in. If you'd needed my help, that is."

"I think that's a foregone conclusion. I'm not exactly what you'd call a . . . a brawler."

"No, but you've got sand."

"Sand?" Moses repeated with a frown.

"Courage," Jamie said.

Moses shook his head slowly. "I don't know about that. I've never been renowned for my bravery."

Jamie hooked his thumbs in his gun belt. "You came all the way to this country from Poland and then set out across it just because that's what your faith told you to do, didn't you?"

"Well, yes," Moses admitted. "But that's my calling, I guess you'd say."

"You joined up with a wagon train full of folks different from you, knowing that some of 'em wouldn't like you, but you're as friendly as you can be toward them and do everything you can to help out."

Moses spread his hands. "What can I say, I was raised to get along with people. And to be practical. I have to get to Oregon somehow, and this seemed like the quickest way."

Jamie sat on the tailgate. "Most of my spiritual beliefs, if you can call 'em that, come from the Indians. They figure we all had to get here somehow, and that somebody put us here. Some of them call him Man Above, some call him the Great Spirit. They have other names for the creator, too. But no matter what they call him, there's always somebody bigger than us, somebody who looks out for us and expects us to be the best folks we can."

"Nothing in my faith would disagree with that," Moses said.

Jamie nodded. "That's what I'm saying. Bradford's got it in his head that he's got all the answers. Me?" The big man chuckled. "I don't reckon I even know all the questions yet. Probably won't while I'm still on this earth. But what I do know is that you'll do to ride the river with, Moses Danzig."

"Ride the river? I'm afraid I don't understand."

Jamie lifted a hand to say good night, and as he turned away he told Moses, "By the time we get where we're going, you'll have figured it out."

CHAPTER THIRTY-SIX

The months she had spent with the theatrical troupe had gotten Savannah in the habit of going to bed late and sleeping late in the morning. She'd had to get over that in a hurry, and after a couple days of being extremely groggy most of the day after being rousted out of her bedroll early, she was starting to get used to the schedule set by Mr. MacCallister.

In fact, she awoke this morning even before he came around to make sure everyone was up and about, getting ready for the day's journey. The pattering of rain on the wagon's canvas cover may have had something to do with that. It was a soothing sound, but at the same time it was different enough to make Savannah want to get up and see how the weather was.

Mr. and Mrs. Bingham slept in an actual bunk built into the side of the wagon, while Savannah rolled up in blankets next to the tailgate. She lifted her head and pushed the canvas flap aside to peer out, only to discover that she couldn't see anything. The thick cloud cover made the pre-dawn hours even darker than usual.

Savannah wasn't sure what time it was, but she suspected it was late enough that Mr. MacCallister would be coming around soon. She pushed the blankets aside, sat up, and dug around in the bag she had brought with her until she found her rain slicker. The idea of going out in the rain to attend to her personal needs didn't appeal to her, but she didn't have any choice.

She pulled the slicker on and climbed out of the wagon, dropping easily to the ground. It wasn't very muddy yet, which told her the rain hadn't been falling for long. It was just a drizzle at the moment, not much more than a fine mist.

Savannah thought she might try to go ahead and rig a cover of some sort so that she could get a fire started using chunks of wood from the supply that the Binghams carried in a rope sling underneath the wagon's body.

That would wait until she had taken care of her other chores. She took a couple of steps away from the wagon . . .

The arm that came out of the darkness

wrapped around her with brutal, startling force, jerking her off her feet. She opened her mouth to scream, but before any sound could come out, a big, powerful hand clamped across her mouth and silenced any cry.

During the night a steady rain began to fall. Jamie wasn't surprised. So far the weather had been cool and clear, almost perfect for traveling. He had known that such a run of good luck couldn't last.

One thing he and the other scouts would have to keep an eye out for was mud. Heavy wagons had a tendency to bog down on muddy ground. Jamie hoped that they could put some miles behind them as long as the rain wasn't falling too hard. With a slow drizzle, it would take a while before the ground softened enough to cause a problem.

"Let's go, let's go!" He called as he strode through the camp, his powerful voice carrying from one side of the circle to the other. "We need to get a move on!"

He heard a thud from the direction of one of the wagons, then his keen ears picked up what sounded like a scuffle. As he swung in that direction his eyes narrowed. The thick overcast made it difficult to see, and so did the water dripping off the brim of his hat.

He was able to make out several figures near the back of one of the wagons, however, and the way they lurched back and forth told him that a struggle was going on.

He broke into a run toward the wagon. He didn't shout or announce in any other fashion that he was on his way, but loped across the ground in near-silence, a runaway locomotive of a man clad in buckskins.

As he came closer, he could tell that one of the struggling figures wore a dress, and he had a pretty good idea who the woman was. She had to be Savannah McCoy. A tall, male shape had his arms around her, and two more men hovered nearby, ready to grab her if she managed to get away.

Jamie targeted one of those other two men first, clubbing his fists together and swinging them with all the power of his brawny arms and shoulders and his own momentum. They smashed into the back of the unsuspecting man's neck with the force of a sledgehammer, causing him to drop like a stone.

The other man yelled in alarm and whirled toward Jamie. The goal of sneaking into the wagon camp during the predawn hours when everybody was asleep, grabbing Savannah, and getting out again without being detected was ruined, so there was no longer any need for stealth. A shot roared as flame gouted from the muzzle of a gun, almost singeing Jamie's face.

Before the intruder could fire again, the fingers of Jamie's left hand closed around the wrist of the man's gun hand. He thrust that arm skyward and gave the wrist such a powerful wrench that bones snapped like kindling.

The man started to scream in pain, but Jamie put an abrupt stop to that with a piledriver punch that broke more bones in the man's face and knocked him out cold. When Jamie let go of him, the man flopped to the ground.

The hombre who had hold of Savannah swept her up bodily, threw her over his shoulder like she was a sack of grain, and took off running through the cold mist.

Jamie couldn't risk a shot with Savannah in the man's grasp, so all he could do was give chase. The man he was pursuing was tall, and his long legs covered the ground quickly. Jamie lost sight of him in the gloom, then spotted him again.

He spotted something else, too: tall, bulky shapes that could only be picketed horses. He grimaced. Sundown and the other saddle mounts were back at the camp. If the kidnapper managed to get on one of those horses with Savannah, he could gallop away into the darkness before Jamie could return to the camp and grab a mount of his own.

Jamie wasn't built for running, and he wasn't as young as he used to be, but he poured on as much speed as he could and saw that he was closing the gap. Savannah was still struggling, and that threw her captor off his stride.

When Jamie judged that he was close enough, he left his feet in a diving tackle that caught the man around the knees. Savannah yelped as the man fell and she went sailing through the air. Jamie hoped she would be all right when she landed, but he didn't have time to check on her. He had his hands full with the man he had just brought down.

The kidnapper rolled over and launched a kick that caught Jamie on the left shoulder. It was powerful enough to make the big frontiersman's arm go numb.

Jamie grimaced but didn't make a sound. When the man tried to kick him again, Jamie caught hold of the man's foot with his right hand and heaved, rolling the man over onto his belly. Jamie scrambled after him, intending to pin the man down with a knee in the small of his back.

His opponent twisted aside and shot a fist upward in a blow that landed on Jamie's jaw, a powerful punch that threw Jamie to one side.

It had been a good long while since he had faced anybody who was almost his equal in size and strength. In a way, he almost looked forward to continuing the battle, he thought as he slapped a hand against the muddy ground and pushed himself up.

The two men came to their feet at practically the same instant, about ten feet apart. Jamie glanced around to see if he could locate Savannah, but it was still too dark. He saw a fuzzy, wavering glow coming through the rain from the direction of the wagon train, though. The shot that had been fired had roused the immigrants and somebody had lit a lantern. He hoped Savannah was already on her way back to them, seeking help.

Then he no longer had time to worry about anything because the other man charged him, malletlike fists swinging dangerously at the end of long, powerful arms.

Chapter Thirty-Seven

They were like two bulls coming together. Jamie blocked the man's first punch, but the second got through and crashed against his sternum, rocking him back a step. Jamie planted a foot on the ground and counter-punched, twisting at the hips as he threw a right that landed cleanly on the man's jaw.

For a long moment, they stood there toe-to-toe, slugging away at each other. Jamie was hammering away at his opponent, do-ing plenty of damage. His massive, heavily muscled form was able to absorb a great deal of punishment, but he knew he couldn't keep it up forever.

The man suddenly changed tactics, feint-ing and then lunging forward to catch Jamie in a bear hug.

The collision knocked both men off their feet again. They rolled over and over on the wet ground, grappling and wrestling and trying to get the upper hand. The would-be kidnapper managed to slide his arm around Jamie's neck from behind, and suddenly it clamped down across the big frontiersman's throat like an iron bar, cutting off his air.

Jamie drove an elbow back into the man's belly, causing him to grunt in pain and expel a big gust of foul-smelling breath. That loosened the grip on Jamie's neck just enough for him to twist halfway around and wedge his elbow under the man's chin. He levered the man's head back and broke free completely.

The separation lasted only a second before they were wrapped around each other again, battling for any advantage. Jamie grabbed the man's hair, hunched his shoulders, and head-butted the man in the face.

He sensed the tide swinging in his direction, but at that moment something smashed against the side of his head with stunning force. The dark predawn lit up with jagged red lightning bolts he knew were only inside his head.

In the few seconds that his muscles refused to obey his brain's commands, the man shoved him away. Jamie knew there was a good chance the intruder had hit him with a gun, which meant the next thing might be a shot. He forced himself to move, galvanizing his muscles through sheer force of will and rolling across the ground.

A revolver went off with a roar like thunder. Jamie saw the muzzle flash, dragged out his right-hand .44, and returned the fire. With rain in his eyes and his head still spinning from the clout he had taken, he couldn't tell if he hit anything.

The next moment he heard hoofbeats pounding against the ground and knew his shot hadn't found its target. The intruder had gotten on one of the horses and was fleeing. Jamie lifted the Colt and triggered three more shots in the direction of the sound, but he knew it would be sheer luck if he hit the man.

As he climbed to his feet, he saw lights from the wagon train bobbing closer. People were coming to see what was going on. They were probably pretty spooked, so to keep them from getting trigger-happy, Jamie called, "Hold your fire! It's MacCallister!"

Bodie Cantrell was in the lead when the group of armed men hurried up to Jamie. "Mr. MacCallister! Are you all right?"

Jamie was covered with mud and he knew that by the next day he would be stiff and sore from the fight. "I'm fine. What about Savannah?"

"She's all right," Bodie said. "She ran back to the wagons and told us you were out here fighting with the man who tried to carry her off. Where is he?"

"Gone," Jamie replied curtly. "He got on a horse and lit a shuck before I could stop him. At least we've got the two I left back in camp."

Bodie shook his head. His face was etched with grim lines in the lantern light. "There's only one man in camp, and he's dead. His neck is broken."

Jamie grunted. Obviously, the man he'd hit in the back of the neck with his clubbed fists had been injured worse than he thought. It wasn't the first time he had killed a man with his bare hands, but it had been a while since that happened. "There was another one. I'm pretty sure I broke his wrist. May have broken his nose or a cheekbone, too. He was out cold when I left him."

"He must have come to, crawled off in the dark, and slipped away," Bodie said. "As soon as it gets light enough, we can search for him —"

Jamie waved away that suggestion. "We've got better things to do. As bad as he's hurt, he's not going to be interested in causing any more trouble for us. He'll probably try to find one of the horses he and his friends brought with them and head on back to Kansas City."

And if the man wasn't able to catch one of the horses, he'd probably die out there, injured as he was. Jamie wasn't going to waste any time worrying about a no-good kidnapper, though.

Bodie said, "They had to be some of Kane's men. They didn't pick Savannah at random to go after."

"I reckon you're right about that. Help me find my hat."

It was Hector Gilworth who found Jamie's hat in the mud where it had fallen off and gotten trampled on during the battle. "Looks like it's in pretty bad shape," he said as he handed it to Jamie.

"The rain'll wash the mud off," Jamie said as he punched it back into shape. "This old hat's been through almost as much as I have. It'll be all right."

They trooped back to the wagons. Jamie told Hector and Jess to make sure everybody was awake and preparing for the day's journey, then he went with Bodie to the Binghams' wagon. He wanted to talk to Savannah and see for himself that she was really all right.

A lantern was burning inside the wagon, its yellow glow coming through the gaps around the canvas flaps in front and back.

Bodie stepped up to the tailgate. "Savannah?"

Leticia Bingham pulled the flap aside. "She's resting. What do you want, Mr. Cantrell?"

"Mr. MacCallister wants to talk to her."

Savannah might have been resting, but she wasn't sleeping. She heard what Bodie said and spoke up from behind the older woman. "It's all right, Mrs. Bingham. I need to speak to Mr. MacCallister, too."

"All right, dear, but you've been through an ordeal. You should take it easy for a little while."

Mrs. Bingham moved back, and Savannah put her head in the opening at the rear of the wagon. "Mr. MacCallister, are you all right?" she asked anxiously. "I heard some shots . . ."

"Nothing to worry about," Jamie told her. "Those fellas are long gone and won't be bothering you again."

"You killed them?" Her voice was hushed.

"Well . . . only one of 'em." But it wasn't from lack of trying, Jamie thought. He would have gladly sent all three of the varmints packing across the divide. "The other two got away, but I don't think they'll be coming back."

"You can't be sure of that."

"Not much in this life is certain. Did you get a good look at any of them?"

Savannah shook her head. "No. One of them grabbed me from behind. The big one who carried me off. I never even saw him. I didn't even have a chance to fight. But I did manage to kick the wagon tongue. I hoped that would make enough noise to attract someone's attention."

"So that's what I heard," Jamie said. "That was fast thinking on your part. If you hadn't done that, they might've been able to drag you off without anybody noticing."

A shudder went through Savannah at the thought. "You said a couple of them got away. You know what's going to happen now, don't you, Mr. MacCallister? Now they're sure that I'm traveling with the wagon train. They'll go back to Gideon Kane and tell him, and since this attempt to kidnap me failed, he'll try something else. Something bigger and more dangerous."

"Let him try," Bodie said. "We'll be ready for him."

"That's right," Jamie agreed. But at the same time he was thinking that Savannah was right. Kane would send a larger group next time, and chances were that they wouldn't be worried about stealth. He would hire gunmen, and their goal would be to catch up to the wagon train and take Savannah away by force.

If that happened — *when* that happened, Jamie amended because every instinct in his body told him that it would — the rest of the pilgrims would be in danger as well.

It was too bad he hadn't taken the time to hunt up Gideon Kane while they were still in Kansas. He could have gone ahead and put a bullet in the varmint then and there.

Sometimes the simplest ways were the best.

Chapter Thirty-Eight

The rain continued as the wagon train rolled northwestward along the Blue River that morning. The sky was such a flat, leaden gray it seemed like the immigrants traveled in a depressing state of perpetual twilight.

The warmth of the sun was nowhere to be found. A dank cold had settled over the landscape, the sort of weather that chilled a person to the bone.

Jamie felt it in his bones, that was for sure. He felt every one of his more than sixty years of life.

But he didn't let that stop him from doing the job that needed to be done. He was out ahead of the wagon train with Hector Gilworth riding beside him as they watched out for muddy areas that the wagons needed to avoid.

The rain grew harder at midday, turning into a slashing downpour that quickly formed large puddles on the already wet ground. Jamie grimaced under the dripping brim of his hat as mud began to suck at Sundown's hooves. "All right," he told Hector. "We might as well turn around and tell the wagons to stop for the day before they get bogged down. If some of those wheels sink down far enough in the mud, it might take days to get them back out again."

When they arrived at the lead wagon and told Captain Hendricks of the decision, the leader of the immigrants wasn't happy. "We haven't covered much distance today," he complained. "Don't you think we can push on just a little farther, Mr. MacCallister?"

"No, I don't," Jamie replied bluntly. "You'll be risking an even longer delay if you do. It'll be better to stay here, hope the rain stops tonight, and that the sun will come out tomorrow and dry the ground some. It hasn't been a very rainy autumn so far, so the dirt ought to suck up most of the water pretty fast once it gets a chance."

Hendricks heaved a sigh and nodded. "Very well. Tell everyone to go ahead and make camp. We're not going to be able to build fires in this weather, though."

"It'll be a cold camp," Jamie agreed. If folks were smart, they would gnaw a little jerky, crawl into their blankets, huddle together for warmth, and wait it out.

Earlier, he had told Bodie to drop back a ways behind the wagon train and watch for pursuers. It was possible the men who had sneaked into the camp early that morning to kidnap Savannah had been part of a larger force. If that was the case, they might make another attempt, and Jamie wanted some warning if that was going to happen.

The other scouts had seen that the wagons were stopped and came on in. Jamie left them to keep an eye on things while he rode back to meet Bodie. He had gone about half a mile before he saw the gray figure plodding toward him on horseback, shrouded in the curtains of rain.

Jamie reined in and waited for Bodie to come to him. He slipped a hand under the yellow slicker he wore and tried to dry it on his damp buckskins. He didn't have much luck with that, but it was better than nothing.

Then he wrapped that hand around the butt of one of his .44s, just in case it wasn't Bodie Cantrell coming toward him through the downpour.

A few moments later Jamie relaxed as Bodie hailed him. He took his hand off the gun.

"Any sign of anybody coming after us?"

Jamie asked as Bodie rode up to him.

Bodie sounded as wet and miserable as he looked. "I didn't see anything but this blasted rain. Ulysses S. Grant could be right behind us with the Army of the Potomac, and I wouldn't know it!"

Jamie chuckled. "I think old Useless S. Grant has his hands full right now being president and dealing with that bank panic back east I heard about. He's too busy to be chasing us, even if he had any reason to."

"Maybe so, but I still say there could be an army back there. You couldn't prove it by me one way or the other."

"We'll figure there's not," Jamie said. "Come on. I'd say you can go get warm, but I'm afraid that may be an impossible chore under these conditions."

"How long do you think it's going to rain?" Bodie asked as they rode side by side toward the wagons.

"Hard to say. I've seen it settle in and rain like this for days. Maybe even as long as a week. Or it could stop tonight. You don't ever know."

"This is why you warned everybody it might be hard to reach Montana by Christmas."

"One reason," Jamie said. "There are still

plenty of other things that can go wrong, too."

When they arrived at the camp, Jamie saw that the wagons had been formed into a circle, as usual, and the men were unhitching their teams. As they passed the Bingham wagon, Savannah stuck her head out the back. "Why don't you two come in here and get out of the rain? It's miserable out there!"

"I'll be back as soon as I tend to my horse," Bodie promised. "How about you, Mr. MacCallister?"

"I'm going to scout around for a while longer," Jamie said. "Then I reckon I'll climb in with Moses, since he's got that wagon to himself." He touched a finger to the broad brim of his hat. "But I appreciate the invitation, Miss McCoy."

Jamie made a big circuit around the camp on Sundown. Satisfied that there were no imminent threats, he rode to Moses Danzig's wagon, tied Sundown's reins to the vehicle, and unsaddled the big stallion. The horses and the other animals were going to be even more wet, cold, and uncomfortable than the humans, but there was nothing that could be done about that.

Hardships were part of life on the frontier. The sooner the immigrants knew and understood that, the better.

Jamie rapped his knuckles on the tailgate and climbed over it into the wagon.

Moses welcomed him. "Come in, Mr. MacCallister. I can't offer much in the way of hospitality other than a canvas roof over your head."

"Right now I'll take it." Jamie stripped off his slicker and hung it over the tailgate.

Moses sat on a crate beside a candle burning on top of a keg and Jamie perched on a second crate. He handed an airtight to Jamie, who opened it with his Bowie knife. Moses then used the candle flame to heat up the can of beans, although it wasn't very effective for that chore.

"All the comforts of home," Moses said with a wry grin. "What do you think, Jamie? Is it going to rain for forty days and forty nights, like in the Old Testament?"

"It better not. If it does, this prairie will get so muddy it's liable to swallow up the wagons whole."

As it turned out, they didn't have to worry about that. The rain stopped during the night. In the wee hours, Jamie woke up enough to be aware that he no longer heard it hitting the canvas cover, then he dozed off again. When he woke up at his usual time, long before dawn, and climbed out the back of the wagon, he tilted his head to look up at the sky.

Stars glittered against the ebony backdrop. The overcast had broken and the clouds had moved on, which meant the sun would be shining later.

The wagons wouldn't be going anywhere for a while, though. The softness of the muddy ground under Jamie's boots told him that. As long as the vehicles stayed put, they would be all right, but if they tried to move their iron-tired wheels would sink deeply into the earth.

There wouldn't be any early start that day.

CHAPTER THIRTY-NINE

Once the sky cleared, the temperature had dropped during the night. Some of the puddles had thin skims of ice on them. But once the sun was up, the temperature began to rise and by noon the day was fairly pleasant.

The ground was still too wet for the wagons to risk moving. Out on the plains, there wasn't much chance for rainfall to run off. Once it fell, it had to soak into the ground, which took time.

Jamie conferred with Lamar Hendricks. "Let's give it until tomorrow. I hate to waste a day, but we don't want to do anything that'll cost us even more time in the long run."

With a gloomy expression on his face, Hendricks nodded in agreement. "I trust your judgment, Mr. MacCallister. I have a feeling that if Jeb Ralston were still our wagon master, we'd be good and stuck here."

"You might be right about that."

Since he had plenty of time to kill, Jamie took Hector and Jess and rode out to make another big scouting circuit. He would have taken Bodie with him, but he was still hanging around the Bingham wagon so Jamie decided it would be better to leave him where he was. Jamie didn't expect any more trouble from Kane's men right away, but if anything came up, he knew he could count on Bodie to protect Savannah, even if it cost him his own life.

Bodie was head over heels in love with that girl.

Jamie and his two companions were riding about a mile west of the wagon train when Hector suddenly said, "Look over there, Mr. MacCallister. Is that what I think it is?"

Hector was smart enough not to lift his arm and point. Instead he indicated the direction he was looking with a nod of his bearded chin.

Jamie didn't have to turn his head to look. He had spotted the Indian pacing them a good five minutes earlier. The lone warrior was riding along the top of a slight rise about a quarter mile away.

"Pawnee, if I had to guess," Jamie said quietly. "He's just taking a gander at us."

"What else can he do?" Jess asked. "There's one of him and three of us."

"There's only one of him that we can see," Jamie pointed out. "Could be fifty more just like him right on the other side of that rise. Maybe more than that."

Hector and Jess got nervous expressions on their faces, and Jamie knew they were thinking about what he had just said.

"He wants us to see him," Jamie went on, "otherwise we wouldn't know he was there. That's his way of making sure we know he's not afraid of us."

"I'm not sure I can say the same thing," Jess admitted. "Redskins make me down-right antsy."

"He's not looking for trouble right now. He's just curious."

"What about later?" Hector asked. "He could come back with a bunch of his friends, and they could be looking for trouble."

"We'll just have to wait and see about that," Jamie said.

After a few minutes, the distant rider peeled away and disappeared from sight. His absence didn't seem to make Hector and Jess relax. If anything, they were more watchful than they had been earlier.

The three scouts rode back to the wagon train in the late afternoon.

Jamie told Hector and Jess, "There's no point in saying anything about what we saw today. People would worry about it and might get all worked up for no good reason. I'll tell Cap'n Hendricks, and we'll let it go at that for right now."

Hector and Jess nodded in understanding.

Captain Hendricks, on the other hand, didn't take the news as well. When Jamie told him about seeing the Indian, he became agitated. "We have to warn everyone on the train."

"So they can do what?" Jamie asked. "Keep their eyes open? They're already doing that if they've got any sense, and anyway, that's what the scouts and I are for, to serve as the eyes and ears of this wagon train. You don't want a bunch of inexperienced pilgrims on edge and ready to start blasting away at anything that moves. That's how innocent folks wind up getting shot."

Hendricks paced back and forth on the still-muddy ground next to his wagon as they talked. "I suppose you're right. You're a lot more experienced at this sort of thing than I am. But I was hoping we could make it through to Montana without encountering any savages."

"We might yet," Jamie said, although he knew how unlikely that was.

"What about the ground?" Hendricks asked. "Do you think it'll be dry enough tomorrow that we can get started again and only lose one day?"

"Maybe. As long as it doesn't start raining again tonight."

Luck held. The weather remained clear, cold, and dry overnight, and the next morning Jamie swung up into Sundown's saddle and rode around the camp, checking the ground. He had waited until the sun was up so he could take a good look at the landscape, and he was satisfied with what he saw.

"We'll have to avoid any low spots that might be muddier," he reported to Hendricks, "but I think if we're careful we can get these wagons rolling again."

Hendricks heaved a sigh of relief. "I'll pass the word. We'll be ready to leave as soon as possible."

Spirits were higher as the immigrants prepared to break camp. They had been able to build fires, cook food, and boil coffee, and even though the air was still cold, not having rain pouring down put people in a better mood. They worked enthusiastically as they got the wagons ready to roll again.

Soon the line of canvas-covered vehicles stretched across the prairie again, rolling slowly to the northwest. Jamie sent out the scouts and took the point himself. Bodie Cantrell rode with him.

"The river's up," Jamie mused after a while. He nodded toward the line of scrubby, bare-limbed trees that marked the course of the stream, about half a mile west of the wagon train's route. "I can hear it."

"Is that a problem?" Bodie asked.

"Not necessarily. We won't be crossing it for a good while yet, so it'll have time to go down. But the fact that it's running like it is means that the smaller streams feeding into it are up, too, and we might come upon one of them and need to get across it."

Jamie's words proved to be prophetic. That afternoon, he and Bodie came to a creek that cut directly across the path of the wagon train. They reined in to study the fast-flowing stream, which was about sixty feet wide, filling the depression through which it ran.

"Normally that creek wouldn't be more than eight or ten feet wide and maybe a foot deep," Jamie said.

"How deep is it now?" Bodie asked.

"Hard to say. Four or five feet, more than likely."

"Will we have to wait for it to go down?"

Jamie rubbed his grizzled jaw as he frowned in thought. "That might be the smartest thing to do, but to tell you the truth, I'd rather keep moving."

He decided to tell Bodie what he and Hector and Jess had seen the day before. "I've got a hunch there's a band of Pawnee in the area, and I'd just as soon move on out, in case they consider this their hunting ground and figure we're interlopers."

"You think they'll attack us?"

"They'll be less likely to if they can see that we don't intend to stay and cause them any trouble."

Bodie looked around. "You reckon they're watching us now?"

"Wouldn't surprise me a bit. Come on. Let's see if we can swim our horses across that creek. If we can, the wagons ought to be able to make it."

Sundown and Bodie's horse swam across the creek without any trouble. Jamie could tell that the water was deep enough to float the wagons. The current was fast, but the oxen and mules would be able to handle it.

The wagons were catching up, and Jamie and Bodie rode back to tell Captain Hendricks what lay ahead. Then Jamie went along the line of wagons, explaining to the immigrants how they would ford the creek.

"We'll take the women and children across on horseback," Jamie told his scouts when he had gathered them around him. "That'll be less weight for the wagons, and it'll be safer for them, too. I think the wagons can make it without any problems, but if any of them get into trouble, I don't want a bunch of kids who maybe can't swim getting dumped in the creek."

Jake grinned at Bodie. "I bet I know which of the ladies you'll be ferryin' across, Bodie."

"I'll do whatever I'm told," Bodie said stiffly.

Jamie jerked a thumb toward the Bingham wagon. "Go ahead and get Miss McCoy, Bodie. Nobody's going to stop you."

Bodie smiled somewhat sheepishly and turned his horse to fetch Savannah.

Lamar Hendricks had his wagon poised at the edge of the stream. As Jamie moved his horse up alongside the vehicle, Hendricks said, "I'm ready to give this a try, Mr. MacCallister."

"Let the team do the work for you," Jamie told him. "Just keep 'em moving as steady and straight across as you can. The current will push you downstream some, but not enough to worry about."

Hendricks nodded. He used the whip on the rumps of the stolid oxen and got them moving. They plodded forward into the creek, obviously a little reluctant to fight the current, but as it took hold of them they began to swim and pulled the wagon into the deeper water. Hendricks perched on the seat looking nervous as the vehicle began to float.

Sundown, with Jamie in the saddle, swam alongside the wagon. Jamie had his lasso ready to throw if the wagon happened to capsize. He figured he could drop a loop over Hendricks and haul him out if necessary.

Hendricks made it to the other side of the rain-swollen stream without any problems. The wagon rolled up the shallow bank and came to a stop as he hauled back on the team's reins. He looked over at Jamie and sleeved sweat off his face, even though the day was still chilly. "I never did like boats, and that's what it felt like I was on when the wagon started floating. I prefer solid ground."

"You did fine," Jamie told him with a grin. He turned his horse, took off his hat, and waved it over his head to signal the folks waiting on the other side. "Come on over, one wagon at a time!"

The crossing proceeded without incident for an hour, with the men guiding the floating wagons across while the scouts ferried the women and children on horseback.

Then one of the women refused to leave her husband to take their wagon across. Hector swam his horse across the flooded creek to report on the situation to Jamie and Hendricks.

"The lady's name is Hamilton," Hector said after he passed along the news. "She's being mighty stubborn about it."

"That's Alice Hamilton," Hendricks said. "She and her husband R.G. were married just a couple days before we left Kansas City."

Jamie nodded. "I remember. You folks were celebrating the wedding the night I met you."

"That's right. I suppose Alice doesn't want to leave R.G.'s side because they're newlyweds."

Hector looked uncomfortable as he said, "I can take her off the wagon seat and bring her on horseback whether she wants to come or not, but I don't know how her husband will feel about that, Jamie."

"I don't reckon we want to go that far. Tell her she can stay with the wagon, but it's her choice."

Hector nodded, wheeled his horse, and urged the animal back into the water.

The Hamilton wagon was the second in

line. Jamie watched as Hector conveyed the message to the young, recently married couple. Alice Hamilton clutched her husband's arm, clearly not intending to leave his side. She couldn't weigh very much, Jamie thought, so it shouldn't really make any difference whether she rode across on the wagon.

A short time later, R.G. Hamilton urged his team of mules into the creek. They swam strongly toward the center of the stream.

The wagon hadn't reached the mid-point, when Jamie noticed that something was wrong. It was riding lower in the water than the others, and he felt a surge of alarm when he saw that it was starting to tilt. The cracks between the boards in these vehicles were supposed to be sealed with pitch to keep water out, but it was possible the Hamilton wagon had sprung a leak.

Jamie cupped his hands around his mouth and bellowed, "Hector!" When the burly scout turned to look at him, Jamie waved a hand toward the wagon, urgently gesturing for Hector to get out there and see what he could do to help. As soon as he had done that, Jamie heeled Sundown into motion and entered the creek from the north side of the stream.

R.G. could feel the wagon tipping underneath him. So could his wife, who grabbed his arm even harder. He lashed the mules in an attempt to get them to go faster, so the wagon might get across the creek before it capsized, but it was taking on water too quickly for that.

Alice screamed as the wagon suddenly rolled to the side. The water caught the canvas cover and pulled it over. Both Hamiltons were thrown off the wagon seat and disappeared into the muddy, fast-moving water.

CHAPTER FORTY

Jamie jabbed his heels into Sundown's flanks and sent the big stallion churning through the creek toward the overturned wagon. Hector was coming from the other direction. So were Bodie and Jake, having heard shouts of alarm from some of the immigrants when the Hamilton wagon rolled over.

Jamie's keen eyes searched the water for any sign of R.G. or Alice popping back to the surface. Even flooded, the creek wasn't really that deep, but it was deep enough for a person to drown in it, especially if he or she was disoriented or had hit their head and was stunned.

Alice Hamilton had bright red hair, so she was easy to spot when she broke the surface. The current was carrying her swiftly downstream. Jamie angled after her.

With Sundown's powerful legs stroking through the water, Jamie caught up with the young woman in a matter of moments. He leaned down from the saddle and reached for her as she flailed wildly in panic.

His hand wrapped around her wrist and he hauled upward, lifting her from the stream almost effortlessly as if she had been a child's toy. Hysterical with fear, she grabbed him, winding her arms around his neck and hanging on in sheer desperation.

"Take it easy," Jamie told her. "You're all right, Miz Hamilton. Just settle down. I'll take you to shore."

His firm, steady voice seemed to penetrate her shocked brain. She still clung to him, but not quite as urgently. She began to shiver from being dunked in the cold water.

Jamie knew she would need to get out of the wet clothes as soon as possible. Some of the women could wrap her in blankets and set her down next to a big fire. That would thaw her out in a hurry.

"R.G.," she said. "Where's R.G.?"

Jamie glanced over his shoulder as he urged Sundown toward the northern bank. Several of the scouts were looking around, but it appeared they hadn't found R.G. Hamilton yet.

"Don't worry, some of the other fellas are helping him." Jamie kept her turned so she couldn't see the search going on in the middle of the flooded stream. It wouldn't do any good to worry the young woman when her husband might come thrashing out of the creek at any moment.

Leticia Bingham and Savannah were waiting on the bank when Jamie got there, along with Alice's mother, who was almost as distraught as her daughter. Leticia reached up. "Let us have her, Mr. MacCallister. We'll take care of her."

"That's exactly what I planned to do, ladies," Jamie said as he gently lowered Alice into their waiting hands. As the women hustled her away, he turned his horse and plunged back into the flooded creek. "Any luck?" he called to the scouts as he swam Sundown out to join them.

Bodie shook his head. "There's no sign of him so far, Mr. MacCallister. He's got to be around here somewhere, though."

Jamie had a bad feeling. If R.G. had been knocked unconscious when he fell from the wagon, he could have drowned in as little as a minute or two. Several minutes had passed since the accident, and the situation was beginning to look bleak.

"Hey, over here!"

The shout came from Jess Neville. He was about fifty yards downstream, where the roots of one of the scrubby trees on the bank extended out into the water. Something was caught in those roots. Grim lines formed on Jamie's rugged, weathered face.

The men on horseback headed in that direction. So did some of the immigrants on the northern bank who had heard Jess's shout. They all got there about the same time.

As soon as Jamie saw R.G. Hamilton's pale face and the wide, sightlessly staring eyes, he knew the young man was dead. The water had washed away the blood, but a large gash was still visible on his forehead. Obviously he had struck it on something when he fell, just as Jamie feared, and that had doomed him.

Jamie didn't think he had said more than a dozen words to the young man during the journey, but he felt sorry for what had happened, anyway.

He had known before they ever left Kansas City that not everyone in the wagon train would make it safely to Montana. Trouble along the way was inevitable, and so were losses.

But Hamilton was the first to die, and that was painful.

Jess Neville looked at Jamie. "What do we do, Mr. MacCallister?"

"Work him out of those roots," Jamie said

flatly. "Hector, give him a hand." To the other scouts, he added, "The rest of you get back to work. We've still got wagons to bring safely across this creek."

One of the people who had come running along the bank, the wagon train captain looked pointedly at Jamie. "We'll get started digging a grave. Reverend Bradford can conduct the service. He's the one who performed the wedding."

It was almost dark before the last of the wagons rolled out of the water and onto the northern bank. Some of the time had been spent hooking up extra teams to the Hamilton wagon and dragging it out of the creek. The men set it upright and examined it for the leak that had caused the tragedy and any other damage. All the goods inside the vehicle had been soaked, of course. Some of them were salvageable, and those that weren't would be discarded and done without.

Jamie assumed that Alice Hamilton would continue the journey to Montana Territory along with her parents and her two younger brothers. There was really nothing else she could do. They couldn't leave her out in the middle of nowhere by herself.

The burial service took place by torchlight that evening. Alice, who had started whimpering and moaning and wailing when she was told of her husband's death, hadn't stopped. Her mother and several of the women, including Savannah, tried to comfort her as best they could, but she was inconsolable in her grief.

Reverend Bradford droned on endlessly. Jamie tried to be respectful as he stood with the others, his hat in one hand and his head bowed, but he would have rather been almost anywhere else.

When the service was finally over, the women led a weeping Alice away while several of the men began filling in the muddy grave where R.G. Hamilton's blanket-shrouded body lay. Somebody had fashioned a marker to put up.

It was a nice gesture, Jamie supposed, but ultimately meaningless. The elements would take that marker in a matter of months. It would fall and rot into the ground as if it had never been there. The mounded dirt would flatten out. And come spring, grass would poke up through that dirt, maybe a few wildflowers. By the next summer, no one would be able to tell there was a grave there.

Maybe that was the way it ought to be. Man was on earth and then he moved on, sometimes after a long, full life, sometimes

313

before it seemed like his days ought to be up. The answers to such things were beyond mortals, mused Jamie. They belonged only to the Man Above.

Bodie came up to Jamie as the immigrants scattered from the grave site and went about their business. "What are we going to do now, Mr. MacCallister?"

"You mean after we try to get some sleep?"

"Yeah."

"Tomorrow morning, when there's enough light to see, these wagons are rolling north toward Montana again. What did you think we'd do, turn around and go back just because one hombre's bad luck caught up to him?"

"No, but —"

"This is the first grave we've had to dig since we left," Jamie said. "I can promise you, it won't be the last."

CHAPTER FORTY-ONE

Gideon Kane sipped from the glass of champagne and watched the woman cross the room toward him.

Her walk was a thing of sinuous grace. Her blue eyes were full of temptation, and her mane of blond hair draped over her bare shoulders, dipping toward the creamy swells of her breasts exposed by the scandalously low neckline of the gown she wore. She could get away with such an outfit because her family was rich. Her name was Deirdre Burton.

Kane had taken her to his bed a couple times, and she had assumed that meant they would get married, creating a marital and a business relationship between their families. He had other ideas, however. He had quickly become bored with her that first night and given her another tumble later on just to make sure it hadn't been just an off night for him.

That experience only confirmed his first impression. The thought of spending the rest of his life with someone as bland and complacent as Deirdre Burton held no appeal for him at all. Good Lord, he told himself when he considered the idea, he'd have to take a new mistress every few weeks just to keep from dying of boredom.

Savannah McCoy, now, she would be a different story, Kane thought as he took another drink of his champagne. Someone as fiery as she could keep him interested.

She was an actress, after all. From one night to the next, she could be anyone he wanted her to be. . . .

"You give the best parties, Gideon," Deirdre said as she came up to him. Musicians played softly on the other side of the big ballroom. "I'd love to dance with you."

"Perhaps later," he told her. "I have a lot on my mind right now. Business matters."

He had expected Eli Harrison to be back with Savannah by now. It had been more than a week since the wagon train had left Kansas City.

Deirdre leaned closer to him and said in a throaty voice she thought was seductive, "I can take your mind off of business if you'd like, Gideon. I guarantee, you won't be thinking of anything except —"

He stopped her by pushing the half-empty glass of champagne into her hand. He had spotted Jenkins coming toward him, and he could tell by the expression on the butler's face that something had happened.

"Excuse me," he said curtly.

She had taken the glass instinctively and stood there with a surprised expression on her face. That look turned angry as he pushed past her and walked away, but he ignored it.

"What is it?" he asked quietly as he and Jenkins met in the crowd of well-dressed men and women — Kansas City's elite — filling the ballroom.

"Mr. Harrison is back," Jenkins said equally quietly.

Kane's pulse surged as he caught his breath. If Harrison had returned, that meant —

He quickly asked, "Is she with him?"

With a doleful look on his face, Jenkins shook his head.

The anticipation Kane had felt was replaced abruptly with fury. "Where is he?"

"In the study."

Kane stepped past the butler without another word. Several of his guests smiled and spoke to him as he left the ballroom, but he paid no attention to them. His rudeness might cause a minor scandal among the city's upper crust, but he didn't give a damn.

Harrison had a haggard look on his ugly face when Kane came into the room. His appearance testified that he had spent several long, hard days in the saddle.

Kane closed the door hard behind him and snapped, "What happened?"

"We trailed the wagon train for a while, like you said for us to do. The girl's there with those immigrants. We saw her. Hell, I had my hands on her."

"But you let her get away?" Kane couldn't believe it.

"MacCallister," Harrison spat out. "He stuck his nose in. The man's as big as a blasted grizzly bear, and even faster than that. We tangled, and I did good just to get away from him. The fellas I had with me weren't so lucky."

"If you didn't get Miss McCoy, it doesn't matter if you got away from him," Kane said coldly. "You failed."

"This time." Harrison's right hand clenched into a huge fist. "I didn't take enough men with me the first time. I'm going to round up some more and go after the wagon train again. I've got a score to settle with that big bas—"

"I don't care about your scores," Kane cut in. "I just want Miss McCoy brought back here, and I won't tolerate another failure, Harrison. Do you understand?"

"You bet I do. I can hire a dozen men?"

"Hire two dozen if you want. Just bring the girl back here."

"And if anybody else gets hurt along the way? There are a lot of innocent pilgrims on that wagon train."

The scornful look that Kane gave him was more than enough of an answer to Harrison's question.

Harrison spent the evening in some of the worst saloons, taverns, and dives in Kansas City, scouring them for gunmen who would be willing to sign on for the job of taking Savannah McCoy away from that wagon train.

He had tried being stealthy, sneaking in and carrying off the girl with no one the wiser until it was too late to stop them, and that hadn't worked at all. Things were going to get ugly next time. There would be gunplay, and people would die. And Harrison didn't care as long as he got what his boss was after.

If he let Gideon Kane down again, he knew he might as well keep going and never come back to Kansas City. He had seen Kane fly into a rage once when a drunken freighter had bumped into him on the street and his filthy boots had gotten dung on Kane's shoes. Kane had beaten the man to death with his walking stick, right then and there.

That wouldn't happen to him; Harrison wouldn't stand still for such an attack, and Kane no doubt knew that. He would just hire as many men as it took to beat Harrison to death rather than do it himself.

Harrison was in a squalid saloon, looking for hardcases willing to hire on to use their guns, when two men sidled up to him at the bar. Harrison barely spared them a glance. They were tough enough in a way, he supposed, but not really the sort of ruthless professionals he was after.

But the smaller one, who had eyes like a pig and a swinish face, said, "Word's gettin' around that you're hirin' men."

Harrison shook his head. "You must have heard wrong, mister."

The man got a shrewd look on his face — if a pig could be said to look shrewd. "You're not goin' after that wagon train Jamie MacCallister's leadin' to Montana Territory?"

Harrison stiffened. He supposed he had

let a few too many hints slip when he was making the rounds of the saloons. But what did it really matter? Where he and the men he recruited would be going, there wasn't much law. In most places, there wasn't any. "What if I am?"

The short, squat man said, "My name's Keeler." He jerked a thumb at his taller companion. "This is Holcomb. We signed on as scouts to go with that wagon train when our pard Jeb Ralston was supposed to be the wagon master. That was before MacCallister broke his leg and stole the job for himself."

That was interesting, Harrison thought. "So you've got a grudge against MacCallister?"

"Damn right we do. But there's more than that, mister. We went over the route with Jeb more'n once. I'd say we know where MacCallister's takin' those wagons just as well as he does. Maybe better."

Going by what he'd heard about Jamie MacCallister, Harrison doubted that, but he was intrigued anyway. "You think you could help me catch up to them?"

"I know we could," Keeler said confidently. "And if you plan on tanglin' with MacCallister . . . well, we wouldn't mind gettin' in on that, too."

He and his men would be able to travel faster if they knew where the wagon train was going, Harrison thought. They might even be able to get ahead of the wagons and set up an ambush. MacCallister would be watching his back trail, but he probably wouldn't expect death to be waiting in front of him.

"Keeler," Harrison said as he stuck out a big paw, "you've got a deal."

CHAPTER FORTY-TWO

Days of searching hadn't turned up any clues to the whereabouts of the men who had stolen the loot from the train robbery. The failure filled Eldon Swint with a fury he was barely able to contain.

When he finally found Lucas, Mahaffey, and Pearsoll — and he *would* find them, he had no doubt about that — he would see to it that they died long and painfully for daring to steal from him. Before he was through with them, they would wish a bunch of bloodthirsty Apaches had gotten hold of them instead.

The problem was . . . he didn't know where they were. The frontier was a mighty big place. Without some sort of trail to follow, it might take months, maybe even years, to locate the thieves.

Swint was sitting in the Bella Royale, seething as usual and trying to distract himself with a bottle of whiskey. It wasn't working. He glanced up as Charley Green entered the saloon and crossed the room toward him. Green looked a little excited about something, which was unusual for him. He was usually about as stolid as a lump of stone.

Without waiting to be invited to sit down, Green pulled back one of the chairs and lowered himself into it. He reached for the bottle, but Swint pulled it out of reach.

"You look like you've got something to say, Charley," Swint told his second in command. "Spit it out first, then maybe you can have a drink."

"I might have a line on where those three varmints took off to with our money."

Swint's bushy, almost colorless eyebrows crawled up his forehead in surprise. He pushed the bottle back where Green could reach it. "Tell me."

"Bodie Cantrell."

Swint's eyebrows came back down in a frown. "What about him?"

"He disappeared the same night, didn't he?"

"Well, yeah," Swint admitted. "But he told me he was leaving the gang. He wouldn't have done that if he was mixed up with Lucas and those other two. That was just a, what do you call it, coincidence."

"Maybe, but Cantrell and Lucas were friends. Lucas could've told Cantrell what he and Mahaffey and Pearsoll were plannin' to do. Shoot, for all we know, stealin' those double eagles might've been Cantrell's idea."

Swint restrained his impatience and the urge to take the bottle away from Green again. "I've been over and over this in my head, Charley. You're not tellin' me anything that I don't already know. Let's say you're right and Cantrell was part of the whole scheme, maybe even the mastermind, although I still don't know why he'd draw attention to himself ahead of time. We don't know where Cantrell went any more than we do Lucas, Mahaffey, and Pearsoll."

"Maybe we do," Green said with a self-satisfied smile. "I talked to a fella who saw Cantrell ride out with a wagon train the same morning that the others vanished with our loot."

Swint leaned forward sharply in his chair, sensing with his predator's instincts that this might be the lead they had been looking for. "How'd you happen to do that?"

"I've still been goin' around town askin' questions, describin' all four of those hombres, not just Lucas and the other two but Cantrell as well, on the chance that he might've been involved. I found a fella who saw him with those pilgrims who were headed to Montana. It was just pure luck, I reckon, Eldon. Luck, and bein' stubborn about it."

"But the man you talked to, he didn't see Lucas, Mahaffey, and Pearsoll with the wagon train?"

Green shook his head. "No, but that don't mean anything. They could've rendezvoused with it later, after the wagons left town. That probably would've been the smart thing to do."

Swint considered the theory. It made sense, but it was far from what he'd consider proof. On the other hand, they hadn't found any other leads so far. . . .

"But that ain't all," Green went on. "There's a fella goin' around town puttin' together a crew of hired guns to go after that wagon train."

Swint's nostrils flared as he took a sharp, angry breath. "Going after *our* money?" he demanded.

Green shook his head again. "No, from what I hear, they're after a girl who joined up with the immigrants here in Kansas City. She's some sort of actress, and they're workin' for a fella who's stuck on her and wants her brought back."

"I don't see what this has to do with us and that missing money," Swint said.

"I talked to some of the boys about Cantrell. They said that *he* was stuck on an actress from that show, too, and I figure it's got to be the same one, boss."

"How do you figure that?"

"Because he quit the gang with no warnin', and then he shows up with that wagon train, too. It's all got to be connected."

Green was a good man, plenty tough, and he followed orders well and could be depended on. Swint had never considered him to be all that smart, though. But as he followed his lieutenant's reasoning, he had to give Green some grudging credit for his intelligence. The theory Green had worked out actually made sense, and it was the best explanation so far for what had happened.

Plus it sure beat nothing, which was what they had come up with so far.

"So what are you saying, that we need to follow that wagon train?"

"Well, it's a place to start, anyway," Green said.

"And if you're wrong," Swint snapped, "we'll have lost a lot of time. Enough time that we might never be able to find those blasted thieves."

"It's up to you, Eldon," Green replied

327

with a shake of his head. "I've never pretended to be in charge of this gang and don't want to be. You're the boss and we'll do whatever you say. I just thought —"

"And you did a good job. I'll admit that." Swint took the bottle back from Green, tilted it to his mouth, and swallowed a long swig of the fiery liquor before thumping the mostly empty bottle down on the tabletop. He had reached a decision. "Round up the rest of the boys. Get some pack animals and lay in plenty of supplies. We're liable to be on the trail for quite a while."

"So we're goin' after the wagon train?" Green asked excitedly.

"We're going after the wagon train," Swint agreed. "And it's a long way from here to Montana Territory."

CHAPTER FORTY-THREE

The weather held for several days as the wagon train continued northward. A glittering blanket of frost covered the ground every morning, but it melted away when the sun came up. Chilly winds blew from the north, sending towering white clouds scudding through the blue sky like tall-masted ships. The thick wool and sheepskin coats worn by the immigrants kept them from getting too cold.

The brisk air didn't bother Jamie. After the rugged life he had led and the iron constitution it had given him, he was practically immune to the weather unless it became really extreme. He enjoyed the cold, clear conditions.

For one thing, the wagon train was making good time again, and he was satisfied with the number of miles they covered every day. There was still a slim chance they would reach Eagle Valley by Christmas.

One of the teenage boys in the group had been recruited to drive R.G. Hamilton's wagon. R.G. had no family and had been traveling alone until romance had blossomed between him and Alice and they had wound up getting married in Kansas City.

Alice insisted on staying with the wagon, even though she could have gone back to traveling with her family. Savannah rode with the grieving widow sometimes, keeping her company. After several days, Jamie sought her out at the Bingham wagon one evening to ask how Alice was doing.

Not surprising, Bodie Cantrell was having supper with Savannah, Edward, and Leticia. Any time he wasn't out scouting, Bodie could be found somewhere near the Bingham wagon. He was so head-over-heels in love with Savannah that Jamie sometimes had a hard time not chuckling at the moonstruck look on the young man's face.

The good thing was that Savannah seemed to return the feeling. There weren't many things worse in this world than being desperately in love with somebody who didn't really give a darn about you.

At least, Jamie supposed that to be the case. He had never experienced such unrequited love himself, since he and Kate had been soul mates right from the start and

330

that feeling hadn't lessened a whit over the years.

It had taken an outlaw's bullet to part them, and Jamie would carry that loss with him for the rest of his life.

"Would you like something to eat, Mr. MacCallister?" Leticia Bingham asked him as he came up to the wagon.

Jamie shook his head. "No, ma'am, but I'm obliged to you for the offer. Moses and I already had supper a little while ago." He grinned. "I'm teaching him how to cook trail grub."

"How's he taking to that?" Bodie asked with a smile.

"Not bad. He's a pretty smart fella. Can do most anything he puts his mind to." Jamie tipped his hat back. "I really came to talk to you, Savannah, and ask how Alice Hamilton is getting on."

Savannah's pretty face wore a solemn expression. "It's been really hard on her, Mr. MacCallister. That's not surprising, of course, losing her husband like that so soon after they were married . . . although I suppose it would be difficult no matter how long it had been."

"Has she said anything about wanting to go back? She might be able to manage that, come spring."

Savannah shook her head. "No, it was R.G.'s dream for them to have a place of their own in Eagle Valley, and Alice seems determined to go through with that. She says she's going to take up the homestead R.G. intended to file. But other times . . ." Savannah looked worried. "Other times she acts like she's too overwhelmed with grief to go on. She says she doesn't think she can make it."

"Probably be a good idea for you to keep an eye on her as much as you can," Jamie said.

"You don't think she'd . . . hurt herself, do you, Mr. MacCallister?"

"I hope not, but you never know what folks might do when they've suffered a bad loss." Some folks might even set out to hunt down an entire gang of vicious killers and outlaws, he thought.

He put that out of his mind and went on. "If you get a chance, tell Alice's folks about how she's acting."

"They already know," Savannah said. "They're worried about her, too. Her mother keeps trying to talk her into coming back to their wagon, but Alice won't hear of it. She insists she's going to stay in the wagon she shared with R.G., because that's where she was happy."

"Seems to me like there would be too many reminders of him in that wagon," Bodie commented.

"People never really know what they'll do until they're faced with something. Then it's too late to prepare. You've just got to do what it takes to survive." That was something Jamie Ian MacCallister knew all about — survival.

The next day dawned clear, but by noon there was a dark blue line on the northern horizon. Within an hour it had grown into a low cloud bank that seemed to be rushing toward the wagon train. To Jamie it looked closer with every minute that passed. He pointed it out to Bodie, who was riding ahead of the wagons with him. "Blue Norther."

"A snowstorm, you mean?"

"Might be some snow with it, might not be. At this time of year, it's hard to say until the blasted thing is right on top of you. But whether it snows or not, we need to stop and hunker down until it's passed us by."

They turned and rode back to the lead wagon. At Jamie's command, Bodie headed on along the line of vehicles, telling the drivers to stop and form up in a circle.

"What's going on here?" Captain Hendricks asked.

Jamie leveled a finger at the onrushing clouds. "We're in for a bad blow. The wind's going to be so hard it'll seem like these prairie schooners of yours are about to lift up off the ground and fly. The temperature's liable to drop forty degrees in an hour, too."

"But it's not much above freezing now," Hendricks protested. "If it drops forty degrees . . ." His eyes widened at the thought.

Jamie grunted. "Yeah. That's what happens when you start out on a trip like this so late in the year."

Hendricks's face hardened angrily, but he said, "What do we need to do?"

"We'll go ahead and make camp. Build fires now while we still can and get some hot food and coffee in everybody. Then tie everything down tight to keep it from blowing away, climb in the wagons, and heap as many blankets and quilts as you can on top of you. It'll be a mighty cold night, but we ought to make it through all right."

Hendricks nodded. "I'll make sure everybody gets busy and does what you said."

For the next hour, as the Blue Norther rampaged closer and closer, the camp was a beehive of activity. Everyone seemed to understand the seriousness of the situation. As the cloud bank swept in, it grew darker and more sinister.

The wind, which had been fairly light, died down to almost nothing as Jamie walked around the circle of wagons, checking to make sure everything was secured as much as possible. Most of the immigrants were worried. He tried to reassure them. They had all been through cold snaps back where they came from, he told them. A great plains norther was a mite more . . . enthusiastic, he explained, but they could ride it out.

"Keep everybody close," he said again and again. "And huddle up together. You'll need the warmth by morning."

Satisfied that the immigrants were as ready as they were going to be, he headed for Moses's wagon. The clouds had swallowed up the sun, and even though the hour was just past mid-afternoon, it was almost dark as night.

The wind hit while Jamie was walking across the camp.

He reached up quickly and grabbed his hat to keep it from blowing away. The wind smacked into his face like an icy fist. By the time he reached the wagon he was leaning forward into it, struggling against the violent gusts.

He climbed into the wagon, ducked

through the opening, and pulled the canvas flap tightly closed behind him, tying it in place with the cords attached to it. He could feel the wagon vibrating from the wind pushing against it.

"You know, I've seen some bad blizzards back in Poland," Moses said. "Is this one going to be worse, Jamie?"

"Don't know. I've never been to Poland. I don't smell any snow in the air, though. I think we're just going to get the cold wind. But it's going to be mighty cold."

"You can smell snow?" Moses sounded like he found that hard to believe.

"Sure. Snow, rain, dust storms . . . you get to where you can smell what the weather's going to do if you stay out here on the frontier long enough."

"Somehow I don't doubt it. I don't think I'd doubt anything you had to tell me, Jamie."

"Oh, I can spin a few windies when the mood strikes me," Jamie said with a smile. "But when it comes to getting by out here, I won't steer you wrong."

The wind began to howl in mindless shrieks that sounded like lost souls being tormented in hell. It made the cold seem even more numbing. Jamie dug an old buffalo robe he'd had for more than thirty years out of his gear and wrapped himself in it. Night closed down quickly, and he slept the way any frontiersman would sleep when he had the chance.

He woke to shouts, stirred himself, crawled out of the buffalo robe, and untied the flap over the back of the wagon. He had just stuck his head out when Savannah Mc-Coy came running toward the vehicle, carrying a lantern and calling urgently, "Mr. MacCallister! Mr. MacCallister!"

"What is it?"

Savannah lifted her stricken face toward him. "It's Alice Hamilton, Mr. MacCallister. She's gone!"

CHAPTER FORTY-FOUR

"What do you mean, gone?" he asked Savannah as he climbed out of Moses's wagon.

"I decided she shouldn't be alone tonight and went over to her wagon right after the wind hit. Alice seemed glad to see me. We put our bedrolls next to each other on the floor. I . . . I tried to stay awake, but I dozed off. When I woke up, she wasn't there anymore." Tears began to roll down Savannah's cheeks. "I'm so, so sorry —"

"Stop that. It's not your fault. Anything you did to watch out for that gal was from the goodness of your heart, and nobody's going to blame you for what's happened."

"Do you think something has . . . happened?"

Jamie didn't answer that question directly. "Let's go take a look around. Maybe we can find her."

Moses was leaning out the back of the

wagon. He had overheard what Savannah said, and asked, "Should I rouse everyone else, Jamie, to help you look?"

Jamie considered for a second. The wind was bitingly cold, and it was only going to get worse. Everybody was hunkered down in their wagons, buried in quilts and blankets, and that was where they needed to stay.

"Get Bodie and that fella Lucas," Jamie decided. "We won't tell anybody else for now." He reached back into the wagon, got his hat, and tugged it down tight on his head. He pulled out the buffalo robe as well and wrapped it around his shoulders. Then he took the lantern from Savannah and headed for Alice Hamilton's wagon.

He studied the ground around the wagon for tracks, but it had dried out since the rain several days earlier and he didn't see any footprints. He found a place where he thought the dry grass had been disturbed, but he couldn't be sure about that.

Bodie and Jake Lucas arrived, looking half-frozen already even though they had blankets wrapped tightly around themselves. Bodie asked, "What can we do to help, Jamie?"

"We're going to look for Miz Hamilton, but we don't want anybody else wandering off and getting lost, so stay close together while we search."

"Do you think that's what happened to her?" Savannah asked. "Do you think she got lost?"

"More than likely. She might've stepped out of the wagon to tend to some personal business, gotten turned around, and started off in the wrong direction, thinking she was coming back. By the time she figured out she was going the wrong way, she couldn't locate the camp anymore."

That explanation was entirely possible, Jamie thought. But his gut told him it wasn't the only explanation.

Since her husband's death, Alice Hamilton had been trying to drag herself up out of a pit of despair. Maybe it had pulled her down so deep she couldn't escape from it.

"I'll help you look," Savannah said.

"No!" Jamie and Bodie said at the same time.

"Get back in the wagon, out of the wind," Jamie told her. "The four of us will find her."

As he, Moses, Bodie, and Jake spread out in a fan shape from the Hamilton wagon, Jamie thought about how the chances of finding Alice would be increased if more people were searching for her.

But the chances of somebody else getting

lost and freezing to death would be greater, too. It was like the old saying about being caught between a rock and a hard place. Whatever he did increased the risk of *somebody* dying.

With the temperature dropping the way it was and the savage wind ripping away any trace of warmth, a person could freeze to death in an hour, maybe less. The frigid cold wouldn't kill as quickly as that flooded creek had, but it could kill just as surely.

Jamie cupped his hands around his mouth and bellowed, "Mrs. Hamilton! Alice!" The other men began calling her name, too. Somebody at the wagon train might hear the shouting and wonder what was going on, but that couldn't be helped. If Alice was lost and truly wanted to be found, the sound of their voices might save her life.

The yelling helped Jamie keep track of the other men, too. He didn't want to lose anybody else.

They spread out away from the wagon for what seemed like a long time. When Jamie estimated that they had covered close to a mile, he called his three companions to him. "I don't think she could have gotten this far. We've missed her somewhere."

"She could have headed off from the wagons at any angle," Bodie pointed out.

Moses suggested, "Maybe we should go back and start over, taking a different direction this time."

"That's all we can do," Jamie said. "Come on."

The night dragged past. First one hour, then two, then three. Jamie's worry had grown with every minute that ticked by. Somebody could survive in the wind for this long — he and his companions were doing it, after all — but they were all bundled up in thick jackets and blankets. Even so, they were suffering. Jamie knew he was going to have to call off the search soon or else risk the men suffering from frostbite.

"I . . . I can't feel my fingers and toes anymore," Moses said, reinforcing Jamie's concern for their safety.

"Let's head on back," he said with a heavy sigh. "We can't do any more."

"Wait a minute," Bodie protested. "You can't mean to just leave poor Mrs. Hamilton out here."

"I don't mean to let you three fellas freeze to death, either. Or lose your fingers and toes."

Moses gulped. "Is that what's going to happen?"

"It could if we don't get you warmed up." Jamie herded them back to the wagon train.

Savannah met them, and the lantern light revealed the worry etched into her face. Her expression fell when she saw that the men were alone. "You didn't find her." It wasn't a question.

"We can't stay out there anymore," Jamie said. "Maybe she found a place to get out of the wind and hole up for a while. There are little gullies and such —"

"You know she didn't," Savannah said. "She didn't get turned around so that she couldn't find her way back to the wagons, either."

"What do you mean?" Jake Lucas asked.

Moses said gently, "I suppose she didn't want to live without her husband. She thought the pain was too much for her to bear and she couldn't go on. So she walked off into the night, never intending to come back."

Savannah started to cry again. Bodie took her in his arms and drew her against him.

Jamie let the young man comfort Savannah for a few moments, then told her, "You'd better go back to the Bingham wagon. The rest of us will hunker down in Moses's wagon. We can start searching again at first light. It'll be easier then."

They would be able to see better in the morning, he thought, but the chances of finding Alice Hamilton alive then would be practically nonexistent.

He didn't sleep much the rest of the night. Along toward dawn, the wind died down, ceasing its eerie howling. The stars came out as the overcast broke. And the temperature dropped harder and faster, like the bottom had fallen out of the thermometer.

Jamie and his companions resumed the search in the gray light of dawn. The air was so cold it seemed to burn their lungs with every breath. Huge clouds of steam fogged the air in front of the men's faces every time they exhaled. It looked like smoke wreathing their upper bodies.

They found Alice about half a mile from the wagons. She was in a small gully, all right, but from the way she was lying there it appeared that she had stumbled and fallen into it instead of seeking shelter. It hadn't saved her. Frost glittered on her open, sightless eyes, and her flesh was cold and hard as stone.

By the time they got back with her body, everybody in the wagon train knew that Alice was missing. Sobs filled the air as the men carried in her blanket-wrapped form. Alice's mother threw herself on her daughter's body and wailed piteously.

Jamie felt the grief that gripped the camp,

but didn't show it. In his life he had seen so much death and suffering that he knew it was inevitable. He drew Captain Hendricks and several other men aside. "It hasn't been cold enough long enough to freeze the ground. We'd better get a grave dug while we can."

"It's a shame the poor girl couldn't be laid to rest beside her husband," Hendricks said.

"I reckon it's a big country on the other side of the divide," Jamie said, "but not so big that the two of them won't be able to find each other."

CHAPTER FORTY-FIVE

As often happened out on the plains, within a couple days the fierce, freezing wind out of the north was replaced by a much gentler, warmer breeze from the south. Jamie knew it would be only a matter of time until the next Blue Norther came barreling down on them, so he wanted to cover as much ground as he could while the weather was decent. He pushed everyone hard and used every bit of daylight he could.

The grinding pace meant there wasn't much time to mourn Alice Hamilton. Her death and that of her husband were tragic and senseless, but those graves were behind the wagon train. Everyone needed to look ahead, because that was where the next challenge would be found.

As Jamie could have predicted, that challenge wasn't long in coming. He was riding the point with Hector Gilworth several days later when he spotted riders paralleling their course about half a mile to the west.

Without saying anything to Hector, Jamie turned his head and looked to the east. He saw more riders in that direction. That came as no surprise to him. He had been expecting something like this. The wagon train was just too tempting a target.

"Ride on back and tell Cap'n Hendricks to have everybody circle the wagons," Jamie said quietly to Hector.

"But it's the middle of the day," the burly, bearded scout protested. "We don't usually circle up until we stop at nightfall."

"Well, we're going to today, because there are Indians on both sides of us."

Hector let out a surprised exclamation. "Are they going to attack us?"

"Too soon to say, but we'd better be ready in case they do. Now git!"

Hector got, hauling his horse around and galloping back toward the wagons.

Jamie reined Sundown to a halt and sat easily in the saddle. As soon as the Indians saw the wagons forming up into a circle, they would know that their presence had been discovered. If they planned to attack, they would probably do it quickly, before the immigrants had time to get set up for defense.

On the other hand, it could be that the

Indians just wanted to parley. Some of the tribes didn't mind the wagon trains passing through their territory as long as they received some sort of tribute in return for safe passage.

They liked to negotiate from a position of strength, though, which is why they usually showed up with a considerable number of warriors, all painted fiercely and bristling with lances, bows and arrows, and occasionally, rifles. They liked to throw a scare into the settlers.

It wasn't just for show. If things didn't go well, the Indians would welcome a fight.

Jamie turned his head slowly from side to side. More mounted figures were visible in both directions, and they were angling their ponies toward the wagon train. The Indians were closing in, but they weren't getting in any hurry about it. Jamie hoped that meant they just wanted to talk.

He turned the stallion and rode back toward the spot where the immigrants were hurriedly pulling the wagons into a circle. Seeing the train stopping, the other scouts and outriders were coming in, too, some of them galloping hard to make it back to the relative safety of the wagons.

Bodie Cantrell rode out to meet Jamie a couple hundred yards away from the wagons. "Hector says there are Indians about to attack us." They both reined to a halt.

"That's jumping the gun a mite," Jamie said. "Right now it looks to me like they don't want to fight. Of course, that could change mighty quick-like."

"What should we do?"

Jamie narrowed his eyes in thought. After a moment he said, "Your friend Lucas is pretty good with a gun, isn't he?"

Bodie looked a little uncomfortable about answering that, but he said, "Yeah, I suppose so."

"He's cool-headed and can take orders?"

"I'd say so."

"Go get him. The three of us will ride out to see what they want."

Bodie nodded. He was aware that what Jamie was asking of him involved considerable risk, but he wasn't the sort to dodge trouble.

When Bodie came back, he didn't have just Jake Lucas with him. Captain Lamar Hendricks rode with them, too.

Before Jamie could say anything, Hendricks spoke up to explain his presence. "If you're going to talk to these savages, I need to be there. I was elected to be the leader of this wagon train."

"And I was hired to be the wagon master,"

Jamie said. "Who'd you leave in charge back there?"

"Hector Gilworth."

"Well, Hector's a good man, I suppose. If we all get killed, he'll put up a good fight."

Hendricks was a little pale under his tan. "Do you think there's a chance we'll all be killed?"

"There's always a chance." Jamie inclined his head toward the north. "I reckon we'll find out pretty soon, because here they come."

About a dozen warriors were trotting their ponies toward the four men. As they drew closer, Jamie saw that they were painted for war. But that didn't have to mean anything, he reminded himself. They might still be able to get out of this without a fight.

"Somebody else is coming from the wagon train," Jake said suddenly.

Jamie twisted around in the saddle to look. It was hard to surprise him, but his eyebrows rose slightly when he saw Moses Danzig riding toward them on one of the extra saddle horses.

Confronting a bunch of potentially angry Cheyenne was just about the last thing Moses needed to be doing, Jamie thought. But it was too late to send the rabbi back to the wagons. Jamie turned back to keep an eye on the approaching Indians.

As Moses came up beside him, panting slightly from the effort of riding two hundred yards on horseback, Jamie said quietly, "Moses, what in the Sam Hill are you doing out here?"

"Hector wanted to let you know that we're all dug in and ready to fight if need be," Moses replied. "He was going to send his cousin to do it, but I suggested that he let me ride out here instead. Jess can use a gun and I can't, so he's of more value there."

"If there's a fight out here, you can't even defend yourself."

"I'll trust in a higher power for that."

Jake said, "On these plains, ain't no higher power than Mr. Colt and Mr. Winchester."

"We'll save the theological debate for later," Moses said. "Oh, my. They're certainly savage-looking, aren't they?"

The Indians were close enough to confirm by the markings on their faces and the decorations on their buckskins that they were Cheyenne, just as Jamie had suspected. As Moses had pointed out, they looked fierce.

Jamie remained utterly calm. That required an effort of will, but he kept his face just as stony as those of the warriors who brought their ponies to a halt about twenty feet away. Beyond them, about as far distant as the wagons were, a hundred more warriors waited on horseback.

Jamie raised a hand in the universal signal of friendship and said in the Cheyenne tongue, "Greetings. We come seeking only a trail to travel peacefully to the north."

One of the older warriors in the group, a man Jamie suspected was the war chief for this band, responded. "This is our land. We have hunted it for many, many moons. It gives my people life. We would not have it taken away from us."

"Nor do we wish to take it," Jamie said with the formality such parleys always demanded. "If we hunt the buffalo, it will be for fresh meat only, and we will kill no more than one."

"You already have the buffalo with sleek hides," the Cheyenne said.

Jamie knew he was talking about the oxen. "We do," he acknowledged, "but we need them to pull the wagons. They are not for eating."

"If you kill a buffalo, you should replace it. Give us one of your animals for this buffalo of ours that you may kill."

Hendricks asked nervously, "What are the two of you saying? It sounds very serious."

"He wants us to give him an ox," Jamie

drawled in English. "I reckon we can spare one. Unless you'd rather fight over one animal."

"No, no. Not at all," Hendricks said quickly. "If that's all it takes for them to let us go on safely, then by all means, give them an ox!"

Jamie conveyed that to the war chief, but before the Cheyenne leader could respond, one of the other warriors suddenly pushed his pony forward and spoke up angrily. "It is not enough! We must have one of their women in trade for their safety as well!"

CHAPTER FORTY-SIX

Jamie instantly knew what the interruption was about. The warrior who had just made the outrageous demand was probably one of the war chief's rivals. He didn't want the encounter with the white interlopers to end peacefully. He wanted a fight, wanted the wagon train wiped out so that he could claim credit for the massacre and further his own cause among the tribe.

The varmint had to know good and well that the immigrants would never turn over one of their women.

"What did that one say just then?" Hendricks asked. "It didn't sound good. What's this about?"

The chief turned to glare at the warrior who had butted in as Jamie said, "The other fella has upped the stakes. He wants an ox . . . and one of your womenfolks."

The men gasped in shock and anger, and Jake exclaimed, "Why, that dirty —" He grated out a curse and reached for the gun on his hip. He had just cleared leather when Jamie leaned over in the saddle and shot his hand out to clamp around Lucas's wrist to keep him from raising the revolver and firing.

It was too late. The damage had already been done. The warrior who had started this ruckus cried out and jerked a rifle to his shoulder, ready to fire.

Jamie heard some rapid words he didn't understand behind him, but ignored them. He was about to reach for his Colts, knowing that in another second the air would be full of gun smoke and flying lead and arrows.

"Stop!"

The voice was old and not exactly powerful, but the piercing timbre of it cut through the air of impending violence and made all the men on both sides freeze in their actions. Another of the Cheyenne pushed his horse forward. He was ancient, his coppery face so lined with wrinkles that he seemed a hundred years old. His braided hair was pure white. But despite his obvious age he sat tall and straight in the saddle, like a much younger man. He leveled a buckskin-clad arm, pointing as he asked, "Who is this mighty shaman?"

Jamie didn't have any idea who the Indian was talking about. Realizing that the man was pointing past him, he glanced over his shoulder and saw Moses sitting on horseback, looking terrified. The young man's lips were moving as he muttered unfamiliar words under his breath.

The war chief reached over and grabbed the barrel of the angry warrior's rifle, forcing it down.

Jamie said harshly to Jake, "Pouch that iron, mister!" They had been given an unexpected respite, and he didn't intend to waste it. "Everybody else, keep your hands away from your guns!"

The tension was still thick as the two groups of riders faced each other.

Jamie went on. "Moses, the old man is talking about you. He says you're a mighty shaman and wants to know who you are."

"A . . . a shaman?" Moses shook his head. "I don't even know what that is."

"A medicine man, like I suspect that old fella is himself. Sort of like the spiritual leader of the tribe."

"Oh. I suppose you could say that, although Reverend Bradford certainly wouldn't agree."

"What was that you were saying a minute ago, Moses?"

"I was praying." A glimmer of understanding dawned on the young man's face. "I was praying in Hebrew . . ."

Before Jamie could stop him, Moses walked his horse forward, putting himself between the two groups. Several of the warriors lifted lances, but a sharp word from the chief made them lower the weapons.

The ancient Cheyenne moved his pony forward until he and Moses sat alongside each other with their mounts facing in opposite directions. Moses began speaking again in Hebrew.

Jamie didn't understand a word of the speech, of course. He didn't see how the Cheyenne medicine man could understand it, but the old man listened attentively. When Moses was finished, the old man surprised Jamie by lifting a hand and launching into a long speech of his own.

Jamie was fluent in the Cheyenne tongue, but what the medicine man was speaking was something else. It was similar to the Cheyenne language, enough so that Jamie thought he caught a word every now and then, but at the same time the words carried a sense of antiquity with them, as if the old-timer were speaking a long-forgotten tongue that had mostly vanished from the face of the earth.

When he was done, he held out his hand. Moses clasped it, and they sat there like that for a long moment. Then the medicine man turned to the warriors and barked words in Cheyenne that Jamie understood.

"What's going on now?" Bodie asked in a hushed voice.

"The old man is telling them to turn and ride away," Jamie explained. "He says that we're among the favored of the Great Spirit and that their medicine will become very bad if they harm us."

"We don't have to give them the ox anymore?" Hendricks asked as the Indians began to turn their ponies and ride away, some with obvious reluctance. They weren't willing to go against the old medicine man's decree.

"No, they won't bother us again, thanks to Moses."

Bodie said to the young rabbi, "What in the world did you *do,* pard?"

Moses shook his head. "I just called down blessings upon him and his people and told him that we were peaceful and would cause no trouble as we crossed the lands that traditionally belong to them." He smiled faintly. "I said it in Hebrew, of course, and made it all sound a lot more flowery."

"And he understood you?" Jake asked, visibly astonished.

"I don't know. He seemed to. Or maybe he just understood the tone of what I was saying."

"How about all that palaver he gave back to you?" Jamie asked. "Did it mean anything to you?"

Moses frowned. "He wasn't speaking Cheyenne?"

"Not the Cheyenne I know."

"That's . . . odd. I didn't actually understand what he was saying, of course, but every now and then I . . . I sort of felt like I ought to understand. Do you know what I mean?"

"Like if you went back far enough, the lingo he was talking had something in common with what you were saying to him?"

"Exactly!" Moses exclaimed. "And that makes perfect sense."

Bodie said, "How in the world do you figure that?"

"Have you ever heard of the Lost Tribes of Israel? In biblical times, the land of Canaan was ruled by twelve tribes. But when Canaan was split into two kingdoms — Israel and Judah — those tribes to the north that formed the Kingdom of Israel vanished from history and are now considered lost. According to legend, they were forced by enemies to leave their homeland and spread out across the world." Moses smiled. "There are some who say that one of those tribes found its way to the North American continent and eventually became the Indians that we know today."

"Wait just a doggone minute," Jake said. "You're sayin' that you . . . and those Cheyenne . . . are related somehow? Like distant cousins?"

Moses spread his hands. "Well, it's just a theory . . . but you have to admit, that old medicine man responded when he heard me praying in Hebrew. The fact that we're all still alive and no blood was spilled . . . I'd say those prayers were answered, wouldn't you?"

Jamie nodded. "I'm not exactly sure how you managed it, Moses, and I don't care."

All the Indians had vanished. The plains were empty around them again.

"Let's get those wagons lined out and rolling again," Jamie continued. "We've dodged a bullet, and we've still got some daylight left. Let's put some more miles behind us!"

CHAPTER FORTY-SEVEN

Even though the encounter with the Indians hadn't resulted in any fighting, the immigrants were more nervous as the wagon train continued on its way. It took a week for them to stop looking over their shoulders and expecting to see painted, war bonneted savages intent on scalping them.

Of course, the more prudent among them continued being watchful as the wagons rolled northward, but that was a good thing. The more alert they were, the better, Jamie thought.

They reached the Platte River and crossed the broad, shallow, muddy stream without incident. From there, the route diverged from the Oregon Trail, which headed west toward South Pass. The wagon train would keep going north for several more weeks.

They spotted their first buffalo herd a few days later. Jamie had expected to run across the shaggy beasts much earlier. The great herds always moved south for the winter, but other than that one cold blast, the weather had been unseasonably warm.

"Good Lord," Bodie exclaimed as he and Jamie reined in atop a ridge and looked at the vast sea of brown in front of them. The herd stretched as far as the eye could see.

Jamie grinned and rested his crossed hands on the saddle horn, shifting his weight forward to ease weary muscles. "You haven't seen buffalo before?"

"Well, yeah, of course I've seen them," the young man replied. "But never that many in one place. There must be a million of them!"

"I wouldn't doubt it. Maybe more than that. I've seen herds go by all day, all night, and all the next day before they finally got out of the way."

"We're going to have to stop and wait for this one to go past, aren't we?"

Jamie took a pair of field glasses from one of his saddlebags and studied the herd. "They're moving southeast. They'll miss us and ought to be out of our way by tomorrow."

With a worried tone in his voice, Bodie asked, "What if they were to turn and stampede toward the wagon train?"

"It wouldn't be good," Jamie replied. "A buffalo stampede is just as much a force of nature as floods, fire, and cyclones. Every bit as destructive, too. You can't stop it, so you just have to get out of its way if you can."

The big frontiersman turned in his saddle to look behind them. "The wagons are about a mile back. Go tell the cap'n to stop right where he is and don't come any closer. Teams stay hitched to the wagons until those critters are clear of us, in case we have to light a shuck and make a run for it. I'll stay here and keep an eye on the buffalo for now. We'll have scouts watching them all the time, just in case something makes them turn toward the wagons. We'll need as much warning as possible if that happens."

Bodie nodded, wheeled his horse, and galloped away.

Jamie turned his attention back to the buffalo. He had hunted the creatures many times, sometimes with his Indian friends using lances and bows and arrows, sometimes with groups of white hunters armed with Sharps rifles.

Even though the sight of a herd like this made it seem as if the buffalo were endless, Jamie knew that wasn't the case. Many of them had been killed already for meat to feed the crews building the transcontinental railroad several years earlier.

They continued to be slaughtered for their hides. Back in southern Kansas, Jamie had seen stacks of those hides piled so high that they looked like shaggy brown hills. It was wasteful and shameful, the unknowable number of carcasses skinned and left to rot, their bones littering the plains. The Indians, at least, used every bit of the buffalo, instead of just taking one part and throwing away the rest.

It was such slaughter, he mused, that would spell defeat for the natives in the end. Without the animals they had depended upon to feed and clothe and shelter them for centuries, they would have no choice but to turn to their white conquerors and change their entire way of life.

Jamie believed in manifest destiny, but at the same time he could share a moment of sympathy for those swept aside in the inexorable tide of progress.

The enormous buffalo herd moved on without menacing the wagon train, and as Jamie had predicted, by the middle of the next day the route was clear again. But they had lost a day to the delay, and with December almost upon them, every day was becoming more and more crucial.

A couple days later, they saw something unexpected: cattle. Not wild cattle, but what appeared to be well-grazed stock with wide, spreading horns.

"Dadgum it!" Jake exclaimed when he saw them. "Those are Texas longhorns. I've seen 'em down in Kansas at the railheads. What are they doing up here?" He and Bodie and Jamie were scouting ahead of the wagon train.

Jamie said, "Some of the ranchers from Texas are moving their herds up here and starting spreads. I've heard tell there are even some in Wyoming and Montana. I'm a little surprised we haven't run across any before now."

"I guess it makes sense," Bodie said. "There's plenty of grassland up here. That's about all there is, in fact."

"Since the farmers haven't gotten this far west yet, it's all open range. I expect that'll change one of these days, but for now this is some of the best ranching country in the world . . . if you don't count the Indians and the blizzards, of course. But you've got problems like that wherever you go, I reckon."

"Those are some fine-looking beef cows," Jake mused as he studied the grazing animals.

"Don't get any ideas in your head," Jamie said sharply. "If we slaughter any of those critters for meat, we'll buy them from their owners first. There won't be any rustling."

"Never said there would be," Jake replied.

Jamie had a hunch that was what had been in the young man's mind, though. His instincts had told him all along that Jake Lucas wasn't the same sort of upstanding young hombre as Bodie Cantrell, even though the two of them were friends.

Where there were cows, there were cowboys, and later that afternoon Jamie spotted riders coming toward them. He reined in and motioned for his companions to follow suit. A few minutes later the horsemen rode up, their chaps and big hats telling him that they were from Texas as he had suspected.

"Howdy," one of the men called. "Mind if we ask what you fellas are doin' riding on Slash M range?"

"That's where we are?" Jamie asked.

"Have been for the past five miles," the puncher replied. "This is Mr. Owen Murdock's spread. I'm Jim Haseltine, his foreman."

"Jamie Ian MacCallister." Jamie nodded. He leaned his head toward the other two and added, "Bodie Cantrell and Jake Lucas. We're scouting for a wagon train that's coming up about a mile behind us."

One of the other cowboys, a lean man

with a dark, hawklike face, leaned to the side and spat. "Wagon train," he repeated scornfully. "That means a bunch of damn sodbusters. You better not be intendin' to stay on Slash M range, mister. You'll get a hot lead welcome if you do."

Anger darkened Jake's face.

Jamie knew the young man was a hothead, so he snapped, "Take it easy. I'm handling the talking here."

He turned back to the cowboys. "I'm not going to argue the idea of open range with you. As a matter of fact, the people with those wagons are bound for Montana Territory, so they shouldn't be any concern to you boys at all. We'll just pass through and go on our way."

Jim Haseltine had a speculative look on his face. "Seems like I've heard of you, Mr. MacCallister. You wouldn't be the one who tangled with the Miles Nelson gang, would you?"

"That was me," Jamie said heavily, recalling the bloody months he had spent avenging his wife's murder.

"Doss, don't go makin' threats against this man," Haseltine said to the hawk-faced cowboy. "He chews up and spits out two-bit pistoleers like you."

Doss exclaimed, "By God, Haseltine, you

367

can't talk to me like that!"

"I just did," Haseltine said coldly. "You can draw down on me if you want. I know you're faster than me. But I don't reckon you'll last long if you do."

"You've just been lookin' for an excuse to run me off."

"I don't need an excuse other than bein' sick and tired of you. Go back to the ranch and draw your pay. You're done on the Slash M."

For a moment Jamie thought Doss was going to slap leather, but the man jerked his horse around and galloped off.

"Looks like we caused you some trouble after all," Jamie said to Haseltine.

The ranch foreman shook his head. "No, that's been buildin' up for a while. I just got tired of that hombre's blusterin' around all the time. Maybe he's right and I was lookin' for an excuse to tell him to rattle his hocks."

"Is he fast on the draw?" Jake asked.

"Fast enough to have killed three men in fair fights," Haseltine answered. "Fast enough to get a swelled head and make a blasted nuisance of himself." He changed the subject. "You need any help gettin' through our range, Mr. MacCallister?"

"You don't have any of it fenced off, do you?"

Haseltine made a face like he had just bitten into a rotten apple. "You won't find any fences within five hundred miles of here, Mr. MacCallister. And that's just the way we like it in these parts."

You'd better enjoy it while you can, Jamie thought, because it won't last. "Then I reckon we'll be fine. Obliged for the offer, though. We might cut out one of these steers and butcher it, if you'll tell me what price your boss would want for it."

"Don't worry about that," Haseltine said. "We can spare one of the critters. And the boss'll back me up on that."

Jamie nodded again. "Obliged." He lifted a hand in a wave of farewell as the cowboys rode on.

"Tough-looking bunch," Bodie commented.

"Texas cowboys," Jamie said. "They're tough, all right. Let's take Haseltine up on his offer and cut out one of these steers."

"Steaks tonight!" Jake said with a grin.

The fresh meat lifted the spirits of the immigrants, even though longhorns tended to be a little tough and stringy. The wagons had been on the trail for a long time, and sometimes it seemed like Montana was still as far off as it had been when they started.

Jamie knew they had made good progress, but there was still a long way to go.

He was standing beside Moses's wagon that evening, sipping from a cup of coffee, when he heard hoofbeats approaching the circle of wagons. He set the cup on the lowered tailgate and turned toward the sound.

The horse came to a stop, and as Jamie walked toward the gap between two of the wagons, a tall, lean figure appeared in it. The cowboy called Doss stepped into the glow from several nearby campfires. When he spotted Jamie coming toward him, he stiffened and his hands curled into claws poised above the black butts of the Colts holstered on his hips, ready to hook and draw.

"There you are!" he called. "They tell me you're one of the big he-wolf gunfighters, MacCallister! Well, I'm here to call you out!"

And with that, his hands streaked for the revolvers.

CHAPTER FORTY-EIGHT

There were too many people around. A group of women stood a few yards behind Jamie, talking. Off to his right several kids were chasing each other around, and one of the big yellow mutts that accompanied the wagon train ran after them, barking. It was a peaceful scene. A stray bullet could alter it suddenly, tragically, and irrevocably.

There was no time to do anything except kill the troublemaker.

Faster than the eye could follow, Jamie's big hands swept down and back up. Even though Doss had already cleared leather before Jamie started his draw, the man never got a shot off. Jamie's Colts crashed, the two shots coming so close together they sounded like one.

The pair of .44 slugs punched into Doss's chest and drove him backward. The back of his calves struck a lowered wagon tongue, and he flipped over it. His guns finally roared as his fingers contracted in death spasms, the shots going harmlessly into the heavens. Doss thudded onto his back and his arms fell out loosely to the sides.

He didn't move again. One of Jamie's bullets had ripped through a lung. The other had pulped his heart. He was already dead when he hit the ground.

The chatter that had filled the camp a couple seconds earlier stopped short, leaving a stunned silence. As the echoes of the shots rolled away, the silence was broken by shouted questions and running footsteps.

Jamie holstered the left-hand Colt and began reloading the expended chamber in the other revolver. Bodie Cantrell, Hector Gilworth, and Jess Neville came pounding up to him with their own guns out and ready.

Bodie asked, "Jamie, are you all right? What happened?"

Jamie leaned his head toward the fallen gunman, whose legs were still visible hanging over the wagon tongue. "That fella Doss came looking for me, I guess he figured he'd add to his reputation by killing me." Jamie paused. "It didn't work out for him."

Hector took a lantern from one of the settlers who had come to investigate the shooting and carried it over to shine its light on

372

the dead man. "It sure didn't. Looks like you drilled him dead center twice, Jamie."

"And the man already had his guns out before Jamie drew," Moses added, having joined the group, too. "I saw the whole thing. It was amazing."

Jamie leathered the right-hand gun and set about replacing the spent cartridge in the other weapon. He turned his head to listen as he picked up the sound of more horses coming toward the wagon train. "I don't know if Doss had any friends, but just in case he did, all these kids and womenfolks ought to get inside where it's safer."

Moses and several of the men hurried to spread the word and hustle the women and children into cover. Jamie, Bodie, Hector, and Jess moved to get ready for whoever was galloping toward the wagons. Jake Lucas, Clete Mahaffey, and Dave Pearsoll hurried up as well, and Jamie waved them into position around one of the wagons. They were a formidable group and if the night riders were looking for a fight, they would get it.

Instead, the hoofbeats stopped, and a man's voice called, "Hello, the camp! Hold your fire! We're friends!"

Jamie grunted as he recognized the voice. "That's Jim Haseltine, the Slash M ramrod." He raised his voice. "Come on in, Haseltine, unless you're hunting trouble!"

"No trouble," Haseltine replied. The man walked his horse forward into the light, trailed by several more members of Owen Murdock's crew. "In fact, we came to warn you. That varmint Doss may come looking for you, Mr. MacCallister. There's a trading post a few miles west of here, and Doss was there earlier tonight gettin' liquored up. He was bragging about how he was gonna find you and kill you, and to warm up for it he shot one of my men who tried to talk some sense into his head."

"Kill him?" Jamie asked curtly.

"No, thank the Lord. Just wounded him."

"Well, Doss won't shoot anybody else." Jamie holstered his guns and pointed. "You want to bury him, or should we take care of the chore?"

Haseltine swung down from his saddle, walked over to where Doss's body lay, and looked down at it. He let out a low whistle of admiration. "He's got his guns in his hands. I hate to admit it, but he was mighty fast. I guess he ran up against somebody faster, though."

"There's always somebody faster," Jamie said. "About planting him . . . ?"

"We'll do it. Shoot, we owe you that

374

much. He was always causing trouble. I'm sorry he came here and caused more."

"Not your fault," Jamie said with a shrug.

"Maybe not, but I hope the rest of your time on the Slash M is a mite more peaceful."

A short time later, the Texas cowboys rode off, taking Doss's body with them, draped over the saddle of his horse. The commotion caused by the gunfight settled down quickly. The immigrants knew that come morning, Jamie would have them up before first light, getting ready to push on toward their destination.

A chilly rain started a couple days later. There was no wind, so it came straight down from a leaden sky, steady but not hard enough to turn the landscape into a quagmire. The wagons were able to continue their journey, although the rain made everyone cold, wet, and miserable.

The sickness started a couple days after that.

Some of the immigrants had been sick at times, but none seriously. As the rain continued to fall, fever raged through the train with little warning. So many people were ill, Jamie knew there was no choice but to stop until the outbreak ran its course.

Around the clock, the sound of the constant drizzle was punctuated by coughing, wheezing, and gagging from half the wagons. Those fortunate enough not to catch the sickness stayed well away from those who had fallen ill . . . with a few notable exceptions.

Moses Danzig seemed to be everywhere at once, doing whatever he could to comfort the afflicted and nurse them back to health. As he explained to Jamie, "For a while back in Poland, when I was younger, I thought I might become a doctor. I even had a little medical training before I accepted the calling to attend rabbinical school. Unfortunately, there's not much even a real doctor could do for these poor people. I just keep them as comfortable as I can and try to help them let their own bodies fight the sickness."

A lot of the time, Savannah McCoy was at Moses's side, helping him despite Bodie's objections. Bodie just wanted her to be safe and not come down with the fever herself, so he urged her to avoid those who were sick.

"I can't do that, Bodie," she told him. "These people . . . they took me in when I had nowhere else to go. They protected me, gave me a new home." She smiled sadly.

"Why do you think I haven't gone back to the troupe? When we left Kansas City, I didn't plan to stay with the wagon train all the way to Montana Territory, you know."

"I know," he said softly as they stood under a canvas cover rigged at the back of the Bingham wagon and watched the rain fall.

"I couldn't leave. I waited until I thought enough time had passed that it might be safe, but by then . . . I just couldn't. I love Edward and Leticia. They're almost like a second set of parents to me. And I've made so many other good friends, like Moses and Mr. MacCallister and the Bradford twins. Alexander and Abigail had been spending a lot of time with me before this rain started, you know, even though they had to sneak away from their father to do it."

Bodie's jaw tightened at the mention of Reverend Thomas Bradford. "Do you know what I heard that so-called preacher saying yesterday?"

"I don't have any idea," Savannah replied. "I think he's capable of saying almost anything."

"He said the rain, and folks falling sick from it, were because we'd offended God by harboring too many sinners among us."

"I'm sure that as an actress I'm one of

those sinners he was talking about."

"That's crazy!" Bodie exclaimed. "You're about the best person I've ever known, Savannah. The way you and Moses have tried to take care of everybody —"

"Reverend Bradford probably thinks that Moses being here is another reason the wagon train is being punished."

"Let him think whatever dang fool thing he wants. All I really care about is you taking care of yourself, Savannah. If anything happened to you . . . if you got sick and . . . and . . . I don't know how I'd stand it." Bodie reached out, drew her into his arms, and cradled her against him.

She rested her head on his chest and sighed. The two of them clung to each other in the gloom as the rain continued to drizzle down.

Four people — two children, a man, and a woman — died during the outbreak of fever. Considering the number of immigrants who had fallen ill, Jamie was surprised the death toll wasn't higher. As he told Moses, "I figure it would have been a lot worse if not for what you and Savannah did."

"I just tried to help," Moses replied with a shake of his head, "and so did a lot of other people. Not just Savannah. Bodie pitched in, and Hector and Jess and so many others. We're past the worst of it now, I think. People are on the mend again. Another few days and we might be able to travel again. That is, if this blasted rain will ever stop."

The rain did stop. And the wagon train moved on, leaving four new graves behind it.

Christmas was less than a month away.

CHAPTER FORTY-NINE

It was a rare sunny day, and as a result slightly warmer, when the wagon train stopped next to a creek so the immigrants could fill the water barrels lashed to their wagons. The creek had some ice along its edges, but it wasn't frozen over as it would be later on in the winter.

All the scouts were out except Jake Lucas and Dave Pearsoll, who had been left behind to keep an eye on the wagons as the pilgrims went about their chores. Jake saw Savannah McCoy walking along the creek bank with the preacher's kids and strolled after them. The youngsters were carrying buckets to help fill their father's water barrels, and he supposed Savannah was watching out for them.

They stopped at the edge of the creek, and when Savannah saw him coming, she smiled. "Hello, Jake." The two of them were on friendly terms, even though Savannah had never been around Jake much when Bodie wasn't there, too.

He returned the smile and tugged on the brim of his hat. "Nice day, ain't it?"

"The nicest we've had lately," she agreed. She watched with approval as Alexander and Abigail Bradford filled the wooden buckets in the stream and then started back toward the wagons with them.

"Why don't we walk down there where those trees are?" Jake suggested, pointing to some bare-limbed aspen that grew about fifty yards downstream.

"Why would we do that?" Savannah asked with a slight frown of puzzlement.

"I want to talk to you about Bodie."

Savannah's frown deepened. "There's nothing wrong, is there?"

"No, not really. It's just that, well, him and me have been friends for quite a while, and there's something that's worrying me a mite."

Savannah hesitated a moment more, but then she nodded. "All right. If it's about Bodie."

The kids came back with their empty buckets. Savannah told them to keep carrying water to the reverend's wagon, then she and Jake walked toward the trees.

The trunks were close enough together

that they formed a screen of sorts and provided a little privacy. When they stopped, Savannah turned to Jake. "Now, what's this about Bodie? What are you worried about, Jake?"

A grin stretched across his face. "I'm worried that he don't know how to take proper care of a beautiful girl like you."

Before she could stop him, he had his arms around her, pulling her against him. His mouth came down on hers in an urgent, demanding kiss.

Savannah stiffened and shoved her hands against his chest, but she couldn't break away from him. Nor could she twist her lips away from his until he broke the kiss and pulled back slightly, grinning again.

Her hand flashed up and cracked across his cheek. "How dare you!" she exclaimed. "You . . . you . . . I never —"

"Maybe that's your problem," he cut in. His hands were tight on her arms. "Listen, Savannah, you can do a lot better than Bodie Cantrell. I can treat you right, and I've got a lot more money than he does." He didn't explain how he had come by that money. "Once we get to Montana, if you stick with me I'll show you a better time than Bodie ever could."

"Let go of me, Mr. Lucas," she said coldly.

"If you don't, I'll scream, and the people at the wagons will hear me. Don't think they won't."

He knew she was right. He wasn't ready to leave the wagon train just yet, so he released her arms, but he didn't step back. He still crowded close to her, and with the icy stream right behind her, there was nowhere she could go.

"Maybe I took you by surprise," he said. "I'm sorry if I did. But I had to tell you how I feel. I had to show you —"

"No, you didn't," she snapped. "You could have had the common decency to respect your friend . . . and me. From now on I want you to stay away from me, Mr. Lucas. Far away."

Jake's face hardened. He asked harshly, "Are you sure about that?"

"I'm positive. And if you don't, I'll tell Bodie —"

"You don't want to do that," Jake told her in a hard, menacing tone. "I know Bodie. If you tell him what happened here today, he'll figure he's got to come gunnin' for me. And if he does, I'll kill him. Simple as that. I'm faster than him, and if he draws on me, he'll die."

He could see in her eyes that she knew he was telling the truth. Fear sprang up in them, fear for Bodie's life.

"If you don't bother me again, I won't say anything."

"We understand each other, then."

"We do," Savannah said quietly.

Jake stepped back to let her go past him. As she did, he told her, "You're makin' a mistake. I can do more for you than Bodie ever can."

She didn't reply, didn't even look around as she hurried back toward the wagons.

Jake stood there glaring and muttering curses under his breath until a sudden footstep from among the trees made him turn quickly and reach for his gun.

"Take it easy," Dave Pearsoll said as he moved out into the open.

"What are you doin' skulkin' around here?" Jake demanded. "We're supposed to be keepin' an eye on those pilgrims."

"You were sure enough keepin' an eye on one of them," Pearsoll said with a sly grin. "A really close eye, looked like to me." His grin disappeared as he went on. "I reckon I understand now why we're still with this blasted wagon train. We could've taken off for the tall and uncut weeks ago, once we were well clear of Kansas City, but no, you insisted that we ought to stay with 'em a little while longer, Jake. But it's just one of them you're interested in. The McCoy girl."

"That's none of your business," Jake snapped.

"It is when you're hangin' on to my share of that money," Pearsoll said. "You're doin' just like Swint, draggin' your feet about divvyin' up. What's the idea, Jake? Are you hopin' something will happen to Clete and me so you can keep all of the loot?"

"That's just loco," Jake scoffed, although in truth such a prospect had entered his mind more than once. "I'm just still not convinced that Eldon won't come after us. Hell, he could be on our trail right now. It makes more sense to stay where we've got friends who'll back our play if it comes to a fight."

"Friends," Pearsoll repeated. "Like the McCoy girl. She didn't look any too friendly when she slapped your face."

Jake felt himself flushing. He blustered, "She'll come around. She just needs some time, that's all."

"And maybe for something to happen to Bodie. That'd make things easier for you, wouldn't it? Maybe more inclined to keep your word to your real friends and honor the deal you made with them."

"Forget it. Nothing's gonna happen to Bodie."

"Is that so? You know good and well that if you're ever gonna get that girl, he'll have to die. You change your mind about that, let me know." Pearsoll turned and walked off toward the wagons, leaving Jake standing there with a worried frown on his face.

He didn't want to admit it, even to himself, but maybe there was some truth in what Pearsoll said.

"I'm getting tired of carrying water," Abigail said. "Can't we do something else?"

"Miss Savannah asked us to do this," Alexander told her. "I don't want to let her down."

Abigail made a face, but she walked back toward the creek with her brother. As they dipped the buckets in the water, she exclaimed, "Alex, did you see that?"

"What?" he asked as he looked around.

She pointed. "I saw something up the creek that way. It looked like a pretty bird with bright-colored feathers."

"All the birds have gone south for the winter," Alexander pointed out. "You're just saying that because you want me to say we can quit fetching water."

"That's not true! I did see it, and if you'll come with me, I'll prove it."

"What are you doing, Abby?" Alexander

asked as his sister set her bucket aside.

"I told you. I'm going to find that bird." She started walking along the creek, toward a bend in the stream a couple hundred yards away where low brush lined the banks.

Alexander looked around for Savannah, but didn't see her. A few minutes earlier, she had been talking to Bodie's friend, that other scout Mr. Lucas. But he wasn't in sight, either.

Abigail was beyond where the wagons were parked, and she wasn't slowing down. Alexander knew how impulsive and dad-blasted stubborn his sister could be when she put her mind to it. She was going to get in trouble if she wandered off. She would get *both* of them in trouble, since their father would take it for granted that Alexander should have been looking out for her.

He trotted after her, calling, "Abby, hold on." When he caught up to her, he frowned. "I'll come with you to look for that stupid bird that's not even there."

"It is, too," she insisted.

He ignored that. "But then we've got to go back. Just a few minutes, all right?"

"I saw it right up here, moving around in those bushes."

Alexander still didn't believe it. Either Abigail was seeing things, or she had just made up the story. If she had made it up and their father found out about it, he would punish her. Making up stories was lying, he always said, and lying was a terrible sin.

Sometimes it seemed to Alexander that most things in life were terrible sins.

The closest wagon was about a hundred yards away when they walked around the bend and into the brush. Alexander looked around. "I don't see anything except a bunch of old dead bushes —"

At that moment, something closed around his right ankle and jerked. Before he knew what was happening, he'd been pulled right off the creek bank. Somebody grabbed him, looping an arm around his ribs and squeezing so tight he couldn't breathe. At the same time, a hand covered his mouth and clamped down equally hard, so he had no chance to yell.

His eyes widened in horror as he saw an Indian standing a few feet away. The man wore buckskins and had feathers in his hair — feathers! — and the worst thing of all was that he had hold of Abigail and was clutching her tightly to him as she kicked and squirmed. The Indian was more than twice her size, and Alexander knew his sister had no chance of getting away.

He knew that an Indian had hold of him, too, and even though he fought, there was nothing he could do. The Indians began walking through the creek, taking their two young prisoners with them.

Nobody at the wagon train even knew they were gone, Alexander's panic-stricken brain screamed.

CHAPTER FIFTY

Jamie knew something was wrong as soon as he got back to the creek where the wagons had stopped to water up. He heard shouting. There was anger in the sound, of course, but there was also something else.

Fear.

He swung down from the saddle and dropped the reins. Sundown would stay ground-hitched. He walked toward the large group of immigrants gathered beside the stream. Several people were talking at once, but the loudest voice belonged to Reverend Thomas Bradford.

"— unforgivable!" he was saying. "I knew I couldn't trust a . . . a shameless jezebel like you to watch my children! I never should have allowed them to associate with the likes of you! I should have put a stop to it as soon as they started sneaking off to visit you!"

The crowd parted without Jamie having

to say anything. It was just a natural result of his imposing presence. He saw that Bradford was shouting at Savannah. The preacher's rough-hewn face was as red as a brick, while Savannah's, by contrast, had all the color washed out of it. She looked frightened.

Moses stepped up. "Please, Reverend, there's no need to browbeat Miss McCoy —"

"You stay out of it, you damned Christ-killer!" Bradford roared.

Moses went pale, too.

Bradford went on. "This harlot was probably seducing some man when she should have been watching my children —"

"That's enough," Jamie said as he moved forward. He hooked his thumbs in his gun belt and confronted Bradford. "There's no need for talk like that. You'd better be glad Bodie Cantrell isn't here right now, mister. If he was, I reckon he'd be going after you for saying such things. I'm tempted to myself."

"You don't know what she did!" Bradford leveled a finger at Savannah. "My children were with her, and now they're gone! Disappeared!"

Now they were getting down to it. Jamie turned to Savannah. "What happened?"

"Reverend Bradford is right," she replied in a shaky voice. "It's my fault. I was supposed to be watching Alexander and Abigail while they fetched water, and they . . . they vanished while I was busy talking to someone else."

"They can't have gotten very far on foot," Jamie said, keeping his tone calm and reassuring. "Where was the last place you saw 'em?"

"They were right here along the creek, getting water for their father's water barrels."

Lamar Hendricks spoke up. "I've been asking around, Jamie, and a couple people saw the children walking up the creek toward that bend." He pointed. "But I looked up there and there's no sign of them."

There might be sign that Hendricks wasn't experienced enough to see, Jamie thought. "I'll take a look." He glanced around, spotted Jake in the crowd. "Come on, Jake."

The young man fell in with Jamie as his long legs carried him along the creek bank. Several other men tagged along, including Hendricks.

The banks deepened around the bend. They were about four feet high, and the ground was covered fairly thickly with brush on both sides of the creek. Jamie studied the growth, looking for broken branches that might indicate a struggle. When he didn't find anything, he turned his attention to the creek itself and the narrow band of muddy earth at its edge.

His jaw tightened as he spotted a familiar-looking indentation. He pointed it out to the men who had come with him. "That's a footprint. The fella who made it was wearing moccasins."

"Indians!" Hendricks exclaimed.

"Looks like it." Jamie nodded and pointed to a vertical mark on the bank. "Something skidded along there. A foot, maybe, like somebody slid down the bank . . . or was pulled." He pointed again. "Another footprint there, but not left by the same man. There were two of them."

Hendricks said, "They lurked here and kidnapped the Bradford children."

"Maybe. I want to look around some more."

It took Jamie another few minutes to locate hoofprints left by unshod ponies on the far side of the creek, beyond the clump of brush. The Indians had left their mounts there, skulked along the creek to spy on the wagons, and then when Alexander and Abigail had come wandering up the creek for whatever reason, had grabbed the kids and carried them off.

This was bad, Jamie thought, but it could have been worse. Indians seldom killed such young captives. They might murder children in the heat of battle, but if they went to the trouble to take prisoners away with them, they usually kept those captives alive. They would either make slaves of the children, or more likely raise them as members of the tribe.

He didn't intend to let either of those things happen. "How long have they been gone?"

"Less than an hour," Hendricks replied.

Jamie jerked his head in a curt nod. "I'll get after them. There's a good chance I can bring 'em back. There were only two Indians. Probably just out hunting, although they could have been scouting for a war party, I suppose. If I can catch up to them before they get back to their village, I'll rescue those kids."

"But what if there wind up being more Indians?" Hendricks asked. "You'll need help, Jamie. I'm coming with you."

Several other men voiced their eager agreement with that sentiment.

Jamie didn't want to be saddled with a bunch of inexperienced pilgrims, but if there was a whole war party out there, he probably couldn't risk taking them on by himself. That would put the children in too much danger.

He compromised. "I'm starting after them right now. Hector Gilworth ought to be coming in soon. Jake, maybe you can go find him and bring him in sooner. Hector can put together a rescue party and lead it after me. He ought to be able to follow my trail. No more than a dozen men, though. The rest need to stay with the wagons. This could be a diversion."

Hendricks said, "What do you mean?"

"They could've grabbed the kids thinking they'd use 'em to lure most of the men away from the wagons, while the rest of the war party circles around and hits the train from another direction. I don't think that's what's happened here, but we can't risk it."

"I understand. We'll do what you say, Jamie."

Jamie's long legs carried him back quickly to the wagons. As he was about to swing up into the saddle, Reverend Bradford stormed up to him and demanded, "What did you find out, MacCallister?"

Jamie knew the truth would just set off the reverend even more, but Bradford would find it out soon enough from one of the others even if Jamie didn't tell him. "It looks like Indians have them, but I'm going after them right now. I'll bring them back."

Bradford looked horrified. "My God!" he burst out. "My poor innocent children, tortured and scalped — !"

"Nobody said anything about them being tortured and scalped," Jamie snapped. "Usually when Indians take white kids like that, they adopt 'em into the tribe."

That seemed to bother Bradford more. Eyes wide, he said, "I'd rather them be killed than see them turned into godless heathen savages!"

Jamie put his foot in the stirrup and swung up onto Sundown's back rather than say what he was thinking. He supposed most people would share the sentiments Bradford had just expressed. That made no sense to Jamie, though. Life was too precious to throw it away that easily.

He turned the stallion and heeled Sundown into motion, splashing across the creek. It took him only a moment to pick up the trail of the two unshod ponies as they headed north. He followed it, his eyes constantly scanning the landscape for signs of danger.

CHAPTER FIFTY-ONE

After following the Indians for about an hour, Jamie came to a spot where the hoofprints of the two ponies joined with those of a number of other horses. He reined in, studied the marks on the ground, and frowned.

The hoofprints confirmed one of his biggest worries. The two men who had grabbed the kids had rendezvoused with a larger party. The prints were such a muddle, he couldn't tell for sure how many there were. More than a dozen, that was certain. Maybe as many as twenty-five or thirty. Even if the group from the wagon train caught up to him, they would still be outnumbered.

But he wasn't going to leave Alexander and Abigail to become part of whatever tribe had taken them.

People usually fell into one of two extremes when it came to the Indians. Most folks considered them filthy, bloodthirsty savages, little better than animals. But some people — usually easterners who had Never actually *seen* an Indian, much less had anything to do with them — claimed that they were noble aristocrats of the plains, living in harmony with nature, the land, and each other.

As usual, both sides were full of buffalo droppings. There were plenty of things to admire about the Indian way of life, but there was no escaping the fact that most of them suffered through hard, short, brutal existences, struggling to survive and constantly warring on each other. The odds of starving to death, dying of illness, freezing in the winter, or being killed in a raid by another tribe were high.

Jamie wasn't going to abandon the Bradford children to such a fate. He would get them back or die trying. Once the two kidnappers joined up with the war party, if that's what it was, the trail was easier to follow. He pushed on, confident that Hector and the others would be able to find him.

By late afternoon Jamie entered a range of small, wooded hills, the highest elevations and the most trees he had seen in quite a while. With his instincts warning him that he might be closing in on his quarry, he used every bit of cover he could find as he continued following the trail.

He smelled the camp before he saw it. Wood smoke, cooking meat, and horseflesh. He dismounted and went up the slope ahead of him on foot, moving in silence over a carpet of pine needles. Before he reached the top he took off his hat and got down on his belly to crawl the rest of the way. When he got to the top, he worked his way through a patch of undergrowth, parted some branches, and looked down into a little canyon where more than two dozen Indians had made camp.

Blackfeet, Jamie thought as he saw the markings on their buckskins and the way they wore their hair. No women and children in sight. It was a raiding party. Several of the warriors sported crude bandages, which meant they had already been in a fight. They'd probably skirmished with another tribe and were on their way back to their usual hunting grounds, taking with them the two white captives a couple scouts had been fortunate enough to come across.

Jamie saw Alexander and Abigail sitting with their backs propped against a fallen log. They appeared to be all right, although their hands and feet were tied and Abigail was slumped against her brother's side, sobbing. Alexander had his head up and Jamie could tell that the boy was trying to be brave, but he had to be scared out of his wits.

Not for much longer, son, Jamie thought.

The trick was figuring out how to get him out.

Jamie studied the landscape around the Blackfoot camp. The canyon was formed by two ridges that dropped off almost sheer for about forty feet. He lay where those ridges angled in and came together. The trail the Indians had used to get into the canyon zigzagged down from that point. Anybody going down it would be in plain sight from the camp below.

At the far end, the canyon ended in a shale slope at the top of which rose a stone wall. The drop from the top of that wall to the shale was about twenty feet. However, the cliff face was rugged enough that it would provide handholds and footholds so that a man could climb down part of the way, leaving a reasonable drop to the shale.

If a man tried that and landed right, he could slide all the way to the canyon floor. If he didn't land right . . . well, he'd probably break an ankle, at the very least.

Jamie didn't see any other way into the canyon. He would have to have help to manage it.

He moved back down the near slope and glanced at the sky. About an hour of daylight was left, giving the other men from the wagon train time to catch up to him. He could finish working out his plan then.

The sun had just dropped below the western horizon when Jamie heard horses coming. He stepped out of the thick stand of pines where he'd been waiting and waved his hat over his head to signal the approaching riders.

They angled toward him. Hector Gilworth was in the lead, with Bodie Cantrell and Jess Neville right behind him, trailed by nine or ten men from the wagon train. Most of them were carrying rifles or shotguns.

He didn't see Lucas, Mahaffey, and Pearsoll and figured those three had stayed behind at the wagons. That was good. Jamie wanted some seasoned fighting men left with the rest of the immigrants.

He was much less pleased to see Reverend Thomas Bradford with the rescue party. He had hoped that Bradford would stay behind. He didn't trust that the preacher would follow his orders. In his arrogant stubbornness — and, to be fair, his legitimate concern for his children — Bradford was liable to try some foolish stunt that would endanger all

401

of them.

Jamie would make sure to tell Hector to keep a close eye on the man.

Bradford crowded his mount ahead of the others and said loudly, "Have you found them? Have you found Alexander and Abigail?"

"Keep your voice down," Jamie snapped. "Sounds carry farther out here than you think they would, and the Indians are right on the other side of that ridge. I figure they'll be posting guards on top of it any time now since it's getting dark, and we don't want them to know we're here."

Bradford was a little quieter as he said, "All right. But what about my children? Have you seen them?"

"I have. They look fine, just a little tired and scared." As the men gathered around him, Jamie went on to describe everything he had seen.

Jess Neville said, "That ain't good, is it? Them Injuns bein' Blackfeet, I mean. From what I hear tell, they hate white folks more than any of the other tribes in these parts."

"That's true," Jamie admitted, "but chances are, if they were going to hurt those kids, they'd have done it before now. We just need to get them out of that camp."

"How are we going to do that?" Bodie

asked. "It sounds like there's no way in there that wouldn't be suicide."

"There's no *good* way," Jamie explained. "But I think a couple men could work their way around to the cliff above that shale slope and drop down into the canyon from there. The rest of our bunch can cause a distraction that'll keep those Blackfeet busy while the two hombres grab the kids."

Bodie shook his head. "No offense, Jamie, but how do they get back out?"

Jamie rubbed his chin and frowned, realizing that he hadn't gotten that far in his thinking. After a moment he said, "We'll have to take ropes with us and tie 'em at the top of the cliff. That'll help us get down, and the kids can hang on to us while we use the ropes to climb out."

"Us?" Bodie repeated with a faint smile.

"I was thinking you might want to come with me."

Bradford said, "I'll do it. They're my children."

"That they are," Jamie agreed, "but how are you at using a gun, Reverend? There's a chance whoever goes into that camp will have to fight their way out."

"I've never believed in violence," Bradford said stiffly.

"And I believe in using whatever does the

job best. Bodie's coming with me. Unless you don't want to, son."

"Try and stop me. Savannah's tearing herself up over this. She'll never forgive herself if we don't get those kids back safe and sound."

Bradford started to bluster something, but Jamie stopped him with a hard look. He figured the preacher was about to say something else bad about Savannah, then Bodie would take offense, and they didn't need that complication.

"What do you want the rest of us to do, Jamie?" Hector asked. "How do we provide that distraction you were talking about?"

"Well, there's only one way to do it as far as I can see. You fellas are about to get your feet wet when it comes to Indian fighting."

CHAPTER FIFTY-TWO

With a faint glow still in the western sky, Jamie and Bodie started out. They circled wide to come at the canyon from the west.

Hector and the other men were dug in behind rocks and trees on the other side of the ridge, waiting for the two rescuers to get into position. Hector owned a railroad watch that had been left to him by his father, and when exactly an hour had gone by, he and the other men would charge the ridge, yelling and shooting, before turning around and dashing back to their defensive positions.

The outbreak of gunfire would be the signal for Jamie and Bodie to make their move.

As darkness gathered, Bodie asked, "How are we going to find our way to the top of that cliff you mentioned?"

"I took a pretty good look at it a while ago," Jamie replied. "Studied the lay of the land while there was still some light in the sky. I'll be able to get us there."

"When it comes to surviving out here, is there anything you *can't* do, Jamie?"

A grin stretched across the big frontiersman's rugged face. "There's bound to be, but since I'm still alive I reckon I've figured it out pretty well so far." He led them unerringly to the foot of a ridge where they dismounted.

"That canyon where the Blackfeet are camped ought to be just on the other side," Jamie said quietly. "Get the rope off your horse and let's go."

The slope on that side of the ridge was too steep for horses, but Jamie and Bodie were able to negotiate it on foot, carrying the ropes with them. As they climbed, Jamie sniffed the air and smelled smoke from the Blackfoot campfire. His instincts had been reliable yet again.

When they reached the top of the narrow ridge, the two men crawled forward until they could look down into the canyon. The campfire still burned, and in its flickering orange light they saw some members of the war party still moving around. Others slept. Jamie spotted the two children, dozing as they huddled against the same log where he had seen them sitting earlier. He touched

Bodie's shoulder and pointed them out to the young man, who nodded.

Moving quickly and silently, they knotted one end of the ropes around the trunks of pine trees that grew atop the ridge. When that was done, they stretched out on the ground again, and Jamie whispered, "Now we wait. Shouldn't be long."

It wasn't. Within ten minutes, gunfire suddenly roared in the distance. Jamie saw muzzle flashes from the opposite ridge and knew the Blackfoot sentries posted up there were returning the fire. In the camp, the rest of the war party grabbed rifles and began charging up the twisting path to the top of the ridge.

"Let's go," he said.

They dropped the ropes over the cliff and swung out onto them, walking down the cliff backwards. It wasn't that far. When they reached the shale, they let go, left the ropes hanging there, and slid down the rest of the way to the canyon floor.

Jamie drew his Bowie knife as he ran toward the log where the children were lying, wide awake because of the yelling and shooting. He had warned Bodie against using their guns unless they absolutely had to, since that might alert the Blackfeet that something was going on behind them.

With a grace and agility unusual in a man of his size and age, Jamie vaulted over the log and dropped to one knee next to Alexander and Abigail. Abigail opened her mouth to scream. From her perspective, all she could see was a dark, giant figure looming over her.

Jamie put his free hand over her mouth. "Hush, Abby. It's me, Mr. MacCallister. Mr. Cantrell is with me. We're going to get you and Alexander out of here."

He started sawing through the tough strips of rawhide with which they were bound while Bodie crouched next to the log and kept a lookout. Jamie had Abigail loose when Bodie suddenly hissed, "Somebody's coming!"

Jamie looked up just as a couple Blackfoot warriors charged into the firelight. The leader of the war party had sent them back to keep an eye on the prisoners. It was a smart move, but it had occurred to the fellow too late.

Spotting the two white men trying to free the captives, the warriors skidded to a halt and tried to raise their rifles. Firelight winked from the blade of Jamie's knife as it flashed across the clearing to bury nearly a foot of cold steel in the chest of one of the Blackfeet. The man gasped, stumbled, and dropped his rifle without firing it. He crumpled to the ground.

Less than half a second later, Jamie's left-hand Colt roared. The bullet ripped through the second warrior's throat and bored through the lower part of his brain. He dropped like a puppet with its strings cut.

Bodie had drawn his gun but hadn't had a chance to shoot. Jamie's blinding speed had seen to that.

Jamie pouched the iron. "Get my knife."

It had taken only one pistol shot to dispose of the second warrior, and neither Blackfoot had gotten off a shot. He hoped the single shot had gone unnoticed by the other Indians, since they were busy trading lead with the rest of the rescue party and things were pretty noisy.

Bodie ran to the fallen warriors, pulled the knife from the chest of the one Jamie had killed with it, and hurried back to hand the blood-smeared blade to the big frontiersman.

While he was cutting Alexander loose, Jamie told Abigail, "You go with Mr. Cantrell now, honey. You'll have to put your arms around him and hang on tight to him while he climbs up a rope. Can you do that?"

"I'd rather you take me, Mr. MacCallister," the little girl said.

"I'm busy with your brother. Mr. Cantrell will take good care of you. You just do everything he tells you, and don't be scared, all right?"

"I . . . I'll try."

"Good girl. Go on, now."

Bodie scooped Abigail up in his arms and ran for the cliff. It wouldn't be easy getting back up that loose shale while carrying the girl, but he'd manage.

A moment later, the last of the rawhide thongs fell away from Alexander's ankles. "You don't have to carry me, Mr. MacCallister. I can run."

"Mighty fast?"

"Mighty fast!"

Jamie grinned in the darkness. "Come on, then."

They hurried to the cliff. Through the moonlight, Jamie could see Bodie climbing the rope with Abigail clinging to his back, her arms around his neck and her legs around his waist.

"I can climb the rope, too," Alexander said.

"I expect you can, but it might be faster if you got on my back, like your sister did with Mr. Cantrell. Reckon you can do that?"

"Sure."

Alexander clambered onto Jamie's back as the big man knelt, then Jamie started up the slope. It took every bit of balance he had not to slip back down the shale. The climb seemed to take a long time, but finally he was able to reach up and grasp the rope. That steadied him the rest of the way and allowed him to go a little faster. He reached the bottom of the cliff, planted a booted foot against the rock, and started that part of the climb. It was the hardest part of the climb, taking a lot of muscle power to lift a man of Jamie's size. Alexander's weight added to the burden.

"Hang on tight," Jamie grated.

"Don't worry," Alexander said. "I won't let go."

Jamie tipped his head back to watch the top of the cliff come closer. Bodie and Abigail reached the rimrock and vanished over it. Jamie was relieved they were safe. In a matter of moments, he and Alexander would be, too.

Below them, a shot suddenly blasted, and a bullet smacked into the rock face less than a yard away from them.

Chapter Fifty-Three

Jamie twisted his head to look down and behind them and saw that several of the Blackfoot warriors had run back into the camp and were pointing rifles at them. Jamie couldn't let go of the rope to grab his guns and put up a fight. He and Alexander would plummet to the ground if he did.

Bodie appeared at the rimrock and shouted at Jamie, "Keep climbing!" Then the revolver in his hand spouted flame as he opened fire on the Indians, spraying the clearing with lead.

That scattered the Blackfeet momentarily, but Jamie knew it wouldn't take long for them to regroup. He redoubled his efforts, grunting with the strain as his thickly corded muscles hauled him and the boy up the rope.

More slugs from below began to pepper the cliff around them. Jamie felt rock splinters sting his cheeks and hands. He called to Alexander, "Hang on tight, son!"

Bodie's gun ran dry. Jamie knew there wouldn't be time for his young friend to reload. Still clinging to the rope with his left hand, he let go with his right and reached down to pluck the .44 on that side from its holster. "Catch!" he yelled as he tossed the Colt the seven or eight feet to the rim.

Bodie dropped his gun beside him and grabbed Jamie's by the barrel, fumbling with it for a second before he secured it. He reversed it, pointed it down into the canyon, and started shooting again.

Jamie heaved, reached higher, heaved again. They were almost at the top. Another second or two . . .

He felt the heat of a bullet as it whipped past his ear. The slug hit the cliff and sprayed grit in his eyes, blinding him momentarily. He clenched his jaw and kept climbing.

He reached up for the rim, only to have a strong hand close around his wrist. Bodie hollered, "Keep coming! I've got you!"

"Grab the boy!" Jamie gasped out.

"Come on, Alexander!"

A second later, Alexander's weight lifted from Jamie's back.

"I've got him!" Bodie exclaimed as he fell

back from the rim, taking Alexander with him.

At that instant, a bullet clipped Jamie on top of the left shoulder. The impact was enough to make his arm go numb. His grip on the rope slipped, and at the same time his toes slid off the tiny foothold where they had found purchase. He yelled as all his weight dangled from the grip of his right hand on the rope.

At that moment, Jamie Ian MacCallister's almost superhuman strength was all that saved him. He hung there with bullets screaming around him and smacking into the cliff for what seemed like an eternity.

In reality, it was only a couple heartbeats before he forced his left arm to work again and grabbed the rope with that hand. He hauled himself up another foot, then Bodie caught hold of the buckskin shirt. Jamie dug his toes against the rock as Bodie lifted him through the air and he rolled over the edge of the rimrock.

His pulse hammered inside his head like a gang of railroad workers driving spikes as he lay there on his back trying to catch his breath. A couple feet away, Bodie knelt and fired down at the Blackfeet, ducking occasionally as one of their bullets came too close to his head.

Jamie rolled onto his side and lifted his head. In the moonlight, he saw Alexander and Abigail watching him worriedly. He grinned at them. "I'm all right, kids. We'd better get out of here."

Bodie threw one final shot at the Indians, then retreated from the edge. "That sounds like a good idea to me." He handed Jamie's gun back to him. "Sorry it's empty."

"I'm not. I hope you hit some of 'em."

The four of them hurried down the slope as fast as they could, heading for the spot where Jamie and Bodie had left their horses. Within minutes they were mounted, with Abigail riding in front of Bodie and Alexander in front of Jamie, as they circled back toward the rest of the rescue party.

Jamie was counting on Hector and the other men to keep the Blackfeet bottled up in that canyon. The Indian ponies could only get in and out of the camp by one route, up that zigzag trail. As long as the men from the wagon train kept raking the top of that ridge with rifle fire, it ought to keep the Blackfeet from getting out.

Once Jamie, Bodie, and the Bradford kids rejoined the others, they would all have to make a run for it back to the wagon train. Jamie didn't think a war party of less than three dozen would dare to attack the entire group of immigrants. The Blackfeet would be angry because somebody had stolen their prisoners from them, but more than likely they would cut their losses and head on back to their home.

That's how Jamie hoped it would play out, anyway. With Indians, it was impossible to predict with absolute certainty what they would do.

As they galloped through the night, Bodie called over to Jamie, "How bad were you hit?"

Feeling had returned to Jamie's left arm. The wound on top of his shoulder throbbed, but he was able to move his arm and roll that shoulder without any trouble other than a twinge of pain. "Just nicked me. It's nothing."

If the Blackfoot who had fired that shot had gotten it off a couple seconds earlier, the bullet probably would have hit Alexander in the head. It had been that close a call. Just thinking about it made Jamie go a little cold in the belly.

They could no longer hear gunshots over the pounding hoofbeats of Sundown and Bodie's mount, but Jamie hoped the fighting was still going on. If not, the four of them might be riding right into trouble.

Finally, the moonlight revealed a saddle

between two hills, one of the landmarks he remembered, and as they rode through it he saw the glow from muzzle flashes in the trees up ahead.

"Who's that?" a voice challenged in the darkness. "Sing out!"

"MacCallister!" Jamie replied. "I've got Cantrell and the kids with me."

"Thank the Lord!"

That was Bradford's voice, prompting Alexander to exclaim, "Pa!"

As Jamie reined in, he scrambled down from the stallion's back and ran toward his father. Abigail was right behind him. Bradford stepped forward and gathered them up in his arms.

The preacher was an unlikable son of a gun, thought Jamie, but he loved his kids and they returned the feeling. He had to give the man credit for that.

"Hector, where are you?" Jamie called.

"Right here," Hector responded as he stepped out of the shadows under some trees. "Are all of you all right?"

"Good enough," Jamie said. "Get the men on their horses. We're lighting a shuck back to the wagon train."

"What about the Blackfeet?"

"When they realize nobody's taking pot-shots at them anymore, they're liable to come boiling out of there and chase after us. It'll be a race back to the wagon train, but I think we'll have enough of a lead to beat them there, and once we do, they'll give up and turn back."

Hector hurried to carry out Jamie's orders, moving through the trees and rocks where the rescuers were forted up. "Back to your horses! Mount up, mount up!"

The men swung into their saddles.

Jamie rode over to Bradford. "Better let Bodie and me take the kids again, Reverend. Our horses can handle the extra weight, and you're not used to riding double, or in this case, triple."

"I can take care of my own children," Bradford snapped. But then common sense prevailed and he relented. "You two go with Mr. MacCallister and Mr. Cantrell."

"I want to stay with you," Abigail wailed.

"Hush now, and do as I say!"

That sharply voiced command got the children to obey. Jamie reached down, grasped Alexander's hands, and pulled the boy up in front of him again. He wheeled Sundown around as the line of men formed and started to leave the shelter of the trees.

They had just emerged into the open when muzzle flame split the darkness, coming from in front of them. Bullets raked through the rescue party, drawing pained shouts and sending two of the men toppling from their saddles.

CHAPTER FIFTY-FOUR

"Fall back!" Jamie bellowed as he hauled hard on the reins. "Back into the trees! Take cover!"

Bullets whined around them as the men hastily retreated. Over the sound of the shots, Jamie heard strident whoops from the unexpected attackers. He knew none of the Blackfeet in the canyon could have gotten in front of them, so that left only one other explanation.

The war party that had camped in the canyon was meeting another group of Blackfoot warriors, and the second bunch had shown up at just the wrong time.

Jamie and his companions, already outnumbered, were caught between the two forces.

Jamie swung Alexander to the ground and then flung himself out of the saddle, taking his Winchester with him. He told the boy to find his sister and make sure both of them stayed down as low as they could on the ground.

Taking cover behind a tree, Jamie brought the rifle to his shoulder, nestled his cheek against the smooth wood of the stock, and began firing at the muzzle flashes from the second group of Indians, cranking off the rounds as fast as he could work the Winchester's lever. More shots rang out as the other men began mounting a defense again.

Bodie Cantrell ran up and knelt behind a tree next to Jamie. "This is pretty bad, isn't it?"

"They've got us pinned down from both directions," Jamie acknowledged. "These trees and rocks give us pretty good cover, so we ought to be able to hold them off for a while, but sooner or later we'll run out of bullets."

"We can't count on any help from the wagon train, either. They don't have any way of knowing we're in trouble, so they won't send anybody after us."

"I reckon not," Jamie agreed grimly.

"If we hit the ones in front of us hard enough, could we bust through them?"

"Not without getting half our bunch killed, including those kids."

"Who are they? What's going on here, anyway?"

"Pure bad luck," Jamie said. "That's what's going on." He went on to explain his theory that the first bunch of Blackfeet had planned to rendezvous in the canyon with another war party.

Bodie agreed that made sense.

The firing from both directions died away.

Jamie called softly, "Everybody keep your head down! They're trying to draw us out into the open, but we're staying put."

Silence settled down over the rugged landscape.

Bodie said in a whisper, "Now we wait?"

"Now we wait," Jamie agreed. But only until morning, he thought.

Some people thought Indians wouldn't fight at night. Obviously, that wasn't true. But they preferred to do their killing during the day, and Jamie figured that's what they had in mind. They would keep the rescue party pinned down until daylight, and once they could see what they were doing, the Blackfeet would attack from both directions at once and overwhelm the defenders in the trees.

When that time came, Jamie and his companions would sell their lives as dearly as possible. There was nothing else they could do.

The hours stretched out uncomfortably.

Jamie heard a lot of frightened muttering from the men. Abigail cried for a while before drifting off into an exhausted sleep. Alexander let out a few sniffles, too, but he was trying to be brave.

Reverend Bradford crawled up to Jamie's position and said in a low, angry voice, "You've managed to get us all killed, Mac-Callister. We'll never get out of this alive."

"I thought you were supposed to have faith, Reverend."

"I have faith in the Lord. I have none in you."

"Well, I'd be the last person to put myself on the same level as the Lord. I'm just a poor sinner trying to make his way in the world the same as anybody else. But I'll tell you the truth, Bradford. I did the best I knew how to do to help get those kids of yours back. Our luck ran out, that's all."

"Our luck ran out when we agreed to let you lead us to Montana," Bradford said bitterly.

Bodie said, "Why don't you just shut your mouth, Bradford? You're always telling other people how they've fallen short, but you're sure as hell not perfect yourself! Those two kids are scared of you, you know that? You're nothing but a damned hardheaded tyrant!"

Bradford started to get to his feet. "You can't talk that way to a man of God —"

Jamie reached over, put a hand on Bradford's shoulder, and shoved him back down. "Stay put, Reverend," he said coldly. "I don't cotton to you, but for your kids' sake I don't want you getting a bullet in the head."

"The Indians aren't shooting anymore. We don't even know they're still out there. Maybe they gave up and left."

"They're out there, all right," Jamie said. "Mark my words, Reverend. They're out there."

However, everything was still quiet by morning. As dawn turned the sky gray and then golden light spread from the east, Jamie scanned the landscape in front of the trees. He didn't see anything . . . but he knew that didn't matter.

He wasn't the only one watching the broad valley between the rolling hills that represented their way out. With no warning, Reverend Bradford suddenly strode out into the open, holding his Bible in one hand and waving it in the air.

"They're gone!" he said loudly. "See for yourselves! The red devils have departed!" He turned to gaze in triumph at Jamie.

"Get down, you fool!"

"The Lord has delivered us from —"

At that instant, a rifle cracked. Jamie saw blood fly in the dawn light as a slug bored into the side of Bradford's head and exploded out the other side in a grisly pink shower. The preacher dropped limply, dead by the time he hit the ground.

Abigail screamed and tried to run to her father. Bodie grabbed her as she went by and rolled onto the ground with her as the Blackfeet opened up again. Bullets thudded into tree trunks and shredded through branches.

The barrage lasted only a moment before ending abruptly. Startled yells came from the war parties in both directions. Guns roared again, but the reports were the duller booms of revolvers. Hoofbeats hammered the ground. Men howled in pain.

The oddest thing was that with all that shooting going on, none of the bullets seemed to be directed toward the trees where Jamie and his friends were.

"What's going on out there?" Hector asked as he knelt behind a rock.

"Sounds like reinforcements showed up," Jamie said.

"Reinforcements? From where?"

"I don't know . . . but I'm glad they're here!"

Stampeding ponies burst into view, along with Blackfoot warriors fleeing on foot to avoid being trampled. With targets out in the open like that, Jamie brought his Winchester up and took advantage of the opportunity. His deadly accurate shots took a toll as .44-40 rounds ripped through the warriors. Around him, the other men joined the battle again, too.

The Blackfeet were the ones caught in a crossfire, and they were smart enough to know that the best thing to do was get out while they could. Several of them grabbed stampeding ponies, hung on desperately to the manes, and swung up onto bare backs. They fled, shouting angrily. The ones who still could, followed that example.

"Must be a cavalry patrol came along and heard the shooting," Bodie said as the gunfire tapered off again. The surviving Blackfeet from both war parties were taking off for the tall and uncut.

"Maybe," Jamie said. "I reckon we'll find out pretty soon."

"What about the preacher?" Bodie nodded toward the body of Bradford.

With a glance at the sobbing Alexander and Abigail, Jamie said quietly, "Leave him for now, until we're sure those war parties are gone."

A few tense moments went by, then Bodie asked, "Who in the world is that?"

A man had stepped out into the open and was walking toward the trees, apparently as casual as if he were out for a Sunday stroll. He was tall and lean and clad in greasy buckskins. His hat was pushed back on thinning white hair, and he sported a grizzled beard. Despite his obvious age, he moved with the ease and vitality of a much younger man.

Another man appeared behind him, leading several horses. He was younger, clean shaven, with sandy hair and a very broad set of shoulders.

Jess Neville said, "We got a couple of hombres comin' in from this other side, too."

Jamie looked around and saw an even more unusual pair approaching the line of trees and rocks. One was a thick-bodied Indian with long, graying hair. Beside him, hurrying to keep up, was a white man not even four feet tall, also dressed in buckskins.

"There's your so-called cavalry patrol," Jamie told Bodie with a grin.

"Four men? That's all? How is that possible? Four men couldn't rout a whole Blackfoot war party, let alone two of 'em!"

"Depends on who they are. I don't know

the young fella, but I'm acquainted with the other three, although it's been a long time since we crossed trails."

Jamie stepped out of the trees and raised a hand in greeting to the skinny, grizzled old-timer.

The man squinted at him. "Well, if that don't beat all! Jamie Ian MacCallister his own self, still big as a mountain and twice as ugly!"

"How are you doing, Preacher?" Jamie grinned and extended his hand. "Long time no see!"

CHAPTER FIFTY-FIVE

The reunion was a happy one, although Jamie's pleasure at seeing the old mountain man called Preacher was tempered by Reverend Bradford's sudden and senseless death. The two veteran frontiersmen shook hands and slapped each other heartily on the back.

Almost forty years had passed since Jamie and Preacher had first met down in Texas. Since then, they had run into each other from time to time, often with years between meetings.

Jamie wasn't sure exactly how old Preacher was, but he knew the mountain man was at least a decade older than him. If anyone had asked him, he wouldn't have been sure whether Preacher was even still alive.

Obviously, Preacher had proven to be amazingly resilient. Jamie wasn't sure the gun or knife had been made that could kill the old buckskinner.

"Who's this?" Jamie asked with a nod toward the young man accompanying Preacher.

"Fella name of Smoke," Preacher said. "Smoke Jensen. We been driftin' around together for the past few years, ever since Smoke's pa got hisself killed by some no-good polecats. Heard a rumor those varmints might be over in Idaho, so we're sort of amblin' in that direction."

"Plan to settle the score, do you?"

"I do," Smoke said curtly.

"Smoke's about as naturally fast on the draw as anybody I ever seen," Preacher said with a note of pride in his voice. "That's how come I started callin' him Smoke. His real front handle is Kirby, but he don't go by it no more. I pree-dict you'll be hearin' a heap about him on down the line."

Smoke shook his head. "I'm not looking for a reputation. Just justice."

Preacher waved a hand toward his other two companions. "You remember Audie and Nighthawk, of course."

"Sure." Jamie shook hands with both men, former fur trappers who were long-time friends of Preacher. "How are you, Audie?"

"Exceedingly fine," the short white man answered. "The fresh air and hardy life I've experienced out here on the frontier seems to have allowed me to stave off decrepitude, at least for the time being."

Audie spoke like an educated man, which was exactly what he was. At one time, he had been a professor at a college back east before he had abandoned that stifling academic life and headed west. Although he was small in size, he had the fighting heart and spirit of a much larger man.

Jamie went on. "You're looking good, Nighthawk."

The impassive Crow warrior nodded solemnly. "Ummm."

"Still as talkative as ever, I see," Jamie commented with a grin. "Fellas, this young scalawag is Bodie Cantrell. Big hombre with the beard over there is Hector Gilworth, and the fella with him is his cousin Jess Neville." Jamie went on to introduce the other men in the rescue party.

"Who's the sky pilot who got in the way of a bullet?" Preacher asked.

"That would be Reverend Thomas Bradford," Jamie said. "Pa to those two youngsters."

Preacher's expressive mouth twisted in a grimace. "Tough on young'uns, seein' their pa gunned down like that."

"Yeah. They got carried off by some of

those Blackfeet, and we were trying to get 'em back when we got pinned down here. It's a mighty good thing for us you came along when you did. What did you do, pull that old trick of yours where you slip into the enemy's camp during the night and cut some throats?"

Preacher chuckled. "It does tend to shake folks up a mite to find a few of their compadres with new mouths carved in their necks. When it got light, Audie and me stampeded the ponies that belonged to each bunch, whilst Smoke and Nighthawk waded in, their hoglegs a-blazin'. Every way those redskinned varmints turned, they was either a bullet or a wild-eyed bronc waitin' to ventilate 'em or trample 'em. Didn't take much o' that to make 'em light a shuck."

"What's left of the two bunches are liable to get together somewhere," Jamie mused. "We'd better get on back to the wagons while we can."

"Wagons?" Preacher repeated. "These fellas are from a wagon train?"

"That's right. Bound for Eagle Valley in Montana Territory."

"Mighty pretty place," Preacher said. "But in case you ain't noticed the chill in the air . . . it's December! What sort of dang fool takes a wagon train to Montana at this time o' year?"

"You're looking at him," Jamie said.

The old mountain man snorted. "I stand by that dang fool business."

"I'm not arguing the point. But we're here, and I'm bound and determined to get those pilgrims where they're going by Christmas." An idea occurred to Jamie. "Why don't the four of you come along with us?"

"Told you, we're headed for Idaho," Preacher said with a frown.

"And that's the general direction we're going," Jamie pointed out. "I wouldn't mind visiting with you for a while, Preacher . . . and having four more good men along for the rest of the trip wouldn't exactly make me unhappy, either."

Preacher scratched his grizzled jaw in thought and looked at Smoke. "What do you think, youngster? It's your pa we're goin' to settle the score for."

Smoke pondered the question for a moment, then said in his grave manner, "Chances are some of the passes where we need to go in Idaho are already closed, Preacher. We knew we might have to winter somewhere. I reckon it might as well be with these folks."

"There's your answer, Jamie," Preacher

told the big frontiersman. "We'll come with you."

Jamie nodded in satisfaction.

Quickly, he got everyone mounted. Reverend Bradford's body was draped over his saddle and lashed in place. Several other men had been wounded in the fighting during the night, but none of the injuries were bad enough to keep them from riding. Bradford was the group's only casualty.

To Alexander and Abigail, though, it was a big loss. The two youngsters were orphans now. The only good thing about the situation was that Jamie was sure one of the families with the wagon train would be willing to take them in.

Jamie and Preacher took the point, and as the two old pioneers rode together, they talked about the things they had been doing since they had seen each other last.

"I was mighty sorry to hear about what happened to your woman, Jamie," Preacher said. "Heard tell you went after the sorry bunch responsible for her dyin' and rained down hellfire and brimstone on their heads."

"I settled the score for Kate as best I could," Jamie said, his face and voice grim. "It wasn't enough."

"No, I don't 'spect it was. I've lost folks I loved, too, and no matter how much vengeance you get, it ain't never enough 'cause it don't bring back them you lost. Nothin' does."

"But that doesn't stop us from trying."

"Nope. Reckon we wouldn't be human if we didn't want to even things up, so we try even though we know it won't really put our hearts at ease."

A chuckle came from Jamie. "Preacher, you're getting profound in your old age."

"Reckon it comes from bein' around Audie too much. That fella goes on and on about philosophy and such-like. And who in blazes are you callin' old?"

By midday, the rescue party, along with its newest additions, came in sight of the wagons parked next to the creek. Several men led by Jake galloped out to meet them and escorted them on in. Everyone gathered around to celebrate the safe return of Alexander and Abigail.

The immigrants were sobered by the death of Reverend Bradford. After his body was laid out on the ground, Moses covered it with a blanket and took his hat off, holding it over his heart. "The reverend might not want the likes of me praying over him, but I feel like I have to do it anyway."

"I don't reckon all those disagreements mean a blasted thing now," Jamie said. "The

435

fella's dead, and I hope his soul is at peace."

"So do I," Moses murmured. "So do I. If it's all right with everyone, I'll conduct the funeral."

"I don't think anybody's going to object. You've got a lot of friends on this wagon train, Moses. Your faith may be different, but after what you did during that outbreak of fever and all the other ways you've pitched in, if these folks have a spiritual leader now . . . it's you."

Moses swallowed and nodded. "I'll try to live up to that."

Jamie nodded. "What we need to figure out now is who's going to take care of those kids."

A voice spoke up from behind him. "That's not going to be a problem, Mr. MacCallister."

Jamie and Moses turned to see Savannah standing there. She had her arms around the shoulders of Alexander and Abigail, whose pale, tear-streaked faces testified to their grief. They huddled against Savannah's skirts, obviously taking comfort from her presence.

"I'm going to take care of them," Savannah went on. "I can handle their wagon and see to it that they have everything they need."

"Are you sure about that?" Jamie asked with a frown. "You being an unmarried woman and all?"

"They were being raised by the reverend alone since his wife passed on," Savannah pointed out. "The children and I have become close, and this is something I'd really like to do."

"Well . . . if that's what all of you want . . . I don't reckon it's my place to say no."

"I'm sure everyone in the group will pitch in to help if need be." Moses paused. "Did you happen to ask Bodie what he thought about this idea?"

"It's not Bodie's decision to make," Savannah replied. "It's mine."

"Sounds to me like it's settled, then." Jamie looked at Alexander and Abigail. "You two have been mighty brave all through this. Miss Savannah's going to need you to keep on being brave. Reckon you can do that?"

Alexander nodded. He used the back of his hand to wipe away a stray tear. "This is all our fault. If we hadn't wandered off and let those Indians grab us, our pa would still be alive."

Jamie shook his head. "There are too many things going on in the world to say something like that for sure. Too many turning points where everything could turn out different. Might as well blame me for not keeping a closer eye on your pa, so that he couldn't step out there in the open where the Blackfeet could get a shot at him. Things happen, and I reckon we just have to tell ourselves that there's a reason for the way they do, and then we go on from there."

"That's right," Moses said. "On to your new homes in Eagle Valley. When do you think we'll get there, Jamie?"

"By Christmas, like I've been saying all along."

CHAPTER FIFTY-SIX

When the wagon train had left Kansas City, Jamie had worried that he might not have enough scouts. With the addition of Preacher, Smoke Jensen, Audie, and Night-hawk, he almost had too many.

On the other hand, he also had four more first-class fighting men to help out in case of trouble. He knew from experience that Preacher, Audie, and Nighthawk were hell on wheels in a ruckus, and it didn't take much time to realize that Smoke Jensen might well be the deadliest of them all.

During one of the wagon train's midday halts a few days after the rescue of the Bradford children, Preacher urged Smoke to get in a little practice with his guns. The old mountain man pointed out a fallen aspen about fifty feet away. "See if you can pick off some of them branches that are stickin' up."

Jamie was close by and heard what

Preacher said. He looked at the fallen tree and saw that the branches weren't much more than twigs maybe half an inch wide. They were barely visible. Jamie figured he could have hit those branches with a rifle, if he'd had time to draw a bead on them.

Smoke swept out one of his .44s and started firing in less than the blink of an eye. He didn't shoot from the hip, but rather thrust the gun out at the end of his arm, taking no more than a split second to aim before the Colt began to roar.

He triggered off five shots. Even with having to cock the single-action Colt each time, the reports sounded so close together they formed one continuous peal of gun-thunder. To Jamie's amazement, five of the aspen branches leaped into the air as Smoke's bullets smashed through them.

Moses had wandered up in time to witness the display. He let out a shrill whistle of admiration and awe. "I never saw such shooting!"

"Taught the younker everything he knows," Preacher said with a proud grin.

Smoke smiled faintly as he reloaded the expended chambers.

Preacher shrugged. "Of course, the boy had some natural talent to begin with."

Moses said, "Mr. Preacher, do you think

you could teach me to shoot?"

"Hold on a minute," Jamie told him. "Moses, you never said anything to me about wanting to learn how to shoot."

"Well, it just seems so foreign to me. But the longer we stay out here on the frontier, the more it seems like maybe it's something I should learn how to do."

"Why, sure, I'd be glad to give you a few leetle pointers," Preacher said. "Don't go to thinkin' you'll ever be as good with a hogleg as Smoke is, though. To that boy, usin' a gun is just as natural as breathin'."

"I just want to be able to protect people who need to be protected," Moses said.

"That there's an honorable goal. There's a heap of bad folks in this world, and it falls to them who have good hearts to stand up to those varmints and do what's right. You got a gun?"

"Well . . . no."

Drawn by the shooting, Bodie walked up in time to hear most of the conversation. He grinned and unbuckled his gun belt. "You can borrow mine, Moses."

"Oh . . . all right. Thanks." Moses took the belt and rather awkwardly strapped it around his hips.

"Hitch that belt up a mite," Preacher told him. "Your holster's too low. You want the gun butt about halfway betwixt your wrist and your elbow, so when you raise your arm your hand'll hit it natural-like. Yeah, that's right," he went on as Moses adjusted the belt. "You saw that log Smoke was a-shootin' at. Pull that hogleg and see if you can hit it."

Moses faced the log, squared his shoulders, and took a deep breath. He made what he probably thought was a quick grab at the gun, although the move seemed painfully slow to Jamie's eyes.

The gun came clear of the holster, and Moses immediately exclaimed, "Whoa!" He grabbed it with his other hand to keep from dropping it. "It's heavy!"

"You'll get used to it," Preacher said. "It's a dang good thing that log ain't gonna be shootin' back at you. Now burn some powder, son!"

Moses pointed the revolver at the fallen tree. The barrel wobbled back and forth violently. He grunted as he tried to pull the trigger, but nothing happened.

Bodie said, "You've got to cock it. Pull the hammer back until it locks into place. Then pull the trigger."

"Oh," Moses said. "I didn't notice Smoke doing that —"

"That's because he does it too fast for the

eye to follow. But you can take your time, Moses."

"All right." Moses looped his right thumb over the hammer and pulled it back. The effort caused the barrel to point upward.

"Straighten it back down," Preacher said.

Still using both hands, Moses pointed the gun at the log. It was still pretty shaky. Seconds stretched out as Moses tried to get the barrel to stop jumping around enough that he could aim.

"Any time now," Preacher drawled.

Moses jerked the trigger.

The Colt boomed. The recoil forced the gun up, and Moses obviously wasn't ready for it. He yelled as the revolver flew out of his hands.

"Duck, boys!" Preacher shouted.

Jamie stepped forward and caught the gun before it could fall to the ground.

Moses had his hands clapped over his ears. "That was so *loud.* It sounds even louder when you're holding the gun."

"Here you go," Jamie said as he handed the weapon back to Moses. Quickly he pushed the barrel down toward the ground. "Don't point it at me or anybody else. Not unless it's somebody who needs shooting."

Moses squinted at the log. "Did I hit it?"

"You didn't even come close," Preacher

said. "Your bullet went ten or twelve feet over it, I reckon. Try again."

By now quite a crowd was gathering. Savannah, with Alexander and Abigail, was one of the spectators. She called, "You can do it, Moses!"

"Yeah!" Alexander added.

"I appreciate the vote of confidence," Moses said, "but I'm beginning to have my doubts."

"A man never knows until he tries," Jamie said. "Sometimes he has to try a bunch of times."

"You're right, of course." Moses took a deep breath and aimed at the fallen aspen again.

Fifteen minutes later, he had emptied the Colt, Bodie had reloaded it, and Moses had emptied it again. He had dropped the gun four times, nearly shot himself in the foot twice, and hadn't hit the log even once.

"Moses, ol' son, I hate to tell you this," Preacher drawled, "but you ain't cut out to be a pistoleer. I reckon if you was to find yourself in a gunfight, you'd be more of a danger to them who was on your side instead of the hombres you're supposed to ventilate."

Moses sighed and nodded. "I think you're right, Mr. Preacher." He unbuckled the gun belt. "I need to be a good sport about it, though. Not everyone can be good at everything."

"That's all right," Bodie told him as he took the Colt back. "You just leave the shooting to the rest of us."

Moses brightened and suggested, "Maybe I could learn how to use a rifle. Or a shotgun."

Jamie felt a shiver of apprehension go through him at the thought of Moses Danzig with a scattergun in his hands. "Not today. Back to your wagons, folks. It's time for us to be rolling again!"

CHAPTER FIFTY-SEVEN

The wagon train turned west a couple days later. If Jamie had figured correctly — and he was pretty sure he had — Eagle Valley was right in front of them, about two weeks' journey away.

Two more weeks for the good weather to hold, he mused as he rode in front of the wagon train. Would that be possible? Already winter had held off with its full force for longer than he had dared hope.

Not that it wasn't cold all the time. Every morning ice had to be broken off the top of the water buckets before the animals could drink. The sun shone most days, but its light was weak and watery and held only scant warmth. The temperature usually climbed above freezing, but not always. People lived in their coats now, not taking them off even at night when they crawled into their bed-rolls.

By the time they got where they were going, the whole lot of them would be pretty gamey, Jamie thought with a smile.

Bodie came up alongside him and waved a hand at the grasslands surrounding them. "It's mighty dry up here. Is there a drought going on?"

"No. The cold's killed all the grass, at least on top of the ground. The snows will come in and cover it up for several months, and then come spring when the snow melts, all that water will soak into the ground, down to the roots of the grass. That's when it'll start budding out again. Once these pilgrims get where they're going, they can plant winter grass next fall if they want to, so they'll have some graze for their livestock almost year-round. Anyway, as I recall, Eagle Valley has more and better vegetation to start with. The foothills get more rain in the spring and fall than the plains do."

Bodie squinted at the western horizon. "If Eagle Valley is in the foothills of the Rockies, like you said, Jamie, shouldn't we be able to see the mountains by now?"

"Be patient," Jamie told him. "You'll see 'em soon enough. When you do, it'll seem like you're never going to get there. They'll sit there in front of us for days without looking like they're getting any closer."

Jamie's prediction proved to be true. A

day later, the immigrants spotted what looked like low-lying white clouds in the distance. Jamie rode along the train to the Bradford wagon, which was being driven by Savannah, who had proven to be an adept hand at getting the oxen to move.

Jamie pointed to the west and said to Alexander and Abigail, "See those white patches up in the sky, way off over yonder? That's snow on top of the Rocky Mountains."

The children were impressed, and so was Savannah.

"It's beautiful," she said. "I never thought I'd see such a sight. When you spend your days in hotel rooms and your nights in a darkened theater, your idea of scenery is a painted backdrop. I like the real thing much better."

"You've changed a mite in the past couple months while we've been on the trail," Jamie said.

Savannah shook her head. "No. I've changed a lot. And all for the better, thanks to you, Mr. MacCallister."

"Not just thanks to me. A certain young fella had something to do with it, too."

Jamie couldn't be sure if Savannah's cheeks were red from the chilly wind . . . or if she was blushing a little, too. But she looked happy, and that was the main thing, he supposed, whatever the reason.

Savannah had gotten Alexander and Abigail nested down in a veritable mountain of blankets and quilts when she heard a soft footstep outside the wagon. The children were asleep, so she moved to the back of the vehicle and whispered through the gap around the canvas flap, "Who's there?"

"It's just me."

The voice was familiar, and it made warmth well up inside her. Not real, physical warmth, although that would have been more than welcome, but rather an emotional one that was quite comforting, anyway.

She climbed over the tailgate and out of the wagon, her movements hampered somewhat by the thick layers of clothing she wore. Bodie reached up, took hold of her under her arms, and helped her to the ground.

That made it easy for him to press her body against his as he hugged her. As many clothes as they both had on, there wasn't anything sensual about the embrace, but Savannah found it very satisfying, anyway.

And when he leaned down to kiss her . . . well, that *was* sensual, and it started her heart pounding harder as their lips clung together.

"I'm sure glad you decided not to leave the wagon train and go back to acting," he said quietly as they held each other and she rested her head against his chest.

"I miss Cyrus and Dollie and everybody else in the troupe," Savannah said. "I'd be lying if I said I didn't. One day I'd like to see them all again. But I've made so many friends here on the wagon train . . . Moses and Hector and the Binghams . . . and you. I can't imagine ever leaving now." She paused. "When we get to Eagle Valley . . . you're going to stay, aren't you, Bodie?"

"I've been talking to Captain Hendricks. I told him I want to claim a homestead, too. I've spent a lot of years on the drift, Savannah, ever since my folks died. I reckon it's time that I settled down."

He wouldn't have to find a homestead to claim, she thought. The one where Reverend Bradford had planned to settle with his children ought to be available. Savannah planned to see to it that Alexander and Abigail got what was coming to them, but they would need a grown-up to help them.

Maybe a couple grown-ups . . . a couple . . . and two children . . .

Well, that made a family, didn't it?

She didn't allow herself to say any of those

thoughts out loud. She didn't want to rush Bodie or pressure him into anything. But he was a smart man, she told herself. He would figure it out soon enough. If the idea hadn't occurred to him by the time the wagon train reached Eagle Valley, surely it would once they had been there a while.

Moses had conducted Reverend Bradford's funeral. Maybe he would be willing to perform a marriage ceremony, too.

The two of them held each other for a time, talking quietly and kissing now and then. Even though the night was very cold, the time they spent together was a pleasant interlude.

Finally Savannah said, "I need to get back in the wagon, I guess. If the weather was nicer —"

"But it's not," Bodie said. "One of these days it will be again, though. When that day comes, we'll spend a lot of time together and enjoy every minute of it."

"I can't wait." Savannah gave him another kiss and climbed into the wagon.

Bodie's heart was light as he walked back toward Moses's wagon. He had come mighty close to asking Savannah to marry him, but he wanted to wait for a better time. For one thing, he wanted to see the look on her face when he asked her that all-important question, and the night was too dark for that.

There would be plenty of chances to propose later, he told himself. Now that they had both decided to remain in Eagle Valley permanently, they had all the time in the world. That thought made him so happy he started whistling a tune. It wasn't a real song, just an irrepressible expression of how he felt at the moment.

It also served inadvertently to cover up the sound of a footstep behind him. He had no warning before something smashed into the back of his head, driving him to his knees.

Pain exploded inside his skull, pain so intense that it blinded him momentarily. He tried to fight his way to his feet, but somebody kicked him in the back and knocked him facedown on the ground. Weight came down on him, a knee digging painfully into the small of his back and pinning him there. An icy-cold ring of metal pressed into his temple.

He recognized it as the muzzle of a gun and stopped trying to struggle. He had no idea who had attacked him, but he sensed that his life was hanging by a slender thread. All that would be required to end it was a little pressure on the trigger. . . .

"That's better," a man said in a harsh whisper.

The voice was familiar, but Bodie couldn't place it right away. The man bent over closer to him, close enough for Bodie to smell the whiskey on his breath.

"Don't give me any trouble," the man went on, "and you might come out of this alive. But I wouldn't count on that, you dirty, stinkin' double-crosser."

Bodie knew the voice, knew who it was that had come out of the cold, dark night to wreck all his plans.

Eldon Swint.

Chapter Fifty-Eight

The outlaw wrapped the fingers of his left hand around Bodie's arm and hauled the young man to his feet, keeping the gun barrel pressed to Bodie's head.

Bodie tried to force his brain to work despite the throbbing in his skull and make some sense of what Swint had said. "Eldon, why are you doing this? I never double-crossed you! I told you I was leaving the gang. I even gave up my share of the loot."

Swint ground the gun barrel against Bodie's temple, making him gasp in pain. "You pretended to give up your share! I'll bet it was your idea for Lucas, Mahaffey, and Pearsoll to steal that whole pile of double eagles!"

Bodie's heart sank. Everything suddenly made sense. He knew why Jake and the other two had left the gang right after he did and had joined up with the wagon train.

He had considered Jake his friend and

didn't like to think that he was capable of such treachery, but Bodie's instincts told him it was true. Jake had been angling to get his hands on more than his fair share, right from the start. Clearly, he had come up with a way to do it.

Swint had figured out who was responsible for the loss of the loot, as well as where they had fled, and he had gotten on their trail like a bloodhound.

"You followed us all the way from Kansas City?"

"Damn right we did," Swint said. "Took us awhile to realize where that money must've gone, and we've run into nothin' but trouble chasin' you boys down. Fever hit the whole bunch of us and laid us low for a while. Killed a couple of the fellas. But the rest of us got over it, and now we've caught up to you at last, you no-good thief."

"Listen to me, Eldon," Bodie said, trying to make his voice as convincing as he possibly could. "I swear I didn't have anything to do with taking that money. I gave up my share, just like I told you back in Kansas City. That's the truth. All I wanted was to come with this wagon train."

"And be with your little whore of an actress." Swint laughed as Bodie stiffened. "Yeah, I know all about her. If you don't want somethin' mighty bad to happen to her as well as you, you'll tell me where the loot is."

"I don't know. I swear I don't."

Swint took the gun away from Bodie's temple, but before the young man could react, Swint raked the barrel across the side of his head in a vicious swipe. Bodie gasped as he felt blood well from the gash that the gun sight had opened up.

"I'll kill you, you damn fool," Swint grated. "You know that, don't you?"

It had been a mistake for him to ever think that Eldon Swint might not be as tough and brutal as he appeared to be, Bodie realized. The man was a ruthless hardcase, through and through, and would do anything to get what he wanted.

"If I knew, I'd tell you, Eldon. I really would. But I can't tell you something I don't know."

"Where's Lucas and the other two?"

Bodie hesitated. If he sold out Jake, Mahaffey, and Pearsoll, it would be the same thing as signing their death warrant. Swint intended to kill them.

But Swint intended to kill *him,* too. Bodie had no doubt about that. And he had threatened Savannah.

"You brought the whole gang with you?"

"That's right, except for the two the fever took. They're situated all around the camp, ready to open fire at my signal. We'll lay waste to this wagon train if we have to, Cantrell. You better believe it."

Bodie believed it, all right, and with a sinking feeling inside him, he realized the situation was worse than he had thought. Swint wouldn't want to leave any witnesses alive, and he wouldn't pass up whatever loot he could find in the wagons. A cold certainty came over Bodie, colder even than the frigid winter temperatures in Montana Territory.

Swint planned to wipe out everyone on the wagon train — Savannah, the kids, Moses, *everybody* — take everything of value from it, and probably burn the wagons behind him as a memorial to his evil.

To give himself time, Bodie took a deep breath and sighed. He suddenly realized Swint's mistake was not knowing who was accompanying the wagon train. He decided to go along with what Swint thought had happened. "Blast it, all right. I should've known all along that I couldn't fool you, Eldon. But just for the record, it was Jake's idea, not mine."

That was the truth, anyway.

"That don't surprise me none," Swint said. "I always thought Lucas was a sneaky little snake. Show me where the loot's hid and I'll let you live. Lucas and them other two got to die, though."

"Fine." The bitterness in Bodie's voice was genuine even if the sentiment he expressed was not. "He never should've been greedy and gotten us into this mess."

"Damn right. Now move, and don't forget that I'll blow your brains out if you try anything funny. I don't really need you. It'll be easier if you show me where the money is, but I'll find it one way or another."

"There's a false bottom in one of the wagons," Bodie said, his brain working furiously as he formulated his plan. It would take a considerable amount of luck to make it work, but he didn't really have any other choice. "It's over here."

With the gun still at his head, he stumbled toward the wagon where Moses was asleep.

Moses . . . and Jamie Ian MacCallister.

Jamie didn't sleep as well as he once had. It was just part of growing older. The cold didn't help matters, either. He felt it more as it seeped into his bones and made them ache and his muscles grow stiff. He was half-awake as footsteps approached the wagon.

Something was off about them. The gait

458

was wrong, causing Jamie's instincts to warn him. Instantly, he was fully awake and alert. His hands reached out in the darkness and unerringly closed around the butts of the .44s he had placed where he could get to them easily.

He rose up, a massive, bearlike shape in the shadows inside the wagon, and moved silently to the rear of the vehicle. Using the barrel of one gun, he moved the canvas flap aside slightly. Two men were coming toward the wagon, one of them stumbling slightly like he was drunk. The other man held his arm as if the first man had imbibed too much.

As clouds moved away from the moon, Jamie saw the second man holding a gun and knew the first man wasn't drunk. Something was very wrong.

The first man said, "I'll show you how to get into that false bottom in the wagon. The loot's hidden there. You've got to give me your word, though, Eldon, that you and the rest of the gang won't hurt anybody."

"Nobody but Lucas, Mahaffey, and Pearsoll," the second man said.

Jamie knew he was lying. He could hear it in the man's voice.

"Those double-crossers got to die."

"Fine, but you've got to get word to the

men hidden outside the camp not to open fire," the first man said.

Jamie recognized the voice. It belonged to Bodie Cantrell. He was doing a good job of letting him know what was going on.

"That's enough jabberin'," the other man snapped. "Anybody in that wagon?"

"No, it's mine. I took it over after the fella who had it died of a fever, too. The same sickness hit us. After that happened, I fixed up the false bottom and hid those sacks of double eagles in it."

"All right, open it up. I want to see that loot of mine . . . and then get down to business."

Killing business, Jamie thought. He could hear the bloodlust in the man's voice.

They were right outside the wagon. It was time to make his move.

Jamie swept the canvas aside and bellowed, "Hit the dirt, Bodie!" He came out of the wagon like a whirlwind, both guns extended in front of him.

Bodie rammed an elbow back into his captor's body and twisted away just as Swint pulled the trigger. Flame spouted from the gun muzzle. Bodie cried out as if he were hit.

Jamie didn't have time to check on him.

He was too busy killing the viper in their midst.

Both .44s roared as he thumbed off shot after shot. Tongues of flame a foot long licked out from the gun barrels. Eldon was tough and stayed on his feet for a moment as Jamie's bullets pounded into him. He even got another shot off, the slug whining harmlessly over Jamie's head.

Then the lead storm took its toll. Eldon went over backwards, shot to pieces.

Jamie rammed the revolvers behind his belt, reached back into the wagon, and plucked his Winchester from the floor. He levered a round into the chamber as he shouted, "Preacher! Smoke! Outlaws around the camp!"

He leaped over a wagon tongue and plunged into the night, ready to do battle. He didn't know how many outlaws were hiding around the camp, but with him, Preacher, and Smoke going after them, to say nothing of Audie and Nighthawk . . .

Well, however many there were, the varmints were outnumbered.

They just didn't know it yet.

CHAPTER FIFTY-NINE

The next few minutes were flame-streaked chaos. Hidden gunmen opened fire on Jamie, and he returned the shots with deadly effect. He hoped all the immigrants were keeping their heads down while the fight raged.

The battle ringed the camp. Jamie heard a rapid fusillade of six-gun fire and figured that was Smoke Jensen getting in on the action. He didn't think anybody else could keep a pair of hoglegs singing that fast.

The Winchester's magazine ran dry. As it did, a man leaped up from the ground nearby and ran at Jamie, thrusting out a gun, eager for a sure shot.

Jamie ducked as the blast rang out, then stepped in to meet the charge. He drove the rifle's butt into the man's face and heard the satisfying crunch of bone. The outlaw dropped like a rock.

"Jamie, look out!" someone called.

Jamie twisted and crouched, and another shot blasted close enough he felt the heat from the muzzle. Before he could do anything else, Bodie appeared, the gun in his hand flaming. The outlaw who had nearly ventilated Jamie went down, twisted off his feet by Bodie's shots.

"Glad to see you're all right," Jamie told the young man.

"Muzzle flash nearly burned my eyebrows off," Bodie said, "but the bullet missed and that's all that counts."

"You're right about that. Let's finish cleaning up these rats . . . and then you'll have to tell me what this is all about."

Just as Jamie expected, the outlaws were no match for the fighting men from the wagon train. Hector Gilworth and Jess Neville had joined in the battle, too, and had given a good account of themselves. Jess might claim to be lazy, but he had tackled two of the gunmen in a fierce shootout and brought them both down, taking a bullet through his left arm in the process. Hector had gotten his hands on one of the outlaws and broken the man's neck.

Preacher, Smoke, Audie, and Nighthawk wiped out the rest of the gang in short order. They weren't the sort of men who asked for or gave quarter, especially when faced with human vermin. By the time they finished sweeping in a big circle around the wagon train, the plains were littered with owlhoot corpses.

Then, as Jamie had told Bodie, it was time for explanations.

The main campfire in the center of the circle was built up until it was blazing brightly and casting light over the gathering. The first thing Bodie did was look around for Jake Lucas, Clete Mahaffey, and Dave Pearsoll.

There was no sign of the three men.

They must have realized what was going on and taken advantage of the confusion to slip away, Jamie decided once Bodie had revealed that they were all former members of Eldon Swint's outlaw gang and spilled the story about the stolen loot.

"I'm sorry, Savannah," Bodie said to the young woman as she stared solemnly at him. A blood-stained bandage was wrapped around his head where Swint had pistol-whipped him. "I hoped you'd never find out about my past. I'm ashamed that I ever got mixed up with a bunch of owlhoots like that."

For a long moment, Savannah didn't say anything. Then, "You could have told me,

Bodie. I thought you trusted me more than that."

"I do trust you," he insisted. "I just didn't want you to think bad of me."

"I've seen what you're really like these past weeks." Savannah looked around at the rest of the immigrants. "We all have. You risked your life to save Abigail and Alexander. You've been a good friend to everybody on this wagon train. I'm sure you've made some mistakes, done some things you regret and wish you could take back . . . but everyone has. I know I have." She shook her head. "But it doesn't make me feel any differently toward you."

Relief washed over Bodie's face. "Thank the Lord! I was afraid you'd hate me when you found out the truth."

Savannah shook her head, moved closer to Bodie, and laid a hand on his arm. "I could never hate you."

Jamie stepped between them and the rest of the crowd, putting his back to the two young people so they could have a moment of privacy as he addressed the group. "Hector, we need to get some horses and rope and drag those carcasses well away from the wagons. I reckon the wolves will take care of them after that."

Moses made a face. "Is it really necessary

to deal with them in such a callous manner, Jamie?"

"The ground's too hard to dig a grave big enough for all of them."

Preacher added, "I wouldn't be inclined to go to that much trouble for such a bunch of polecats, anyway. Nature's got its own way of dealin' with varmints like that, and I don't figure on losin' a second's sleep over how they end up."

"What about those other three Bodie mentioned?" Smoke asked. "The ones who made off with that money to start with and started all this trouble."

A grim smile touched Jamie's mouth. "I thought you and me and Preacher might take a little hunting trip."

"That sounds like a mighty fine idea to me," the old mountain man said with a savage grin of his own on his grizzled face.

"I told you we should've gotten far away from that wagon train a long time ago," Clete Mahaffey groused as the three men rode through the dawn light.

"Yeah, and you've said that how many times since we lit out?" Jake Lucas shot back at him.

Dave Pearsoll said, "Look, we're all lucky to be alive. If Swint had gone after us first

466

instead of Cantrell, we probably wouldn't be. We've still got the loot, so let's count our blessings. We're on our own now, and from the sound of the shooting back there when we rode out, at least some of Swint's gang have to be dead. Maybe all of 'em if they went up against MacCallister, Preacher, and that Smoke kid."

Pearsoll had a point, Jake thought. If he was being really honest with himself, he had to admit that he had hung around the wagon train for as long as he had only because of Savannah McCoy.

Even after the unsatisfying incident along the creek where the Bradford kids had been snatched by the Blackfeet, he had harbored feelings for her. Clearly, though, the little tramp was never going to see that she ought to be with him instead of Bodie, so staying with the wagons was a waste of time.

Hell, he was a rich man, he mused. He could find all the willing women he wanted. Women a lot better looking than Savannah McCoy . . .

He wasn't convinced of the truth of that last part, but he could tell himself that, anyway.

Fate had taken a hand and forced their separation from the pilgrims.

Jake said, "You know, I've heard about a

place over in Idaho we ought to look for, a settlement called Bury. From the sound of it, gents like us are welcome there."

"Bury?" Mahaffey repeated. "What sort of name is that for a town?"

"Don't know and don't care, as long as that's not what they do to us there," Jake said with a grin. He didn't feel too bad any longer.

Sure, it was bothersome that Eldon Swint had trailed them all that way. But luck had been on Jake's side, as it always was, and he was convinced that Swint and the other outlaws had been wiped out in the fighting around the wagon train. From here on out, he and his two pards could just enjoy life.

He died with the grin still on his face as an arrow struck him between the shoulder blades with such force that its flint head drove all the way through his body and ripped out from his chest. Jake's body toppled loosely from the saddle and hit the ground beside the spooked horse as shots, war cries, and, ultimately, screams filled the cold morning air.

CHAPTER SIXTY

Preacher sniffed the air. "I don't know about you fellas, but that smells like snow to me."

The morning had dawned clear as Jamie, Preacher, and Smoke set out on the trail of the three outlaws, but thick gray clouds soon had moved down from the north, obscuring the sun and making the cold wind seem more frigid.

"Yeah," Jamie agreed with the old mountain man's prediction. "Not today, I don't reckon, but it wouldn't surprise me to see some snow tonight."

"How far you reckon we are from Eagle Valley?" Preacher asked as he squinted at the sky.

"Three days, maybe. I've known we were getting close for a while now, but I didn't tell those pilgrims just yet."

Smoke said, "I'm pretty sure this is December twenty-first."

The two older men looked at him.

Smoke's broad shoulders rose and fell in a shrug. "Just pointing out that three more days will be Christmas Eve. You said you wanted to get there by Christmas, Jamie." A rare smile touched the young man's face. "You're cutting it a mite close."

"Yeah, but Bodie and Hector will keep those wagons moving as fast as they can until we get back."

Preacher suddenly drew back on his reins and frowned. "Danged if I don't smell somethin' else now. And it ain't nothin' good, neither."

Jamie and Smoke reined in, too. Jamie took a deep breath, and his face was as grim as Preacher's. "Gun smoke."

They hadn't heard any gunfire. Whatever had happened was over, leaving only faint traces in the air.

All three men drew their rifles and laid them across the saddles in front of them, then rode forward, still following the tracks. The trail led over a gently rolling hill. As they crested it, they brought their mounts to a halt again.

About a hundred yards in front of them, at the bottom of the grassy slope, lay three bloody, huddled shapes that had once been human.

Jamie took a pair of field glasses from one of his saddlebags and used them to study the dead men. They had been scalped and mutilated. The blood that covered their faces was already freezing in the cold air.

"Is that the three we're after?" Smoke asked.

"Just going by what's left of them, that's hard to say," Jamie replied. "But I recognize the clothes. That's Lucas, Mahaffey, and Pearsoll, all right."

Preacher said, "From the looks of 'em, they run into a bunch of Blackfeet. Might be the leavin's from those war parties we scrapped with awhile back."

Jamie grunted. "Let's take a closer look."

They rode forward, eyes constantly scanning the landscape around them for any sign of an attack. Jamie spotted a double eagle lying on the prairie and pointed it out.

"The Blackfeet scattered that money those fellas had with them," he said. "They let the earth have it. That's their way of showing it didn't mean anything to them."

Jamie's instincts told him that the Indians were gone. They'd had their brutal sport with the three luckless outlaws and then moved on.

The question was, where had they gone?

Once Jamie got a closer look at the bodies,

he was convinced that they were Lucas, Mahaffey, and Pearsoll. The gruesome sight didn't particularly bother him; he had seen plenty of violent death in his time.

What worried him were the tracks of the unshod ponies they found around the mutilated corpses. He gestured toward the hoofprints. "Looks like there were forty or fifty Blackfeet. That's more than we left alive in that battle."

"The ones who got away met up with some of their pards," Preacher suggested.

"And then what?" Smoke asked.

Jamie rode in a big circle and found tracks moving away from the place where the three outlaws had been killed. He pointed them out to his two companions. "It looks to me like they angled off on a course that'll cross the path of the wagon train."

"Chances are that was what they was after all along," Preacher said. "They're mad about gettin' whipped before, and they're goin' after the whole wagon train this time. They just happened to run across these three varmints along the way and took advantage of the chance to kill 'em."

"Come on," Jamie said as he wheeled Sundown. "We'd better get back there as fast as we can."

A grim hunch filled him as he rode, a

hunch that said they might already be too late.

Bodie rode out in front of the wagons with Audie and Nighthawk. He enjoyed talking to the little mountain man, who seemed to know something about almost everything. No matter what the subject was, Audie could converse on it. Bodie didn't always fully understand what the former professor was saying, but it was interesting, anyway.

"And that's why I believe it's imminently possible that life may exist on other planets in our solar system," Audie said. "If we can ever develop telescopes powerful enough to study them more closely, we may see the evidence of great civilizations with our own eyes. Don't you agree, Nighthawk?"

"Ummm," said the Crow warrior.

"Yes, but you like to argue just on general principles, my friend. You'll see, one of these days. The evidence will prove me correct, as it always does."

"So, let me get this straight," Bodie said. "You're saying there are people like us on other planets?"

"Well . . . not necessarily like us. Different conditions might produce different sorts of life. But they could still be self-aware and highly intelligent. More intelligent than we are, perhaps."

"Wouldn't that be something?" Bodie mused. "I'm not sure I'd want to meet a man from another planet."

"I would," Audie said. "I would consider it a great privilege and honor, not to mention the most scientifically intriguing encounter of our age or any other."

"Ummm," Nighthawk said.

Audie turned to frown at his friend. "What do you mean, we have bigger prob— Oh, Lord. Bodie, look at that."

The three men reined in. Bodie's breath seemed to freeze in his throat as he saw the dozens of mounted figures on a rise to their left. Even at that distance, his keen eyes could make out the feathers in their hair.

"Blackfeet," Audie said. "We need to get back to the wagons — *now!*"

The three men wheeled their horses and kicked them into a gallop. As they raced back toward the wagons, Nighthawk pointed to a group of Indians closing in from the other direction.

"Make some racket!" Bodie yelled. "We've got to warn the train!"

They pulled their guns and started firing into the air. Bodie was confident that Hector Gilworth would hear the shots and order the immigrants to stop and pull the wagons into a defensive circle.

He glanced over his shoulder at the pursuit and saw puffs of smoke as the Indians opened fire on them. At that range, shooting from the back of their ponies, the likelihood of any of those bullets finding their targets was extremely small, but Bodie couldn't rule out pure bad luck, though. His muscles were tense as he halfway anticipated the shock of a slug hitting him.

The wagons came into sight. He felt a surge of relief when he saw that they were already forming into a circle, just as he'd hoped. The Blackfoot war party was a large one, but the men of the wagon train had some experience at fighting Indians. They would give the Blackfeet a hot reception.

In fact, shots had already begun to crackle from between the parked wagons by the time Bodie, Audie, and Nighthawk reached the train. They leaped their horses through one of the gaps as gunfire and shrill war whoops filled the air and lead tore through the canvas covers on some of the wagons. Hector Gilworth ran along the line of wagons, bellowing, "Everybody keep your head down!"

Bodie threw himself out of the saddle, dragging his Winchester from its sheath, and looked around frantically for Savannah. He spotted the wagon she had been driving and ran toward it, but before he could get there he heard Jess Neville shout, "Bodie! Over here! Those red devils are chargin'!"

Bodie swung around and saw a large group of Blackfeet thundering toward a gap in the circle. If they broke through and got inside, it would be bloody chaos. Bodie sprang to join Jess and several other men in defending the opening. He brought the rifle to his shoulder and began firing as fast as he could work the lever. Clouds of powder smoke rolled around him, stinging his eyes and nose, and the constant roar of shots deafened him.

The savages wouldn't get through, he vowed to himself. They would never reach Savannah or any of the other women and children. He would stop them.

Or die trying.

CHAPTER SIXTY-ONE

Jamie, Preacher, and Smoke heard the shooting before they came in sight of the wagon train. The immigrants had had a little warning, because they'd been able to pull the wagons into a loose circle. They were defending that stronghold from at least fifty Blackfoot warriors who were galloping their ponies around and around the circle.

Jamie drew rein and lifted his rifle. "Let's see if we can pick some of them off and even the odds a little."

Three Winchesters cracked as the frontiersmen opened fire. With all the shooting already going on, the Blackfeet didn't notice right away that some of the bullets were coming from a different direction. That gave the three men a chance to do some real damage before they were discovered.

Jamie fired, saw a warrior throw up his arms and pitch to the ground from his pony's back as the .44-40 slug bored through him. By the time that Blackfoot hit the ground, Jamie had worked the repeater's lever and shifted his aim. The Winchester blasted again, and another of the attackers fell.

The shots from Preacher and Smoke were just as deadly. Nearly a dozen members of the war party died before the Blackfeet realized what was going on. Shrieking in outrage, a group of them peeled off and charged toward the three men.

"Time for us to light a shuck," Preacher drawled as he slid his rifle back in its saddle boot.

"I want to get back to the wagons," Jamie said. "Let's take them by surprise and plow right through them."

"Sounds good to me." Smoke pulled both Colts from their holsters.

Preacher did likewise.

Jamie filled his hands with his .44s and dug his boot heels into Sundown's flanks. The big stallion leaped forward.

It was a mad, outrageous maneuver, filled with gun thunder, swirling clouds of powder smoke, pounding hoofbeats, and the constant whine of bullets slashing through the air around them. The three men never broke off in their advance, smashing into the group of Blackfeet and scattering them. The hail of lead from six revolvers shredded through the warriors, and several of those who escaped being ventilated were knocked from their ponies and trampled.

As Jamie's Colts ran dry, a mounted Blackfoot with his face painted dashed in from the side and thrust a lance at him. Jamie twisted away from the deadly weapon and as the warrior came within arm's length, Jamie reversed his left-hand Colt and crashed the butt into the man's forehead, crushing it and driving bone splinters into the man's brain. He grabbed the lance away from the dying warrior.

Preacher and Smoke were slowed down by hand-to-hand battles, but they broke through and galloped toward the wagons. Jamie was right behind them. As he charged past another of the Blackfeet, he threw the lance like a spear. His massive strength put so much power behind the throw that it tore all the way through the man's torso and stood out a foot on the other side.

The wagon train's defenders saw them coming and intensified their fire, giving cover to the three men. One after another they leaped their horses over a wagon tongue and into the circle.

As they piled off their horses and ran to join the defenders, Bodie, who was a couple wagons over, called to them, "You got back just in time!"

"Durn right we did!" Preacher responded. "We was about to miss all the fun!"

If it was "fun" the old mountain man wanted, he got plenty of it for the next few hours. With their initial charge beaten back and their numbers cut into by the unexpected attack by Jamie, Preacher, and Smoke, the Blackfeet settled down to a waiting game, continually circling the wagons just out of easy rifle range. From time to time, some of them would dash in and concentrate heavy fire on one part of the wagon train, then pull back sharply as the immigrants mounted a stronger defense at that position. Then, mere moments later, the Indians would attack somewhere else.

The Blackfeet suffered losses with each foray, but so did the immigrants. Several men were killed, and a dozen more were wounded.

During the afternoon, Jamie was able to talk to Bodie and tell him about finding the bodies of Jake Lucas, Clete Mahaffey, and Dave Pearsoll.

Bodie sighed and shook his head solemnly. "I know that they nearly got all of us killed and that Jake never could be trusted after all, but there was a time when I considered him a friend, Jamie. I don't think he was all bad. He was just too weak where money was concerned."

"Most folks have their weak spots. You've just got to learn how to keep from breaking at those spots."

"I suppose. I'm sorry for what happened to Jake, anyway." Bodie's voice hardened. "But if I'd had the chance, I might have shot him myself."

"Reckon I know the feeling."

Moses kept busy bringing water and ammunition to the defenders. At one point in the afternoon as he handed a box of cartridges to Jamie, he said, "I wish now I'd been able to learn how to shoot. I feel like I'm useless."

"Not hardly." Jamie hefted the box of ammunition. "I didn't have to go fetch this myself. I was able to keep fighting."

"Remember what Preacher said when he was trying to teach me? Maybe I should volunteer to fight on the side of the Blackfeet. Then they'd be wiped out for sure!"

Jamie laughed. "You stay right where you are, Moses. We need you to send up a few prayers for us."

"I can do that," Moses said. "In fact, I have been for several hours now!"

A short time later, during a lull in the

fighting, Preacher came over to Jamie. "What do you reckon the chances are they'll give up once the sun goes down?"

Jamie glanced at the sky where the thickening clouds meant that it would get dark earlier than usual. "I got my doubts." Something caught his eye, and he pointed it out to Preacher. "Even more so now."

"Dadgum it!" Preacher exclaimed as he looked at the column of gray smoke that was starting to thicken and climb into the equally leaden sky. "You don't think they've started a prairie fire, do you?"

"No. I think they've started more than one," Jamie replied grimly as he pointed out several more clouds of smoke in different directions. "They're putting a ring of fire around us, Preacher. If they can't kill us one way, they'll do it another."

"We got to get movin'. If we just sit here whilst them blazes join up with each other and completely surround us, we'll never get out. All that grass is dry as tinder this time of year."

"I know," Jamie said with a nod. "But if we start to hitch up the teams, the Blackfeet will come charging in while we're busy with that and overrun us."

Preacher's eyes narrowed. "Not if some of us keep the varmints busy."

"You mean take the fight to them again?" Jamie pondered the idea for a second, then nodded. "The ones who do that probably won't stand a chance, but the wagons might be able to get away. I seem to recall there's a little river a mile or two from here. If the wagons can get on the other side of it before the fire pins them in, those folks could make it."

"Well, I'm goin', that's for durn sure," Preacher declared.

"So am I," added Smoke, who had come up in time to hear the two older men formulating the plan.

"We'll need seven or eight other men," Jamie said, "all of them volunteers." He sighed. "I'll spread the word."

Everybody had seen the smoke and was worried about it. Within a few minutes, Jamie had put together a force of volunteers who would attack the Blackfeet and keep them occupied while the wagons made a dash for the river.

It wasn't a surprise that Bodie was one of the volunteers. Savannah clung to him for a long moment, sobbing, but she didn't beg him not to go.

Bodie was relieved by that. She had Alexander and Abigail to think of, and anything that gave the children a better chance of getting through this ordeal alive had to be done.

Hector and Jess were going along, too, as was Captain Lamar Hendricks. "These people elected me to lead them. I don't know of any better way to do it than to do whatever I can to see that they get where they're going."

"I wasn't too sure about you starting out, Cap'n," Jamie said. "I reckon you'll do, though. Yes, sir, you'll do."

Half a dozen more men joined the group. They were all mounted and ready to charge out of the circle. Edward Bingham had been put in charge of getting the teams hitched up and leading the race to the river. He shook hands with Jamie. "Buy us some time, Mr. MacCallister. We'll do the rest."

"Never doubted it," Jamie said.

They were just about ready to launch the counterattack when Moses appeared, also mounted on a saddle horse and carrying a rifle.

"Blast it, Moses!" Bodie exclaimed. "You shouldn't be doing this."

"We're causing a distraction, right? Keeping the Indians busy? I can give them something to shoot at. Don't worry, I won't shoot any of you by accident." Moses grinned. "This rifle isn't even loaded!"

Jamie moved Sundown over next to Moses's horse. "You've been a mighty good friend to all of us, and I appreciate what you're trying to do here. You ready, Moses?"

Moses swallowed hard and nodded. "I'm ready."

"Good." Jamie's arm shot out and he hit Moses in the jaw, a crashing, big-fisted blow that knocked the young rabbi out of the saddle and sent him sprawling on the ground, out cold. "Somebody put him in a wagon. I reckon he'll forgive me when this is all over."

He turned to the other men, looped Sundown's reins around the saddle horn, and drew both revolvers. With a rebel yell, he sent the stallion lunging forward and led the attack as the men galloped toward the startled Blackfeet, guns blazing.

CHAPTER SIXTY-TWO

It was even more loco than the earlier dash through the war party ringed around the wagon train. They were outnumbered at least three to one.

But the Blackfeet weren't the same sort of fighters on horseback that, say, the Sioux or the Comanche were. More used to battling on foot, they didn't respond quite as quickly as they might have. The men from the wagon train were among them almost before the Blackfeet knew what was happening.

Not only that, but Jamie Ian MacCallister, the old mountain man called Preacher, and the young gunfighter named Smoke Jensen were veritable engines of destruction. The guns in their hands roared again and again, left, right, left, right, and each time flame spouted from the muzzle of a Colt, one of the warriors cried out and died as a bullet ripped through him.

Bodie, Hector, and Jess fought savagely,

desperately, too. So did Captain Hendricks and all the other men. Seeing their fellow warriors being slaughtered, the rest of the Blackfeet closed in, surrounding the men from the wagon train. Jamie couldn't see the wagons anymore, but he hoped they were on the move.

Truthfully, he couldn't see much of anything because of all the smoke around him. Suddenly, he realized that it wasn't all powder smoke.

Like a runaway freight train, a wall of flames swept over the top of a hill and barreled down on the fighting men.

Some of the Blackfeet were too slow to get out of the way, and the fire engulfed their shrieking forms. The rest of the war party broke and ran. Their strategy had worked too well. The thick grass was so dry the flames had moved faster than they'd expected.

The smoke made the horses panicky. Jamie fought to control Sundown and hauled the big stallion around. He waved an empty gun at Preacher and Smoke and shouted, "Head for the river!" He spotted Bodie, Hector, and Jess and repeated the command to them, then rounded up the rest of the men from the wagon train. Some of them were wounded, but managed to stay

in their saddles as they fled from the onrushing flames. Those who had been shot off
their horses lay lifelessly on the prairie.

Jamie saw the wagons moving fast up
ahead. The sky was filled with smoke, and
the oxen and mules pulling the wagons were
as frightened as the horses were. Every
instinct they possessed told them to flee,
and they were doing it rapidly.

Jamie galloped past the Bingham wagon
in the lead and saw the line of trees that
marked the course of the river. But he also
saw fires closing in from both sides. His
heart sank as he realized they weren't going
to make it. The flames seemed to race
toward each other with supernatural
speed . . . and the gap he had counted on
closed, forming a fiery, impenetrable wall.

Groaning, he hauled back on the reins.
Despite everything they had done, the
wagon train was completely surrounded by
barriers of flame and smoke. Most of the
flames were still half a mile or more away,
but it wouldn't take long for them to continue their inexorable advance until that
whole part of the country was burning, with
the wagons and the immigrants right in the
middle of the inferno.

The sky overhead was black as midnight
from the smoke and the clouds, but the

plains and the hills were lit up by the blazes so it looked like the landscape of hell. Jamie wheeled Sundown and saw that the wagons had come to a stop. So had the men who had attacked the Blackfeet. Everyone realized that they were trapped. There was no way out.

They had come so far only to meet a fiery death days before the holiest time of the year.

Jamie rode back to the wagons, not getting in any hurry. His eyes searched the landscape around him, what he could see between the clouds of smoke, anyway. He didn't see any sign of the Blackfeet. Any of them who had survived the battle had either been swallowed up by the fire or managed to find a way out, so they were on the other side of the flames and no longer a threat.

Seeing quite a few people gathered beside the Bingham wagon, Jamie headed for them. He dismounted, and the crowd parted to reveal Jess Neville lying on the ground with his head pillowed on Savannah's lap. She was crying. Bodie and Hector knelt on either side of Jess. Burly, bearded Hector was bawling like a baby.

"D-don't worry about it," Jess said in a weak voice.

Jamie hadn't noticed him being wounded

before, but Jess's coat was pulled back and the shirt underneath it was sodden with blood.

Jess went on. "The way I look at it . . . I'm finally gonna get plenty of . . . rest now."

Hector took his cousin's hand and held it tightly. He said in a voice choked with emotion, "That's right, Jess. You just rest. You . . . you've got it comin'."

"Yeah . . . just a nice long . . . sleep . . ." Jess's eyes closed, and a final sigh came from him.

Bodie reached over and squeezed Hector's shoulder. "I'm sorry, Hector. He was a heck of a fine fella."

Moses came up behind Hector. The young rabbi had a bruise forming on his jaw, courtesy of Jamie's fist earlier. He rested a hand on Hector's other shoulder. "He died trying to save us all. No man could ask for a more honorable end."

"I reckon not," Hector agreed with a heavy sigh. He lifted his head and looked around. "But it won't be long before all of us are crossing over the divide, will it?"

One of the men burst out, "I can't stand this! We're all going to burn to death! I won't let that happen to my wife and kids. Where's my gun? I . . . I'll end it for all of us!"

Jamie grabbed the man's arm and jerked him around. "No, you won't. Nobody's going to give up hope. Not yet."

"But we're trapped," someone else said. "The fire's all around us. We can't get away."

"No, but look at the smoke," Jamie insisted. He had just noticed something. "It's going almost straight up now. That means the wind isn't blowing as hard. If the wind's not blowing as hard, the fire won't move as fast."

"So it gets here in fifteen minutes instead of five," one of the men said bitterly. "What difference does that make?"

"That's ten more minutes to say goodbye," Jamie said. And ten more minutes to hope for a miracle, he thought.

He was a pragmatic man, always had been. He looked at life as it was, not as he wished it could be. He had stared death in the face on many, many occasions. He knew that when his time was up, his days on earth were going to come to an end.

But he also knew that when that time came, he would lie down for his eternal rest next to his beloved Kate. They would be together again, never to be separated. He knew that with every fiber of his being — which meant that it couldn't be the end. It just couldn't.

Blamed if he could see any way out, though.

He stood there as the immigrants slowly dispersed, going back to their wagons to be with their families for what they believed would be their final minutes on earth. He saw Bodie huddling with Savannah, Alexander, and Abigail.

"You reckon this is the end of the trail?" Preacher asked from beside him.

Jamie looked over at the old mountain man and shook his head. "No. For some reason, I don't."

"Neither do I," said Smoke, who came up on Preacher's other side. "I've still got too much to do."

Audie said, "We all know Preacher here is just too stubborn to die."

"Ummm," Nighthawk added.

They stood there together, five of the more formidable fighting men the West had ever known. Between them they had killed hundreds of badmen, had risked their lives to protect the innocent countless times, had seen things and done things that few other men ever had. Even though Smoke Jensen was still young, he was one of them as much as any man could be. It was bred into his blood. If Smoke survived, Jamie was sure he would go on to carve the most illustrious career of them all.

The flames crept closer.

"Dang, I'm sure glad we got to fight side by side again, you ol' hoss," Preacher said.

"I am, too," Jamie whispered.

Something touched his cheek.

He lifted his head. It wasn't an ember that had come swirling down from the sky to land on his rugged face. That would have been hot. The thing that had touched his cheek was . . . cold. Then he felt another and another.

Preacher said, "What in tarnation?"

Jamie looked up into the sky and saw more of the fat white flakes, heavy with moisture as they tumbled down from the heavens. Dozens, no, hundreds, thousands, millions, were falling almost straight down because there was no wind, already blanketing the ground.

A smile spread across his face. "It's snowing."

Chapter Sixty-Three

It wasn't a blizzard, but the snow fell so thickly that it was hard to see more than a few feet ahead. At first, the terrific heat of the fire melted the snow as it fell and vaporized the water, but there were just too many flakes. When the flames reached the unburned ground that was covered with a couple inches of snow, they couldn't go any farther. Soon they began to sizzle and go out.

The danger was over. It might not be Christmas yet, Jamie reflected as he stood with his friends and watched their salvation piling up whitely on the ground, but it was sure close enough to call it a Christmas miracle.

Moses, Bodie, Savannah, and the Bradford children came to stand with the frontier men. Jamie rested a big hand on Moses's shoulder. "You were the most valuable fighter of us all, amigo."

"How do you figure that?"

"You fought for us with your prayers." Jamie swept his other hand at the deepening snow. "If this isn't an answered prayer, I don't know what is."

By morning, the snow was a couple feet deep, completely blanketing the landscape so that there was only a vast expanse of pristine white around the wagon train. The ugly swath of black, burned ground was hidden underneath the snow.

Jamie worried that if the drifts got much deeper, the wagons wouldn't be able to move. They would be stuck there, maybe for weeks.

The snow stopped falling not long after dawn. It would slow the wagons' progress, but it wouldn't stop them. They could still push on to Eagle Valley.

The immigrants took half a day to bury Jess Neville and the other men who had been killed in the fighting. Some of the bodies were badly burned from the prairie fire, which made the grisly task even worse. It wasn't easy chipping graves out of the frozen ground, but they did it.

With the sun starting to peek through the thinning overcast, they moved on, bound for their new homes.

Late in the afternoon of December 24, 1873, Jamie Ian MacCallister reined Sundown to a halt at the top of a saddle between two hills and looked down into a broad, fairly level valley bounded by wooded slopes on the north and south. The valley stretched for fifteen miles before more hills gradually rose into the snowcapped peaks looming over it. A twisting line of trees showed the course of the stream that meandered through the valley. Frozen over now, come spring it would thaw and water the land, turning it into a verdant oasis. Protected from the worst of winter's storms by the heights around it and fertile in the summer, Eagle Valley was one of the prettiest places Jamie had ever seen. It would make a fine home for the pilgrims in the wagon train rolling slowly up the trail behind him.

He looked to his right and saw a lone pine tree growing there. Snow dusted its branches. A smile spread slowly across his weather-beaten face as he looked at the tree.

Bodie rode up to him. "What are you thinking, Jamie?"

"I'm thinking we'll camp right here tonight. It's Christmas Eve, and there's our tree. We'll celebrate here and thank the Good Lord for getting us this far."

"That's a fine idea," Bodie agreed. "I'll go tell the others." He turned his horse and rode back to the wagons.

Jamie stayed where he was, resting his hands on the saddle horn, easing weary bones and muscles. He looked up at the mountains and the towering vault of sky above them. "I figured it was loco, starting out with those pilgrims so late in the year, but that was Your plan all along, wasn't it? You got us through, and now You'll watch over these folks while they make their homes here. I'm glad I could be a part of it."

The children improvised decorations and tied them to the branches of the little pine tree. Everyone gathered around that evening and sang hymns and Christmas carols. As the strains of "Silent Night" drifted out across the valley, Jamie walked over to Moses, who stood watching silently.

"Must be sort of hard on you, seeing them like this when your faith doesn't agree with what they're doing," Jamie commented.

"Hard?" Moses smiled and shook his head. "Not at all. I'm happy for them. They have their beliefs to sustain them, just as I have mine. The differences . . . well, right now they're not as important as the things we all have in common. Love one another, your scriptures say, and that's what matters the most."

"Remember when I told you you'd do to ride the river with, Moses? I reckon that's more true than ever."

"And you as well, my friend. We've been to see the elephant together, haven't we, Jamie?"

Jamie laughed and slapped Moses on the back. "You're learning, amigo. You're learning."

They were still standing there a few minutes later when Bodie and Savannah came over to them. Bodie shook hands with Jamie and Moses. "We've got a favor to ask of you, Moses."

"Anything," Moses answered without hesitation.

"We'd like for you to perform our wedding tomorrow," Savannah said.

"A Christmas Day wedding?" Moses said, smiling. "Well, that should be easy for you to remember."

"We figure we'd better be married," Bodie said, "since we're adopting Alexander and Abigail. I'm not sure how we'll go about doing that legally, but —"

"Don't worry about that," Jamie said. "I've got friends in the territorial capital. We'll see to it that it gets done. I don't reckon a piece of paper will make much difference, though. In all the ways that count, you two are already mother and father to those kids."

Savannah said, "I don't want them to ever forget their real parents. Reverend Bradford had his faults, but he loved them and I'm sure their mother did, too. They'll grow up knowing that."

"They won't have to worry about knowing they're loved," Moses said. "I think you and Bodie will handle that just fine."

"So you'll do it?" Bodie said. "You'll perform the ceremony?"

"Of course. Tomorrow, before everyone spreads out across the valley to find their homesteads. It's my Christmas gift to the both of you."

Most of the snow from several days earlier had melted, but there were still patches of white here and there, enough to make the valley beautiful on Christmas morning. Jamie was up early, as usual, and was sipping a cup of coffee when Preacher came up and helped himself to a cup from the

pot sitting at the edge of one of the campfires.

"Well, you done it," the old mountain man
said. "Got them pilgrims here by Christmas."

"With a lot of help from you and Smoke."

"I got a hunch you'd have brought 'em
through somehow even if we hadn't come
along. I'm glad we got to help out, though."
Preacher sipped the hot, strong brew. "As
soon as ol' Bodie gets hisself hitched to that
pretty little Savannah gal, Smoke and me
are gonna be movin' on. We got places to
go." He paused. "Varmints to kill."

"I could give you a hand with that," Jamie
suggested.

Preacher shook his head. "Nope, but I'm
obliged for the offer. This is just too personal. The fellas we're after killed Smoke's
daddy. Score like that, an hombre's got to
settle his own self. I'll do my best to help
him catch up to those murderin' skunks,
but once he does, he'll want to take 'em on
alone."

"I reckon I can understand that," Jamie
said.

"How about you? I recollect how fiddle-
footed you can be. You'll be movin' on, too?"

"Maybe when winter's over," Jamie
mused. "Reckon I'll stay long enough to see

to it that these folks get established all right. And then come spring, I'd like to make sure Moses gets to where he's going. He has a calling of his own he needs to answer." Jamie thought of something else. "What about Audie and Nighthawk?"

"Those two are gone already."

"What?"

"It's true," Preacher said with a nod. "They drifted out last night. Audie said they was gonna spend Christmas in the high country, then maybe winter with Night-hawk's people."

Jamie shook his head. "Wish I could've told them so long."

"That's just it with them two," Preacher said with a chuckle. "They'll turn up again one o' these days. They got a habit of showin' up when their friends need 'em."

At mid-morning, the immigrants began assembling in the center of the camp for the wedding. Bodie had no suit, but he had cleaned up his clothes as best he could. Savannah left the Bingham wagon wearing a white dress that Leticia had altered to fit her. Bodie stood with Moses, waiting for her, a big smile on his face.

Savannah stopped short as she started to walk up the aisle formed by the gathered immigrants. With a worried frown on her face, she asked, "Where are Alexander and Abigail?" She raised her voice. "Bodie, where are the children? I thought they were with you."

"I thought they were with *you.*" Bodie started toward Savannah. "Where in the world —"

"Right here," a man's harsh voice called out.

Tall, powerfully built, and ugly, he stepped out from behind one of the wagons with his right hand clamped around Alexander's arm, his left holding Abigail equally cruelly. Behind him loomed a large group of men bristling with guns. "And unless you want them to die on Christmas Day, Miss Mc-Coy is coming with us."

Jamie, Preacher, and Smoke stood to one side. Bodie had taken his gun off for the wedding, but they were all packing two irons apiece, as usual. They couldn't slap leather with those kids in the line of fire, though.

"Kane!" Savannah gasped. "Kane sent you! You're the man who tried to kidnap me before!"

The big stranger grinned, but that didn't make him any less ugly. "That's right. It's taken us a long time to catch up to you." He glanced at two of the men with him.

"My so-called guides didn't really know where they were going, after all. But this time I'll be taking you back to the boss, just like I promised."

Jamie recognized Keeler and Holcomb, the former scouts. Somehow the treacherous varmints had thrown in with Gideon Kane's men, he thought.

Hector growled, "Jamie, what do you want us to do?"

"Have everybody back off," Jamie ordered. "If bullets start to fly, we want as many folks out of the way as possible."

Hector prodded the immigrants back, leaving a rough triangle with Jamie, Preacher, and Smoke at one corner, Bodie and Moses at another, and Savannah, the two youngsters, and the gunmen at the final point.

Moses suddenly stepped forward, putting himself between Jamie and his companions and the hired killers. He held his hands up and said quickly, "Let's all just settle down here. It's Christmas Day. A holy day for these people. We don't want any bloodshed or violence."

"There doesn't have to be, as long as Miss McCoy comes with us," the leader of the gunmen said.

Moses came closer, still with his hands

lifted beseechingly. "Please be reasonable. You can't expect to come in here and steal a bride away from her groom."

"We're taking her," the man grated. "No matter who we have to kill do to it."

Moses sighed. "I was hoping I could get through to you, talk some sense to you. I really hoped it wouldn't come to this."

The man sneered at him. "You're some sort of sky pilot, aren't you? What the hell are you gonna do?"

"This," Moses said softly.

He launched himself into a diving tackle. His arms, already spread out, went around Alexander and Abigail and jolted them loose from their captor, knocking them to the ground. As he shielded the children with his body he cried out, "Now, Jamie!"

The hired killers already had their guns out. They were completely ruthless men, eager to slay without conscience or hesitation.

But they were facing Jamie Ian MacCallister, Preacher, and Smoke Jensen.

They never had a chance.

It was a gun battle that would be talked about in that part of the country for years, even decades. Less than two hundred people actually witnessed it, and of those, many caught only brief, chaotic glimpses because they were too busy ducking for cover as shots rang out. But even so, over time thousands of people told friends or children or grandkids about how, yep, they were there when Jamie, Preacher, and Smoke faced thirty hired killers. Or forty. Or a hundred, depending on how the story got inflated. The important thing was Jamie, Preacher, and Smoke all suffered wounds that laid them up for a while.

And all the gunmen who had come to kidnap Savannah died.

The stuff of powder smoke legends, to be sure . . . but only one more adventure in the lives of those three frontiersmen.

When the guns had fallen silent, the wounds had been bound up, and the dead dragged away, a man and a woman stood together and pledged their love for each other, in front of God and their friends, and for two young children, that union and the family it created proved to be the greatest Christmas gift they ever received.

EPILOGUE

Montana, 1947

Alexander Cantrell sighed.

Beside him, his sister Abigail said, "Are you all right, Alex? Are you having a touch of that angina again?"

Alexander shook his head. Mere moments had passed, although to him it was as if he had traveled back in time seventy-four years. He looked down at the graves of his parents. "I was just remembering again."

"The wagon train?"

"Yep. And everything that happened on the way up here."

Abigail shivered. "Some of those times were awful, like when the Indians got us. And that terrible fire . . . I never saw anything like it."

"I thought about those things," Alexander said, "but mostly I thought about Ma and Pa . . . and the Reverend . . . and Moses . . ."

"And Jamie," Abigail whispered.

"And Jamie," Alexander agreed.

Although it still seemed hard to believe, less than three years after that fateful Christmas Day, Jamie Ian MacCallister was dead, struck down in 1876 by bushwhackers who had mistaken him for his son, the famous gunfighter Falcon MacCallister. When they had heard that awful news in Eagle Valley, Bodie had wanted to strap on his guns and leave the Diamond C ranch to track down Jamie's murderers. Hector Gilworth, Lamar Hendricks, and a number of the other settlers in the valley had been ready to saddle up and go with him.

Before that could happen, they got word that Falcon had wreaked his bloody judgment on the killers. Jamie's death was avenged, and he slumbered peacefully, eternally, under the earth of his home range, next to his beloved wife Kate.

From time to time, they had gotten news of Smoke Jensen, too, and knew how the young man had settled the score for the death of *his* father. For many years, Smoke continued to be the deadliest gunfighter the West had ever known . . . but he was also a devoted family man, marrying twice, raising a whole passel of children and grandchildren, and establishing one of the finest ranches in Colorado.

As for Preacher . . . well, for a time he had been thought to be dead, but as it turned out, the old mountain man was too tough to kill. His friends in Eagle Valley never did know for sure what happened to him. For all Alexander knew, Preacher was still out there somewhere, roaming the wild places and getting into one scrape after another. That idea was pretty farfetched, of course. Downright impossible, in fact. But when Alexander thought about Preacher . . . well, it was hard to rule out anything completely.

Moses Danzig had visited the Diamond C now and then and enjoyed the time spent with his old friends Bodie and Savannah. Cyrus O'Hanlon, who had recovered from the beating he'd received from Kane's men, his wife Dollie, and the rest of the troupe had come to Montana, too, and performed in the Opera House in Billings. Savannah had joined them for one night and thoroughly enjoyed being an actress again, but that was enough. She had an even better life on the ranch, she told her old friends, being married to Bodie and raising a fine pair of twins, although she and Bodie were never blessed with children of their own.

Alexander's parents never spoke of Gideon Kane, but years later, giving in to curiosity, Alexander had looked into the situation and found out what had happened to the man from Kansas City. He remembered Jamie saying something ominous about paying a visit to Kane, but that hadn't come about. Some woman whose affections Kane had spurned had killed him in February 1874, sticking a knife in his chest. As far as Alexander was concerned, it was a more merciful end than the lowdown snake deserved.

The farms and ranches in Eagle Valley were some of the best in the territory, and then later, in the state, and the Diamond C was the best of them all. Years passed, and Alexander and Abigail grew to adulthood, married fine partners, and raised families of their own. Some of those children and grandchildren had brought them out to the old burying ground on the ranch.

It was the tenth anniversary of Bodie Cantrell's death. His beloved wife Savannah had gone to be with the Lord a couple years before that. Alexander missed them every day. He would for the rest of his life, however much of it was still allotted to him.

He took off his hat as Abigail leaned over and placed one bouquet of flowers on her father's grave and another on her mother's. Bodie and Savannah had adopted them, but as Jamie had once said, the piece of paper didn't matter nearly as much as the love, and they always had that.

Oh, they had that.

"Dad . . . ? We'd probably better be starting back to town."

Alexander nodded, tightened his arm around his sister's shoulders for a moment, and then put his hat on. He turned and told his son, "You're right, Jamie. Let's go. Come along, Abigail."

"You think we can make it home without the Indians getting us?"

"I reckon," Alexander said.

They walked away, cradled in the memories of days gone by, of days when true heroes walked the earth under the big Montana sky.

The employees of Thorndike Press hope you have enjoyed this Large Print book. All our Thorndike, Wheeler, and Kennebec Large Print titles are designed for easy reading, and all our books are made to last. Other Thorndike Press Large Print books are available at your library, through selected bookstores, or directly from us.

For information about titles, please call:
(800) 223-1244

or visit our Web site at:
http://gale.cengage.com/thorndike

To share your comments, please write:
Publisher
Thorndike Press
10 Water St., Suite 310
Waterville, ME 04901